LEGACY OF POWER

Season One

C.C. Bolick

LEGACY OF POWER: SEASON 1

Dirt Road Books

ISBN 978-1-946-089-28-1

Cover Design by Fiona Jayde Media

Edited by EbookEditingPro
Edited by N.N. Light Editing Services

Books by C.C. Bolick:

Leftover Girl Series:

Leftover Girl
Secrets Return
Prison of Lies
Illusion of Truth
Fate of War

The Agency Series:

Run Don't Think
Love Don't Wait
Fight Don't Fear
Heart of a Traitor

The Fear Chronicles:

Fear Justice
Fear Power
Fear Darkness
Fear Tomorrow

Legacy of Power: Season 1
Legacy of Power: Season 2
Legacy of Power: Season 3

For Milly,

Because no one who has touched a person's heart is ever really gone

EPISODE 1
Revelations

April 1990

Grief touches each of us in a different way. For some it brings the end and for others the beginning. Grief magnified the world around me and brought my worst fear into sharp focus. My mother was dying, and I had no way to stop the cancer destroying her body.

Mom was my closest friend and the only person who seemed to understand I felt different from everyone else. Not that the brown hair falling just past my shoulders or my normal jeans and t-shirts were weird compared to the other tenth graders, or that I dreamed of a life other than college and two-point-five kids. I cried when the space shuttle Challenger fell out of the sky. Video from a California earthquake made me shudder every time I rode over a bridge. And, like other fifteen-year-olds, I couldn't wait to turn sixteen and get a driver's license; nothing strange about that.

But there were instances, especially late at night, when I had this nagging feeling I'd been born in the wrong time. Or the wrong place.

On one spring afternoon, as the oppressive Alabama heat took hold, I rode the bus home alone. My younger sister, Lorraine, had stayed at school to practice for a math tournament. Patches of blue were visible through the thickening clouds, almost as blue as the paint Dad had used on the outside of our house.

The bus dropped me off at the end of the dirt road that doubled as our driveway. I climbed into a single-cab Toyota pickup in the grass near the road's edge. Digging in my purse, I found the keychain and cranked the engine. Although I didn't have a license, Dad let me use the truck to make the two-mile trip every morning and evening since the bus refused.

I kept my speed at a minimum because of the slick mud caused by rain from that morning. With the darkening clouds, it could rain again soon. When I reached the house, I parked and entered through the front door. Sounds drifted from the living room as I kicked off my shoes. Typical music from the sixties that Mom enjoyed, a record of Elvis she'd played so many times static crackled in the background. I couldn't believe she clung to old technology like a record player when all of her favorites were available on cassette. CDs would be better, but she'd never agree to get a CD player. The tape player sat on the shelf next to the record player. Lorraine and I were the only ones who used it.

Lifting the needle gently, I slid the arm to the side and turned off the record player. The turntable coasted to a stop. I preferred Tom Petty or Guns N' Roses any day, but my mother would crinkle her nose at the 'newfangled' rock, as she called it.

I found the TV remote and turned on a news story. Only five channels came in clear with the outside antenna; Dad had bought us an enormous satellite dish but had not yet finished the project. At Mom's encouragement, he kept us all trapped in another decade. It had been that way since Darla died.

In front of the console TV, I dropped into Dad's recliner and watched a man who insisted a crowd sighted aliens on an Atlanta street. There was some huge cover-up after an earthquake occurred in Atlanta, about two hours from our insignificant town. Secret government agents came and erased his friend's memory, the man claimed. Like me, the news anchor suppressed a grin.

"These agents wore all black," the man insisted, his voice rising with each word. "And the alien—I swear I saw a laser gun."

"Did you say laser?" the anchor said.

"Yes, like on *Star Trek*. Or is it *Star Wars*?" He scratched his head. "I'm not sure, but it had a red beam."

Where was Mom? She could easily tell the difference between the two space shows, and the laughter would be good for her. Hopefully, she hadn't spent the entire day in bed. I held up the remote to change the channel, and that's when I noticed the mud.

Not just mud, but a shoe print of the same red clay from our yard. Across the floor, next to Lorraine's Nintendo, were another two prints side-by-side. They were too big to be Dad's. The rest of the floor was clean. I leaned forward, deep in thought. There should be more prints…

"Mom?" Glancing into the kitchen, I saw more mud. My heart raced. I ran to her room down the hall, but the bed was perfectly made. The breathing machine next to her bed sat silent and beside it was a bottle of pills. Where could she be? "Mom?" I yelled as fear took hold.

The grandfather clock at the end of the hall came to life, and I jumped. Four o'clock. Dad wouldn't be home for at least an hour.

I raced back to the kitchen and stopped at the mud. Two prints side-by-side with no other prints around. It was like someone had dropped out of the sky, made the huge prints, and then flown away. The only sound was my laughter, a mixture of disbelief and fear. This day was getting stranger by the moment.

At the back of the kitchen was a door that led to the garden behind the house. I ran to the door and turned the handle, only to realize the door was slightly open. My heart thudded in my chest.

I stepped outside and scanned the garden. My mother's bench sat to the left of the garden. Thick azalea bushes made a row on either side of me, lining the edge of the porch. In the garden, tomato plants hung from their ties to wooden stakes and huge leaves from the patch of cucumbers waited patiently. There was no wind and no noise, not even from birds. No squirrels racing across limbs of pine trees in the woods behind the garden. It was as if everything but the damp heat had been sucked from the air. The clouds above had thickened and now threatened to rain down.

Was she out here? The woman rarely went outside until after dark.

A low whistle split the air. I glanced around, but nothing moved in the garden.

"Mom?" I yelled again and held my breath.

A hand gripped my arm. Mom spun me so I could see her eyes. "Get down," she said in a steely tone that sounded like a stranger.

Instead of moving, I stared into her eyes. Then I noticed the gun in her other hand. She shoved me down behind one of the azalea bushes and ran toward the garden.

My butt landed on gravel and sharp rocks cut into my palms. Instead of crying out with shock, I sat shaking on the ground.

What was happening? Why the gun? For that brief second, I'd witnessed a woman holding a gun as if she'd been trained in the military. The coldness in her eyes and strength as she forced me away—this couldn't be my frail mother whose body died a little more each day.

Why push me out of the way?

My hands were shaking; I couldn't speak. But I had to get up and see what the heck was going on. Instead of jumping to my feet, I rolled over and pushed myself up on my knees. I crawled around the edge of the bush and scanned the garden.

Mom stood at the center of the small patch, her brown hair barely long enough for the tie at the back of her head. Tendrils of hair blew around her face as she stood like a statue, her pale skin and fragile figure reminding me of her sickness. She shouldn't be in this garden alone, but for sure not staring at a person in a gold uniform and gold helmet with a shield across the face. It had to be a man since he stood more than a foot taller than her. Holding a weapon, he was dressed like no military I'd ever seen. A gun, but not exactly like hers. This gun looked expensive and fake, like something from one of her space shows.

In all my years, I'd never seen her with a gun. Never seen a gun in our house. Now she faced off with a man in this comic book gold outfit as if he'd materialized from the sky.

Thunder rumbled in the distance. The clouds above raced across the sky, coiling with a madness that matched what I felt inside. Any moment it would rain. Any moment I'd wake from this nightmare. The two faced each other, neither moving, neither breathing nor speaking. I tried to catch my breath. Where was Dad, and why had my world shifted on its axis?

I crawled forward, a stick breaking beneath my hand, sounding unnaturally loud in the silence. The man glanced my way. Before he could say a word, Mom fired a single shot, and he crumpled to the ground.

"Oh my god," I screamed. "You shot him."

She turned slowly, as if seeing me for the first time. Then she kicked his black boot with her favorite pink slippers. Why was she in the garden with plush slippers that were soaked in mud to her ankles? The man made no movement as I stumbled toward them, nearly falling as I struggled to catch my breath. The first drop of rain landed on my nose.

Mom turned, one hand holding the gun, and the other arm she wrapped around my shoulders. "You can't understand, but he wouldn't have stopped. Now that he found us, he never would have left us alone."

"Is he dead?"

"Yes."

My teeth chattered as she tried to comfort me. A note of sorrow entered her voice. "Charlene," she whispered and kissed my hair. Without warning, she spun me around behind her.

Another man stood a few feet from her, pointing a similar gun to the one on the ground next to the dead man. He wore the same gold uniform and helmet.

I closed my eyes and leaned my head against her back. She had to feel my entire body shaking.

The man said words I couldn't understand.

"Speak in my language," she said, deadly quiet.

"Your language?" he asked with a laugh. "You claim this place?"

"This is my home. You are invading my property and you will leave."

"A daughter?" he asked. "Does she have your power?"

Power? What kind of drugs was this guy on?

"No." She moved forward. "I knew there would be two of you, but I never imagined *you* had the guts to come here. Get out before I kill you."

The man laughed louder, which brought my desperation to new heights. He loomed over her; like the other man, he stood more than a foot taller. What was happening?

Before I could ask my question aloud, Mom spun and pushed me to the ground. The man fired his weapon and a red beam sliced through the air, hitting a tree along the edge of the garden. She landed on her side and aimed her gun at him. His entire body, every trace of him, faded from sight.

Okay, I'd finally lost my mind. Seeing a person transported like on *Star Trek* was one thing, but seeing a real person disappear before my eyes… it wasn't possible. And yet, here I was on the ground, witness to this amazing event.

Mom climbed to her feet and did a dance, spinning around as she surveyed every angle of the garden, arms extended, and gun held tight in her hands.

"Mom," I groaned.

"Stay down," she hissed. "This isn't a game. He means to take me away."

"Where?" I asked. "Who is he?"

Rain fell harder, soaking my hair and running down my face. Above me, Mom didn't seem to notice the rain.

The man reappeared, this time behind her.

"There," I gasped.

He removed the helmet, which dropped into the mud, and revealed a hardened, wrinkled face with a beard of silver.

His skin held a deep tan and his eyes a fire that made me think they were actually glowing red.

Mom swung around and aimed her gun at his head. Her voice left no room for doubt. "I will kill you."

"Knowing who I am, you still plan to kill me?" He watched her, still as a statue in his glittery gold suit. Rain slid down his face and he shook his head, transferring the weapon to his left hand while he moved hair from his eyes with his right hand. "There's no reason for more blood. I will claim my bounty for returning you alive."

"Try. We'll see how you compare to the others."

He coughed and stood straighter. "Candorice Reisten, by order of the king of Golvern, you will relinquish your weapon and accompany me to my ship."

Candorice was my mother's name, but Reisten… she'd never told me her maiden name. Could this man really know her? Would he shoot her with the ray gun?

Mom ducked and spun. He disappeared as she barreled through the empty air where he had stood.

"Get on the porch," she yelled at me.

Despite the force in her voice, I couldn't move from where I lay across the ground. The man reappeared behind her and I yelled. She fired the gun at him, and he stumbled backward, knocking over several of the stakes with tomato plants. The small fruits weren't even red yet.

"Your family will pay for your disgrace," he cried out.

In response, Mom shot him again. Her hands gripped the gun, and she didn't move as he fell to the ground, his chest heaving with breaths that made me pity him. Then he went limp.

Finally, she let out a breath and lowered her arms. The gun hung loosely at her side as she approached and kicked his boot. Then she bent over and felt for the pulse along his neck. Despite the water pooling around her feet, she dropped to her knees and lowered her head as if praying. She said a few words I didn't understand.

"*Fatle en lanre.*"

"What did you say?"

Mom raised her head and turned toward me. "Your way with fate."

All of this was so foreign, I'd given up on trying to decide if I was dreaming. "His language?"

"It once was mine."

"You know him?" I asked.

"His name was Yens Sortico." She stood and walked toward me, holding a hand out. "He was once a friend of mine, many years ago."

With the way her voice deflated, I remembered she was sick with cancer. "You mentioned fate?"

"There's not much comfort in facing death where he is from. I much prefer the teachings of eternal life from the many religions of this planet."

This planet? She'd moved beyond just scaring me. I sat up and wiped the strand of hair from my face. "How many years ago?"

"He and I were born in the same city, a long way from here."

"I don't understand."

Mom turned and made her way to the bench. It was where she always sat after sunset and where she watched the stars. It was her favorite part of living so far from the city. She wanted to live where the stars were the only lights in the sky.

While rain trickled down my face, a scary sense of realization crept into my thoughts. Either I was crazy or all of this had really happened. My life had changed in those quick moments, and I felt nothing would ever be the same. I thought back to the man's words. He'd known her name.

He'd mentioned a place called Golvern and a king. But what had she done to deserve a gun in her face?

At the bench, she sat and patted the spot beside her. As she laid the black gun across her lap, I knew one thing for sure. My mother was not who I thought she was. How could she be so calm? My entire body shook as I stared at the two lifeless forms. Two men she'd shot dead in our garden. Already, a stream of red stained the surrounding grass.

"Sit by me," she said.

I stared at my mother. Of all I feared for that moment, the dismantling of what I'd come to believe as truth bothered me most.

"What happened?" I asked and sat next to her.

She tried to put an arm around me, but I pulled away. "I shot two men who came to take me away."

"Take you… where?"

"To another planet."

"You killed two people. Where did you learn to shoot?"

"I've known how to shoot a gun *with precision* since I was twelve."

Precision? What a stupid word to latch onto after watching her kill. What would happen when the police found out my mother was a murderer? Earlier thoughts of her two favorite space shows came flooding back, and I laughed uncontrollably. Thinking about the police suddenly seemed as absurd as concentrating on how she learned to *precisely* aim a gun. The men in gold had mentioned a ship, and now she was talking about another planet. I pointed at the men. "None of this is real. It can't be."

Mom caught my fingers in hers. "My hand is real. The bench beneath us is real. The men I shot are real, and I'd shoot them again to protect you. That instinct is in my blood. Our blood."

"I don't understand."

“Which is my fault. I shouldn’t have kept the truth from you this long.”

“What truth?” I asked.

She smiled and put a hand on my shoulder. “I wasn’t born on Earth.”

EPISODE 2

Cold Truth

Rain soaked through my clothes as I sat on the bench next to Mom. Across the yard lay the bodies of two men dressed in gold uniforms, one near the porch and the other at the far end of the cucumbers. As if they were sleeping in our rain-drenched garden.

Breathe in. Breathe out.

Maybe all of this could be okay. Somehow.

I turned to Mom, but she continued to stare straight ahead. One of these men must have made the mud prints in the house. What a strange thought. Lightning flashed, and I counted the seconds. One-thousand-one, one-thousand-two, one-thousand-three, one-thousand—thunder rumbled, a low sound that barely tickled the sky. It didn't make Mom move from her spot on the wooden seat.

"Who are you?" I asked.

One-thousand-one, one-thousand-two—

"The name I was born with is Candorice Reisten."

"But you weren't born on Earth." Saying the words made the air feel lighter and the rain not so cold. Maybe I'd finally crossed a line with no return. "This other planet…"

"Golvern."

"Golvern," I repeated. "Where is this planet?"

"Forty trillion miles away."

How could I even imagine that distance? "Farther than the sun?"

"Farther than all the planets you've seen in satellite pictures on TV. Farther than any of Earth's probes have traveled. Golvern is on the other side of the galaxy."

"How did you get here?"

"In a spaceship."

"Of course." I leaned my head back and closed my eyes, welcoming the pelts of water against my face. "Why were those men here?"

"I told you. They wanted to take me back. They were under orders."

"From who?"

"The government of Golvern. My power to shoot with precision is rare. They were upset when I left and wanted me back."

"When you left…"

"Eighteen years ago." When several moments of silence passed, she put a hand on my knee. "Do you believe me?"

I opened my eyes and looked over her face. "Do I have a choice?"

The door to the porch creaked open and Dad raced across the garden. He examined each of the men at length before continuing to where we sat on the bench.

As he approached, Mom looked up at him. "I'm sorry for the mess, Gregory."

Dad glanced around the garden, taking in a three-sixty view of the soggy mess and then the pine trees beyond the garden. Rain soaked his honey-colored hair, plastering the tips to his face, as his blue-gray eyes stopped on me. Then he looked to Mom, his tall frame holding still despite the steady downpour. “It’s been a long time, Candy. I thought they’d given up on you.”

She looked at her feet, the pink fur of her slippers soaked with mud. “I hoped they would. I never should have brought this conflict to your door.”

“Our door,” he said.

“You knew about… these people?” I let out the breath I’d been holding. “Is it true they’re really from space?”

He nodded. “I’m sorry, Charlie. You shouldn’t have found out this way.”

My teeth chattered. Why did Dad’s words make the situation deadly real?

“Are there any more?” he asked.

Mom shook her head. “There were two. They always come in pairs.”

“Did they see Charlie?”

“They did.”

He put his hands in the pockets of his jeans, most likely filled with sawdust from a day at his woodworking shop, and looked at the ground. From one foot to the other he rocked, as if trying to reach a conclusion. Dad raised his eyes to me. “How are you feeling?”

“Scared,” I said.

“Understandable. The first time I saw those men in gold, I thought I was losing my mind.”

“Mom says she was born on another planet.”

“She was.”

I took a deep breath. “Are you human?”

Dad gave a serious look, the one usually reserved for when I got in trouble. “Yes.”

“You should be upset.” My voice shook. “Does this seem normal to you?”

He turned to Mom. "You're tired. Let me take you to bed."

Coughs rocked her body as she tried to catch her breath. "I'll clean up this mess first."

I turned to her. "The way that man disappeared and reappeared. He faded out."

"We call it teleporting," she said.

We? "You mean like your favorite space shows?"

"Nothing like those shows. I've always found humor in the way humans think of aliens."

Hearing the words humans and aliens in the same sentence, coming from her, was more than I could handle. "You're saying you're an…" I couldn't get the word out.

"An alien, yes."

"Can you teleport like he did?"

"It drains my strength, but yes I can. The ability to teleport is a power everyone from that planet has." She squeezed my hand. "I'll show you."

"That's unnecessary," Dad said. "You're weak enough as it is. I'll deal with this after I take you to bed."

Another round of coughs rocked Mom. Tears formed in my eyes, but maybe they wouldn't notice with all the rain. "Deal with this?" I asked. "Two dead bodies?"

Dad sighed. "This isn't the first time we've had to make bodies disappear."

"What if someone finds out?" I asked. "You could go to prison."

Mom shook her head. "I've killed no one born on Earth. Those people weren't in the system and there's no traceability."

"System?" I asked.

"No birth certificates or social security numbers," Dad said. "Hopefully no one else will come looking for them."

It couldn't be that easy. "You said something about a spaceship. If they're dead, what happens to the spaceship that brought them here?"

"I have a friend who can take care of that," she said. "There are others here like me. Most don't want to be bothered."

Was I going crazy or having some type of mental breakdown? A picture of a guy slinging an ax in a Stephen King movie flashed in my head. Jack Nicholson. Was I going crazy like him?

Dad grasped Mom's arm and lifted her to stand. "I'll walk you to bed, Candy. You get some rest, and Charlie and I will take care of this."

She looked at me. "I'm sorry you had to find out this way." Mom glanced around as if suddenly realizing where we were. "Has Lorraine come home?"

"Not yet," I said in a small voice. "She was staying after to practice for the math tournament. She won't be home until six or seven."

Mom nodded, and they turned toward the house. Dad didn't say a word until he'd settled her in bed and walked back to the garden. I remained on the bench where they'd left me.

"Tough day," he said.

"Are you going to sit down? Mom wanted me to believe everything is okay, but I don't think it is."

"No, but we can get there. Come help me in the shed."

I nodded and followed him to the twenty-by-twenty building to one side of the house. Inside, he flipped on the lights and reached for a row of plastic milk containers. He'd removed the tops of these jugs before filling the insides with concrete. Dad called them 'poor man's anchors' and used them anytime we went fishing in the boat. He pointed to a wad of clothesline for me to grab.

Pain tightened in my throat. What did he plan to do with these supplies? I waited in silence as he pulled his Chevy Bonanza around and backed up to the first man. The sky had darkened, not quite reaching nightfall but still thick with clouds. Rain had subsided and now sprinkled in a light mist.

He lowered the tailgate. "Charlie, I need your help loading him up. I'll grab his arms and you grab his feet."

I reached for the man's black boots and helped Dad lift the man's body. It felt like he weighed a ton. As we pushed him into the truck's bed, the body slid back toward me. Blood from his chest splattered my face and arms. Dad maneuvered him away from me and toward the front of the bed. I wiped at the thick crimson, as red as any blood I'd seen.

"Sorry about that."

"Their blood is like ours." I took the rag he offered and wiped my face.

"She shot them in the heart, which is located in the same side of the chest."

We repeated our moves with the next man and loaded him into the bed behind the first man. Dad closed the tailgate and we both climbed inside the truck. He cranked the engine and set us in motion toward the dirt path that wound to the back of our property.

"If those men hadn't appeared, would you have told me?" I asked.

His silence was my answer.

When the lake came into view, an eerie calm filled my veins. Maybe the shock had overwhelmed me. We approached the seven-acre lake where Dad often took me fishing on weekends. He stopped the truck near an aluminum boat alongside the far stretch of the bank.

My strength was almost gone by the time we had both men loaded into the boat. Dad dropped in the concrete anchors and I grabbed the clothesline. He pulled the cord on the motor three times before the sputters turned into a continuous roar. The smell of gas and oil surrounded us in the remaining light of day. Water gurgled as he pointed us toward the deepest part of the lake. A trail of foam followed the boat as we slid across the water.

At the lake's center, he cut the motor and stripped the gold suits off both men. Because of the dim light and the rain, there wasn't much to see that would embarrass me. Perhaps it was my continued state of shock. After watching my mother shoot these two men, why would seeing them in their underwear bother me? The remaining articles were solid black and not much different from the men's underwear I'd seen in commercials.

I moved the uniforms into a pile at the front of the boat. Dad bound both sets of hands with the clothesline. Then he tied one end of rope to one set of hands. He tied the other end to an anchor and repeated this process for their feet.

With a heave, I helped him shove the bodies into the murky water. We followed this with the anchors, which helped to pull the men beneath the surface. When their faces had completely faded from sight, I sat on one of the boat's metal seats.

Dad rinsed his hands in the water. "They'll be fish food now."

"What about their clothes?" I asked.

"I'll get rid of their uniforms and their weapons. Don't want to poison our fish."

"Uniforms, as in some type of military clothes?"

"From what I understand, these soldiers serve Golvern's government. They were sent to bring your mother home."

The second one had also mentioned a bounty. "What did she do?"

He sat on the seat across from me. "She left."

"That's it?"

"Candy wanted her freedom, and she fought for it. That was eighteen years ago. After killing several of these soldiers, they left her alone."

"What happens when they find out she killed again?"

"I don't know. Every soldier who dared step foot on our property over the years has died a quiet death."

"How many have come?"

"Dozens."

"She shot better than all of them?"

He nodded as he stared at the water. "She never misses. It's a rare gift many wish to control."

I thought about the soldier's words and shivered. *Your family will pay for your disgrace.* "She should have told me."

"Don't be mad at your mother. She wanted us all to live and die as normal people."

"Is she really dying? The cancer—"

"Yes." He cleared his throat. "I'm glad you got to see this side of her."

"How did she get this power?"

"From what she's told me, the power passed down through her family."

"How long have you known?" I asked, not sure if I wanted the answer.

"Since the day I met your mother, I knew she was different. But I vowed to love every part of her, and I've kept my promise."

"She said the instinct is in her blood. Our blood."

He took a deep breath and slowly exhaled. "Until now it's always been her legacy. I have a sneaking suspicion it may also be yours."

*****

The house was dark when we returned. Only the TV chattered from the living room; I'd left on the news from earlier and now contestants clapped and shouted letters on a game show. The clock in the hall chimed. Six o'clock and Lorraine hadn't come home yet. Dad suggested I get cleaned up before he disappeared into his bedroom.

In the bathroom, the lights around the mirror made me squint. A mixture of blood and mud covered my arms and clothes. A splatter of dried blood brushed my cheek. I wiped the blood, only to realize it had crusted on my skin despite the rain.

My skin looked pale and my eyes bloodshot. This morning I was human and now… I wasn't sure what I was. If Mom wasn't from Earth, that meant a part of me wasn't either. I shivered. Who could have ever thought a normal fifteen-year-old like me would face this impossible situation? Not just impossible, but who would believe me?

Not that I'd tell anyone. I groaned as I thought of what tomorrow would bring. This morning I'd cried in the bathroom at school because Mom had been so sick yesterday, she skipped dinner. Dad told me and Lorraine to prepare for the end.

Prepare? He loved Mom, and yet he'd accepted the fact her life was fading fast.

I turned on the faucet and filled the tub; steam rose, and the room felt thick and hazy. A deep breath of the steam calmed my racing heart. I stripped off my clothes and threw them in a pile near the laundry basket. Would the blood come out of my U2 t-shirt?

After tonight, I never wanted to see blood again.

Sinking under the water, I ran my fingers through the hair that floated around my face. It was the same thick brown as Mom's and Lorraine's. Everyone who saw us together knew we were family, from the sharp features of our nose to our cheekbones and brown eyes. My chin was about the only thing I inherited from Dad. I tugged at a tangled wad of hair above my ear and choked as red clouded the water. Blood from the men we'd dumped in the lake. Tears filled my eyes—all the pent-up fear and shock I'd been feeling since finding the house empty this afternoon. The tears flowed as if they'd never stop.

Mom had been sick for the last two years.

She was from another planet. How could that be a real thing?

Dad knew the truth for eighteen years.

We were normal. We had to be normal.

Except she wasn't, which meant I wasn't. I climbed from the tub and drained the water, watching as the blood-tinged liquid faded from sight.

Pounding came from the door. "Charlie, I need to use the bathroom," Lorraine called. "You locked the door."

"Go away," I yelled.

"I need to get in."

"I'm taking a bath," I said, trying to keep the tears from my voice.

"What's wrong?" Lorraine's voice went from demanding to filled with fear. She sounded younger than the almost thirteen-year-old who wanted to do everything like me. "Where did Mom and Dad go?"

"Don't worry about it."

I wanted to refill the tub and stay there forever, but the water would eventually get cold. Cold like the truth we all must face. Even Lorraine. My anger at her subsided as I realized Mom's legacy was as much about her as it was about me. I wrapped a towel around me and wiped up the water I'd dripped on the floor. Gathering my blood-stained clothes, I rolled them into a ball and opened the door for her.

"Thanks," Lorraine said as she ran by me.

I closed the door and went to my room. Inside, I grabbed a flannel set of PJs even though Dad usually kept the air turned up to eighty. With the PJs on, I felt an odd calm as I sat on the bed.

Lorraine pushed open my door. Her brown hair looked faded, with lighter streaks. Anger filled me since she'd gone against Mom's wish that Lorraine never dye her hair. I hated to admit the new look made her even prettier than before. Not that Lorraine needed help since her huge brown eyes and long eyelashes always had guys staring at her face. Despite the fact she wasn't more than five foot tall, her body was mature and her curves defined in a way mine never were at twelve.

"Don't tell Dad," Lorraine said, "but Sheila got sick after lunch. Her mom didn't bring me home."

There wasn't room for more secrets in this house. "How did you get home?"

"Joel drove me."

"You took a ride from a stranger?"

She laughed. At least the fear in her voice was gone. "Joel's not a stranger. You have lunch with him and Carmen every day. Plus, he's on the math team. I was going to call, but he offered to drop me off."

"Dad wouldn't approve of a boy bringing you home."

"He's just a friend, not a boyfriend. Not even my friend yet; he's mostly yours. You don't have to run him off like the others."

I'd chased off several guys interested in Lorraine. She couldn't help the fact she was prettier than most girls, including me, or that she looked more like fifteen than twelve. "How did you get inside without Dad seeing the car?"

"I had Joel stop before the last curve. I walked the rest of the way."

Walked through the mud and darkness all alone when men had come with guns to grab Mom only hours before. "Joel was okay with leaving you?"

"I told him he didn't want to meet Dad."

"Don't ever do that again," I said.

Lorraine peered closer at me. "Something's wrong. You don't look right."

"Mom wasn't feeling well and went to bed early."

She dropped onto the bed next to me. "I can't stand being sad all the time. Is that selfish?"

I put an arm around her shoulders. "Sometimes I feel the same way."

"I just want us to be a normal family again."

Over the years, I'd gone to every length to protect my younger sister, but no one could protect her from the truth.

EPISODE 3
Visitor

When I woke the next morning, the sun had yet to rise, and the house was silent. Events of yesterday came rushing back. Since sleep was impossible, I tiptoed down the hall while trying not to wake anyone. Had I imagined the men from another planet?

In the kitchen, light from above the stove cast shadows around the room. A set of muddy footprints stopped me in my tracks. It wasn't a dream. I grabbed a broom and swept until the mud loosened from the tile. Then I cleaned up the remnants of our intruders and disposed of the mud. Leaning against the counter, I closed my eyes and shivered. The mud meant the face-off with Mom was real, that seeing her precisely fire a gun—when I'd never seen her shoot a day in my life—was real. It meant the men who invaded our property were real.

It also meant she wasn't human.

Dad walked into the kitchen as the sky glowed behind the trees. He said nothing as he made coffee and sat at the table while it brewed. When the aroma of coffee filled the room, I asked, "How is Mom?"

"Still sleeping." He filled his mug and went back to the table. "Are you going to be fine at school today?"

"I don't know." The only thing I knew for sure was I had to get out of this house. "I'm not going to tell anyone."

"Good."

He drank his coffee in silence as I made breakfast, bacon and biscuits. Would my stomach handle any food this morning? So many questions remained from last night, but Lorraine bounced into the room before I could ask any of them. She sat in the chair next to Dad and spent the next twenty minutes talking about her upcoming math tournament.

She looked around. "Is Mom going to get up?"

Dad patted her hand on the table. "We'll let her sleep late this morning. Yesterday was a rough one."

No joke. I wanted to say something smart to Lorraine, but the haunted look in her eyes kept me from speaking. She worried about our mother as much as I did, maybe more.

Lorraine barely said a word as I drove to the end of the driveway and the bus picked us up. The school in Credence housed every grade on the same property, which meant the bus carried all ages. I took a seat near the back and stared out of the window. After a thirty-minute ride, my life would be back to normal.

At least I hoped it would, because I really needed normal.

Focusing on the trees, I blocked out all thoughts of blood on my hands until we passed the sign for a county road where my family had lived until the night Darla died. I pictured Lorraine with her identical twin sister playing on the swing set Dad built in our backyard. I was seven the night our house burned, and they were five. Lorraine and Darla both suffered burns, but Darla died in the hospital.

Sounds of screaming filled my mind, along with the smell of burning flesh, as Dad pulled her out of the house.

Lorraine didn't speak for a month afterward. Mom insisted I couldn't understand the depth of her devastation because I didn't have a twin. I'd never known the close connection cut from Lorraine's life forever. I guess it was why I always shielded Lorraine from the world, no matter how often she aggravated me by dominating a conversation. She always had to be the center of attention. That night changed every facet of our lives.

Our mother had blamed herself, as if there was some magical way she should have been able to save Darla. The truth smacked me so hard I sucked in a breath. With her power, she probably felt guilty. Nights when Dad told Mom she couldn't have saved Darla, quiet conversations they didn't realize I overheard, came flooding back. How often had they discussed the truth right under my nose?

I pushed thoughts of Darla out of my mind. It had been months since I let myself think of her. Dad often said to look to the future, but the past seemed to be catching up at a frantic pace.

What if someone found out what Mom did? The bus stopped for a pickup, and I watched as rays of sunlight reflected on a lake. Thoughts of murky water, of the faces fading from sight, made me shiver.

Lorraine leaned over the seat in front of me. "Are you okay?"

"Yes," I said. "What makes you think something is wrong?"

"You've barely said a word all morning."

"I'm fine."

She turned around and sat down. I had to get a grip; otherwise, these thoughts would torture me for the rest of the day.

At school, I went straight for my locker. Unlike most people, I had one to myself since my best friend had moved three months ago. We'd exchanged letters and a few calls, but I cut off communication. I couldn't deal with her asking if I was okay, if I'd found more friends.

Truth is, having more friends meant more questions. I didn't like people who gossiped, and I didn't need questions, especially not with bodies in our lake.

A few weeks ago, Carmen sat with me at lunch like I was a charity case. She didn't have many friends either, but at least she understood what I was going through with Mom. Her mother was sick more days than she wasn't. Since it was just the two of them and her mom ran a florist shop downtown, Carmen spent every afternoon working to help out. Turns out people were always getting married or dying, so business was good.

Carmen sat with me every day since, along with her boyfriend Joel. That day was no different, although I'd never wished for privacy more. Right after I took my seat in the cafeteria, they showed up and sat across from me.

She put her tray down and gave me a warm smile. There wasn't a mean bone in Carmen's body. With her soft voice and the same beautiful dark features as her mom, who'd moved from Puerto Rico, she could have more friends if she tried. However, Joel was the only person she seemed to notice and they made a cute couple. At six-four, he looked like a giant in the seat next to her. She often wore one of his jackets and had to roll up the sleeves.

I poured ketchup on my plate and dunked a French fry. "Thanks, Joel."

"For what?" he asked in a teasing voice.

As usual, he'd get more words out of me than I felt like speaking. "For bringing Lorraine home."

"It was no problem."

"I didn't realize she'd be stuck at school. My mother—"

"It's okay," Carmen said. "Really. Let's change the subject."

The last thing I needed was Carmen and Joel thinking there was a problem. I didn't need anyone thinking we had a problem. "Lorraine was silly to ask you to drop her off before the house."

Carmen turned to him, twirling the end of her cocoa-colored braid on her finger. "You dropped the poor girl off in the woods? You should have dropped her off at the front door and watched her walk inside. That's what a real man would do."

Joel shrugged. "I didn't want her dad to shoot at me. I've heard fathers do that sometimes."

Carmen rolled her eyes. "I wouldn't know. My dad lives in another state."

What a laugh. This huge guy was worried my dad would shoot him. As I pictured my mother holding a gun, I stifled a grin.

"Besides," Joel said, "they live in the country for a reason. No one is going down to that house to cause trouble." He lowered his voice. "Would your dad do anything if I dropped Lorraine at the door?"

"Probably just warn you to stay away from his twelve-year-old daughter," I said.

Joel's jaw dropped. "Twelve?"

"Well, she'll be thirteen in a few weeks."

He did the math on his hands just to be sure. "How can she be twelve in eighth grade?"

"Because she skipped a grade," I said. "Lorraine was so smart, especially in math, that they moved her up three years ago."

"I knew she was smart," he said, "but I didn't realize Lorraine skipped a grade. No wonder she tries so hard to act older. Bet that's been weird."

Weird? That was nothing compared to what happened yesterday. "My parents admitted they'd made a mistake by allowing it, but she can't go back now."

Joel stopped eating and stared at me. "She's worried, I think. You never talk about it, but Lorraine told me how sick your mom is."

"If I talk about it, that means I have to think about it. The only good thing about coming to school is I don't have to think about home." A flash of red caught my eye, and I jumped to my feet, shaking off my hand.

Carmen jumped up and so did Joel.

"What's wrong?" she yelled.

The surrounding noise disappeared. Everyone faded to black. All I could see was blood on my hands and in my head. My chest tightened and I gasped. Before I realized what was happening, Carmen put her arms around me and forced me back into my seat.

"It's okay," she said. "Take a deep breath. Tell me what's bothering you."

"Blood…" I held up my hand and took several deep breaths.

"It's not okay," Joel said to Carmen before shoving a napkin at me. "It's ketchup."

My cheeks flamed as Carmen helped wipe the ketchup from my hand. "Don't worry. We all feel like screaming sometimes."

"Did I…" I swallowed and peered around. Several students looked our way. "Did you hear me scream?"

She nodded. "Everyone in the cafeteria heard you scream."

"You don't have to talk about your mom," Joel said. "I understand."

The edge in his voice turned my embarrassment into anger. "Understand?" What did he know about me or my family? "What about *your* mom?"

His expression clouded. "Let's not talk about my mom either."

The chill in his voice stunned me. "I didn't mean—"

Joel grabbed his tray and stood. "See you later, Carmen."

Carmen said nothing as he dumped his tray and left through the main doors.

"What did I say?" I asked.

She turned to me. "Joel notices everything. He wants to know everyone's problems and thinks he can fix most of them, but he never talks about his own family."

"What do you know about them?"

"He lives with his aunt."

"He doesn't live with his mother?"

Carmen shook her head. "His mother works in some government building in Atlanta. He used to stay with her, but he had trouble in school. That's why she sent him here."

I couldn't imagine my parents sending me away. "Does he ever see her?"

"Sometimes he goes back for the weekend." She lowered her voice. "He doesn't consider Atlanta home."

"What about his father?"

"Never heard his name. Joel's mother gave him the name Greene. It's her last name."

I thought about the secrets my parents kept. "Maybe he feels like he can't tell anyone because he's protecting his family."

"At least I have one friend who doesn't have to keep secrets."

This wasn't good. I was keeping secrets and so was her boyfriend. How could I be the friend she wanted without betraying my family?

Her smile didn't calm the churning in my stomach.

*****

That afternoon, I drove down the dirt road with a sense someone might be watching us. Could more of those soldiers return? Maybe I'd pull up in a yard filled with flashing cars from the sheriff's office. I gripped the steering wheel and pushed down on the accelerator.

"Why are you acting strange?" Lorraine asked.

I shifted the truck into third gear. "I'm not."

She crossed her arms and stared ahead. "You've been acting weird all day."

At the house, Mom waited for us in the living room. Lorraine ran ahead, and Mom pulled her into a warm hug. "Rainey, glad you could make it."

Lorraine laughed. "Where else would I go?"

Mom released her and held out two arms for me. As I walked into her embrace, I glanced around the room. No mud. "Feeling better?" I whispered.

"Much." She pulled away. "Lorraine, I did laundry today. Your chore is to fold all the clothes on the couch."

My sister's eyes widened as she surveyed a mountain of jeans and shirts, plus towels and socks that spilled onto the carpet. "This will take me an hour."

"It will take longer unless you get started now."

With a nod, Lorraine set her shoulders and approached the clothes. Usually, I folded clothes on laundry day. "What should I do?" I asked.

She led me into the kitchen, and the humor faded from her voice. "We'll talk in the garden."

Again, I scanned the room for any lingering mud. "We should talk here."

With a smile, she pointed at the door to the porch. "See you outside." Before I could answer, she disappeared.

My mouth fell open, and my backpack dropped to the floor. Mom had teleported out of the room as the man had yesterday. I glanced at the door to the living room. Muffled singing from Lorraine drifted through.

I snatched open the porch door and ran outside. She stood near a sprinkler at the center of the garden. A mist of water fanned out as the sprinkler turned, dousing the tomato plants. Every stalk in the garden, along with every hill of dirt, had been repaired since her altercation with the soldiers. "Don't do that," I yelled.

"Why?" she asked. "It's who I am."

"You're not the same person who raised me. What if Lorraine saw you teleport?"

"Maybe it's time I tell her the truth."

"Not yet." I gritted my teeth. "Lorraine isn't ready to know what you are."

"You mean what *we* are." She arched an eyebrow. "You think to buy her time? Do you wish for more time?"

"With you? Yes, but this power is scaring me."

"She fears the future," said a female voice with a strange accent.

Across the garden, a woman sat on the bench. I blinked with a wary feeling at the pit of my stomach. "Was she here a minute ago?"

"Maybe," Mom said with a twinkle in her eyes. "Maybe not."

"This isn't funny."

"I'd like you to meet Keva," my mother said.

The woman shaded her eyes from the afternoon sun, which had finally sunk below the trees. I looked at Mom.

"You rarely come out here until after dark. That's two days in a row."

"Keva's visit is special," she said. "I needed help to make sure more of the men who came yesterday won't return."

"They were pawns in a deadly game," Keva said. "Your mother's power is rare on our world. As long as they believe she can be recovered, more will return."

I walked to her, shocked at how human she seemed, on the surface at least. Even while sitting, I felt sure she was shorter than me. Her skin was radiant with a healthy glow. At a size two max, the way she held herself made me think of a firecracker about to go off. Brown hair fell to her shoulders, thin strands with streaks of silver. Not silver as in gray hair, but a sleek silver that glistened in the light. Her eyelids shimmered with the same shade of silver. Keva's eyes were the only part of her that made me shiver. There was a depth to her brown eyes, a sharp intelligence focused on me.

"You speak English?" I asked.

She nodded. "Golvern has one language for the entire population, but we maintain close ties with Earth. We speak many of your languages."

Amazing. She could probably speak dozens of languages when I could only speak one. "Can I learn to speak Golvern's language?"

"In due time," she said.

Mom sat to Keva's right. "Keva got rid of the ship those men brought. No one will know what happened yesterday. I thought that might make you feel better."

Keva held out her hand.

I studied her slender fingers. We weren't that different except for being from different sides of the galaxy. She wore no rings, but a web-like tattoo covered the last two fingers on both hands. When she motioned for me to take her hand, I glanced at Mom. "What does she want?"

"To shake your hand. You must grant her permission."

Permission to shake a hand? What other strange rules did this planet have? I gathered my courage and raised my hand. Her firm grip held my fingers for several seconds as she closed her eyes and seemed to meditate.

Without warning, she released me and turned to Mom. "My journey was not wasted."

Mom hugged the woman and Keva stood. "Until then."

Keva gave me a solemn glance. "Until then." She faded from sight, leaving me alone with Mom in the garden. The only sound was the sprinkler.

Mom shaded her eyes as she watched the sunset. She said a few words under her breath and then looked up at me.

"Where did she go?" I asked.

"Keva teleported back to her ship."

I glanced upward. "Ship?"

Mom pointed toward the sky. "She's parked there, I think, behind that cloud."

"Really?"

She laughed. "Don't be so gullible."

We both laughed, hers satisfied and mine nervous as I processed the fact my mother had friends from space. Maybe it was time to accept my life would never be normal again. "Did I do something wrong? She shook my hand and then couldn't get out of here fast enough."

"You did nothing wrong," she said. "When Keva touched your skin, she saw your future."

You must grant her permission. "Another power?"

"The power to see the future is almost as rare as my power."

The future. Keva was from a planet called Golvern, and she had the power to see the future. "You mean the future as in what could happen tomorrow at school?"

She smiled. "I mean what will happen since you've inherited my power."

EPISODE 4

Reasons

Mom watched her words sink in. She motioned for me to take the seat beside her on the bench, but I couldn't move.

I mean what will happen since you've inherited my power.

For a moment, I stood in shock, turning the words over in my head as if I'd realized something vital to my existence. "How do you know I'll have your power?"

"Keva has the power to see the future of people she touches."

"Any people?"

"Will you please sit down?" Sighing, Mom leaned back against the bench and looked toward the sky. "I know this isn't easy."

Slowly, I sat next to her, but not close enough she could brush against me.

"That's better," Mom said. "Keva's power doesn't work on everyone. We didn't know if she would get a read on you, but she was determined to try."

"Why?"

"Don't you want to know if you're like me?"

"Like an alien?" Several repercussions for those words flowed through my head along with a laugh that escaped my lips.

"You don't believe me." She sighed again. "Maybe you don't want to believe."

I leaned back and stared at the clouds, unsure of what she saw above us. "I watched you teleport."

"Sometimes you have to see the truth to believe."

"It's not that I don't believe or I don't want to believe. You can't spring this truth on me and expect me to immediately accept. You say you're from another planet, but nothing about what that means or how you got here."

"On a spaceship. I thought we'd discussed how I arrived."

"You mentioned a spaceship, but I haven't seen it." I leaned forward to stand. "What do you want from me?"

Her hand shot out and gripped my arm, but she didn't have the strength to keep me in place. "I want you to try to teleport."

Again, laughter caught me on the raw. I sank back onto the weathered wood. "You want me to teleport? You haven't even explained how this power works."

"That part *is* easy. All you do is think of another place. Close your eyes and picture yourself there."

I closed my eyes and thought of the living room. No, Lorraine might see me. Maybe the kitchen or my bedroom. Maybe down by the lake, but I didn't want to think of what existed under the surface of that murky water. With a sigh, I opened my eyes.

"What's wrong?" she asked.

"I can't think of any place to go."

Her chuckle was low and filled with the same warmth as the hand that gripped mine. "Only you, Charlie. Anyone else could think of a dozen places they'd rather be. Lorraine could probably name a hundred."

"We never take vacations and I go nowhere but to school and the store downtown."

"Your father and I have always avoided attention."

"Now I know why."

Mom turned to me and held out a hand. A gun appeared in her palm, which she offered to me. "Imagine this on the counter in our kitchen."

My breath hitched as I stared at the gun. It was black like a pistol used in one of those TV police shows. I reached for the gun and gripped the cold metal in my palm. My finger twitched where it landed near the trigger, a surprisingly natural fit and lighter than I'd expected. Imagining I actually had the power to move an object with my mind felt uncomfortable. On the one hand, having this power would be exciting. On the other, soldiers may come for me like they did for Mom. "Is this the gun you used to shoot those men?"

"Don't worry about them." She held up a hand when I tried to speak. "I can hear the waver in your voice. Focus on moving the gun and nothing else."

Concentrating, I focused on the gun, but the metal remained in my hand. "I don't want to be like you. They may come for me next—"

Gently, she took the gun from my hand while pointing the barrel away from us. "You're not ready and we have little time. Charlie, dear, you've got to put this fear out of your mind."

"If you already know I can teleport, why worry now?" This conversation had moved from strange to ridiculous. How much did she think I could believe? "You could have showed me years ago, but you didn't. Instead, you left me in the dark and suddenly it's so important for me to try. Now that you're out of time…" My voice cracked on the last word. Her sickness, along with this crazy business about soldiers with laser guns and alien powers, was too much.

"Those men didn't come after me because I can teleport. Everyone from Golvern can teleport. They wanted my power to shoot with precision, which everyone *isn't* born with." Her voice dropped, and a note of sadness entered. "I hear there are only eight of us left."

"Eight?" I choked. "How many people live on this planet?"

"Golvern is less than half the size of Earth and the surface is mostly water. While Earth is home to more than a billion people, Golvern has far less."

"What do you think Keva saw?" I asked. "Can you trust her?"

"I've known Keva since before you were born. She hasn't told me the details of her vision, only that you'll have my power. I trust her with my life."

"Which power?"

"The rare one."

I jumped to my feet. "That was the first time I've ever held a gun. How soon do you expect me to shoot one?"

"With my training, by the middle of next week."

She had to be joking. "You might show me how to aim straight, but I'll never be able to shoot anyone."

"Never let fear or any other emotion dictate your life."

Fear? As I walked, I wiped tears from my eyes. I wouldn't let the threat of some power that didn't exist last week dictate my life. When I reached the porch, she called my name. I turned and Mom pointed the gun in my direction. Looking at the barrel, all I could do was stare as she fired off one bullet aimed for my head. A split-second later, the bullet stopped between my eyes, mere inches from my nose.

As if the entire world had stopped, the bullet hung in the air and stared me down. I couldn't breathe or think or speak. Mom appeared next to me and took the bullet, closing it tightly in her palm.

"Y-you could have killed me," I stuttered. "H-how did you stop the bullet?"

"With my power to control the bullet's velocity. It's about more than just aiming straight." She grinned. "Are you still afraid?"

I wasn't sure how to answer her question.

*****

Middle of *next week* for me to stop a bullet in someone's face? Tomorrow was Friday and next week I'd learn how to shoot a gun. Mom leaned on me as we entered through the kitchen; Dad walked in as the door closed behind us. He gave us a knowing look as he shifted her weight to him. Her arm went around his waist.

Mom was honest when she said using the power drained her strength. I didn't like the fact she skipped dinner that evening, and Dad wasn't the least bit happy about how tired she looked. While I waited for his return, I heated up leftover spaghetti sauce and boiled water for the noodles.

Lorraine stuck her head in the kitchen. "What's for dinner?"

"Leftovers," I said.

She glanced at the table. "I talked to Dad when he came home. Did he take Mom to bed already?"

"She was tired."

My sister's face fell. "I don't think I'm hungry tonight. Will you tell Dad I went to bed?"

"Fine." Water boiled in the pot before me. I broke the noodles in half and dumped them into the water, stirring as the angel hair pasta returned to a boil. When I glanced up again, the doorway was empty.

After I poured up the noodles, Dad returned and made himself a plate.

"Lorraine's not feeling well," I said.

"These days haven't been easy for any of us." He glanced at the long table, a solid oak masterpiece he'd built himself. "How about we eat in the living room, just this time?"

I grinned because of the softness in his voice and a distinct hint of mischief. We ate at the kitchen table as a family every night; it was Dad's rule. He always knew how to make me feel better. "Are you sure?"

He sprinkled cheese over his plate and headed for the living room, dropping into the recliner while spilling none of the sauce. I made a plate and sat on the couch. The evening news came on, and I relished these moments of feeling normal. I'd welcome any hint of normal in the months to come.

After a few minutes of world news, the show reported a bank robbery in New York City. One of the men moved faster than humanly possible, even faster than the cameras could keep up with. The anchor interviewed a woman who swore she saw the man disappear before her eyes. Pictures of people screaming and escaping a building with their hands up flashed across the screen. I shot Dad a look, but the TV had his complete attention.

"Could the man who disappeared be an alien?" I asked.

Dad took a bite of spaghetti. "Your mother has told me of others, but they want to be left alone as she does. Most likely it was a sophisticated plot to steal money and nothing more."

The way he accepted Mom's origins bothered me. Now he mentioned others like he was an expert on aliens. "How many others?"

"To tell you the truth, I'd rather not know."

A different news anchor interviewed a man who described agents dressed in black. A feeling of déjà vu made me shiver. "Who are these people?"

"Could be FBI or another agency. Your mother has stayed clear of the government for the last eighteen years. No one knows she's here, and we'd like to keep it that way." When he finished his spaghetti, Dad turned off the TV and put his plate in the sink. He checked on Mom and Lorraine, returning after I'd dumped the rest of my sauce in the trash. "Let's go for a ride."

"Now?" I asked.

He grabbed the keys for the Toyota from the hook near the door. "I'd like to visit the shop. You can drive."

Without a word, I left the house, and he followed to the truck. I climbed into the driver's seat, buckled the seatbelt, then cranked the engine. He dropped in next to me and pulled on his belt.

"What happened in the garden?" Dad asked when we'd reached the road.

"Mom showed me her power. She fired a bullet at my head and stopped it within inches of my nose."

He stared through the windshield at the dark highway up ahead. Dad observed the edge of both sides of the road for a reflection of light. Whenever we rode at night, he always scanned the trees for the eyes of deer that could dart into the road. "It's amazing to watch. She's tried that trick on me several times."

"Were you scared?"

"Were you?"

"I didn't have time to decide if I felt scared. She plans to train me to shoot like her by the middle of next week. I don't think I can."

"Why not?"

I gripped the steering wheel and looked away from the bright lights of an approaching car.

"When I first taught you to drive this truck, I figured you might struggle with shifting the gears. Instead, you did great. Do you know why driving came easy for you?"

"Because you were a brilliant teacher?"

"You made me look like a brilliant teacher, but the biggest reason is you didn't fear driving."

"She told me not to let fear dictate my life."

"Your mother understands the pitfalls of letting her emotions get the best of her."

"Why?" I asked.

"I think she should tell the story."

Fifteen minutes later, I stopped the truck along one of the streets in downtown Credence. Some considered the center of the town a historic district; the brick railroad station had once been a hub for travel in our region. I parked across from Dad's shop, near the railroad tracks.

He unlocked the front door and opened it to flip on several overhead lights. A florescent glow reflected from the smooth surface of an oak table similar to the one in our kitchen but not big enough to seat eight. Six handcrafted chairs sat around the table.

Beyond the table were wood bunk beds, a bedroom suite, and coffee tables for a living room. The room, full of Dad's creations, smelled of pine, but also a hint of my favorite wood—cedar. To my right was a chest he'd designed with intricate carvings along the edges.

"I thought you'd like to know how your mother and I met."

I pushed happy thoughts of playing in the store as a kid out of my mind. "How?"

He sat in a wood swing he'd built and motioned for me to sit next to him. "Your mother came to Earth on an educational trip of sorts. It sounds strange, but people from that planet found interest in studying Earth. Their technology is hundreds of years more advanced, but they enjoy our literature and entertainment."

"Weird," I said.

"I'd run this shop for two years, ever since my dad died of a heart attack. That morning, I put a new table and chairs in the front window as a display. She saw the furniture and fell in love. Apparently, they didn't cut trees where she was from and wood furniture was highly sought after. Only the elite members of society furnished their homes with wood."

"Then she was poor like we are."

He laughed heartily. "Watch who you're calling poor. Haven't you always gotten everything you needed?"

"That's not what I mean. Is this society like ours?"

"There are different social levels, if that's what you're asking. When she first walked into my shop, I saw this girl about eighteen who truly lit up the room. I'll never forget the look on her face. She focused entirely on the furniture, while my attention was on her. Someone could have walked out with the entire store and I wouldn't have noticed."

"Would you call it love at first sight?"

"I don't know what I'd call it. All I knew was I couldn't let her leave without a promise we'd meet again. We spent the next week together, and it was the best week of my life. When I asked her to marry me, she showed me her power to teleport. I was… surprised. Her second power was more to take in. I'd known folks from the military who could shoot, but she was truly an expert marksman."

"She never went back?"

He sighed. "For two years, soldiers came to take her back. That marksman power was one her government liked to control. Eventually, she decided they'd never stop and went home. But it wasn't home anymore. Three months later, she returned."

I smiled. "Because she loved you."

"That and she was pregnant with you."

My eyes widened. "You mean I was... She was... You think she came back because of me?"

"That's how it works with love, Charlie. You never know what's in the cards, but you've got to be prepared for anything. She decided to stay and fight anyone who came our way. I promised to protect Candy with my dying breath. Turns out the one thing she didn't need was my protection." He gripped the arm of the swing. "We kept the table from the window, since it's the reason we got together. Unfortunately, it burned in the fire."

The sadness in his voice brought tears to my eyes. "You made another, didn't you?"

He nodded. "The one in our house now is a replica. I never forget a piece of furniture I've made. Each is its own work of art—my small contribution to this life."

I squeezed his hand. "You have more contributions."

"Whenever I think of the past, this shop has always been my rock. For the three months your mother was gone, crafting this furniture kept me sane. Find something you love, Charlie, and give it your all." Dad winked at me and stood. "Even if it's not shooting a gun, but maybe give that an honest shot, too."

Maybe he was right. Even if I didn't have Mom's power, even if shooting a gun made me shake inside, I owed it to myself to find out. He cut off the lights, and I stared at the table while trying to imagine my mother walking into this store for the first time. As he locked the door and we walked across the street to where the truck waited, a deputy sheriff approached.

Dressed in a uniform with tall black boots, he closed the distance between us in record time. A gun hung from the belt at his waist, along with a walkie-talkie and a set of handcuffs.

"Gregory," the man said. "We need to talk."

"That sounds ominous," Dad said.

The walkie-talkie crackled with a voice calling dispatch, and the deputy turned down the volume. "Someone's been asking questions about your wife."

My heart pounded. Could someone know about Mom's power or that she killed those men?

EPISODE 5

Sneaky Business

Someone's been asking questions about your wife. The deputy's words made me shiver. Dad held out a hand, and the two men shook. "How are you, Roy? Nancy doing well?"

The calm in his voice shocked me when I couldn't trust my voice enough to open my mouth. I schooled my features and took a few deep breaths. Roy Parker went to high school with Dad back in the sixties. He wasn't a person I should fear.

Roy nodded. "We're doing fine. How is Candy?"

"She's seen better days, but we're thankful for each one we mark off the calendar together."

"I don't know what I'd do as a man in your position, but I'd be blessed to have half of your faith and her willpower."

"Life is what we make it." When the other man stayed silent, Dad said, "Shoot with whatever you've got to say."

Lifting his wide-brimmed hat, Roy wiped sweat from his brow and replaced the hat. "A man came around asking questions about a woman who might have come to town eighteen years ago. Maybe you saw him?"

"No," Dad said.

"Parts of his story rang true, and I thought of Candy. Can't remember anyone else showing up around that time. That summer was the worst drought in a hundred years."

"Nothing grew well that year except pecans," Dad said. "What did he want?"

"Information, as far as I could tell. He was looking for a woman he claims is his sister. That part of the story was hard to swallow. Clearly, his job was mercenary."

"We're Candy's only family." With a glance at me, Dad said, "Any idea who he was?"

Roy lifted a cigarette to his lips and lit the end with a long drag. "The only name he gave was Smith."

How convenient this man had such a common name. "What did he look like?" I asked.

Both men glanced at me. Roy took another drag on the cigarette and Dad stared across the street. Lights in the florist shop were still on. A lone car crawled through the nearest intersection. Otherwise, the street was empty. Had Carmen stayed late to help her mom again?

"He stood about five-eleven with brown hair. Black suit, mid to late twenties. Couldn't see his eyes behind the sunglasses."

"Anything else?" Dad asked.

"Didn't flash around a badge, but he smelled like a fed."

"Thanks, Roy."

Roy finished the cigarette. "Didn't have any type of accent I could place, but he got aggressive down at the diner. Ma Turner didn't like him asking about strange events, including some missing men, insinuating there could have been murders. I let him know we're a small town and our residents look out for each other. Not like we keep a stash of bodies around here."

A picture of our lake flashed in my head, along with two faces as they disappeared below.

Dad put an arm around my shoulders. "It's why I'm proud to have grown up in Credence. I can't think of a better place to raise my kids."

I let out a breath of relief as the deputy assured Dad he'd keep an eye out for the guy.

"If there's anything I can do to help, Greg, please let me know. I don't like outsiders coming around with questions."

"No one does," Dad said.

The deputy turned away. "If the man returns and gets aggressive with you, give me a heads-up and I'll take care of him."

"How do you do it?" I asked Dad when we were alone.

"The trick with lying is it has to center around truth to be effective. I've only ever lied when I absolutely had to; everything else remained true. Keep it simple."

A movement caught my eye in the doorway for the florist shop. Carmen emerged, and Joel followed. She noticed me and waved.

"Isn't that your friend?" Dad followed as I crossed the street in her direction.

"Hi, Mr. Conners," she said. "This is my boyfriend, Joel."

He and Joel shook hands. "How long have you been in town?" Dad asked.

"A few months. Glad to meet you, Mr. Conners." Joel cleared his throat and straightened to his full height, which was taller than Dad. "I thought you should know I gave your daughter a ride home this week."

Dad glanced at me and then up at Joel. "Which daughter?"

"Lorraine," Joel said. "She was stuck at school after practice for the math tournament. Her friend went home sick at lunch, and I didn't want her waiting there alone."

"You're on the math team?" He waited for Joel's nod. "I don't recall you stopping in our yard. How old are you?"

"Sixteen. I have a class with Charlie."

"You're in tenth grade?" Dad asked, his eyes wide. "Why didn't Lorraine ask you to come inside and meet me?"

Joel rubbed the back of his neck. "When we reached the driveway, she said you might get mad about me bringing her home. I didn't want to take a chance on getting shot."

"I guess you're in luck. Guns aren't my specialty."

Carmen laughed. "What is your specialty, Mr. Conners?"

"Anything that can be built with wood," Dad said in a teasing voice. "Is Joel trustworthy?"

"Yes," she said. "He'd never hurt anyone. I'm glad he gave Lorraine a ride. He wanted to make sure she got home safely."

"Then I guess I owe you thanks, Joel."

Joel seemed to relax. "If you don't mind, I could use your help with moving a table for Carmen's mom."

"I'd be glad to help." Dad followed Joel inside the store.

As soon as they disappeared into the store, Carmen turned to me. Her hazel eyes reflected the streetlight above, intensifying her stare. When she spoke, I felt her anger. "Joel told me he gave Lorraine a ride home because someone on the math team was bothering her."

"Who was it and what do you mean by bothering?"

"Steve Gerber had a hand on Lorraine's arm."

"Who is that?"

"Some eleventh-grader with a death wish. He doesn't realize Lorraine has a sister like you. Joel warned him, but Steve laughed it off. Said he always gets what he wants." Her voice lowered. "It's why Lorraine was upset on the way home."

I made fists at my sides. "Anything else?"

"I saw you talking with the deputy. Did you hear about the man in the black suit?"

"He was asking questions." I thought about Dad's words. *Keep it simple.* "The deputy said to let him know if the guy returns."

"That's what he told my mom."

"Did Joel see him?"

Carmen glanced toward the window where Joel and Dad were moving a display. "This was before Joel came by. He had a long-distance call with his mom this afternoon and wasn't in the mood to talk afterward." She looked at me. "When I told Joel the man looked like some kind of secret agent, he got all wound up and made me promise to page him if the guy showed up again. Said not to worry, he'd deal with it."

"The deputy said he might be some kind of federal agent. How do you think Joel will deal with the guy?"

"Who knows what's going through Joel's head. He seems like he wants to protect me. It's cute most of the time."

"Did mister agent say anything?"

She leaned close. "The guy was a creep. He knocked over a vase, and we both reached for it at the same time. His hand brushed mine, and he gave me the strangest look. It was like he could see into my soul."

"That's weird," I said.

"I told him to leave me alone and then the phone rang. He checked his watch as I took an order. When he pulled up his sleeve, I saw a tattoo. Didn't recognize the words, but I've always heard it's good to take note of details in case someone needs them later." She reached in her pocket and unfolded a sheet of yellow paper. "Here's what it said."

In her beautiful cursive scrawl were the words *'Fatle en lanre'*.

Your way with fate.

"Not sure what that means," she said. "Maybe it's Latin or something."

If only I could tell her the truth. Those words meant whoever this guy was, he knew about Mom's power. Maybe even what she'd done. I thought of Keva reading my future and wondered if this guy had the same power. Could he be from that other planet? "Guess we could research it at the library."

She shook her head. "Maybe you can. Credence has three weddings and two funerals this weekend. I'll be busy until Sunday night." Carmen reached for the paper. "Unless you need to keep it."

"No, I'm good." I'd never forget those words as long as I lived.

* * * * *

When we reached the house, Mom slept soundly in her bed. I wanted to tell her about the man's tattoo, but that would have to wait.

Lorraine was in her room; I wondered if she'd ever eaten. Instead of finding my sister tucked tightly in bed, she sat with her back to me, staring at moonlight drifting through the window. Sounds of muffled crying filled the room.

I sat down beside her. "You don't have to cry alone."

She gave me a sad smile and took my hand. "I was waiting for you, but it got late and I was alone…"

Touching her cheek, I wiped away the tears. "You're never alone. Don't forget you've always got me."

Lorraine sighed. She was probably thinking about how I could never replace the twin sister she lost. It didn't matter if I couldn't; I'd never stop trying.

"Worried about Mom?" I asked.

"Always." Her grip tightened. "She was sick in the bathroom and I tried to help her. I don't know what I'll do if she…"

"Carmen told me about Steve."

She froze. "I asked Joel not to tell anyone. Then he rats me out to Carmen and now she told you. Wait until I see him again."

"Don't be mean to Joel. He's worried about something Steve said."

"He shouldn't worry. No guy will ever put a hand on me again."

I glanced at her. "Did he hit you?"

"No, but he tried to keep me from leaving with Joel. Said we were meant for each other, that he'd known all year. If I told my parents, he'd get his gang friends to pay them a visit."

"That would be interesting."

She looked up at me. "What do you mean?"

I couldn't tell her about our family protection plan yet. How would she process the truth when I still couldn't wrap my mind around it all? "I'm sure Dad wouldn't let anything happen to us."

"With Mom being so sick, I don't want anyone coming here."

That made two of us. "You should have let Joel drop you off at the house. He and Dad met when we went downtown. I think Dad likes him."

She wiped a tear that trailed down her face. "Dad wasn't my biggest worry. I didn't want you to know about Steve."

"If someone is hurting you, I've got to know."

"But you always take things too far. Remember that boy last year?"

I crossed my arms. "Has he talked to you again?"

"Nelson looks the other way when I walk down the hall. So does Horace and Billy and that tenth grader you punched in the face."

"He was too old for you."

"We've only got a few more weeks of school. Maybe Steve will find some other girl and leave me alone."

"Does Steve talk to you in school?"

"Only if I stay at the locker long enough. That's why I've been keeping most of my books in my backpack."

Talking was one thing, but Steve was following my sister around. I needed to follow him around and put a stop to his attention. "Get some sleep and don't worry about Steve or Mom. There's nothing you can do about either tonight."

She nodded and crawled into bed. I pulled the sheet over her but stayed by the door until her breathing relaxed.

By the time I reached my room, I'd devised a plan to learn more about Steve. Eleventh-grade classes were in a building on the far end of the campus. There wasn't enough time between classes for me to watch him, even if I ran.

I could only think of one way to make this work. I'd have to teleport.

Mom suggested emotions could be my issue, but I needed to think about this logically. I'd seen her disappear before my eyes. If this was my legacy, I had to find a way to use this power. It might be the only way I could help Lorraine. As I dressed in shorts and a t-shirt for bed and brushed my teeth, I made up my mind.

Closing my eyes, I pictured myself outside of our front door. Lorraine's window was on the back side of the house. She wouldn't see me even if she woke. I focused harder, pushing all emotion out of my mind. This was normal. It was possible. I could do it.

The power was in my blood.

A strange warmth swirled in my stomach, like when I knew I was about to win a game. At the last possible second, a murky view of the lake replaced the scene outside the house. My eyes shot open and darkness surrounded me… as my body dropped into the water.

Cold, dark water.

I'd followed my vision of the men disappearing beneath the surface .and realized my worst nightmare. I fought against the water as my head sank beneath the surface. My lungs burned, demanding air, but I could only see darkness. I kicked my feet and waved my arms through the water. Somehow, I brought myself back to the top and choked on a breath of air.

As I tried to catch my breath and paddle enough to keep myself above the surface, I thought of the bodies below. Unseen hands that could grab my feet and pull me under…

Again I choked, but my eyes were finally adjusting to the moonlight. I found the closest bank and treaded water until I could touch bottom. I'd never wished for shoes more. Mud squeezed between my toes and I slipped, flailing my arms to keep from falling backward. I thought of the bodies and propelled myself toward the shore. Stalks of grass stuck to my legs as I stumbled up the bank.

I'd teleported.

Why wasn't I bursting with excitement? My world had shifted again and now I officially had a power. Seeing me teleport would thrill Mom, but all I wanted was a shower and my bed.

Next time I tried this experiment, I'd be sure to wear shoes.

My feet slid as I climbed the shore and weaved through the grass. Slimy green algae clung to my hair. The moon lit the water and the ground around my feet but seeing the woods beyond the lake didn't steady my racing heart. An owl hooted from the trees, which danced in the same breeze that chilled my skin. I jumped at the sound and put a hand on my chest. If only I could picture myself back in my bedroom and teleport there. I closed my eyes, but nothing.

Instead of teleporting back, I walked down the dirt road toward welcoming lights from the house up ahead. My toes ached by the time I walked through the garden and up on the porch. At the kitchen table sat Dad.

He glanced up as I walked in. "Go for a swim?"

"I imagined myself at the lake."

Dad leaned his head back and roared with laughter. "Don't you mean *in* the lake?"

"I didn't know how this was supposed to work."

"Well, you made something happen. Your mother will be proud but don't wake her tonight." He pointed at my head where a wad of algae hung from my hair. "You brought part of the lake back with you. Hope you were alone down there."

I stuck out my tongue. "I swam to the shore. Didn't touch the bottom."

"Good," he said. "There's no telling what's at the bottom of that lake."

EPISODE 6

Exposed

Despite teleporting myself into a lake in the middle of the night, I slept soundlessly after a long, hot shower. No nightmares of drowning in dark water or bodies kept me up.

The next morning, I cooked sausage and eggs while Mom sat at the table. As I flipped the sausage, I described the man from town and his tattoo. "Carmen said it was on his wrist. She noticed the tattoo when he checked his watch."

"Keva has a similar tattoo," Mom said. "People with the power to see the future live by those words."

"Do you think she knows him? Maybe they're related."

Mom glanced up. "How old did Ron say this man was?"

"Mid to late twenties. Is it someone you know? Dad said there were others living on Earth. Last night, the news talked about a man who robbed a bank in New York. He could move faster than the cameras. A few nights ago, it was the cover-up of an earthquake in Atlanta."

"Hmm." Mom took a sip of her coffee. "I don't know anyone with the power to cause an earthquake, but I do know a few people who can teleport."

I sat next to her. "People on TV suggested there's a government agency involved, a secret agency. The man yesterday wore a black suit like those agents on the news. He said he was looking for his sister."

"Since my brother has been dead for years, I don't think he came to Credence looking for me."

"Aren't you worried this man might know who you are? Maybe he could bring more soldiers."

"If someone from Golvern had found me, they'd be here by now."

"Don't you worry about humans?" I asked. "What if the government finds out about us?"

"Humans like to think they're advanced enough to deal with aliens, but their technology is hundreds of years behind. I've stayed away from human trouble over the years, and you must do the same. Never reveal your powers to any human. Then these agents will have no idea you exist."

I thought about the tattoo. "But there are others with the future power, right?"

She nodded absently as she stared into the cup.

The liquid seemed thicker than normal and had a yellow hue. "What are you drinking?"

"A special delivery from Keva. She brought one of my favorite drinks from back home."

Her words left me feeling disappointed. "I thought Earth was your home now."

She smiled and patted my arm. "I stand corrected. We'll call it my favorite imported drink."

"There's one more thing." I took a deep breath as Mom gave me a questioning look. "I teleported last night."

"Where?"

"Down to the lake. I had to walk back in the dark, but I think I can do it again."

"Of course you can do it again. I knew you'd find the power if you could only focus and believe in yourself."

The happiness in her voice made my insides glow. "I couldn't wait to tell you."

"This evening we'll test your abilities. You must practice often." She finished the drink. "After mastering this first power, we can work on finding your second power."

"Don't get ahead of yourself." I slid back from the table and stood. "What if I don't have a second power? I don't want to upset you."

Her eyes gleamed. "You'll never upset me, power or no power. I want what's best for you, but I also want you to know yourself fully. It's hard to flourish within limits you don't know exist."

"You want me to push the limits? Okay." I waved my hand at the stove and one of the back burners twisted on. Gas lit a circle of flames. "That actually worked."

"Since you didn't *assume* you couldn't turn the stove on, you had no reason to doubt."

"I can move anything with my mind?"

"As long as you believe you can. That's how greatness is won."

I wasn't sure about greatness, but I'd push the limit of this teleporting power to figure out how to stop Steve from threatening my sister.

*****

On the drive to the bus stop, Tom Petty came on the radio. I sang "I Won't Back Down" while drumming on the steering wheel. It was exactly the song I needed to prepare for the day ahead.

"Why are you in such a good mood?" Lorraine asked.

Because I had the power to get rid of Steve for good. "It's Friday."

"Thank goodness." She slid on her backpack and climbed from the truck.

The backpack looked like it weighed more than she did. "Need some help with your books?"

"No, I'm good."

As the bus bounced along the road to school, I considered the best time to find Steve and put my own brand of fear in him. My first and second classes had a test. I was supposed to cook a cake in home economics, but it wouldn't take a great deal of thought. Cooking had always come easy for me.

I could skip lunch, but then I'd miss talking with Carmen. Had she remembered anything else from meeting the man with the tattoo? Any details were important to figuring out if he was looking for Mom. Even though my mother didn't seem worried about a possible connection to her past, he hadn't been far from my mind all morning.

During each of my normally boring classes, I found a way to use my power without catching anyone's attention. With a casual flip of my hand, I made a stack of folders fall from my math teacher's desk, along with the chalk he was holding. Everyone laughed as he said 'silly me' in good humor. If only I could figure out his secret to being stress free.

In home economics, I made a mess of bread baked by a girl who'd teased me for most of the year. She couldn't figure out how the temperature got turned down or why the timer went off early.

Since using the power drained Mom's strength, I expected exhaustion to take over before the afternoon. However, with each new task, I felt energized.

At lunch, I dropped into my usual seat and Joel sat across from me. "Where's Carmen?" I asked.

He lifted a burger from his tray. "She stayed out to help her mom at the flower shop. Only missed two days all year so there shouldn't be a problem."

Which meant no more details from the visit to her shop. I took a bite of my burger. What could I talk to Joel about for the next twenty-five minutes? "Tell me something funny. I need a good laugh."

He finished his burger and started on his fries. "This girl in the cafeteria thought ketchup on her arm was blood. I thought she was going to run out of here. Haven't seen anything funnier in weeks."

"You're making fun of me after you ran out when I mentioned your mom?"

His eyes darkened. "You don't want to know about her."

"Carmen said she works in Atlanta. What does she do?"

"Boring stuff, really. She works in a government building."

When I felt sure he wouldn't elaborate, I asked, "That's it?"

"Yeah." He finished his fries and then his drink. "She writes reports and follows up when people don't pay their taxes. That's it."

"Do you ever get to see her?"

"Sometimes on the weekend, but I'd rather be here. I don't want to think about summer."

"Can you do me a favor?"

"What?" Joel asked.

"I want you to show me Steve Gerber."

"Carmen told you about him too?"

I nodded. "He was bothering my sister and I want to make sure it doesn't happen again."

Joel raised an eyebrow.

"You don't believe me?"

"I do. That's the problem."

"Will you help me?" I asked.

"Sure, but don't try to fight him."

"What makes you think I'll try to fight him?"

He smiled. "Because if Lorraine was my sister, I'd fight him."

"Thanks, I think."

"Look across the room, at the last table by the exit to the office. Steve has blond hair and a blue shirt. Someone at the tournament practice called him 'pretty boy' Steve."

I burned an image of Steve's face into memory. Now I had what I needed to find him later.

"Whatever you're planning, please keep me out of it. I don't want to get kicked out of this school."

"Would you have to go back to Atlanta?"

Joel lifted his tray and stood. "I'm not going back to school there."

*****

I left the cafeteria before lunch was over and shoved my books in my locker. Several of the eleventh and twelfth graders left at lunchtime for jobs, and I found Steve walking with a group toward the parking lot. Instead of walking into the rows of cars, I waited behind a building under construction.

One day, the school would have a new room for the band to practice. Work had stopped for the day; maybe the construction crew got an early start on the weekend. Behind the building was a stack of blocks as tall as me. It was the perfect place to hide.

Steve left the crowd headed for vehicles. He walked down the sidewalk and away from the building, along a row of busses already in line for the afternoon pickup. Where was he going?

I followed, creeping down the side of the building while keeping enough distance he wouldn't notice me. He turned once and I ducked behind a bush large enough for me to hide. After passing six busses, he stepped off the sidewalk and walked behind one with the rear emergency door open. I stayed back, tiptoeing until I reached the bus. I leaned against the side and listened for him.

After a few minutes, he hadn't emerged. I moved around the back of the bus, ducking under the open door. Maybe someone had been cleaning the bus. I peeked around the side and Steve stood with a cigarette. Smoke rose from the cigarette, twisting in the air above his head. So, he'd ditched class to smoke.

I waved and the cigarette disappeared from his hand. Steve looked around in shock. Then he was dumbfounded. I put a hand over my mouth to keep from laughing. He bent to study the ground, and I pulled back out of sight. When I peeked again, he pulled a pack of cigarettes from his pocket and opened the lid to retrieve a lighter. He noticed me as he lit another cigarette.

I crossed my arms over my chest and stepped closer. "I'm Lorraine's older sister. I want you to leave her alone."

He looked confused. "Who?"

"The girl you grabbed at the tournament practice. I want you to stop bothering her."

"Bother her? Lorraine is in love with me."

This time I couldn't stop the laughter. Steve didn't seem threatening at all. Maybe I'd call him 'pretty dumb' Steve instead of 'pretty boy' Steve. How had he made it on the math team? "If she doesn't like you, why bother?"

He rose to stand at his full height, at least six inches taller than me. "She's the prettiest girl in school. I'm going to *have* her and there's nothing you can do about it."

"Lorraine's younger than she looks. She's a kid."

"She won't be for long." Steve blew smoke in my face and took another drag. "Can't you see I'm busy?"

Disgust rippled through me. "Stay away from her or I'll punch your face."

He reached for me, and I aimed a fist at his head. I landed a blow on his cheek, and Steve shoved me against the bus. My arm scraped a sharp edge along one of the windows. I cursed and shoved an elbow into his side, hard enough he pushed me away and ducked between the buses. He stumbled onto the sidewalk, near a broken chunk of concrete. I waved and the concrete appeared in front of his feet. Unaware, he tripped and fell on his face.

I closed my eyes and pictured myself behind the stack of blocks at the construction site. As I opened my eyes, I laughed with relief at the sight of the blocks and spun to make sure no one saw me. My heart dropped to my feet as I realized I wasn't alone. Someone saw me teleport.

Joel leaned against a nearby tree. "I was waiting for you to come back. I wanted to make sure you were okay, but I never expected…" He glanced at my arm and rushed forward. "You're actually bleeding this time." Joel dropped his backpack to his feet. From the front pocket, he pulled a box with a roll of gauze and wrapped my arm.

"You carry a first-aid kit in your backpack?"

His voice was harsh. "I like to be prepared for anything."

Despite Joel's size, he handled my arm with great care. The way he wrapped the gauze seemed almost professional. "Where did you learn this?" I asked.

"I took some medical classes."

"For school credit?"

"The cut doesn't need stitches, but you should see the nurse."

"Thanks," I said, "but I don't want anyone to know where I was."

Joel's eyes flickered over me. "Fine," he said, dropping my arm.

I swallowed. "Do you want to know—"

He held up his hands. "I didn't see what happened and don't want to know anything about it."

"What?"

"You heard me. I'll never speak of this day and neither will you."

"But you must have seen—"

"I didn't see anything." He turned and ran down the sidewalk.

Joel didn't look back at me.

*****

That evening, Mom and I sat on the bench after the sun had set. We talked about how I used my power to scare the guy that was messing with Lorraine. The only part I left out was Joel seeing me teleport. I still hadn't figured out how he wrapped my arm so calmly or why he ran off. Maybe Joel didn't do deep conversations. Carmen had suggested he looked for ways to fix people's problems.

There was no fixing mine.

"You should be careful," Mom said. "Some things we can explain away, but you don't want anyone finding out about your power. Especially someone in a position of authority. If our government found out about your power, they'd use you for their own agenda. You'd be a guinea pig for their experiments."

Good thing Joel wasn't a threat. His mom did work in a government building, but who in a tax office cared about impossible powers like mine? I breathed a sigh of relief. Maybe on Monday I could convince Joel he saw nothing bizarre like me teleporting.

Mom stood and pulled me up with her. "I want to show you something."

Before I could answer, the dark garden disappeared, and an open landscape surrounded us. The sun sat low on the horizon. I squinted at trees in the distance. "Where are we?"

"Wyoming. This is a remote location where I've often come to think." She pointed to a bench like the one from our garden. "The stars are brighter here."

For miles in either direction, there was nothing but rocks, grass, and this lone bench. At the edge of sight were mountains. "I can use my power to teleport someone else?"

"Yes, but you must touch them."

"How often do you come here?"

"I haven't in months. We're two thousand miles from home. Do you think you can take us back?"

"Maybe."

"If you think about it, you'll always find a way to tell yourself no."

Perhaps she was right. I reached for her arm and closed my eyes, focusing on a picture of the garden. When I opened my eyes, we stood in the same spot as earlier, next to her bench at home.

Pride shone in her eyes. "You conquered your fear of this power better than I ever imagined."

"I'm not afraid. Why is that so important?"

"Any strong emotion can interrupt your focus, but fear is the worst. It speeds up your heart rate and makes tapping into your power harder. The easiest way to use your power is when you think only of the one goal."

"Is fear why you blame yourself for Darla's death?"

She sat on the bench and put her head in her hands. "When your father woke me that night, smoke filled the room. My first instinct was my girls, but fear of what may have already happened to you paralyzed me. It all happened so fast. I couldn't teleport and he took me out first. It was the logical choice, and I coughed on the ground as I tried to catch my breath. He ran back in and pulled you out. By the time I found control and helped him pull Lorraine and Darla out, it was too late."

"It's not your fault she died." I sat beside her. "Wasn't there an electrical storm? Lightning hit the house—"

"If I hadn't lost my focus, I could have saved her. I've blamed myself every day since."

For several minutes, we watched the stars. Crickets chirped and unseen animals rustled the grass behind us. Lightning bugs flashed along the edge of trees.

She clenched her fists and stood. Mom walked to the end of the garden, face set with determination, and I followed. Along six of the wooden fence posts were glass coke bottles. In her hand, a black gun appeared, which she handed to me.

"Don't think about it," she said. "Just shoot."

I held up the gun and fired six bullets, one at each of the bottles. All other sounds faded from the night as bullets cut through the trees beyond the fence. "Guess I don't have the power." Tears filled my eyes. "That means I'm not like you."

She put her arms around me. "You've made extraordinary progress in the last twenty-four hours."

Maybe teleporting so often that day finally caught up with me. "I'm tired."

Mom pulled back. "Whatever happens, don't give up. You'll find this power."

"How can you be sure? I'm half human."

"On Golvern, I was called a Protector because of this power. I had the strongest bloodline ever known. It's why those soldiers came after me and why they'd come after anyone with my legacy. Human or no human, you have the gift."

"What if I don't want to be a Protector?"

"You'll be powerful," she said and turned away to cough. "But not powerful enough to challenge fate. Not even I could win that fight."

EPISODE 7

Bullseye

I thought about Mom's words. *Not even I could win that fight.* "You've mentioned fate several times. Why is this word so important to you?"

She took my hand and led me to the bench. We sat side-by-side as she pointed to the sky. "Do you see that hazy group of stars near the horizon?"

I stared at the dark landscape as my eyes adjusted. The stars became distinct instead of blotches of light that faded together. "Is that where Golvern is?"

She chuckled. "You can't see Golvern from here. Those stars represent a gateway that allows travel between the two planets. It turns a forty-year trip aboard a spaceship into less than an hour."

"Gateway?"

"A collapsed star. You could call it a black hole with a cylindrical shape. One end is at Golvern and the other is at the edge of this solar system. The gateway was discovered hundreds of years ago. It's how people from Golvern started visiting Earth."

"Dad said they have advanced technology. Why come here?"

"Golvern is a smaller planet and more advanced, but the people there love the variety of entertainment created on Earth. Literature from this planet is consumed with a hunger and many precious metals like gold and silver don't naturally occur on Golvern. There is an elegance in many human works of art that citizens of Golvern adore."

"What do people there look like?"

She blinked. "Same as you and me. The entire planet speaks the same language, but there is a variety of sub-cultures readily accepted by all. Most citizens of Golvern believe people should be treated the same regardless of the way they look or the color of their skin. It's the harmony Earth could only dream of, but just for those with Golvern blood."

"What about money?" I asked.

"There is always an advantage to having money. I can't imagine a society without some consideration of wealth."

"How many planets have you seen?"

"With people like us? Only Earth and Golvern. It's strange that the people are so similar with one big difference. Many of those on Golvern detest humans."

"I thought you said they like our literature."

"Humans have been brought to Golvern over the years, but they don't have the powers held in high regard. They can't do the most basic task—teleport. Some believe over the centuries human DNA has weakened Golvern's greatness."

I considered her words. "Dad said you went to Golvern after you'd married him but came back after finding out you were pregnant with me. If you never had me, would you have stayed?"

"I loved your father. When the soldiers kept coming, I decided staying here wasn't worth putting his life in danger. That's why I left."

The thought of growing up on another planet made me shudder. "Were you worried about me being different?"

"Almost everyone on Golvern is born with a twin. You weren't and that fact alone would have made your life unbearable."

"Even with your strong bloodline?"

"I'm afraid so. The human part of you would have been shunned for being different. I didn't want that life for you."

"Did you ever think of going back?" I asked.

"Once you were born, I was never going back." She hesitated. "The government sends people without a twin to special schools, separate from the general population. They don't get to choose their careers and they never own property. Once in the system, you can never advance beyond a low-paying job. Life is tough for anyone with human blood. The lucky ones are born with a twin and able to hide who they are."

"Why not send them back to Earth?"

"The court of public opinion would never allow that. Which brings me to another point. People with rare powers are also treated differently."

"Like you?"

"The government wanted to control my Protector power. It's why I left the first time and why their soldiers wouldn't stop coming after me."

My mouth felt dry. "What about the advanced technology? Is there a way to cure your cancer?"

"I'm long past the point of no return. No technology could save me now."

"Maybe they could have caught your cancer earlier."

Mom gathered my hands in hers. "Charlie, the illness I have isn't what humans consider cancer."

"What?"

"True, it's eating me up inside, but it's not the same." She took a deep breath. "On Golvern, we have two suns. Neither are as strong as Earth's sun."

"Does Golvern have two of everything?"

"One might think so. Earth's sun produces more radiation and affects my cells differently than it does humans. People from Golvern will eventually die from exposure to this radiation."

How could she explain so calmly? "Being on Earth is making you sick?"

"That's right."

"What about me and Lorraine?"

"The human part of your DNA protects you from the radiation. You might develop skin cancer over time like humans, but the sun won't ravage your body as it has mine."

"You need to go back."

"Technology can do nothing for me now. I've come to terms with my fate. I only worry about yours."

*****

Mom stayed in bed most of the weekend. Dad took Lorraine fishing and that afternoon she bragged about catching three large catfish. He skinned the fish and cut the meat into fillets, a useful skill when wanting to avoid bones. I soaked the fish in a mixture of egg and milk and then coated it with flour and cornmeal. Though the smell of the fish frying in the deep pot of grease made my stomach growl, I couldn't bring myself to eat the first bite.

Not after knowing what the fish had eaten.

While they were gone, I practiced teleporting myself to various places throughout the woods where no one would be watching. I spied on Dad and Lorraine down by the lake. Once, I think he noticed me hiding in the trees. He looked in my direction and stared long enough to make me grin. Maybe he knew I'd be testing myself or maybe he knew these woods better than anyone. His knowledge of the different trees had always impressed me, along with how he could pick up the sounds of particular animals.

I finished my chores in record time. If only Mom could have seen me relaxing on the couch while the vacuum maneuvered itself around the room. Every time I pointed at the vacuum, it did my bidding. I found I didn't have to move my hand every time I wanted something to happen, but the motion helped me to focus.

On Sunday, I moved the rug near the stove and froze at the sight of mud. I fought tears that sprang to my eyes as I thought of those men invading our lives.

The nightmare would never end.

I'd always look over my shoulder and wonder if someone was watching us.

Even though the floor already gleamed from where I'd mopped the tile, I kneeled and scrubbed every square inch with my hands. By the time Dad and Lorraine came back from another morning of fishing, my fingers cracked and bled.

He grasped one of my hands and gave me a look of concern. I pulled the hand back and went to my room.

Something about that day with the mud had changed me forever. Now I saw dirt and filth wherever I looked. Even in my room, I couldn't lay on the bed without straightening every item on my dresser at least twice. I organized my closet until I'd grouped the clothes by color and length. Shoes thrown randomly in the corner had to be scrubbed until each pair shined and was grouped in a neat row along the wall. One shoe was missing the mate, and I threw it away.

Finally, I sat on the bed and stared at my walls. A cobweb in one corner of the ceiling made me shudder. I'd never paid attention to details like they might be dangerous. If any item was out of place from now on, I'd wonder if an unwanted visitor could lurk in the shadows of my life.

By cleaning, there'd be no more shadows to hide.

I glanced down at the cut on my arm. Already healing, I wondered if Joel had told someone about seeing me teleport. Deep inside, a voice said I could trust him.

Under the pillow I slept on every night, I found the picture.

Visions of the house burning that night flashed before me. Screams, though I wasn't sure who made them. Maybe all of us. Seeing Lorraine and Darla loaded on a stretcher and shoved into an ambulance. Nine years ago felt like yesterday.

Months later, after Lorraine was home, I found her staring at a picture of our family Dad salvaged from the ashes left where our old house once stood. In a rage, she lifted the frame from the fireplace and busted it against the rock ledge. Mom rushed forward as Lorraine pulled the picture from the frame and ripped it into several pieces.

Lorraine couldn't stand to see Darla. After she broke the rest of the pictures in the house, our parents gave up on hanging new ones. They said it was Lorraine's way of dealing with Darla's loss. She deserved closure after losing the closest person in her world. That's when Mom first revealed having a brother who died years before. Twins ran in her family even though I didn't have one. Now I knew it wasn't just Mom's family. Lorraine was born with a twin for the same reason Mom was. I was the odd one.

Other parents might have taken their child to a psychologist but not my family. Dad's solution was to put his camera away and make no more pictures of us.

Years later, I found a Polaroid of us he'd kept hidden in his shop. It was from the summer before the fire. Three girls smiled, wrapped in their parents' arms. I asked Dad for the picture, and he gave it to me, with the stipulation I never show Lorraine.

Flames had licked the edges of the picture, but all of our faces were intact. I'd kept this picture under my pillow to look at whenever I wanted to see my family as we had been.

Lorraine would have been fine on this other planet. They wouldn't have treated her differently, like me. If I'd never been born, Mom could have gone back to Golvern and raised Lorraine. Maybe Darla wouldn't have died.

These thoughts were pointless. I slid the picture under my pillow and went to work cleaning the cobweb.

*****

For the rest of the week, Mom made me shoot every evening after dark. She lined up the coke bottles, as before, with one on each of six fence posts. I aimed the gun and tried to focus, but I missed every shot. On Thursday, she went to bed early and Dad tried to offer advice on how to aim.

"I know I'm not a marksman like your mother." He fired the gun, and with six tries, hit two of the bottles. "But I know how to shoot." Dad spent the next hour helping me feel more comfortable holding the gun. He told me how to breathe, to concentrate, and to aim a little higher because of the wind.

Still, I couldn't hit a single bottle.

At lunch on Friday, Carmen gave me an orange rose. She'd talked to me during lunch all week but seemed to force out her words when Joel and I both stayed silent.

"My favorite color." I smelled the sweet petals. "What's the occasion?"

She peered at her boyfriend, who'd been studying the pizza on his tray. He'd yet to take a bite. "I've been pestering Joel to tell me why he's been so quiet. He told me what happened last Friday."

My breathing stopped. "What did he say?"

"That Friday was a bad day. You went after Steve."

I glanced at Joel, and he raised his eyes. "I punched him in the face and told him to leave Lorraine alone."

"Is that why you've been quiet?" she asked.

"Yes," I said. "I didn't want to worry you with my problems."

"That's what friends are for." Carmen smiled. "The flower was to make you feel better. You shouldn't blame yourself for helping your sister."

She thought I was blaming myself? "I thought you might not have lunch with me anymore. Who would want to associate with the girl who beat up 'pretty boy' Steve? I think I'll start calling him 'pretty dumb' Steve instead."

Carmen bent over her tray in laughter. "Steve is a jerk, and he deserved you standing up to him. Didn't you think I'd be supportive?"

"I can punch him too," Joel said. "If it will make you both feel better."

"I appreciate the offer, but I think he's going to leave Lorraine alone." She glanced at her tray. "Crap, I forgot my drink."

Joel rose. "I'll get it for you."

With a wave, she jumped to her feet. "I'll be right back."

When she was out of earshot, he sat down and looked at me. "I'm not sure who or what you are, but I don't want Carmen knowing anything about what happened Friday. For some reason, she's set on keeping you as a friend."

"She thinks I'm her charity case. I think it's because her mom is sick like mine."

"I'm not sure what it is, but she likes you."

"You really care about Carmen, don't you?"

"I love Carmen," he said. "When we get eighteen, I plan to marry her. Until then, I'm going to do everything I can to protect her."

The idea of anyone in school thinking about marriage shocked me. That was years away. Would Joel make up something like that? No, the look in his eyes told me this was the truth. "I would never hurt Carmen. I know you don't like me—"

He leaned forward. "I never said I don't *like* you. I don't understand you, and I want to make sure Carmen is safe."

"I won't tell Carmen about… Maybe you can just forget what you saw."

"If only I could forget," he said.

"What did I miss?" Carmen dropped into her seat, and we talked about random gossip for the rest of lunch, anything but what was on my mind. From the way Joel watched me, I could tell seeing me teleport wasn't far from his mind either.

*****

That evening, we finished dinner and Dad asked Lorraine to ride with him to the store.

She glanced at the table in confusion. "It's my turn to wash dishes."

"It's okay," he said. "Charlie will take care of it."

Lorraine made a face but didn't argue. She shot me a look before following him out of the kitchen. Jealousy or anger, I couldn't tell. Since there weren't many dishes, it would be an easy night. After a week of trying to hit the bottles and missing, I was ready for an evening of TV.

When I'd finished the dishes, Mom suggested we go into the garden.

"I thought I'd get the night off."

She took my hand. "No nights off until you conquer this power."

I followed her into the garden, where a metal table sat with the tape player from the living room. An extension cord stretched from the porch and the screen lit with a blue glow.

"What's all this?" I asked.

"Music helps me concentrate and appreciate the beauty of life. I thought we'd give that a shot. Literally."

"I doubt your music will help me."

Mom smiled with understanding. The love in her face and her heart—this is how I always wanted to remember her. "It doesn't matter if the sounds and words touch my soul or yours. What matters is that you find peace." She motioned to the six bottles waiting, illuminated by the moonlight. The same gun I'd used all week appeared in her hand. "This will be yours one day."

"I know you want me to have this power, but what if I can't shoot like you? What if I'm normal like Dad?"

"Charlie, I've always known you're anything but normal." She held up the gun and aimed it toward the fence. Then she lowered the gun. "Tonight is perfect. I'm sorry for missing practice yesterday."

"Since you weren't feeling well, Dad helped."

She gave me a strange look. "Your father was teaching you how to shoot?"

"He showed me to aim higher because of the wind."

"I told you before, this power isn't about aim. Focus on the bullet and bend the air around it so you can make the bullet stop wherever you please."

"Bend the air?"

"Close your eyes."

I closed my eyes and took several deep breaths.

"You have the power to teleport, as I do. You also have something more."

Crickets chirped as I stood perfectly still. A gentle breeze touched my hair.

Mom placed the gun in my hand, still warm from her grip. "Feel the gun as if it's an extension of your arm. Consider it will be a part of you for the rest of your life."

I took another deep breath while gripping the gun. "You sound so sure."

"Aren't you?" She sighed. "When you pull the trigger, feel the bullet. See it in your mind. You are in control. Never let someone take that from you."

After a week of shooting this gun, the shape fit my palm perfectly. I pictured what a bullet would look like.

"Now picture the glass. Don't think about how small the bottle is or how far. Think about your bullet hitting the center."

A vision of the bottle flashed in my mind, then the bullet, and the path it would take. Music began and Tom Petty sang "I Won't Back Down." Energy surged inside of me. "That's my song."

"I have my taste in music, but I also pay attention to yours."

"Didn't realize you could operate a cassette player. Thought you only listened to records." My eyes fluttered.

"Don't open your eyes. Feel the music and clear your mind. Don't think of my next command but be ready."

I hummed along with the first verse.

When the chorus started, she yelled. "Pull the trigger. Now!"

I pulled the trigger, and the sound of a bullet rang out in slow motion. Even with the music, I heard the bullet whoosh through the air, currents I imagined myself controlling. I felt as it strummed through my veins. Then an explosion of glass as the bullet found its mark.

Opening my eyes, tears blurred my vision. Only five bottles remained. I wiped the tears and fired five more shots in quick succession, each sending a bottle flying from its pedestal. The garden waited silently as I stared at the empty fence posts in awe.

"It can make you emotional." She gripped my shoulders and leaned her head against mine. "The energy is a greater rush than any drug."

"I have the power?"

"You have the power."

My heart pounded in my chest. I wanted to do cartwheels around the garden and scream at the top of my lungs, but I stood there, letting her hold me.

"You're everything I could have hoped for."

"What's next?" I asked, my voice cracking.

"Next you learn how to hit all six bottles with the same bullet."

I laughed and threw my arms around her. Mom hugged me tight, her happy tears mixing with mine in the moonlight.

EPISODE 8

Training

The day after I found my power to shoot was Saturday. Dad took Lorraine fishing, and she made a point to ask why I wasn't invited. She'd become distant over the last week, as if she was jealous of the time Mom spent with me. I couldn't help Mom and I needed this time to train together. Telling Lorraine why was out of the question.

After sounds of Dad's truck faded as they headed for the lake, Mom pulled me away from dish duty.

"You cooked breakfast," she said. "That's enough."

I glanced at the plates with dried egg and the greasy skillet. Leaving a pile of dirty dishes in the sink was out of the question. "It won't take long."

She looked at the mess. "Is something bothering you? I've noticed your dedication to cleaning lately."

"It was the mud."

"Mud?"

"When those men came, I knew someone was in the house because of the muddy footprints they left. The shapes were too big to be Dad's boots. Every time I look at the floor, I find more mud."

"I'm sure it's simply a trick of the mind."

"Before we dumped them…" I took a deep breath. "The blood got on my arms and in my hair. Even though the blood is gone, I still see it sometimes. My heart races and it's hard to breathe."

"I'm sorry you have to face this now." Mom put an arm around my neck and kissed the side of my head. "Let me help you."

I shook my head. "No need for you to get tired. Then you might skip training."

"We're not skipping your training today. I'm looking forward to showing you the book."

"Book?" I turned on the water and added soap. "I thought we'd be shooting again."

"We'll do plenty of that." She took a seat at the table. "First, we'll start with the basics."

"Don't you think I've already mastered the basics?"

"As you'll learn, there's far more to being a Protector than hitting your target."

I scrubbed the plates and then the silverware. "Where does the name Protector come from?"

"We protect those who can't protect themselves. There are three other powers on Golvern besides the Protector power and the ability to teleport. We'll cover those when Keva returns."

"When is Keva coming back?"

"Keva likes to appear when I least expect her, but it will be soon."

When I finished the dishes, I expected another session in the garden. Instead, she held out her hands. "I'd like to take you to my special place. I call it our cellar."

My eyebrows shot up. "We have a cellar? Where's the door?"

She took my hands. "There's no door. Only I can visit this place."

The surrounding room faded, and we appeared in a room three times the size of our kitchen. White lights illuminated the room from a strip around the ceiling. Guns of all shapes and sizes covered the four walls, from small pistols to automatic rifles. There were no windows around this room and no door.

At the center of the room sat a long metal table that seemed to be a workbench, with a vice grip and precision tools mounted in holders. The metal was chrome, along with various drawers in two large cabinets behind the table. Next to one of the cabinets was a welder and machining center with a computerized screen.

"What is all of this?" I slid my hand across the table's surface. "Where are we?"

"Your father has his shop and I have mine."

"You make guns?"

"If my power is shooting a gun with precision, why not find a similar hobby? I've designed guns for years and sold them to collectors around the world. You don't really think your father's shop financed the two-hundred acres we live on? Or building this place?"

"I didn't know."

"This is where I designed your gun, one of my greatest achievements."

"You know how to use these tools?" I lifted what looked like a caliper from a holder on the table. After pressing the button, a blue light lit a small screen. "Is this Earth technology or Golvern technology?"

"Why choose when I've had access to both?"

I shook my head as I spun, taking another sweeping view of the room. "How did this place get built?"

"Your father's best friend was a foundation expert. The county thought we were building a basement."

"We're under the house?"

Mom smiled. "Gregory's friend poured the concrete, and they worked for weeks to complete the structure. Afterward, they covered it with forty feet of dirt and built the house on top of it. You might remember Hugh."

My thoughts went back to construction of this house. We lived in a small trailer on the property while they completed the work. Dad had a friend that helped throughout. "He had a son my age."

"The two of you played together. Hugh and junior moved to Virginia after inheriting some property from his grandmother. Haven't seen them in years."

"Dad didn't worry about him telling anyone? Did he know what you were?"

"Hugh didn't know why we needed this room, but he always had an interest in structural design. He pressed your father to tell him how we'd get in with no door, but Gregory kept a tight lid on those details."

"You didn't want anyone to get in unless they could teleport."

"You can only teleport to a place you've seen. Since I'm the only one who's been down here other than your father, I was the only one who could enter. Until now."

I let out a long sigh. "You won't make me build guns now, will you?"

"I want you to follow your own dreams." She gripped my shoulders. "But this is your legacy. Everything in this room will be yours after…"

"Can we not talk about that today?"

Instead of answering, she walked to one cabinet. She lifted a tiny box from the top of the cabinet and removed a needle.

"What are you doing?" I asked.

"This cabinet is bio-metrically coded."

"Which means?"

"The drawers only open with a sample of my DNA. Nothing can be teleported in or out."

"Did you build all of this?"

Laughing, she pricked her finger and pressed a single drop of blood against a flashing circle. "Someone great with technology owed me a favor." The circle turned blue, and she slid open the second drawer. Inside sat a pink gun and hard-bound book with a gold cover. A keypad appeared next to the blue circle, and she typed several strokes. Some symbols were neither letters nor numbers. "With a sample of your blood, you'll have access to my most prized possessions." She reached for my hand and pricked my index finger. "Besides my daughters and the love of my life."

When my finger touched the circle, it changed to green and then back to blue. "Now it recognizes you," she said.

"This technology is crazy."

She lifted the pink gun. "This is for your sister. I designed two guns especially for my daughters in case you inherited my power."

"I think the pink suits her."

Mom chuckled.

"What's so special about these guns?"

"To start, they're weighted properly. I designed the clips myself to hold more bullets. The bullets are smaller, with the best aerodynamics possible. You won't find a gun like this at Hillyer's Sporting Goods downtown."

She lifted the book and placed it on the table. I returned the gun to the drawer. Inside the book were thick yellow pages covered with drawings of anatomy. The pages smelled like a library and were hand written in a foreign language. The pictures showed various marks over the bodies.

"This book contains patterns you will memorize. Certain points of the body are of more interest while shooting."

"You mean like pressure points?"

"With the points in this book, you can immobilize a person without taking their life. Near the end starts the kill shots. Hitting your mark is only important when you know where to land your bullet."

Immobilize. Kill. My world had changed fast in a matter of days. "Why is shooting a gun with bullets so important? They have lasers."

"Lasers can paralyze a person temporarily or kill, but technology always needs a power source. Your gun does not."

"It's just a gun."

"That's right. What's that word you like to use? Old-school? When the power is out, old-school never fails." The black gun appeared in her hand and she gave it to me. "From now on, this is yours."

"But you—"

"I have my own favorite to fight with. Keep the gun on you when possible. When it's not, hide the gun in a place only you can find. Call it when you need it."

"Call it," I said. "With my power."

She held out her hand, and another gun appeared with a chrome finish. "This is the gun I've used since I first learned the knowledge you now have." Mom opened a lower drawer in the cabinet and pulled out a mannequin that looked like an actual person.

"Don't tell me you have a dead body that's been preserved."

"It's not real, but the features have to be as close as possible to real anatomy for this training to work."

I lifted my gun as Mom hung the mannequin.

She pushed the barrel away. "Never point a gun at someone you don't intend to shoot."

"Sorry," I said with a laugh.

With a laugh of her own, she flipped the pages and stopped on a figure of a man's head, with a mark over the ear. "This training is important. Teaching Lorraine our ways will be your responsibility."

"Are you sure she'll have the power?" I aimed for the mark and pulled the trigger. The bullet moved in slow motion, and I twisted the currents of air to guide it home.

"Excellent shot. Lorraine will have the power. How she'll develop will be entirely up to you."

I lowered the gun. "You're talking like you have days left. You owe it to Lorraine to train her yourself."

"Always fighting fate," she whispered and raised her gun.

*****

On Sunday, Lorraine and I worked on a China cabinet for Mom's birthday at Dad's shop. The wood store was a much calmer experience than shooting with Mom in her high-tech cellar. Dad had built the cabinet weeks before. We'd sanded the surface and applied stain, and today we added polyurethane, which made the wood shine. The smell of the spirits we used to clean the brushes made me dizzy. I welcomed the fresh air as I stepped outside.

Lorraine went down the street to buy an ice cream. I noticed Carmen in the doorway of the flower shop and crossed the street. When I reached the sidewalk, Steve

Gerber approached. I glanced down the street, but Lorraine was nowhere in sight.

"Stay away from me, *Charlene Conners*," he said.

The way Steve said my name made me want to hit him again. "You're the one who stopped *me*."

He raised a hand. "Do you think anyone can get away with hitting me, even a girl?"

Before I could answer, Carmen pulled me into the flower shop. From inside, we watched Steve point at the window and yell as if he might break the glass. After his tantrum, he climbed into a silver car and squealed tires out of there.

"You should stay away from him," she said.

"I'm not arguing."

She glanced at the phone on the desk. "I've been trying to call Joel all day, but he's not answering. He'll want to know that Steve came by."

"Steve isn't Joel's problem."

Carmen lifted the phone and dialed. Her fingers twisted the cord as she watched me. "Still no answer." She hung up the phone. "Maybe we should go over there."

"We?"

She laughed. "I'm not going by myself."

"Haven't you been?"

"Every time I mention visiting Joel's house, he always comes up with an excuse for why I can't come over. Once a pipe burst and flooded the house. Another time his aunt forgot to pay the bill and there was no electricity."

"Sounds strange." As if I had any right to call this family strange.

"I know, but he makes a cute face when he tells me these stories. Truthfully, I don't know if I should believe him or not. Maybe he's stringing me along."

I thought about when Joel mentioned Carmen at lunch. "I think Joel really loves you."

"Well," she said with a smile, "that's sweet of you to say. Go with me to his house. I hate to admit that after everything I'm kind of afraid to go alone."

I laughed. "You think your mom will take us?"

She hit my arm. "We don't need my mom. I got my license last week."

My eyes widened. "When did you turn sixteen?"

"A week ago. Hey, I know that face. Don't be mad since I didn't mention my birthday. There's been so much going on, I didn't think it was a big deal."

"Happy birthday," I said. "I'd love to get you a present."

Carmen walked into the back of the store and returned with a set of keys. "Mom's not feeling well. I told her we'd take the van and deliver the last of the flowers. We can stop by Joel's afterward."

Lorraine returned with her ice cream as we left the store.

"Tell Dad I'm helping Carmen deliver flowers," I said.

"Can I come?" she asked with a burst of excitement.

I shook my head. "We'll be back soon."

Her excitement faded and her face took on a look of hurt. Without a word, Lorraine turned and crossed the street in the direction of Dad's store. I'd hear about this later, but I couldn't deal with her riding along to Joel's. There was no telling what we'd find at his house.

I climbed into the passenger's seat of a van with decals of flowers on the side. The seats sat higher than the Toyota's did, but not as high as Dad's Bonanza. Carmen cranked the van, and I turned on the radio.

"Every rose has its thorn," I sang along with the radio. "This should be your theme song."

"Ha, ha." She shifted the van into gear with a jerk.

"Are you sure you know how to drive?"

"Mom made me chauffeur her around for the last six months. What about you?"

"I can drive a stick."

She glanced at me. "That's impressive."

I pointed to the windshield. "Eyes on the road, please."

"Oh, yeah."

Carmen dropped off the flowers at a church across town. I helped her carry in the arrangements, and after accepting their thanks, we headed for Joel's. "Are you sure you know where he lives?" I asked.

"I know about where he lives." She drove down several roads, then the same one twice, and finally found a street with six houses. Separated by trees, the homes sat back from the road with thick woods in the backyard. At the last one, she pointed. "There's Joel's truck."

The drive was made of stone, leading up to a two-story brick house. Magnolia trees lined the drive and shrubs grew in a neat row along the front of the house, where the stone ended at a porch with two rocking chairs. A red Toyota sat in the driveway, newer than mine but similar in size, and a black car with tinted windows. Carmen pulled up behind the truck and turned off the engine.

"Well?" I asked.

"My stomach is flipping over and over. I'm not sure what to do now."

"Knock on the door. Go inside if he invites you. I'll go with you in case anything happens."

"What can *you* do to protect us?"

I stepped from the van and turned to hide my hand. The black gun appeared, and a thrill shot through me. No need to worry about danger ever again. Just as quickly, I sent it back to the underground room. For now, Mom and I agreed that would be the safest place to stash my gun. She'd given me a drawer in a cabinet that wasn't secured so I could picture the gun there anytime.

Carmen got out of the van and walked toward the steps. I ran to catch up as she reached the door with an oval stained-glass window. The white rockers on the small porch looked as if they'd never been used. With a deep breath, she raised her hand and knocked. A moment later, the door opened and Joel stared at us in confusion.

"What's going on?" he asked.

"I've been calling all day," Carmen said. "You weren't answering and we were worried about you."

Joel turned to me. "We?"

"She was worried about you," I said. "Carmen asked me to help deliver flowers."

"Then we saw your truck and stopped," she said.

He glanced at the van. "You were riding by and saw my truck."

Loud voices came from inside the house, and he looked over his shoulder. "Now isn't a good time."

"You never invite me here," Carmen said. "You tell me you love me and then you disappear."

"I didn't disappear," he said in a patient voice. "I would never leave without saying goodbye."

"But you would leave," she said.

Joel sighed with frustration and opened the door wider. "Since you're here, why don't you come inside?"

Carmen nodded and slowly entered the room. I followed into the dim light as Joel closed the door behind us. A TV sat on a table along one wall and a couch along the other. The room smelled as if someone had baked cinnamon rolls, but the air was freezing compared to the heat outside. To our left, stairs led to another floor. In front of us was the doorway to a kitchen with a table and white fridge visible.

To our right, a doorway led into a room decorated as an office. Three screens rested atop a massive desk with a black office chair. A shelf over the desk was filled with books, but I couldn't make out any of the titles.

"Are those TVs?" Carmen asked.

"Those are computer screens," Joel said. "Most of Latasha's work can be handled from home."

"Those are thin screens," I said. From this distance, each one seemed only a few inches thick. Nothing like the thick glass of a TV screen and the huge picture tube that hung out the back.

"Latasha gets the latest technology."

Voices sounded again, louder this time—two women arguing above us, followed by the sound of something crashing to the floor. "Latasha is your aunt?" Carmen asked.

"No." Joel struggled to remain patient as he eyed the stairs. "She's my mom's coworker."

"At the tax office?" I asked.

His eyes narrowed. "That's right. She's a genius at finding money in bank accounts."

"Why are you living with your mom's coworker?" Carmen asked.

"I didn't want to tell you—"

"Why?" she demanded.

"Because you might think I'm weird. My mom works crazy hours and Latasha works mostly from home. It made sense for me to come down to Credence so I could attend a normal school."

Carmen rubbed her arms. "What's wrong with your AC?"

"Waiting on the repairman," Joel said.

"What happened to your phone?" she asked. "Let me guess. It's broken too."

A ringing sounded. Joel looked skyward in disgust and headed for the kitchen. "I'll be right back."

Carmen shot me a look of concern as the voices from above became louder. One of the women was screaming. The air seemed to get colder and goosebumps rose on my arms.

Joel returned. "I'm sorry, but you picked a bad time to come. Maybe we can try another day."

"Who's screaming?" I asked.

"Latasha's sister."

"Her sister lives here?" Carmen asked.

"No, her sister doesn't live here." He waved us toward the couch. "Maybe we should sit down."

She shook her head. "Steve Gerber threatened Charlie."

"What?" he demanded.

"He yelled at her outside of Mom's store."

Joel rubbed his temples. "I'll deal with Gerber. You won't hear anything from him again."

A door opened on the floor above and a woman walked down the stairs. She wore a black shirt that hugged her curvy form and a black skirt that stopped above her knees. Her short black hair was tied behind her head. I glanced at Carmen. From the look on her face, she had to be reading my mind. This woman couldn't have been older than twenty-five and looked more like a model than someone who typed on a keyboard all day.

"Didn't know we had company," the woman said.

"This is my girlfriend, Carmen, and her friend, Charlie. They're not staying."

Latasha glanced up the stairs. "That's probably for the best. My sister is in a terrible mood." She held out a hand for Carmen. "I've heard so much about you. I can already tell we'll be great friends."

Carmen glanced at me before shaking the woman's hand. After Latasha offered us cinnamon rolls she made that morning and encouraged us to return another day, Joel led us outside.

"I'm sorry you came at a bad time," he said.

"Will there ever be a good time?" Carmen took a bite of the cinnamon roll she held. "This tastes amazing."

"Latasha's a good cook." He kissed Carmen's cheek and watched her face for a long moment. When Joel spoke again, his voice was calm and collected. "Not all of us have a happy home life like you. But yes, there will be a good time."

She gave him a hug. "I'm sorry to barge in."

"Don't worry about it." He walked us to the van and gave her a kiss on the lips as he closed her door. "I'm working on a normal life." With a smile, Joel stepped away and watched as Carmen cranked the van and we backed out of the driveway.

"Is it just me or does Joel have more secrets than I thought?" she asked when we reached the street.

His family was strange but so was mine. "I wonder how he'll take care of Steve."

She took one last glance at the house. "We might not want to know."

EPISODE 9

Discovery

On Monday, Joel didn't show up at lunch, which was a relief. However, on Tuesday, I was first to the table. Joel arrived before Carmen and dropped into the seat across from me. "Why were you at my house?"

I put my fork down. "Carmen needed help to deliver flowers."

"And you happened to be hanging out at her mother's store."

"I was across the street at my dad's store."

His voice lowered. "Is he like you?"

What kind of question was that? "I thought you didn't want to know anything about me."

Joel watched long enough to make me squirm. "Is he?"

"No," I said.

"Can Lorraine do what you…?"

Hearing her name made me cringe. My one experience with teleporting myself at school had turned into a disaster. "No."

"What's your interest in Carmen?" he asked. "Do you plan to hurt her?"

"Hey, I didn't pick her as a friend. *She* insisted we sit together for lunch. You were part of the deal since she can't seem to stop thinking about you." I sighed in frustration. "What's *your* interest in Carmen? Do you plan to hurt her?"

"I would never hurt Carmen."

"Then why are you so obsessed with me hurting her?"

"People who have a power like you can hurt others."

"How would you know?"

He cleared his throat. "I've read plenty of comic books. Someone who can disappear and then reappear has a dangerous power. Those stories never end well."

This conversation was falling apart fast. I thought of the shock on his face the day I teleported. "You should forget you ever saw… I didn't mean for you to get involved in my problems."

"I wish I could forget. With my memory, forgetting isn't likely."

"Do you know Carmen was afraid to show up at your house? There's something wrong with that picture."

He crossed his arms over his chest. "Don't bring her into this."

"*You* brought her into this."

"Don't come near my house again. If someone finds out—"

Carmen flashed a smile as she sat down next to him. "Did you tell her about Steve?"

"Steve?" I asked.

"You haven't read today's paper," she said.

Dad bought a newspaper daily, but I rarely read the columns of Credence's primary news source. "No."

"Latasha checked up on Steve's family," Joel said. "She found problems with his dad's business accounts and an enormous tax bill. They arrested his dad yesterday and Steve's on the way to Louisiana to live with his mom."

"What?" I glanced at Carmen. She had to realize this made no sense. "Who gets arrested over taxes?"

"Be thankful," Carmen said. "Now Steve won't be bothering Lorraine."

"Do you think it's fair?" I asked. "You talk to Latasha—whoever she is—and suddenly they arrest Steve's dad."

"Because he was involved in dirty deals. He's guilty." Joel sighed. "If you saw the way Steve talked to Lorraine and heard how he's been bragging…"

Bragging? "What did he say?"

Carmen coughed. "That he took her… you know."

"She'll be thirteen in two weeks," I said. "I can't believe this is happening."

"It's not happening anymore. Joel fixed everything." She reached for his hand. "Thank you for helping Charlie's sister."

He nodded. "It was the right thing to do."

For the rest of lunch, Carmen and Joel chatted about everything, including our strange visit. Joel invited Carmen over for the upcoming weekend. He wanted to spend as much time with her as possible before school ended. We had only three weeks of classes left. Both would go their separate ways—Carmen to Seattle to spend the summer with her dad and Joel back to Atlanta to stay with his mom. Carmen smiled at him playfully, but I didn't feel good about them making up.

The more I thought about Steve, the more my stomach churned. If Joel got rid of Steve so easily, what would happen when he decided I was a threat to Carmen? What if he went after my family next?

If someone finds out.

Those words made me shiver.

*****

After dinner that night, Mom planned to show me how to knock down all six bottles with one bullet. Lorraine started to clear the table, but Dad insisted she ride to town with him instead. The look on her face twisted my insides; Lorraine didn't plan to ride anywhere.

When she refused, Dad used his stern voice. Mom stared at the floor and Lorraine looked as if she might burst into tears. My sister stomped out of the room.

"I don't know how much longer I can lie to her," Dad said.

Mom stood and put her arms around him. "We'll figure out how to handle Lorraine. I've wondered when we should tell her, but I'm not sure how she'll process the truth."

"Can we make it soon?" Dad asked.

She nodded and waved for me to follow her as he left. We'd just reached the garden when sounds of his truck revving filled the muggy air and faded into the night. Mom waved and six coke bottles appeared, each one on a fence post.

"This won't be easy," she said. "You'll have to curve the bullet to approach the first bottle from the side. Afterward, you must apply enough force to pierce each bottle. If the bullet doesn't make it through all six bottles, you'll try again."

I called my gun, and it appeared in my hand. As I raised the gun, gripped with both hands, I positioned my feet. With one foot in front of the other, I felt in control. I thought of the surrounding air, thick with moisture, and pictured the currents I'd need to curve the bullet to do my bidding. My finger grazed the trigger. Almost time. One more glance to make sure I was ready—

The sound of an engine approached. I lowered the gun as Dad drove the truck around the house, to the side of the garden, and slammed to a stop. Bright lights flooded our sight. The driver's door opened and he jumped out.

Mom ran to meet him. "What's happened?"

"I lost Lorraine," he said, out of breath.

"Lost?" I yelled. "She ran away?"

"Lorraine told me she wanted to go back to her room. Then she teleported out of the truck."

With a look of shock and amazement, Mom put a hand over her mouth. "She must be terrified."

I glanced at the house. "Think she's in her room?"

"This could be good or bad," Dad said.

Mom gripped his hand. "When Darla died, Lorraine destroyed every picture in the house. With this new power, she could destroy everything else."

"Let me talk to her," I said.

They both looked at me. "What will you say?" he asked.

"Something like I understand, blah, blah… I don't know. What I do know is how it feels to learn you've kept this secret from me."

Dad nodded. "Let's give her a chance."

I got rid of my gun and ran into the house, down the hall and to Lorraine's room. My heart pounded in my chest at her door. I knocked, but no sound came from inside. After knocking again, I opened the door. The room was dark; I squinted at the dim light from the window where Lorraine sat. She'd wrapped her arms around her knees and rocked back and forth.

"Lorraine," I whispered as I kneeled next to her.

The grandfather clock in the hallway chimed, but she didn't move.

"Are you okay?" I asked.

She laughed as if the whole world had gone crazy. "I must be dreaming. This can't be real. I was in the truck and now I'm… here."

"You teleported here. Mom and I both have the power; now so do you."

"Okay."

"That's it? I freaked out when she told me."

"This is a dream, right?" she whispered.

"It's not a dream."

She pinched herself. "Ouch, but this can't be true." Her voice rose. "What did you call it? Teleport?"

"You're starting to freak out," I said.

Lorraine looked around the room, then at her hands and mine. She attempted to talk normal, but her voice shook. "I'm fine."

I shook my head. "You can freak out; I won't laugh."

She stood and walked around the bed. Pacing the floor, she didn't look at me for several minutes. Eventually, she returned to sit by my side. "I thought about it and you've never made up anything like this before."

"No."

"You don't have that big of an imagination, so this must be true."

"Thanks a lot," I said.

Without laughing, she closed her eyes and disappeared from the room. Lorraine returned before I could stand and dropped down on the floor next to me. "I went to the cafeteria at school. Everything was dark and I came back here."

"This isn't a dream."

She turned to me. "Did you know Steve is gone?"

I gathered her hands in mine. "What happened with Steve?"

"He kissed me, at a practice for the math tournament. Joel saw, and that's why he insisted on driving me home. I didn't want him to tell you because I knew you'd worry."

Was she still freaking out? Her voice was steady as she told me about Steve, as if teleporting had helped her find a new courage. "You're my sister and you're way too young for a jerk like Steve. Did he ever ask your age?"

"No, and I didn't tell him." Lorraine leaned into me. "I only told him to leave me alone."

I wrapped my arms around her. "Steve won't bother you anymore. I heard he moved to Louisiana." Gentle sounds of her sobbing surprised me. Despite her need for attention, she rarely showed weakness. I smoothed the back of her hair. "Did Steve hurt you in any way?"

"No," she cried. "But he told everyone that we… I didn't do what he said."

"I know. Don't worry, I'll make sure everyone knows."

For several moments, her tears soaked into my t-shirt. Finally, the shaking subsided, and she pulled back to wipe her face. "Thanks."

"Anytime." I watched as a weary smile crossed her face. "Is there anything else?"

"Anything…"

"I thought you might, well, want to talk about how this teleporting power works."

Lorraine looked at her hands. "I was in the truck and I thought of myself in this room. Here I am. Then I went to school and brought myself back, just by thinking of this room." She took a deep breath. "You said you can do this too?"

Standing, I took her hand and pulled her up. This was going better than I'd hoped. I pictured us in the garden and the surrounding walls of her bedroom disappeared.

Lorraine glanced around with wide eyes. "We're in the garden."

Mom and Dad walked out of the house and crossed the grass to meet us. Lights from the truck, which still ran where Dad stopped, illuminated the ground. They took turns hugging Lorraine.

"Are you good, Rainey?" Dad asked.

My sister nodded. "Since this is probably a dream, I'm going to say yes."

"I'm afraid it's not a dream," Mom said.

Dad ran to the truck and killed the engine and lights, before walking back to stand next to Mom.

Lorraine pointed at the fence. "What's with the bottles?"

I held out a hand, and my gun appeared. "Target practice."

Her eyes nearly bugged out of her head. "Is that a real gun?"

"I just teleported you to the garden," I said. "And you're only worried about the gun?"

She looked from Mom to Dad. They nodded to me.

I turned and fired a single bullet that knocked down all six bottles in succession.

Lorraine's jaw dropped. "Did you…" Again, she looked at Mom and Dad for an explanation. "Did she…"

"Your sister has a special ability to shoot," Mom said. "So do I, and I believe so will you."

"We have powers?" Lorraine asked. "Like in the comic books?"

"That's right," Dad said. "You girls and your mother. I'm normal."

Excitement grew on Lorraine's face. "I thought something strange was going on. Daddy kept forcing me to go fishing and to the store. When I asked what you two were doing, he'd give me an answer like cleaning the fireplace. We've never even lit a fire in there after all these years."

"Your father was never a good liar." Mom slapped him across the chest.

Dad laughed. "You don't give me much to work with."

"All of this is real?" Lorraine looked at the gun, the bottles, and then at her hands. "I can teleport and maybe shoot perfect like someone in a movie?"

"I'll take that as a compliment," I said.

"It's a lot to believe." Mom glanced at me. "She's doing so well; I think we should show her the cellar."

"We have a cellar?" Lorraine put a hand on her forehead. "I think I'm going to be sick."

"You take Lorraine," Mom said. "I'll take your father."

I grabbed Lorraine's arm, and we all appeared in the room below. At the table, I took a seat on one of two swivel stools and Dad took the other. We watched in amazement as Mom sped through what took her two weeks to tell me. Lorraine watched it all with wide eyes.

At the end, she presented Lorraine with the pink gun and made her shoot. To my surprise, she hit Mom's target on the first try.

Mom hugged her, and Lorraine burst into happy tears.

"Possibly she's stronger than you," Dad said. "Don't be jealous. More likely it's her age. She doesn't have the experience you do or the fear."

Lorraine turned to me. "I don't think I'm stronger or better. If I'm unafraid, it's because Charlie gave me the courage to believe."

I smiled at her. For once, Lorraine wasn't trying to be the center of attention. This legacy of power was hers as much as it was mine. Just because I was the oldest didn't mean we couldn't share. "We can be stronger together."

Dad stood. "Sounds like our girls have this under control."

Mom put her arms around him. "I guess a girl can have everything she's ever wanted." With those words, they disappeared, leaving me and Lorraine alone in a room filled with guns.

"How is all of this possible?" Lorraine asked.

"Mom is from another planet. We can talk about the details later, but that's where her power comes from."

"Like Superman. I can't believe I'm not dreaming." She glanced at me. "How long have you known?"

"A few weeks."

"That's why you've spent every moment with her." She smiled. "I was so jealous."

"She's been training me to shoot."

"Do you think she'll train me?"

"Maybe we'll both train you."

"I'd like that." Her smile died. "What if… I'm more powerful than you? I'm not saying I want to be, but do you think you'd hate me?"

I laughed and put an arm around her neck. "Hate you? I'd hide behind you and make you shoot first."

*****

When we'd talked so long Lorraine yawned, I offered to take her back to the house. "Meet you in the kitchen," she said as if it were a game and disappeared.

I found her next to the stove. "You know, I did actually have to practice this. You could stop making it look so easy."

"I don't think I'll ever get used to traveling this way." Lorraine laughed. "What do you call it again?"

"Teleporting."

Music drifted into the kitchen, and I followed the sounds to the living room. At the doorway, Lorraine and I watched Mom and Dad dance in the light from a stained-glass lamp in the living room. Their shadows moved along the far wall. A record spun as words from Elvis reverberated through the room. As often as Mom had played the song, I knew the words to "Only Fools Rush In" by heart.

"I can't help falling in love…" Dad sang in a soft voice.

Mom rested her head on his chest. "…with you."

For the first time, I felt the rhythm of her music in my heart. Seeing how they looked at each other, I understood what these songs meant to her. They represented love for a man she'd crossed the galaxy to come home to.

"If only I could be so lucky," Lorraine whispered. "To find a man who will love me like he loves her."

Unlikely, I thought. What kind of movies had Lorraine been watching to talk like this? I rarely thought about getting married, but for once I did let myself dream of dancing with someone who would accept me for who I really was. No matter what planet I was from or what power I had.

Someone who wouldn't judge me for wanting to be normal.

Too bad that was no longer possible.

EPISODE 10

The Code

After Lorraine learned the truth, the following days were the best we'd known as a family in years. Dad came home from the wood shop early, and all four of us worked to throw dinner together. Laughter filled the house with a warmth missing since the night Darla died.

Cleaning up took no time, and we finished before sunset. When the sun sank behind the trees, we'd start our training exercises.

Dad offered his advice, and Mom encouraged him to join in our fun. Lorraine would shoot or I'd take the lead. It didn't matter who was better or faster or how many shots we each landed on the mark. I didn't know how many bullets Mom had built and stored, but we never ran out.

Mom seemed energized when we started but would tire after an hour or two. With each day that passed, she seemed older and less able to handle the power, even missing a few shots toward the end of each night. She played off the misses as if she'd planned to let us shine. Lorraine didn't seem to notice, and I didn't want to say a word that might end our time together.

One night, the three of us girls sat along the bank of the lake, sweating from the thick air and swatting mosquitoes. As I stared at the dull outline of trees reflecting on the lake, I told Lorraine about the day I first learned of the powers.

"You and Daddy really dumped bodies in the lake?"

"They had no choice," Mom said.

"Are we safe here?" Lorraine asked. "Do you think they might—"

Mom grabbed her hands. "We're safe. Others have come for me over the years, but I've dealt with them. That's the advantage of learning how to wield our power and why your training is crucial."

My sister made a face and crawled back from the water's edge. "I've eaten fish from this lake."

"It never hurt us," Mom said.

"I'm officially grossed out." Lorraine yawned. "I think I've heard enough to give me nightmares."

"Go to bed," Mom said. "We'll continue our training in the morning."

Lorraine hugged us both and teleported home.

The water sat as still as glass before me. Somewhere a coyote yipped in the darkness. "When will the soldiers return?"

Mom stared at the water for so long I thought she might not answer. "They'll be back soon, I fear."

"Is that why you've been pushing yourself?"

She turned to me. "I could always hide from Lorraine but never from you."

"Be honest. We deserve the truth."

"We have to be ready when they arrive. My strength is fading. I need you and Lorraine both able to defend our home."

"What if we can't?" I asked.

"If they learn of your power, they'll take you back to Golvern. There's a bounty for my recovery, but you and your sister are unknown there. People with our power are rare, and like me, your command of this power is strong. The person who brings you back will be rewarded on a grand scale."

"You mean money?"

"Money, power. Use your imagination. You and your sister are still young enough to be wards of the government. You'll be forced into service at sixteen."

"Why sixteen?"

"Sixteen is the age of majority on Golvern."

"You mean in a few months I'd be an adult there?"

"In a few months, you'd be forced to live on your own and fight for your life."

"Maybe the school in Credence isn't so bad."

Mom pulled me close. "I was forced into service. I've never wanted that for you."

"What if they capture me and I don't have a choice?"

"Never let them use your power to kill for their reasons. It's like someone taking a piece of your soul."

* * * * *

That night, I slept maybe two hours. The thought of someone stealing me from bed and forcing me to fight haunted me. I climbed from bed before the sunrise and found Mom at the kitchen table with Keva. Both had a mug of the strange yellow drink.

Keva wore white pants and a green shirt with long sleeves. Green streaked her brown hair this time, the exact color of the shirt. On the table next to Keva sat a square device about the size of her hand.

I sat across from them.

"Good morning," Mom said.

Keva smiled at me and took a sip from her mug.

The device made a sound like cymbals crashing and glowed with a picture before fading to dull black. "What is that?"

"Touch it," she said.

I turned the device over in my hand. It didn't have any buttons, only a glass screen. "Is this some kind of phone?"

"It's a communication device."

Again, I flipped over the device. No thicker than my pinkie finger and far lighter than the phone that hung on the wall in our kitchen. I slid my hand over the smooth face. "Where are the wires?" I asked.

Keva's eyes glistened. "We must get you up to speed."

When she reached for the communication device, the sleeve of her shirt slid up enough to reveal black markings near her wrist. I thought of the agent who questioned Carmen at the florist shop.

"Can I see your tattoo?" I asked.

"Another time." She pulled her sleeve down and covered the tattoo. "This table is beautiful. Did Gregory make it?"

"Of course," Mom said. "He's a master of woodworking."

"You're a lucky woman," Keva said with admiration.

I swallowed. "How long have people from Golvern visited Earth?"

"Hundreds of years," Mom said. "Our technology is a thousand years more advanced than Earth's."

Her use of the word 'our' made me shudder. Even after living on Earth for almost two decades, Mom still considered herself one of them.

"Our technology may be more advanced," Keva said. "But this doesn't include the treatment of humans on our planet."

"Mom told me how humans are treated. I wouldn't have been accepted without a twin."

"No," Keva agreed. "Even with your power, you'd be an outcast."

But something still bothered me. I turned to Mom. "You could go back. A thousand years of technology could heal you, right?"

We sat in silence as the grandfather clock chimed.

"Why not go back and let them heal you?" I asked.

Mom's voice filled with sorrow. "I've taken treatments over the years to extend my life here. Otherwise, I'd already be dead."

"That's not what I asked."

She put a hand over mine. "We've discussed this already. If I go back, they'll question me about the last eighteen years. I'm not the only person forced into service by the government. They have people who can read emotions. I won't be able to lie about my time here. They'll figure out you exist, along with Lorraine. They'll force you into service."

"If it will keep you alive—"

"It won't. I'll die inside to see you held hostage by Golvern's government."

I turned to Keva. "If she's really your friend, talk her into going back."

Keva finished her drink. "I'm not the person to convince her."

"Why not?" My voice rose. "You can see the future."

"I've tried to explain your gift," Mom said.

"You told her of an Olsandyol's power?"

"Olsandyol?" I asked.

"We are keepers of the future," Keva said. "Like Protectors bend air currents to move bullets, we manipulate time to preserve the future."

"The future hasn't happened yet."

"But it will," Mom said. "Those with Keva's power make sure the future happens as it should."

"That makes no sense. How can the future happen as it should?"

Keva's eyes twinkled. "Sometimes you must sacrifice the present to secure the future."

"What does the future have to do with saving my mother's life?" I stood and filled a glass of water at the sink. My hands shook with rage as I leaned against the counter and stared through the window into darkness. There was a way to save Mom's life; I knew it. Why were they giving me non-answers? "She should go back. Now."

"If I go back now, I'll undo the future Keva has seen."

I glanced at Mom. "Couldn't someone bring technology here to treat you?"

"I have weeks, maybe. Time we are wasting."

"Weeks?" The word cut deep into my heart. "You won't change your mind?"

She shook her head. "My purpose in coming to Earth was a noble one. I've enjoyed every minute with your father and my girls. Let's not waste the time we have left."

"Have you taught her about the other powers?" Keva asked. "The lesson is important."

Mom smiled. "You know I haven't. Go ahead."

I dropped into my seat. "You said everyone there can teleport."

"But there are four other powers that only show up in certain bloodlines. These powers are rare."

"One is the Protector power," I said. "The second is your power to see the future."

"The third is a Strategist," Keva said. "Those people are geniuses with technology."

"Like the folks at M.I.T.?" I asked Mom.

"Even better," she said.

Keva leaned back in the chair. "The last power is a Sensory. They can read the emotions from a person's face."

"They'll know what I'm feeling?" I looked at Mom. "You said something about people who can read emotions. They'd know if you lie about us."

"Simply by reading the lines on her face," Keva said. "I've learned to avoid these people when possible. Anyone who can read your emotions will never have the best for you in mind. They'll always know when you oppose them and how to take advantage of you. You can't hide from a Sensory."

"You've seen my future, right?" I asked.

Keva nodded. "All of it."

"What do you mean, all of it?"

"I've seen your greatest triumphs and the day you'll take your last breath."

Stunned, I opened my mouth but couldn't reply.

She looked at Mom. "You've made progress with her training, but she's not ready."

"Not ready for what?" I demanded.

Mom bent over as coughs rocked her body. "My time… is short."

"You've given her what she needs to start. Paleris will finish her training."

"Paleris?" Mom asked in surprise. "He would never come here."

It was as if they'd forgotten I sat at the table. "Who is Paleris?"

Silence filled the room.

"Paleris and I trained together," Mom finally said. "He believed we should use our power to serve Golvern's government. When I turned down the life of service they offered, he turned his back on me."

"Did he come here to take you back?"

She shook her head. "Several fighters came but not Paleris. My leaving tarnished what he stood for. Even though we trained for years as fellow Protectors, maybe even friends, he didn't agree with my stance. To my knowledge, Paleris has never stepped foot on Earth's soil."

"Could he have forced you to go back?"

"No," the other woman said. "Your mother is the strongest Protector Golvern has ever known. He would not come because he knows she would beat him."

"Paleris would not come because he couldn't stand to look at me."

"He will," she said.

Mom narrowed her eyes. "To Earth? It's not possible."

"You won't see him, but he will return. He will come for your daughter."

"No," she stammered. "I… came here…" Another round of coughs shook her. "I stayed to protect my children. They will never know servitude as I have."

The device made a sound, and Keva tapped the screen. She lifted it to her ear and spoke in a language I didn't understand. Mom watched with a look of fear as Keva placed the device on the table.

"Tell me," Mom said.

"Six of Golvern's best fighters will come to take you home."

"No," Mom said. "Earth is my home now. It's where I'll spend eternity."

Keva watched Mom before nodding. "Eternity may start sooner than you think. You're outnumbered."

"Three Protectors against six of Golvern's best soldiers means good odds for us."

"Do you think your girls are ready to fight?"

"I am." I turned as a noise from the doorway caught my attention.

Dad walked into the room. "For years we've lived as a family. Now we'll fight as one and die as one, if necessary."

* * * * *

After Keva left, Mom sat next to me on her garden bench as we watched the stars. "There's one more lesson you need to hear."

I'd given up on trying to figure out the mystery of space travel. "I've learned all I want to know about Golvern."

"You've read the book, but I never told you about our code."

"Code?"

"Do you remember the phrase we discussed for those like Keva?"

"Fatle en lanre. Did I pronounce that right?"

"Close enough. Protectors also have a code. After living by the bullet, there's no better fate than dying by it."

"How do you follow this code?"

"Protectors want to die from a bullet. To kill a Protector with a laser or any other method is a stain upon their legacy. A laser killed my brother, from someone he trusted."

The pain in her words brought tears to my eyes. "Do you know who killed him?"

"That person no longer breathes." She wound her arm around mine. "When my father's life was almost complete, he suffered. He asked me to end his pain with a bullet mark of his choice."

"Did you?"

She let out a long sigh. "For a Protector, a family member is always the first choice for this honor. If there is no living family, the honor falls to another Protector. I felt pain, but I also celebrated the passing of his legacy."

"You shot him?"

"He was dying."

"But you killed him."

"I gave him a choice. He wanted control of his fate."

"Too much death." I wiped at the tears that streamed down my cheeks. "I want happiness from life, not pain."

"I found happiness with your father. One day you'll meet a man who will love you like your father has loved me. Then you'll understand."

"I don't want to get married. Ever."

She held up her left hand. "On Golvern, people don't wear rings to celebrate marriage. Do you know what this ring is worth?"

I studied the golden band with carvings along the edges and a tiny row of diamonds at the center. "Probably a few hundred dollars."

She put her hand over her heart. "Your father gave me this ring. It means more to me than our land, our house, and even that cellar where I get to do what I enjoy. It's a part of me. When I'm merely a thought in your mind, this ring will serve as a reminder."

"Of what?"

"Coming to Earth changed the course of my life. On Golvern, I became disillusioned with the politics and treatment of people like me. I couldn't find a purpose."

"With all the advanced technology, you couldn't find a purpose?"

"For a long time, I hated the planet I called home. I didn't know I'd been on a journey to find your father all along. He healed my heart and proved love existed." She wiped her eyes. "People from Golvern are romantic by nature. They want to know love exists and how to find it."

"I'm not sure I'd know what love is *if* I found it."

"One day you'll meet a man who can take care of you, even if you don't need him to. Until then, save your heart."

"There's no one like Dad."

"Maybe fate will surprise you. Maybe he'll even sing Elvis to you."

I laughed. "Did Keva put you up to this?"

She laughed with me. "You'll know one day. I hope you think of me."

"I'll always think of you." I sighed. "Do you ever regret not going back to Golvern?"

"No. Earth gave me so much more." With those words, she hugged me, and we watched the stars until dew fell and sunlight glowed on the trees.

EPISODE 11
Warning

Lunch that week was filled with Carmen's anxiety about going home to Seattle. She spent every summer with her dad, and this summer would be no different. Joel promised to call her every night, though he seemed more distracted than normal.

"Why aren't you talking?" Carmen asked me. "I'm sure you have plans for the summer."

"Yeah," I said. "Spend as much time with my mom as possible."

Her face twisted with remorse. "I'm so sorry. What a terrible friend to ask a question like that. Of course you're going to spend time with your mom. How is she doing?"

I hated when people asked that question. "She's doing the best she can. Like my dad says, 'we take our days one at a time.'"

"I'm sorry to hear that," Joel said.

"It's not like she's getting better." Tears filled my eyes, and I hid my face. The last place I needed to cry was in the lunchroom. "There's no cure for her..." That last word caught in my throat.

"Hey, it's okay." Carmen rubbed my back. "I'm here whenever you need to talk."

Wiping the tears with my hands, I looked at Joel. The way he watched me brought an unexpected rush of anger. "I don't need your pity."

"You don't have it," he said in a firm voice. "My dad died before I was born. At least you've had fifteen years with your mom and hopefully many more."

He was right, but I'd never think of life as fair. I deserved every moment of every day with my mom. What right did this sickness have to take her away? Why did she choose to stay on a planet that was killing her?

Though I knew the answer, I didn't want to admit the truth. Her time was getting close. I knew from the way she slept past noon some days and went to bed before dinner. The days of our training had been wonderful, but I knew I couldn't keep her to myself forever.

Carmen and Joel thought they had problems as they mulled over two months of separation. I had to face a future without my mom. Joel handed me a napkin, and I wiped my eyes and nose.

They exchanged a look, and Carmen took a sip of her drink. She coughed and gave Joel a bright smile. "Will you go back to Atlanta? Or is there any way you can stay here?"

Joel shook his head. "I have to go back. It's part of our agreement."

"With who?" I asked.

"My mom," he said. "She agreed to let me stay with Latasha until the last day of school. Then it's back to Atlanta until August."

"I don't know if I should be happy or sad," Carmen said.

He pushed his tray away. "What do you mean?"

"Latasha is hot." Carmen looked at the table. "I don't know how I feel about my boyfriend living with a woman who looks like that."

Joel glared at her. "It's a temporary situation. If you want to know the truth—"

"Yes, Joel," she said, looking up. "I want to know the truth."

"Latasha stuck her neck out for me and offered me a place to stay. She knew I wanted to get out of Atlanta, but my mother didn't want to let me leave."

"They both work in Atlanta, right?" I asked. "For the tax office?"

He nodded. "I hate that place, and she knew I'd do anything to get out."

"Why does it sound like you were in some kind of prison?" Carmen asked. "Are the schools that bad?"

"Let's just say I have more freedom here. No one knows who I am or that my mother works for the government."

Carmen stacked her tray on top of Joel's. "Why does it matter what she does?"

"She has enemies," he said.

I laughed while imagining a woman who looked like Joel, maybe Mom's age. She sat behind a wooden desk, maybe in a cubicle like one of those TV shows, and balanced ledgers until the numbers blurred. At least soldiers weren't showing up from another planet prepared to drag her back. "People threaten her for looking at their tax forms?"

He hesitated. "It's more than that. She sends people to prison for crimes and sometimes they want revenge."

Carmen's eyes widened. "Are you in danger?"

"No one knows where I am." Joel took a sip of his drink. "Besides, the worst thing that's happened in this town since I arrived was someone stealing a car and leaving it on the train tracks downtown."

"Credence can be dangerous," I said.

A grin spread across his face. "Be serious. No one ever gets hurt here."

Laughter tickled my throat, and I put a hand over my mouth. They looked at me as if I'd gone crazy.

If only Joel knew about our lake.

"What about that man in the suit poking around the store?" Carmen asked. "He was asking questions and they weren't about flowers. You should have seen the creepy way he looked at me."

Joel's grin faded. "Has he been back?"

"No."

"Good. If he comes back, let me know."

Laughing, Carmen stood and lifted her backpack. "What are you going to do, sic your mother on him? Maybe have her audit his taxes?" She looked at me. "Maybe Latasha could get rid of him like she did with Steve."

He pulled her back down on the seat. "Lower your voice. This isn't a joke."

"Have you remembered anything else about the tattoo?" I asked.

"What tattoo?" he asked.

Carmen rolled her eyes. "You remember, the tattoo on his wrist."

"You told me he wore a black suit, broke your mother's favorite vase, and gave you the creeps. If you'd told me about a tattoo, I'd remember. What did the tattoo look like?"

"Three words in some weird language. I can't pronounce them. Maybe Charlie can try."

I didn't want Joel's prying eyes on me, and speaking an alien language was the last thing I needed to show off to someone with his connections. He'd seen my power and knew enough to put *my* family in danger.

Danger from what, asked the voice in my head. I had no logical explanation for the fear making my skin crawl, just a feeling.

"Sorry, gotta get to class." I grabbed my bag and left the cafeteria without looking back.

*****

That evening, we made dinner as a family. I fried chicken and made mashed potatoes while Mom gave Lorraine directions on how to cook the gravy. Luckily, Mom caught her just before she burned the bottom of the thick liquid.

"Stir it faster," Mom said.

"I'm trying." Lorraine scraped the spoon in circles as Mom added more water. The mixture of flour and seasonings bubbled as Lorraine vented her frustration.

I said nothing. Lorraine burned the pan the last three times she'd tried to make gravy. Why did Mom talk with this level of patience, as if Lorraine had to get the hang of it tonight?

The gravy thickened as I lifted chicken from the skillet and put it on a plate with paper towels to soak up the grease. Mom turned off the pan with gravy and removed it from the heat.

"See there," she said. "Perfect."

Lorraine stared at the gravy in wonder. "Are you sure it's right?" She dipped a spoon in and tasted their creation. "It tastes like gravy, even has enough salt."

Mom placed a kiss on her head. "Cooking may never be your strongest talent, but that's okay. I want you to remember it's never too late. With patience and effort, you can do anything."

"Making gravy isn't like shooting a gun," I said.

"I'd rather shoot," Lorraine said.

"Your mother's trying to make a point." Dad stood at the counter to my side, slicing tomatoes and cucumbers from the garden.

"What point?" I laughed. "That Lorraine could kill someone with gravy as easy as with a gun?"

He and Mom exchanged a glance, and he turned back to the tomatoes, slicing with a practiced motion. Though his words were calm, the turmoil in his eyes brought back the anxiety I felt at lunch.

Mom smiled. "If you put your heart into it, making gravy can be just as rewarding."

Her voice sounded upbeat, despite the way she leaned against the counter. As if she was trying to make us believe everything was fine.

Something was wrong. I couldn't put my finger on it, but I felt the change in the air like a jolt of electricity.

Lorraine bounced around the table while humming, in her usual annoying 'everyone look at me' good mood, while setting out plates and silverware.

"Set a fifth place," Mom said.

My sister looked up in confusion but set an extra plate and fork at a spot we never used.

"Who's coming?" I asked.

"I am."

In the doorway stood Keva. Green streaked her short brown hair, and she wore a long-sleeved crimson shirt with solid matching pants. Her face showed the same weariness from our last meeting, when she'd predicted more soldiers would come for Mom.

Lorraine froze. "Who are you?" She turned to Mom as if realizing the magnitude of Keva's appearance. "How did she get in here?"

"Her name is Keva. She has the power to teleport like we do." Mom took a seat at the table, and I helped Dad place the dishes with food at the center.

"You're like us?" Lorraine dropped into her usual seat and glanced at the spot next to her, set for Keva. She pulled her plate a little closer to Dad's.

"She's from the other planet," I said.

"Oh." Her eyes were wide as she turned to Mom. "Are you friends? Did you grow up together?" Before Mom could answer, Lorraine looked at Dad. "How long have you known Keva?" Before he could answer, she cut her eyes to me. "How do *you* know Keva?"

"Calm down, Rainey." Dad sighed and waved for Keva to sit down. "This isn't the time to show off your special personality."

Keva chuckled. "My oldest son was like her. Never met a stranger." She shot Mom a pointed look. "We need to talk."

"Food first," Mom said. "Then we'll talk."

With a glance at her watch, Keva took my usual seat next to Mom. "As you wish."

I sat next to Lorraine and we all filled our plates. Mom waved her hand, and a mug with one of the special yellow drinks appeared next to her plate, and then one next to Keva's. Our visitor closed her eyes and groaned with her first bite of chicken. She seemed to enjoy the food so much; I wondered what they ate where she was from.

Everyone stayed quiet as Dad described an incident from the store where he accidentally destroyed a table he'd almost finished.

"The break wasn't clean," he said. "The piece was a total loss."

"I wish you hadn't said that." Mom shook her head. "The destruction of perfectly good furniture hurts my feelings."

He laughed. "Your obsession with wood never ceases to amaze me. I hope it's not the only reason you married me."

"Tell me about your younger son, Keva," Mom said. "You never speak of him."

"He's cold. Calculating. He has infinite patience for achieving his goals." Keva took a long sip from the mug. "He's too much like his father for my comfort." She looked at me. "You're lucky, Candorice. Your girls will make you proud."

"What's wrong with his father?" Lorraine asked.

I kicked her under the table. She knew better than to ask an adult that kind of question.

"Nothing now," Keva said. "He's dead."

"Dead?" A bite of chicken lodged in my throat, and I choked. Dad stood and hit my back until I could breathe.

Keva watched me over the rim of the mug she held. "One well-placed bullet did the trick. He'll never hurt me again."

"Bullet?" I looked to Mom.

She nodded. "When I had to choose between her life and his, I made the only choice I could live with. It's why we've remained close over the years."

Lorraine pushed her plate away. "I don't think I can eat anymore."

The grandfather clock chimed from the hall. No one said a word as we all digested Mom's words. She'd used her power and killed to protect her friend.

Dad broke the stunned silence. "As long as you don't feel a need to return the favor."

Keva laughed, a deep sound that surprised me. "No, Gregory. You'll always be one of my favorite humans."

"Now," Dad said, "I'll let my daughters talk about their day."

Not like I planned to tell anyone about my day. "How can either of us follow that?"

As Keva checked the silver watch on her wrist, I tried to glimpse the tattoo. "Why do you keep checking the time?"

"For someone with my power, time is everything."

Mom finished her plate and sat back in her chair. "Shall we discuss why you're here?"

Dad stood. "Help me clear the table, Rainey."

My sister stood and grabbed her plate and Mom's.

Keva fingered her watch as if unsure. "Candorice," she finally said. "Tonight will be the last time we meet."

Mom lowered her head. "I had a feeling you'd say that. I've enjoyed your friendship."

Last time they'd meet? Did she mean Mom was going to… "Don't talk that way," I said.

"She hasn't accepted her fate," Mom said. "Or mine."

"She will," Keva said. "Your daughter is young, but she'll be forced to grow up sooner than she realizes."

I slammed a fist on the table. "I'm not losing her."

With a glance at Mom, Keva said, "It might not seem so, but fate has smiled upon you."

"I'm sick of hearing about fate," I yelled. "How can you talk like this is a normal conversation?"

Mom reached for my hand. "Because I've known this day would come. Keva, how long do we have?"

Keva checked her watch once more. "Soldiers from Golvern will arrive in one hour and seventeen minutes."

Lorraine ran back to the table with a look of horror. "More of those soldiers are coming? How do you know *exactly* when they'll arrive?"

"She has the power to see the future," I said.

"Another power?" Lorraine asked.

A chill went through me as Dad's words replayed. *For years we've lived as a family. Now we'll fight as one and die as one, if necessary.*

This was the last fight Keva predicted.

"Do you know who will come?" Mom asked.

How could Mom sound so calm? Lorraine dropped into the chair next to me and wrapped an arm around mine. Her whole body shook, and I tried to steady her.

"You have everything you need." Keva stood. "Thank you for the wonderful dinner."

Before anyone could reply, she disappeared.

"What's going on?" Lorraine asked.

Dad put a hand on her shoulder and squeezed. "Tonight we must fight."

"With g-guns?" she stuttered. "I'm not ready."

"We have an arsenal below this house," Mom said. "We have all we need to be ready. I can get—"

"Send the girls," Dad said. "Tell them what to get. You should save your strength."

She sighed as she looked at me and Lorraine. "I'm sorry it ends like this."

"We're not finished yet," I said.

"*The cellar*," Lorraine said. "What if we hide there and the soldiers arrive and they can't find us and—"

"They must find me," Mom said. "Keva told me this truth many years ago."

My eyes widened. "You knew all along this would happen?"

"I knew Keva said it would happen, and I've always trusted her."

"What if she lied? What if she made this up for—"

"What?" Mom stared at the door to the garden. "Keva has no reason to lie. Her job is to make sure the future happens as it should."

I jumped to my feet. "Why does she get to make that decision?"

"One day you'll understand." When Mom looked at me, a fire had lit in her eyes. "But not today."

Lorraine turned to Dad. "Say something."

"Your mother makes the calls," Dad said. "We follow her plan."

"We won't hide," Mom said. "Tonight, we end this."

EPISODE 12
Fight

We had to get ready to kick the asses of six soldiers from another planet. They were coming tonight, in a little more than an hour.

The clock was ticking.

Lorraine and I teleported to the cellar and brought back all the guns Mom requested. She sat in a chair at the kitchen table with Dad by her side. He'd made a pot of coffee and steam rose from the mug in his hands.

They watched as Lorraine and I laid the guns across the table. Over two dozen guns waited for her command. Clip after clip filled with the special bullets she'd designed.

Anyone looking on might think we were about to rob a bank or clear out an entire block of downtown Credence.

Each time I returned, I checked the clock and another few of our precious minutes had disappeared. We were under an hour now. Dad lifted an assault-style rifle from the table.

"Do you know how to shoot that?" Lorraine asked.

"I may not be an expert marksman like your mother, but I learned how to shoot a gun."

"Okay," Lorraine said with a nervous laugh. "Just asking."

I checked the time again. Forty-six minutes. "Are you sure they're coming?"

"They're coming," Mom said. "When they arrive, I want you girls to stay out of sight."

My stomach churned at the thought of more soldiers invading our house. Our lives. They would come with lasers, advanced technology from another planet, and try to steal our mother away.

She would either kill them or be killed. By this point, I understood Mom wasn't going back.

Mom waved her hand over the table. "You can shoot any of these guns, but I designed yours especially for size and weight. Keep those close and only choose another if necessary."

Forty-four minutes according to the clock on the wall.

"Would you stop checking the time?" Dad asked. "You're going to make yourself sick."

"I'm already sick." I held up a shaking hand. "I'm not sure if this is a dream or if soldiers in gold uniforms are really on their way to our house."

"They're on their way." Mom grasped my hand.

"We can go anywhere with our power," I said. "Why don't we leave?"

"One day you'll realize it's not the power that sets us free." She pointed at my chest. "It's what's in here." Mom put her hand to her chest. "And here. I don't want to run. Making this stand will ensure they don't return. It will mean freedom for you and your sister."

The phone rang and I jumped. The ringing sounded again.

Lorraine snatched the phone from where it hung on the wall. "Hello?" She looked at me. "It's Carmen."

Talking to her was the last thing I needed in this state. However, as soon as her voice came through the phone, I felt better. Something about her words put our crazy situation into perspective.

"Hey," she said. "What are you doing?"

"I'm, um, family stuff."

"How's your mom?"

I glanced at Mom's tired face. "She's worn out."

"I just wanted to make sure you were okay. After lunch, I worried about you."

"No need to worry about me."

"But I do. Sometimes it's good to have a friend. You know we can talk whenever you need me. Charlie, you can tell me anything."

Anything but the fact my mom was from another planet and soldiers with lasers were about to break down our door. "Thanks, Carmen."

"For what?"

"For being my friend."

A smile sounded in her voice. "You're welcome."

When I hung up the phone, Lorraine asked, "What was that about?"

"Just Carmen being Carmen. She wants to make sure I'm okay."

Dad laughed. "She picked a hell of a night to do it."

I nodded and laughed with him. "Her timing has never been good."

We all laughed, and Dad rose to pull me and Lorraine into a hug. He dragged us to where Mom sat and squeezed all of us together.

Mom sighed. "I'll never forget this night. This is why I came to Earth."

"I'm sure there are other good things about our planet," I said, pulling away.

"It doesn't snow on Golvern," she said. "And they don't make ice cream."

"That's awful," Lorraine said. "Not the snow part, since it almost never snows here. But no ice cream?"

I crossed my arms over my chest. "Good thing I'm never going there."

The laughter faded from the room.

"You will, one day," Mom said. "Never forget I told you that."

There was no point in arguing, but I was never leaving Earth. I swore to myself as I took an inventory of all the guns. This life wasn't for me, and an alien government wouldn't force me to kill.

Dad motioned for me and Lorraine to follow him into the living room. He opened the door to a closet next to where the hall began. "The two of you will hide here." After removing the vacuum cleaner and two boxes to make room, he held the door as Lorraine and I squeezed in. "Stay inside. Your mother said she wants you to hear everything that is said. Do you have your guns?"

I held out my hand, and my gun appeared. Lorraine did the same.

"Keep those with you at all times," he said. "If your life is in danger, go to the cellar."

"Stay in the closet, no matter what happens out here." Mom leaned against the doorway from the kitchen. "I love you girls."

Dad went to her side and helped her to the couch.

"Do not under any circumstances sacrifice yourself to save me, understand?" she said.

Lorraine and I both nodded slowly.

"My life is over, but I will continue living through you. Protecting you two girls is my most important objective tonight."

"I thought you wanted to let them know you're not going back," Lorraine said.

"All of this is for nothing if either of you die. Do you understand?"

Lorraine bit her lip and nodded.

I looked away. "All of this is for nothing if *you* die."

"Charlene," Mom said.

She rarely called me that. "What?" I asked, like a kid about to be sent to her room.

"Remember the cost of freedom."

"We will follow your wishes." Dad crossed the floor and closed the door, placing me and Lorraine in darkness. "Watch and listen but stay quiet and don't open this door for any reason."

Dropping to sit, I pulled my knees close to my face.

Lorraine did the same next to me, but she reached for my hand. "Do you think they'll take her back?" she whispered.

"No."

"Do you think they'll take us?"

"They're not taking me."

She squeezed my hand. Maybe my strength brought her comfort. I'd always tried to protect Lorraine, though tonight might be more than I could handle.

For several minutes we waited in the darkness; our only light seeped through gaps in the panels of wood that were part of the door. I checked each gap and found one large enough to see through while on my knees.

Dad paced the floor, and Mom watched from the couch. She talked in a low voice I couldn't understand. More seconds ticked away.

"What are you seeing?" Lorraine whispered.

"Nothing yet."

When I looked back at them, I jumped. The room was full of people in the same uniforms as the soldiers Mom killed in the garden. "They're here," I whispered. "Six, no seven dressed in gold."

She shoved me aside to get a look. Lorraine put a shaking hand over her mouth.

Six of the soldiers stood with lasers in their outstretched hands, their faces hidden behind gold helmets. Mom stood from where she sat on the couch. Dad stood next to her, holding the automatic rifle.

My heart slammed in my chest. I tried to catch my breath while not making any noise.

Apart from the soldiers with lasers stood the seventh person in gold. This body was shorter than the rest, closer to Mom's height. The soldier walked in front of the others, standing between the lasers and my parents. Why hadn't Mom pulled a gun yet?

When the short soldier spoke, it was definitely a female voice. I couldn't understand her words.

Mom lifted her head. "You will speak to us in my language of choice." The force of her words left no room for argument.

The soldier lifted her gold helmet to reveal a face that was younger than Mom's. Bright orange hair spilled over her shoulders.

"Amelia," Mom said with surprise. "It's been many years. You're the image of your mother."

"I have her power," the woman said. "Golvern's government ordered me to ensure your return."

"Like her, you choose duty."

"For a Protector, duty is the only choice."

"You will fight me?" Mom asked.

"I was hoping you'd come without argument." Amelia turned to Dad. "I'm sorry to intrude on your life, but I have my orders."

Dad lifted the gun in an attack stance. "And I have mine."

Mom's gun appeared in her hand. "The battle for my power ends tonight."

The sounds of gunfire exploded in the room. The other soldiers teleported out of there as Amelia and Mom faced off. Dad ducked beside the couch. More bullets were fired, but still the two stared each other down.

A thrill shot through me as I watched this amazing fight. Each was controlling the direction of the bullets. Theirs and the bullets coming at them, so that neither could hit her opponent.

As I listened to the bullets zip through the air, I wondered what getting struck would feel like.

"We've got to help Mom," Lorraine said.

I grabbed her arm. "She told us to stay in here."

"That woman has the same power we do. Mom didn't know she was coming. She needs our help."

Before I could argue, Lorraine shoved open the closet door and ran with her gun pointed at the woman with orange hair. Amelia. Mom knew her name. Did she know this woman would come tonight?

I followed with my gun gripped tightly in my hands.

The bullets stopped as Amelia looked at Lorraine, who stood a few feet away. Then she took me in before turning back to Mom. "You have children? Daughters?"

Lorraine opened her mouth to answer as a soldier appeared behind her with a laser. I pointed my gun at the man, and she turned as he aimed the weapon to fire.

I pulled my trigger and focused one hundred percent on the bullet, ramming it at the man's chest. The sound when it hit barely registered, but I *felt* the bullet strike as if a bomb had exploded and continue through to the man's heart.

In a split-second, I'd shot a man, maybe killed him. I didn't have time for shock or remorse to register.

As I fired, Lorraine teleported out of the room before the laser's beam could strike her. I let out a breath of relief. At least she took Mom's advice. But did she go to the cellar?

A devilish grin spread across Amelia's face. "She's an inheritor."

Mom looked at me with anger. "What part of staying out of sight did you miss?"

Two soldiers in gold appeared by Mom's side. "This was a trap," she said. "Get out."

Before I could move, more soldiers appeared. Dad stood with his gun and started firing automatic rounds. Everyone dropped to the floor as Amelia tried to take him down. I fired at her, striking the arm she used to hold the gun, and she disappeared.

A laser fired at Mom, and she spun to face two soldiers. "Left, Charlie!"

Side-by-side, the two of us fired and guided our bullets to hit their marks. The soldiers fell to the floor. That left three plus Amelia.

Shooting together with Mom, making the bullets follow our commands in unison, was the best feeling of my life. She glanced at me with a smile and misty eyes.

There was no denying the love and pride she felt.

A hand went over my mouth, and the room faded. In an instant, I was somewhere else, somewhere dark… in the garden. The soldier had teleported me out into the night. I fought against the arms trying to strangle me. I couldn't breathe.

I kicked and tried to scream. I clawed at the arms that held me, muscular arms from someone twice my size. My fingers slid along the gold uniform of the soldier's arms.

Crap, I needed to learn how to fight. My mind spun with too many thoughts to control. The world was getting darker.

My strength was fading. Then came the sound of a bullet.

The arms loosened until my feet touched the ground and I staggered forward, gripping my neck as he fell. Had I almost died?

Lorraine stood over the soldier with her gun. "Are you okay?"

I rubbed the skin around my neck and coughed. "I think so."

"Did I just kill someone?" she asked in a pained voice.

I glanced around for more soldiers before kneeling at his side. He wasn't moving, and I checked for a pulse at his wrist like they did in the movies. I wasn't getting anywhere near his neck.

Down to two.

We ran inside the kitchen, but the house was silent.

A soldier appeared beside Lorraine and grabbed her hair. The gun dropped from her hands as she tried to punch him, kick him, bite him.

I imagined my gun in my hand. No telling where I lost it after the man grabbed me. The gun appeared, and I lifted to shoot, but felt a shiver run through me. My hands shook and I couldn't aim. Lorraine screamed.

Fear was crippling me. This one emotion was more than I could handle. I closed my eyes and thought about how Lorraine was depending on me. I thought about the gun in my hand and grasped the metal. A surge of excitement flowed through my veins as I opened my eyes and pointed the gun at the soldier.

I pulled the trigger and the bullet cut through the air, piercing his heart before I could take a breath. He fell on his side, unmoving, as his hand slammed against the floor. I kicked the laser out of his hand, and it slid across the floor, coming to a stop against the wall.

Lorraine put her hands on her face. "I can't handle this."

"We're down to one plus Amelia," I said in a shaking voice. "This is almost over."

But where were Mom and Dad?

We raced into the empty living room. The gun Dad had used lay on the floor next to the couch. The bodies of the other soldiers lay on the floor, but one was still missing.

Lorraine and I checked every room in the house and the cellar before returning to the garden. There, Mom stood with Dad at her side. Amelia stood before her with glowing moonlight making her long orange hair look as if it were on fire. Up close, this woman wasn't much older than me, maybe twenty. Her chrome gun hung at her side, about the size of the pistol Mom held.

"I'm never going back," Mom said.

"You have to," Amelia pleaded. "The government won't stop. This is about more than you and me."

"They may force us into service, but they don't own us. When did our power become theirs to control?"

"They need us." Amelia took a step forward. "Please, for the sake of your children, return. If you go back, no one will come here and learn your secret."

I approached and stood on Mom's other side. Lorraine went to Dad's side, and he put an arm around her. "We stand as a family," Dad said. "I don't have your power, but I have what's important."

Amelia sighed as she watched Mom. "I didn't know you had a family. When I took this assignment, I thought it was a simple matter of bringing you home."

"The government has been sending soldiers for years," Mom said. "I killed all of them."

"No," Amelia said. "That's not what they told me. For the last eighteen years, you've been lost."

"For good reason." The last soldier appeared behind Mom and shoved a syringe into her neck. She grabbed for the syringe, but he emptied it and pulled away.

Lorraine shot the man before anyone else could. He fell back, and the syringe hit the ground beside his arm. His life faded with his eyes wide-open, staring up at the stars.

I aimed my gun at Amelia. "What did he give her?"

"A stabilizer." She held up her hands. "It was a last resort meant to force Candorice to return."

Mom put a hand over her chest. "I'm… having trouble… breathing." She reached for Dad's arm, and he helped her to the bench.

Amelia stared at me but didn't draw her gun. "If your goal is to be the last one of us standing, kill me. For betraying a fellow Protector, I deserve that fate."

"No," Mom said. "There are… so few… of us… left."

"What does this stabilizer do?" I asked, still gripping the gun.

"If we don't return to Golvern within the hour, it will kill her."

EPISODE 13

No Choice

If we don't return to Golvern within the hour, it will kill her. "I don't understand," I said. "Why would anyone go this far to force my mom to return?"

Amelia's eyes glistened as she watched Mom, who sat on the bench. "They told me you betrayed Golvern."

"It was a lie," Mom said. "I would never betray Golvern."

"Your leaving betrayed Golvern," Amelia said.

"All I wanted was my freedom."

I glanced at the soldier who'd shoved a syringe in Mom's neck. He'd injected her with something Amelia called a stabilizer. I kicked his foot, but he didn't move. If he had, I would have fired the gun in my hand and made sure he was dead.

Dad sat next to Mom, gripping her hand. "What's in this stabilizer?"

Amelia sighed in defeat. "Once it mixes with your blood, the stabilizer thickens."

"How long do I have?" Mom asked. "Worst case?"

"One hour. They designed it for you, to give us enough time to return to Golvern where you can get the reversing agent."

"This reversing agent will save her?" Lorraine asked.

"Our orders weren't to kill her," Amelia said. "The government wants her back alive."

"What else can we do?" I asked.

Amelia shook her head. "There's nothing anyone can do. He didn't bring the reversing agent. I felt sure you would return after we spoke."

"I won't return," Mom said.

"Then you'll die," Amelia said without emotion. "There's not enough time for me to travel to Golvern and return with the serum. Giving you the stabilizer was meant to force your hand."

"Like I said, I'm not going back."

"You have to," Lorraine said. "If not, you'll die."

"I'm already dying." Mom looked up at Amelia. "What are the stages?"

"First you struggle to breathe. Then your blood thickens and your heart beats faster. It's extremely painful by simultaneously thickening your blood and speeding your heart so it can handle the load. You won't die until the hour is up, when your heart explodes."

Tears ran down Dad's face. Lorraine sat on the bench next to him and gripped his arm while laying her head on his shoulder.

"Take a message to Golvern's government," Mom said defiantly. "Let them know that even under the threat of impending death, I refused to answer their summons. Tell them I died free."

"What of your legacy?" Amelia asked.

Shock hit me. I tucked my gun into the waistband of my jeans and grabbed Amelia's arm. "You can't leave her; she'll die."

"Nothing can stop Fate," said a voice behind us.

I turned as Keva approached. "You can see the future. You knew this would happen."

Keva stopped when she reached me. "Sometimes I wish I could turn back time and not know what awaits. Ignorance is truly bliss."

Amelia swung around to face her. "You're an Olsandyol?"

"Yes. We weren't supposed to meet tonight, yet here I am."

Amelia looked to Mom and then back at Keva. "This is my fault. Tell me how to repair the damage I've done to her family."

"You're trusted by the government," Keva said. "Tell them you confronted Candorice and she chose death over their ultimatum of service."

"Protests will start anew," Amelia said. "People will hear the story and blame the government for her death."

"I don't understand," I said. "Why would anyone on that planet care what happens to my mom?"

"Don't tell them about my daughters," Mom said.

Keva and Amelia exchanged a glance. Nodding, Keva turned to me. "Her sacrifice will protect you and your sister until the day you can protect yourselves."

Tears filled my eyes. "You're going to let her die?"

"In the future I've seen, your mother dies today. I'm sorry."

"No," I said. "I won't accept it."

"The future has chosen you," Keva said.

"For what? To watch my mother die and know it means nothing?"

"It means everything." Amelia stood proudly, with a smile of understanding. She touched her forehead in a salute to Mom. "The story of how you stood against the government alone will be told for centuries."

Mom smiled as she leaned on Dad. "As long as my daughters carry on my legacy, my story doesn't end."

Amelia's eyes shimmered. "I won't betray a fellow Protector. I'll follow the code and keep your daughters safe until they can stand as Protectors and fight in their own way." She took a deep breath. "Do you want me to—"

"No," Mom said. "That is not your honor."

Amelia nodded.

"Fatle en lanre," Keva said. "When we meet again, you will understand why."

With a final long look at Mom, Amelia disappeared.

I turned to Keva. "She's your friend," I said in agony. "Why didn't you stop them from hurting her?"

"Knowing what would happen meant I couldn't stop them. I wish I could show you the future."

Mom reached out a hand. "Charlie will understand one day."

"Yes, she will." Keva kneeled before her and took Mom's hand. "I've seen that day."

Mom looked at me. "We talked about sacrificing the present to preserve the future." She coughed, and Dad held her as she shook. She turned to him. "I'm sorry it ends this way."

With tears in his eyes, he nodded. "I always knew this day would come, but I'm not ready to lose you. I never will be."

Mom glanced at Keva. "You've done what you can to help us. Tell me about your sons. You once predicted they may be your greatest downfall."

Keva's voice dropped. "They are trying to change the future we've seen. I'm in a fight against them."

I thought of the man who questioned Carmen with the tattoo Mom didn't want to discuss. Could this man have been one of Keva's sons?

"Will you be successful?" Mom asked.

"I'm not sure, but I'm willing to fight them for the future. They've entered into a contract with someone who wants to sever all contact between Golvern and Earth."

Mom coughed again. "Who contracted their services?"

Keva glanced at me. "I'd rather you die not knowing."

"Your answer is truth enough." Mom reached for me and Lorraine, taking one of our hands in each of hers. "I'm so proud of my girls. We won this fight together."

The pain was tearing me apart. "At what cost?"

"We should go inside," Dad said. "It's cooler and maybe you can breathe easier."

Mom shook her head. "This is how I want to spend my last hour. With the people I care about, in the garden I've enjoyed over the years."

*****

For forty-five minutes we talked about whatever we could think of, anything but the end of my mother's life. As the time ticked away, I realized even if she left at that exact moment, there was no reaching Golvern and saving her.

Tonight was the last time I'd see my mom.

Keva said her goodbyes to her friend and left my family alone in the garden. Before disappearing, she looked at me and said, "This may seem like the end, but it's only the beginning."

To Mom she said, "Fatle en lanre."

Mom repeated the phrase with tears in her eyes. In the wake of Keva's exit, she asked Lorraine to sit beside her. My sister pulled away from Dad and took the seat next to Mom.

"You should sit with us," Dad said to me.

I looked at the bench and thought of the irony he made it the exact size needed for all four of us to sit. On Mom's bench, on her last day, we could watch the stars together.

Mom hugged Lorraine, and I took the seat next to Dad. He put an arm around me and kissed my forehead. His eyes were red from crying, a sight I'd never seen.

"You have one more lesson," Mom told Lorraine.

"No," Lorraine said. "We won't spend these last minutes talking about a lesson."

A round of coughs rocked Mom, and she struggled to catch her breath. "Your last… lesson… is the code…"

"Of the Protectors," I finished.

"That sounds medieval." Lorraine choked on her tears. "If Charlie knows, she can teach me."

"We live by the bullet," Mom said. "At the end, our greatest honor is to die by it."

"Please," Lorraine said, "can we not talk about dying?"

"This is important." Mom's voice dropped to a whisper as I strained to hear. "When a Protector gets too old or sick to go on, another Protector ends their suffering with a bullet."

"You mean…" Lorraine looked at Dad and then at me.

"The honor falls to family, unless there are no additional members of the lineage." Mom reached for my hand. "Today, the honor belongs to you."

Tears pooled in my eyes. "You want me to shoot you?"

"This is what I've wished for ever since learning of my power. My father had the gift and so did my brother. They both lived by the bullet and wished to die by it with glory, protecting those who needed their help most."

"No," Lorraine cried.

Mom squeezed her hand. "I escaped that life when called upon to protect members of the royal family. I should have complied, but I loved your father and returned here instead."

"That's enough, Candy," Dad said.

She shook her head. "There will never be enough to undo the damage I've done to my family's honor."

"Why couldn't they leave you alone?" I asked.

"The first few years after I came to Earth, the government sent soldiers after me. They hoped one would bring me back. When I returned to Golvern, they welcomed me and never spoke of the lives I erased from existence."

"You came back to Earth because of me," I said.

"It was my choice," Mom said. "Never forget that. When I came back to Earth, the government didn't want anyone to know about my refusal to do their work. They feared the fact I stood up to them would cause revolts."

She coughed again, her whole body shaking. "This last round of soldiers was their acknowledgment of my betrayal. They made our shame official."

"Who cares what they think?" I asked. "That government is on another planet."

"Many care," she said. "There is a group that opposes the government. They fight for freedom for all humans living on Golvern."

"You've helped them?"

"Never, but I fear they will make my stand against the government a battle cry. You must stay far away from anyone who stands against Golvern. Don't let them make you fight like the government would."

For several moments, we sat and listened to the only sound—crickets beyond the garden, in the dark trees. The moon cast a strange halo of light on the surrounding grass.

If only I had a way to slow time. I wiped at the tears now streaming down my face.

"Get me the book," Mom said.

I pictured the book in the cellar drawer where it stayed. The drawer was biometrically coded, which meant I couldn't call it; I'd have to go below. I appeared in the cellar and ran to the drawer, quickly gaining entry. With the book held close to my chest, I returned to the garden and opened it for Mom. She flipped to the last pages.

The kill shots.

Mom chose a page and pointed at the drawing. A small weakness in the skull that required the utmost precision. "This is a painless way to die. It's my choice."

I'd known what she wanted when I went for the book. The reality of what she was asking hit me. We'd fought soldiers that night, killed men who came for her, like this was all a game. Or a dream.

At school, my class had discussed the moral and legal implications of euthanasia. I'd never imagined I'd be faced with making the choice myself.

Mom looked up at me. "This is what I've always wished for. My brother died by a laser, and I don't want the same dishonor."

"I can't do this," I said.

Lorraine put her hands over her face and shook her head.

"No one will know you did this but us," Mom said.

"Then how does that make it honorable?" I wiped my face on my arm. "*I* don't want to know."

"But I will," she whispered.

I turned to Dad. "Tell her this is too much to ask."

"Too much to ask?" Dad gave me a look of agony. "Your mother deserves her last wish."

"Get my record player," Mom said.

Dad rose and crossed the garden to the house.

"Please, not from me." I kneeled in front of her. "I can't live with this."

"It can't be Lorraine. You're the strong one." She wiped the tears from my face. "You're the one who can use this experience to make the universe a better place. From what Keva has said, you're going to make me so, so proud, Charlie-girl."

I opened my mouth, but she put a finger over my lips.

"I can already feel my veins turning to stone. I have little time and I don't want to die like this." She brought my hand to touch her neck.

Beneath my fingers, her pulse raced faster than I thought possible.

How could I make this choice, even if it was what Mom wanted?

The truth hit me.

I didn't have a choice.

The rest of what she said, I tuned out. My thoughts were all I could deal with. Mom hugged Lorraine and they appeared to be saying their goodbyes. The buzzing in my head made me feel disconnected from everything.

Dad returned with the record player and a long extension cord. He placed it on the bench, hooked up the cord, and helped her to her feet.

Finally, her words cut through my mental fog. "I love you, Charlie."

"The powers, what we are… I can't do this without you."

She hugged me despite the lack of strength in her arms. I pulled her to me and made sure she knew how much I loved her.

"If anyone comes from Golvern, don't trust them," she whispered in my ear. "Keva is the only person you can trust.

If anyone tries to capture you, teleport yourself to another place. Promise me."

"I promise."

She turned to Dad. "I want to stand on my own."

He hugged her and they said goodbye, followed by a kiss. Dad smiled at her. "It was all worth it, Candy. Every minute."

Mom smiled back. "You were everything, Gregory. I'd do it all the same if I could."

Dad started the record and reached for Lorraine. The record spun, and he lowered the needle. Sounds of static crackled as the first notes of 'Spirit in the Sky" filled the air.

An old song, but one of her favorites.

With an arm around Lorraine, Dad pulled my sister away from the bench and held her tight. His chin rested on her head as tears streamed down her cheeks.

Mom closed her eyes and lifted her head. "I'll let you know when I'm ready."

The song played through the first two verses as I looked on. My tears had stopped as a bitter numbness set in. She hummed the tune and sang along with some words.

As the third verse began, she opened her eyes. "I'm ready."

I raised the gun and turned away. Tears swam in my eyes, a drenching rain that never spilled down my face. I took ten steps toward the row of trees beyond the garden.

The hum of the electric guitar sent lightning through my veins, and I no longer felt in control of my body. As if I was only a visitor here, watching a movie I couldn't stop.

I thought of the dot on paper while picturing her face in my mind. Hitting this minuscule part of her skull would mean no pain, according to the book, but the entry had to be perfect.

"I love you," Mom said.

Dad and Lorraine stood to my right. Facing the trees, I pulled the trigger.

The bullet sliced through the air in slow motion. Even though I couldn't see the bullet, I felt its velocity as I commanded the air currents and grieved for its deadly force.

Behind me, the sliver of precision metal curved back to find its mark.

Lorraine cried out in anguish and buried her face against Dad's chest. I let out the breath I'd been holding. The gun slipped from my fingers. The only sound was Lorraine's sobs and the metal barrel crashing to the ground.

I walked out of the garden without looking back.

EPISODE 14
Flight Risk

The day after my mother died, my father had her body cremated. No need to wait for an autopsy. Everyone knew she died of the cancer she'd been fighting for years.

Not my bullet. Dad had connections with the entire town; he'd lived in Credence all of his life. In ways I never questioned for fear of learning the truth, he made sure no one had a reason for investigating her death. Thankfully, he kept those details to himself and no one from town asked me anything. For a town that loved to gossip, people were surprisingly respectful.

I'd thought Mom and I would have so much more time.

Dad got rid of the soldiers' bodies before the sun rose that next morning. Lorraine and I helped him dump the bodies in the lake as we did that first night. For Lorraine, her emotions were a mix of pain at Mom's death and fear at someone discovering our crime.

For me, it was numbness and wishing that night was over.

During the next two days, I wavered between anger at the world and regret for all the things I didn't think to say or do. We'd never given Mom the China cabinet for her birthday. She would have loved this piece of wood furniture I'd worked on with Dad and Lorraine.

Mom would never have that birthday. Tears streamed down my face.

For the service, Dad's friend from Virginia returned. Hugh Flint built the cellar under our house before leaving town years before. He brought a preacher, Wynn, who took charge of the details and made Mom's send-off to the next life beautiful. At least for those who believed in a next life. I wasn't sure.

It was enough that the preacher seemed to believe. Wynn didn't fit any of my notions of a preacher, starting with the fact he wore brown pants and a white-collared shirt with the sleeves rolled up to his elbows. Nothing fancy.

Wynn had helped Hugh drive all night. Once they got the word from Dad, they wasted no time in coming down.

During the service, Wynn talked about Mom as if he'd known her personally. He read the twenty-third Psalm and brought me some measure of comfort with promises of how her walk through the valley of death wasn't a lonely one.

At the end, he played Mom's song again. "Spirit in the Sky" revved through the room with sounds of the electric guitar. As the tune played, I thought of her eyes as I turned away, of her look of gratitude that I'd been willing to fulfill her wish. I remembered each step I took.

And my finger on the trigger as I tugged. The bullet flowed through the air, turning with the air currents I controlled.

I felt the bullet when it struck.

Even though I didn't understand this strange culture, it was what she wanted. I'd made her final wish come true.

After the song finished and Wynn brought the service to a close, he approached me. "You look like your mother."

"Did you know her?"

"I met her many years ago, long before I knew Hugh."

"How well did you know her?"

He smiled. "I'm a man of God, but I've seen things no person can explain. I knew she was different from us. She saved my life once, and I asked if there was any way to repay her."

"What did she say?"

"Though she wasn't raised with religion as I was, the idea of life after death brought her comfort. She asked that I perform her funeral when this day arrived."

Shock filled me. "She knew when she would die? Years ago?"

Wynn nodded. "I don't know how, but Candy knew her fate rested in this small town. She told me when the day would be, and I was ready."

How long ago did Keva tell her?

Although I wanted more answers from him, the sound of my name made me turn. He slipped away to talk with my father and Hugh.

"Charlie," Carmen said, throwing her arms around me. "I was so sorry to hear about your mom."

I patted her back. "It's okay."

"We all knew she was sick, but I didn't realize she was this close." She released me. "If you need anything, please call. Treat me like the friend you need."

Nodding, I wiped tears from my eyes.

Joel held out a box of tissues, and I grabbed one to wipe my eyes.

Carmen's mother put her arms around me next. "I'm sorry. We'll all miss your mother."

"Thank you," I said.

"You should come over for dinner," she said as she pulled back. "Or we can come over and cook at your house. That might be better."

I nodded through the tears. Maybe I was wrong to keep Carmen at arm's length. Having a friend sounded good. Someone I could talk to, confide in.

Joel gave me a brief hug. He looked over my face as I drew back. "It's not your fault she died. It's not anyone's fault."

The way he got so close to the truth made me laugh. All three looked at me strangely, but they couldn't know the truth. No one would understand.

Mom died because she came back to Earth. She returned to give me a better life.

"I know." It was a lie, but it was all I could think of.

*****

That night, Dad sat at the kitchen table with Hugh and Wynn. Lorraine and I sat in our normal seats. We left Mom's seat empty.

A stream of visitors had drifted through the house that afternoon and left us with a mountain of food that covered the counters. Everyone from teachers at school to customers Dad had known for years, even the mayor who Dad went to school with. And the deputy, Roy, and his wife Nancy. I wondered what he would think if he had a look in our lake.

The mood was sad, but mostly a celebration of Mom's life. I never realized my family had this many friends.

Now that we sat at the table and the other visitors were gone, the silence wasn't the calm I'd hoped for.

"Do you have anything to drink?" Hugh asked.

Dad thought for a moment. "I have something Candy brought me. It's a few years old—"

Hugh laughed. "The older the better."

My father rose and pulled a bottle from the top shelf of one of the cabinets. I'd never noticed the square shaped bottle with dark brown glass. The words seemed to be printed on the glass instead of a label.

Hugh took the bottle. "What is this, Russian?"

"Something like that," Dad said. "It's smooth." He handed a shot glass to Hugh and Wynn, then one to me and Lorraine.

Lorraine's eyes widened. "You're going to let *us* drink?"

"Tonight we take a shot of our own, to toast your mother. I wish you could've been older for this, but she didn't believe fate gives us choices."

"Very appropriate for Candy," Wynn said.

Shock filled me. Would this preacher really take a shot with Dad?

Hugh filled the glasses and raised his. We all followed, raising our glasses high.

"To Candy," he said.

"To Candy," we all said.

The men drank theirs in one gulp. Lorraine tasted the liquid, made a yuck face, and then finished it all at once.

The aroma tickled my nose. I sipped the liquid at first, but Dad was right. Though I'd heard alcohol could burn all the way down, this drink tasted almost sweet.

"I'm not a drinking man, but that was smooth." Wynn turned the glass in his hand. "Did Candy ever tell anyone about saving my life?"

Dad shook his head. "No and neither did I."

"Probably better you didn't." Wynn looked at me. "One day when you're older, I'd like to show you a place in

West Virginia. That's where I'm from. There's a house you should see."

"Why?" I asked.

He gave me a thin smile. "You'll know when you see it."

Hugh turned to Wynn. "I didn't think you were going back to West Virginia."

Wynn shrugged. "We all go home at some point."

With another shot, Dad sat back in his chair. "You did a great job with the service, Wynn."

"It was from the heart."

"Even though Candy wasn't raised with any type of religion, she always said that song made her wish she could have been."

"She lived a good life," Wynn said. "It's all any of us could hope for."

"One thing still bothers me," Hugh said. "We built a room under this house with no way inside. I'm assuming Candy used the room."

Dad poured each of the men a shot and drank his in one gulp. "She did."

"Can you explain how?"

Wynn chuckled and drank his shot.

Looking over at me and Lorraine, Dad said, "Girls, I think it's time for bed."

With his words, the weight of the world seemed to fall on my shoulders. The day was finally over. I'd find my bed and sleep until I couldn't any longer.

I wouldn't even change clothes, though I'd always taken a shower before bed. After all the scrubbing and crazy amounts of cleaning I'd done in the last few weeks, I was finally wiped out.

The mess of a world around me would have to wait.

*****

When I woke the next day, at almost noon, I found Dad at the kitchen table with a cup of coffee in his hand. The kitchen was clean, and someone had arranged all the containers with food in the fridge. Had he cleared it all by himself?

I sat down beside him. "Where are your friends?"

"On the road. Some folks are early risers, unlike my daughters."

"They went home?"

"No need for them to stay any longer."

The edge in his voice bothered me. "Are you okay?"

Dad hesitated. "I will *be* okay, one of these days. How about you?"

"Same for me. How much does Wynn and Hugh know about Mom's past?"

"Last night, I let Hugh in on how she could teleport. He doesn't know where she was from, and I think we'll keep it that way."

"But Wynn knew. How?"

"There was an accident years ago in Wynn's hometown in West Virginia. Your mother was there meeting a buyer for a special gun she'd made."

"What happened?"

"The man's younger brother was trapped in a mine. The buyer took Candy down into the mine and they used some fancy technology to search. When they found his brother, Candy teleported both of them out. Wynn was the brother."

"Didn't she worry about getting hurt? Or that someone would find out about her?"

"She left before anyone else saw her. Wynn's brother used his influence to make the story disappear. Your mother has used her power over the years to save lives. She pulled several people from a burning building a few years ago. They were too high to be reached in time and she teleported them to the ground. You had no idea she was gone."

"No one knew she saved those people?"

He shook his head. "The people she saved were too frantic to worry about getting a good look at her, but she covered her tracks in any case. There's no way she could ever take credit. She had to be content with me knowing."

"You make it sound like Mom was some kind of superhero."

"I guess you could put it that way."

"Why didn't she tell me?" I asked.

"Because she didn't want you to do anything risky. She took every precaution to keep people from finding out who she was."

"What about Wynn?"

Dad smiled. "Wynn was the one exception to the rule. He wanted to know how her power worked, and for some reason, she trusted him. Your mother brought Wynn here to meet me."

"Wynn never told anyone?"

"Not that I know of. When Candy first stayed on Earth, it was hard not using her powers. Saving lives gave her a purpose. As you got older, she focused less on the outside world and more on the inside of our house."

"I still don't understand why she told Wynn the truth."

"It had to do with him being a preacher. The truth of her powers went against the core of his beliefs. The irony is she wanted him to teach her more about his beliefs. She wanted religion. Something to believe in."

Maybe I didn't know my mother as well as I thought. What other lives had she touched beyond our small family? How many ways had she truly made a difference?

Keva and Amelia had discussed Mom's legacy on a planet across the galaxy. What did her life really mean to them?

"We should talk about today," he said.

"What happens today?"

"After Lorraine gets up, I want to spread your mother's ashes."

Tears filled my eyes. "I'm not ready."

"The sooner we do this, the sooner it can be over."

I shook my head and stared out of the window into the garden. "I'm not sure what 'over' means. She's never coming back."

"We take this one day at a time." He took a deep breath. "Your mother wanted her ashes spread in the lake."

"No," Lorraine said from the doorway. "We're not doing that."

The thought of pouring her ashes in that dark water made me shiver. "Why did she choose the lake?"

"Your mother never wanted to kill those men. She did it to protect herself and hide the two of you. To her, dying meant ashes to ashes."

Lorraine took a seat at the table. "Like in the fire?"

"Death is a part of life," he said. "You are both young, but you must come to terms with the reality of death. In that we are all the same. Placing her ashes in the lake proves she's no better than those men. Her life wasn't worth more. In the end, their final resting place will be the same."

"I don't care what she wanted," Lorraine said. "She loved our garden. Her ashes should go there."

They stared at each other across the table.

"Maybe we can put some of her ashes in the garden and some in the lake," I said.

They both looked at me.

"I think that's fair," Dad said.

Reluctantly, Lorraine nodded.

She said nothing for the next hour. So unlike Lorraine to stay quiet, but I could tell she needed space. After Dad pulled out leftover trays of food for lunch and no one ate a bite, we drove down to the lake and dumped part of the ashes.

When we reached the garden, Lorraine poured out the rest of Mom's ashes. I took a handful and a gentle wind blew the ashes from my hand. Like a song Mom loved, "Dust in the Wind." I sang a verse of the song as the wind carried the last of her ashes away.

She knew about my music, and I'd always remember hers.

Next to me, Lorraine wiped her eyes. "How will I go on?"

"Like you always have," I said. "As the center of everything, as long as you don't stop being you."

"How will you go on?"

I stared at the trees until she sighed. "I don't know."

The only answer I could think of was getting as far away from Credence as possible.

*****

That night, I sat on the bench in the garden and watched the stars. Here I felt closer to Mom than I had for the last two days. These were the stars she'd never travel back to or see again.

This would be the last night I'd sit here, I decided as I watched the sky twinkle.

Keva appeared on the bench at my side. "A beautiful sight."

I turned to her. "I thought you might have returned for her funeral."

"Candorice was my friend. I paid my respects in my own way."

"Did Amelia go back to Golvern?"

Keva nodded. "She told them your mother didn't have any children to carry on her legacy."

"She lied to help us?"

"For Amelia, it was a matter of honor. She will hide your existence for now. Unfortunately, there are some with the power to see through her lie. They'll read the truth on her face."

"Then we're not safe." I stared across the garden. "What should I do?"

"Train. Practice. Get stronger with your power. It's the only way you can protect yourself and those you care about."

"I don't want to train anymore. I don't want to use this power ever again."

"But you will. Remember, I've seen your future."

"If someone from their government comes for me, am I strong enough to fight them?"

"You need time, but you also need direction. Your mother had a friend on Golvern."

I thought back to the night Mom and Keva talked at the table. This was the friend who couldn't stand to look at her, who blamed her for avoiding her Protector duty. "She mentioned the name Paleris."

"He has the Protector power." Keva hesitated. "Training with him can strengthen your ability."

"I don't want to go there. My mother didn't want me to go there. It's why she fought and died here."

"Your mother chose her fate, but she cannot choose yours."

"I thought both of you said I wasn't strong enough to fight fate."

"Candorice was," Keva said softly.

"I'm not leaving Earth. Ever."

"You may change your current path, but you won't alter fate, not in this case. This only ends one way, and that's with you on Golvern."

When I looked back at Keva, the bench was empty.

EPISODE 15

Don't Look Back

After we said goodbye to Mom, I spent the next two days in my room. I didn't clean, watch TV, or read anything. Only the necessities brought me out, and I didn't spend over ten minutes away from my room each time.

Dad left me alone. On day three, I came out of my darkness and thought of my younger sister. How was Lorraine dealing with our mother's death? Since the house had been quiet, she wasn't breaking pictures or anything else the way she did after Darla died.

I found her downstairs watching music videos on MTV. She stared at the TV with a blank expression, and I waved my hand in front of her face. Aerosmith jammed on the screen, but she didn't notice me.

Lorraine noticed nothing until I shook her arm.

"What?" She pulled away, grasping her arm as if I'd hurt her.

"Where were you?" I asked.

"I was thinking."

"This isn't good for you."

She glared up at me. "You're not my mother."

Those words made me snap. I slapped Lorraine's face.

My sister jumped to her feet, gripping her cheek. "You have no right. You've been in your room since we dumped her ashes."

The tingling of my hand was an ugly reminder I'd lost control. Guilt drove me to look at the far wall, the TV, the floor… anything but her angry eyes. Justifiably angry since I had no defense for my actions. "I'm sorry."

"I lost her too," Lorraine whispered.

Hot tears filled my eyes. "Don't you get it?"

"Get what?"

"She came back to Earth for me. You had a twin. You would have been fine growing up on Golvern, but they would have put me in a special school. I would've been an outcast for the rest of my life."

She reached for my hand. "You would have had us. Plus, I don't think Dad would have left Earth."

"Charlie," Dad said.

I turned, and he motioned for me to follow him into the kitchen. He sat at the table, but I stood by the door.

"Violence isn't the answer," he said. "Haven't you realized that after everything your mother went through? She killed so you wouldn't have to."

As the tears threatened to trail down my face, I stared at the floor.

"You've spent two days in your room. Are you done sulking?"

I couldn't speak, only shake my head.

"This isn't what your mother fought for. She wanted you to have the life *you* wanted."

"This is the life I want."

"Not wasting away. There are so many things you can do with your life, so many opportunities. You can go to college and have any career. You can go places you've never seen."

"I don't want to do any of that."

"What do you want?"

"I'm not sure."

His voice softened. "We've all been through an ordeal. All of our lives changed that night, not just yours. Healing will take time."

"I know."

"Look at me."

Slowly, I shifted my eyes to meet his.

"We're a family. We'll help each other through this, do you understand?"

I nodded. "Can I go back to my room?"

He sighed. "Go."

When I'd reached my bedroom and climbed into bed, I realized this life wasn't for me. Credence wasn't a place I wanted to stay. This house, my family… I felt as if I was suffocating.

The memory of Mom's last night haunted me. Pulling the trigger, controlling the bullet… No, I wouldn't think of it again.

Ever since Keva left, I'd felt fear every time I thought of using my power. The man she mentioned, Paleris—could he come for me? Would Amelia change her mind and bring more soldiers to kidnap me for Golvern's government?

What if anyone else from that planet showed up in our living room?

Keva said I needed to train to protect those I care about. What if I couldn't protect my sister?

I teleported myself to the cellar. The glowing lights where the walls met the ceiling reminded me of Mom's smile as she showed off her 'shop.' She'd been proud to show me her work.

She'd also been proud of me the day I found my ability to shoot.

I took my gun to the garden and fired an entire clip. It didn't matter what I aimed for, I just needed to feel the power of the gun in my hand.

"Why?" I yelled.

Another clip emptied before my eyes. I was wasting the precious bullets she made. Bullets she could never make again.

If only I had enough time to learn how she made the bullets or the guns. I'd never thought about making her teach me. Back in the cellar, I dug through the drawers until I found a book she hadn't showed me before.

Inside the solid black cover were directions on how to make a gun and formulas to achieve her perfectly balanced weights. Drawings on how to fashion the bullets. On the last page was a note for me.

Charlie,

My girl, this is your legacy. I'm watching you from a special place where no one feels pain. Wynn promised me this place exists.

Take your time and learn these skills. You don't have to build guns like I did, but the knowledge is here if you choose to. I'll be proud of you either way.

Love,

Mom

Her words were supposed to make me feel sure of myself. To push me toward doing what was right.

Instead, a part of me broke inside.

*****

That night, I tiptoed through the house after Dad and Lorraine went to bed. The floors were filthy, but I wasn't there to clean. I shoved the neat-freak bug out of my head.

In the kitchen, I found Dad's cash jar and filled a zipper bag with all the bills. I also shoved in the stack of cash I'd saved from doing chores. Maybe I should have counted the money, but I was afraid to know how little I had.

I stared at the phone on the wall. A good friend would call Carmen, even though it was after ten.

She'd probably cuss me out.

Lifting the phone, I dialed her number. After four rings, her tired voice came over the line. "Hello?"

"Hey," I said.

"Charlie?" She seemed to wake up. "Charlie, is that you? Are you okay?"

"I'm fine. Just wanted to tell you I'm sorry."

The line went quiet. "For what?"

"Not being the friend you deserve."

"I've never asked you to be anything you're not. But you've been a good friend."

"You're just being nice." I laughed. "Thanks for being nice to me."

"Hey, maybe we can meet tomorrow and have lunch. There's an Italian place downtown I think you'd like."

"Sounds good," I said. "Call me tomorrow, but not too early."

"Sure. See you then."

I hung up the phone and smiled. It was good to hear her voice one last time.

On the fridge, I left a note for my family.

Dad and Rainey,

Sorry I can't be the daughter and sister you need. I can't explain why, but I have to go. One day I'll come back.

Love,

Charlie

Back in my bedroom, I emptied the contents of my backpack and filled it with three days' worth of clothes. I threw in the bag of money along with several clips of bullets and pulled on a jacket despite the heat outside. The gun I wore.

If I needed more ammo, I knew how to get back.

At the door to Lorraine's room, I stopped to listen. Her breathing was soft in the night. I wanted to see the outline of her face, but I couldn't take a chance on getting close enough to wake her.

Downstairs, I slid on my most comfortable sneakers. I opened the front door and locked it behind me. The muggy air wrapped around me like a wool blanket and sweat beaded along my brow, but I felt an odd sort of comfort. Maybe I'd tie the jacket around my waist for now. Ahead of me was a dark drive, which led to a dark road. Then an entire world.

I walked; luckily, the sky was clear, and the moon and stars would be my friends tonight. The darkness was filled with birds crying out, crickets making their nightly dance, and coyotes yipping in the distance.

None of that scared me.

Where was I going? I wasn't even sure. I laughed as I walked down the dirt drive until the road came into view. At the pavement, I had a simple choice.

Left or right. Either way would take me out of there, so I chose the right. I didn't bring a watch, but maybe I should have. It was well after midnight before I tired.

Lights came around a curve up ahead. I stepped off the road into the grass as a truck approached. The black, rusted Chevy was as big as Dad's Bonanza. It crawled to a stop by my side. In the moonlight, I made out an Army outfit as a man leaned his head out of the window. He was older than

Dad, with graying hair and deep wrinkles, but not anyone I'd seen in Credence.

"You need a ride?"

The hairs on my arms stood. An alcohol smell drifted through the open window, and I cringed when I noticed a machete hanging over the rack in his back window. At least it wasn't a gun.

I wasn't going anywhere with this guy. "I'm good."

"You can't be out here walking, all alone. It's late."

Actually, it was early. "I said I'm good."

"Look, darling," he crooned. "Get in the truck."

I drew my gun and aimed it at his face.

He threw his hands in the air. "I didn't mean… I'm sorry."

"Get out of here," I yelled.

He swore and slammed a foot on the gas. The truck sped away from me, and I tucked the gun back in my pants. What a relief.

My relief didn't last long. As soon as he was out of sight, clouds covered the moon. I walked on while trying to decide where to go. An entire world awaited me, a place where I could forget about the past, but where?

Maybe an hour later, I'd reached the outskirts of town. A few more miles and I'd find the highway. Rain began to fall, seeping through my hair and clothes.

I smelled the clean air and thought of my freedom.

Lights flashed behind me as another truck approached. This time, the truck was the same body style as my Toyota, but with an extended cab. The truck slowed and a young man rolled down his window.

"Did you break down?"

I glanced both ways. "I need a way to town."

"You don't have a car?"

"No."

"You're getting soaked. Town is back the other way," he said, pointing behind him. "I'm on my way to Atlanta."

From the jersey he wore and the mop of shaggy hair beneath a college ball cap, the guy had to be a student. "I need out of this town. Atlanta sounds good."

He smiled and reached across to open the passenger door. "Get in."

I ran around the truck and climbed in. With the overhead light on, I wrinkled my nose in disgust. The backseat overflowed with empty coke bottles and fast-food bags. Cigarette packs littered the floor around my feet.

I'd reamed Lorraine after riding home with Joel, and here I'd climbed into a truck with a guy I'd never met. His truck was filthy and smelled worse than fish from the lake, but at least it was dry.

He narrowed his eyes as the light faded. "How old are you?"

"Eighteen."

Seeming to relax, he shifted the truck into drive, and we moved forward. "What are you running away from?"

"Who says I'm running away?"

"You've got one bag, and you were walking down the highway. Hey, the cops won't—"

"No one will look for me if that's what you're asking."

"What's the deal?"

"I'm never going back to that town."

He laughed. "Never is a long time. I'm Scott, by the way."

"Hello Scott, nice to meet you. I'm…" I said the first thing that came to mind. "Charlie."

"Well, Charlie. I'm headed for the airport. Is that a good place for you to stop?"

Airport? I bit my lip to keep from laughing. Charlene Conners, with the power to teleport anywhere in the world, was on her way to an airport. "It's perfect."

For the next twenty miles, Scott told me all about his classes and why he was looking forward to going home for the summer. When he pulled into a gas station to refill, I went into the store for a snack and to use the bathroom. Would he still be waiting when I returned?

I kept my backpack on, just in case.

He'd finished at the pump and went inside by the time I returned to the truck. With relief, I opened my door and tossed my bag inside. The rain made the air so thick and hot, steam rolled off the pavement in the bright lights from above the pumps. Good thing this truck had a working air conditioner.

And I'd planned to walk all night. What was I thinking?

A man approached and reached inside the bed of the truck. His hands went for what looked like a red toolbox.

"Get out of here," I yelled.

He glared at me, and I pointed my gun at him. His face turned to shock as he ran away with empty hands. I slid the gun into my pants as Scott ran across the parking lot.

"What happened?" he asked.

"A man tried to grab your tools. He ran off."

"What made him leave?"

I shrugged. "I think I scared him."

He laughed. "Makes perfect sense. Your face is scary like Freddy Krueger."

Rolling my eyes, I climbed in the truck. "You're such a dork."

I ate the bag of chips from the store and laid my head back. For the next hour, Scott told me his life story. Everything and then some. My only regret was I couldn't go to sleep.

Eventually, the highway opened to more lanes, and the buildings looked brighter and spaced closer together. We were approaching the city and the airport, as shown by signs along the interstate.

I'd never been to an airport before; I'd barely been anywhere. Lights flashed on planes as they rose into the night and landed, flying so low they barely cleared the truck. The rain had stopped, and the clouds thinned, but not a single star winked at us from the darkness above.

I watched, wide-eyed, as Scott took the exit and followed the signs to park. We passed row after row of cars, and then more cars, before reaching an open lot. A control tower to our right stood proud against the night sky, with lights that flashed continuously.

Scott talked until he found an empty spot and parked the truck. People walked by us as they headed toward signs for a terminal. If the airport was this busy at night, the place must be packed during the day.

I climbed out with my bag. He pulled out two suitcases and moved the toolbox from his bed into the cab. After locking the doors, he turned to me. "I've got to catch a plane. Will you be okay?"

"I'll be fine. I'll probably get a ticket when I figure out where to go."

"If you want to come to Denver—"

"No. I'll find my place."

He flashed a relieved smile and held out a hand. "It was nice to meet you, Charlie."

I shook his hand. "Thanks for the ride and thanks for not being a serial killer."

Laughing, Scott checked his watch and said goodbye before heading to the terminal.

Then I was alone.

It wasn't like I could catch a plane. Did I have enough money? Probably not. I thought of the I.D. I'd need to buy a ticket. In my wallet was the learner's license with my picture.

If I planned to start a new life, I had to first erase who I was. I threw the license in the closest trashcan. As of that moment, Charlene Conners no longer existed.

Someone walked past me to the automatic doors. My stomach growled at the smell of the box of food she carried. My choices were slim. Either go inside or stand out here all night.

Inside were people and food. There I could figure out my next move.

I'd find a good meal and make a plan. Someone like me could blend in as long as needed. Hiding my powers and acting normal should be easy. I'd been normal nearly all of my life until a few weeks ago. No shooting and no teleporting.

The fact I might not be the only one here with powers? Never occurred to me.

EPISODE 16

Regrets

The airport was packed with people, even with multiple displays showing a time of 4:35 a.m. People in suits, people in PJs. People with kids in tow and some speaking languages I didn't understand.

Most entering the building carried bags and pulled suitcases toward a long counter. On the other side, reps sold tickets and tried to sound awake at this early hour.

I passed the ticket sales and headed for the smell of bacon. Signs above directed me to a food court. Pictures on the wall showed mouth-watering meals that made my stomach growl louder. With this many people, at least one restaurant had to be selling a breakfast plate with pancakes.

Pulling my jacket close, I felt thankful for remembering to bring it. The air in this place made me shiver.

Or maybe it was the memories I tried to hide. I'd walked out on my sister and my dad, less than a week after my mother died. What kind of person did that?

Even Carmen and Joel would feel abandoned. Well, maybe Carmen. Joel would probably feel relief after learning the weird girl with a power to teleport had disappeared for good. Guess I'd never know.

I passed a sign with the picture of a teary-eyed child, maybe three, and the words, 'Have you seen me?'

Would that be me next week? Would Dad call the cops and have everyone search for me?

Probably not, knowing I had the power to return home with a simple thought. My walking out of a perfectly good home on two hundred acres would shock Dad. He'd always insisted our lives were easier than what he'd known growing up. This would be a deep cut so soon after Mom's death. Maybe I should call and let him know I was alive.

Or maybe not. I was a terrible daughter.

And sister. I couldn't think of Lorraine without hearing tears in her voice. She'd be angry and hurt to find me gone.

Mom's last words repeated in my head. *I love you.*

How could she love me after pulling the trigger? It didn't matter that's what she wanted. Or that she was already dying.

I couldn't get past the fact I carried out her wishes. Killed my mother.

What would she think if she could see me now, carrying a backpack with clothes and a bag of money I'd burn through in a matter of weeks, maybe days?

I'd have to find some kind of job. Except I no longer had an I.D. I was nobody and nothing to anyone.

At a cluster of restaurants, I settled for eggs and biscuits. I stood in the long line quietly while waiting for my turn. A few people looked at me strangely, then took a glance around to see if I was alone. Most didn't notice me.

I bought a plate with three scrambled eggs and a sausage biscuit. The food had no salt and not much taste, but it did stop my stomach from growling. It cost me six dollars, which was more than I'd imagined.

My money might not last a week.

With my stomach full, I explored the airport while looking for the best place to hide. In the area marked baggage claim, people hurried through the walkway while looking over revolving conveyors for their bags. Though I'd never been to an airport, I decided the best place to hang out was in a high-traffic area. People would rush through and never pay me any attention. After grabbing their bags, they'd head toward the signs marked 'exit' and never look back.

Plus, that put me close to the exit if I needed to run. At one end of the baggage claim area, I found a row of six seats. A woman and two kids occupied the seats to my right. To my left sat an older couple with suitcases at their feet. The center seat was mine.

I dropped into the seat and laid my head back. My whole body ached. The time on the wall showed six twenty, and I wondered if Lorraine was up yet. Had Dad read my note?

Outside the window, sunlight glowed on planes landing and bouncing along the concrete toward gates. I'd watched enough TV to know the basics of an airport. The ceilings would be taller than any room I'd seen. And the electronic screens would display flight destinations and codes in bright colors.

However, the noise and amount of people felt like ten times more.

A family passed in front of me, with four kids laughing as they headed toward a security checkpoint. Above that doorway was a sign with a gun symbol. A red circle surrounded the gun with a line through it.

Guns weren't allowed at the airport. I patted the barrel tucked into my jeans, completely hidden by the jacket. Yes, they had every right to worry, but I wasn't letting go of my only protection. I'd never let the gun Mom gave me out of sight.

A blast of air came from somewhere far above, and I shivered. Slouching down, I pulled the jacket closed.

For the first time in days, I felt a wave of regret for killing those soldiers. Shock too, as I realized my shots took them down. They were on Earth hunting for Mom. Capturing her was their job.

Did that mean they deserved to die?

I closed my eyes. If I kept thinking horrible thoughts, I'd never get out of this airport.

A guard dressed in navy blue pants and a jacket passed by. He glanced down at me as he walked but didn't stop. Twenty minutes later, another guard in the same uniform walked through with a dog. Neither stopped, though I made eye contact with the second guard.

One kid beside me screamed and the second chimed in. The mother yelled at them in another language. I didn't understand her words but felt her frustration. To my other side, the couple waiting quietly stood and pulled their suitcases in the opposite direction.

Maybe staying in this spot wasn't such a great idea.

The first guard weaved back through the crowd, this time stopping in front of me. "You're a little young to be here alone. What are you doing?"

"Waiting for my family," I said.

"They're on a flight?"

I nodded. "From Denver." Scrambling, I searched for a monitor with flight numbers and arrival times.

He hesitated as his radio crackled and a voice asked him to check another terminal. "Stay out of trouble." The man walked away, and I headed for the other end of the baggage claim. In an empty row of seats, I leaned my head back with my bag gripped in my arms. It made the perfect pillow.

No more screaming kids. A few minutes to rest would be great.

I'd just close my eyes and try not to fall asleep.

*****

Voices shouted, and I jerked to attention, dropping my bag to the floor. People around me screamed and ran toward the exit signs in a massive flow.

Alarms sounded, and red lights flashed. A family ran by me, almost shoving me from the seat.

Above all the noise, the cracking of an entire clip of bullets reverberated through the air. More screams followed as people tripped over bags and shoved others in their frantic bid to escape.

I gripped my bag close to my chest but didn't leave the seat.

A motion to the left caught my eye. Approaching was a man dressed in a sequined white jumpsuit with his arm around a woman's neck. I blinked and looked again. Was this a dream?

No, the man had definitely dressed like the cover of one of Mom's Elvis albums. The legs of his pants flared around his white boots. Lights from above sparkled along the sequins. His black hair was cut like I'd seen in pictures, and he even had the sideburns. The only thing missing was a guitar hanging from his shoulder.

He dragged the woman while he pranced through the room, glancing around as if looking for fans to take his picture. She was at least a foot shorter than him, dressed in a black suit, and kicked at his legs as she gripped the arm around her neck. In his other hand was a gun.

The scene was so bizarre, I wanted to laugh with humor and disgust at the same time. Instead, I hugged my bag as he passed between me and one of the luggage carousels.

Laughing like a true villain, he barely looked my way. The woman twisted with a burst of strength, almost breaking free. He wrenched her closer and put the gun to her head. I thought of the soldier who grabbed me the night Mom died.

A man in a black suit approached from the other direction with a gun in his hand. His face was clean-shaven and hard as stone; his dark hair was cut military-style. Broad shoulders and thick upper arms gave the impression he knew how to fight.

If he noticed me, he didn't look my way. Elvis turned, with the woman still in his grip, and the approaching man stopped and aimed his gun. The three stood about thirty feet to my right, near the next luggage carousel.

"Not so close, Agent Mason," Elvis said.

Agent, I thought. Like FBI?

Agent Mason kept the gun trained on him. He spoke in a deep voice, filled with anger, but his movements were slow and cautious. "What's with the suit, Faulkner?"

Elvis smiled. "If I'm going out, it will be in style. And I won't be alone."

I glanced around in shock. No one sat in any of the seats. Luggage made circles on the conveyors with no one there to grab the bags. The room had cleared completely except for two more agents dressed in black near the main doors. And another three watching from across the room.

Mom would have loved to see this.

Another man in a black suit entered the room. He was shorter than Agent Mason and not built in the arms. As he walked by me, he leaned down. "Now is a good time to disappear."

Disappear?

He motioned for the door and kept walking, drawing his gun as his pace slowed. His hair was brown, he wore dark sunglasses, and he walked with confidence. Everything else blended into the black suit. In fact, all the agents looked like emotionless minions in their black clothes.

"Faulkner, you don't have to do this." The new agent approached and stood by Agent Mason. Both aimed their guns at the man dressed like Elvis.

I should have taken his advice.

I should have run. Or teleported. Anything to get out of there.

But one thought I couldn't ignore. Was there any way I could help? If I pulled out my gun and fired, these people would see.

Was this woman's life worth exposing my power?

I thought of my mother dying. Maybe saving another life could wipe out a fraction of the grief I felt. Mom had saved others. She'd used her powers like a superhero.

Elvis pressed his gun into the woman's black hair, the short strands jutting out in every direction from where they'd fought. Her dark complexion made a sharp contrast against his sequined white sleeve. "You know I'm going to kill her. I don't understand why you think we can negotiate."

"Faulkner," the woman groaned. "We can make a trade."

"You have nothing to bargain," he said.

The two agents moved closer, their guns never wavering from the target.

"No," she yelled. "Don't come any closer. Let me deal with him."

"Deal with me?" Faulkner's body shook with laughter. "My arm is wrapped around your neck. You think you can move fast, that the power you have is stronger than mine. Now we know the truth."

"You don't need to kill her," Agent Mason said. "I'm the one you want."

"I'll kill you next," Elvis said, tightening his grip. "This woman is never coming after me again."

"You killed my partner," she managed to say.

He tightened his elbow around her neck until she choked. Faster than I could follow, the man released her, ran across the room, and shot the two agents near the exit. He returned and regained his grip. "Who's faster now?"

I put a hand over my mouth. The two agents fell to the floor. It took a few moments for me to digest everything I'd seen.

The man moved faster than my eyes could. At first, I thought he was teleporting. Then I remembered the news story about a bank robbery in New York. The man could move faster than anything alive. Faster than the cameras.

"You should have left me alone, Sylvia," he yelled.

She closed her eyes as he loomed over her, or maybe it was because he seemed to spit each word.

"Why haven't you killed me?" Agent Mason yelled.

"Delayed gratification," Elvis said.

A bullet was fired; the force as it cut through the air sent a ripple effect my way. Possibly a sniper from above. Glancing around, I couldn't find the shooter, though the effort was useless. Elvis moved before the bullet could hit him.

Agent Mason lifted a radio and pressed the button. "Don't. You might hit Sylvia."

"Yes," Elvis said. "Wouldn't it be ironic if her own agents killed her? Great story to tell around the next potluck."

The agent who'd talked to me waved for Agent Mason to calm down. "Tell me about this outfit, Faulkner. I didn't realize you had an Elvis fetish."

Elvis held up the hand with the gun and smoothed the hair on the side of his face. "If you live through this, make sure they log it in my file."

"The details in those sequins are amazing. Did you sew them yourself?"

"I made the entire thing." Elvis held up a leg. "Agent Payne, tell the truth. You're a fan."

Now, the other agent had a name. Agent Payne removed his sunglasses. "How did you guess?"

Elvis moved again, this time toward the three agents near the far wall. They'd drifted closer while he talked. I didn't see him move, only felt the rush of air left in his wake. When he'd returned to grip Sylvia's neck, all three agents slumped to the floor.

Blood pooled around one agent, a woman, drifting outward on the tiled floor. With her wound, she might die before an ambulance could arrive.

"Agent Payne, tell me your favorite Elvis song."

Agent Payne glanced at the other agents, lifeless on the floor. His body went rigid as he gripped the gun, though his voice remained warm and friendly. "The one where he's in prison."

Elvis belted out a laugh. "You've always seemed more of the romantic type."

Turning his head to the side, Agent Payne said, "Elvis seems to know me better than I know myself."

"This isn't the time for jokes." Agent Mason took one step closer to Elvis. "Release her or I *will* kill you. Even if you take her down, I'll bring you to justice. I'll find a way."

"You'd best stop the threats. I've run out of other people to kill first."

That's when his eyes stopped on me. "Or maybe not." He dragged the woman closer to me and pointed his gun in my direction.

"No," she screamed, a sound that went straight to my heart.

I took a deep breath. Now that he was threatening me, I couldn't teleport out of there with everyone watching.

He fired the gun, and a bullet sped toward my face. I felt the bullet slice through the air, worked the surrounding air currents. The deadly shot of metal slid by me and went through the seat at my side.

Elvis blinked. The smile faded. "I never miss."

"Maybe you're not as fast as you think," Agent Payne said.

Agent Mason fired several shots and Elvis moved, barely missing each bullet.

"Missed me by a mile," Elvis said.

I found my voice. "He almost hit you."

Glaring down, the man stalked toward me and pointed the gun at my face. "Shut up. This time I won't miss."

My breath caught. He was going to shoot at me again. Would I have enough time to curve the bullet at this close range?

Jumping forward, Agent Mason slammed into Elvis and the woman from the side. Although Elvis didn't lose his grip on her neck, he stumbled backward.

I shoved my jacket aside and pulled the gun from my pants. The metal felt at home in my hands. For the first time since this nightmare started, I felt safe and in control. I didn't hesitate to pull the trigger.

He dodged the first and second bullets. Holy crap, this man was fast, but I could control the air currents and force the bullet in his direction. While time slowed for me to follow the bullets, I found I could also follow his movements.

My third bullet struck his head.

Elvis's arm loosened enough the woman stumbled away, gripping her neck. He crumpled to the ground in his sequined white suit and his head lobbed to the side. The gun fell with his arm, crashing to the floor.

She found her balance and kicked the gun out of his hand. The two agents rushed to join her, holding out their guns as if Elvis might rise from the dead.

He wouldn't. I'd aimed for the same spot on the skull I used for Mom. His death was quick and painless.

Anger flooded through me. After shooting those other people, he didn't deserve quick or painless.

Silence fell over the baggage claim area. The room, which had been bustling with life earlier, felt huge. The alarm still buzzed and red lights flashed. Luggage piled up on the carousels.

In the distance, a siren wailed.

The only people left were dressed in black suits and staring at me.

EPISODE 17
Agents

As Dad would say, the day had gone to hell. I'd exposed my power by shooting a man dressed as Elvis. Now he lay dead and the woman he *was* choking had a gun pointed at me.

An alarm echoed through the baggage claim area, this monster of a room nearly empty. Annoying red lights flashed in time with the alarm. Lists of flights lit up screens with endless delays. The nearest clock showed nine fifty. Sirens wailed from beyond the exit door, where more people in black entered with guns in their hands.

How many more waited outside those glass doors? I kept thinking, why not teleport somewhere? Anywhere? Several ran across the room to check the agents who'd been shot. Paramedics rushed in with bags of supplies and gurneys.

I thought of Mom's words from the night she died. *If anyone tries to capture you, teleport yourself to another place. Promise me.*

Already, I was breaking my promise by not leaving. With all the people dressed in black suits, I thought of the news reports with secret agents and a cover-up to hide alien activity. Were these people rushing past me FBI, like in the movies? Glancing around, I didn't see anyone wearing an outfit or badge that showed FBI.

The one Elvis called Agent Mason stopped close enough to touch me. "Lower the gun," he said in a deep voice, radiating control.

Like an idiot, I stood there with shaking hands, gripping the gun.

Agent Payne raised his hands in a motion meant to calm me. "Be a good girl and give my partner the gun. Then we can talk and everything will be okay."

"Okay?" I asked. "How can any of this *possibly* be okay?"

"Calm down," Agent Payne said. "That's all we're asking. No one is going to shoot you if you cooperate."

"Will you shoot me if I don't?"

He looked skyward and shook his head in frustration. I held my breath as I waited for his answer. With a nod to Agent Mason, he grabbed my gun and wrestled it from my hands. I yelped with surprise and stumbled backward.

The woman Elvis was choking—Sylvia—caught my arm to keep me from falling.

"How could you be s-sure I wouldn't s-shoot?" I stammered.

Agent Payne examined my gun before turning to me. "I don't believe you came to this airport with any intention of killing. You were in the wrong place at the right time." He glanced at Sylvia. "You saved one of our own."

"That man was shooting at everyone," I said. "He moved faster than my eyes could follow."

"His power allowed him to move faster than any of us," Agent Mason said. "More than a hundred agents have tried to take him down."

All three looked at me as if waiting for an answer.

I peered at Agent Payne. "Could I have my gun back?"

Agent Mason raised both eyebrows. "First, guns aren't allowed at this airport. It's a federal crime." He pointed at one of the signs. "In case you can't read, the picture is obvious. Second, you need a permit to carry a gun. I don't suppose you have one?"

"No." Was it a federal crime or was he just telling me that? The second part I couldn't argue with. Good thing I'd get my gun back whenever I was ready. The teleporting power would make sure of it.

"Third," he said, "this weapon was discharged at a crime scene. We'll have to log it as evidence."

Evidence? I swallowed down the bile rising in my throat. Why hadn't I thought about the investigation that would follow a man being killed in an airport, even if he was the bad guy?

With a smile, Sylvia patted my arm. "Why don't you have a seat? We'll be here for a while."

No, I needed to get away from this circus of people already filling the room. With my hands shaking again, I dropped into the seat I'd used earlier. Sobs rose in my throat, and I struggled to maintain control. Better to remain silent than let them see my fear.

A paramedic approached us, along with another agent. The agent looked down at the man in the Elvis suit with disgust. "Do you need medical help?"

The men shook their heads. Sylvia glanced down at me. "Are you hurt?"

Instead of answering, I hugged my bag close and sank lower in the chair. I wanted my gun back, the only thing I had left from Mom.

"I'll take that as a no," Sylvia said.

The paramedic checked Elvis for a pulse before he and the agent continued toward a group of people clustered around an injured agent.

"What's your name, kid?" Agent Mason asked.

"What's *your* name?" I shot back.

He stared at me for several seconds before holding out a hand. "You can call me Agent Mason." When I didn't respond, he said, "Or just Mason."

I looked at him while thinking of all the places I could teleport to get out of there. Instead, I shook the massive hand that gripped mine gently. "Call me Charlie."

"Now, that wasn't so bad." He motioned to the man beside him. "Charlie, this is my partner, Agent Payne."

"Where are you from?" Agent Payne asked. He didn't offer to shake my hand.

"Texas," I said.

"That's an interesting accent you have," Agent Mason said. "Can't say I believe it's from Texas."

Crap, I never considered my accent would give me away as being from Alabama. Maybe I could keep my voice neutral. "That's where I'm from."

Agent Payne reached for my backpack. "Do you mind if I look in your bag?"

"Hey, that's my stuff."

"We need to make sure you're not carrying any more weapons." He moved the bag into the seat next to me. From his pocket, he pulled on a pair of gloves and dug through my clothes. He set the bag of money to the side and handed my wallet to his partner. Next, he lifted the extra clips of bullets. "You came prepared."

Agent Mason whistled as he looked over the ammo. "Seems we're dealing with a pro." He opened my wallet. "No I.D. How old are you, Charlie?"

"Eighteen," I said.

"Do you have any other abilities?" Agent Payne asked.

"No." It was better if they didn't know I could teleport. I froze when I noticed the gold watch on his wrist. Carmen had described a watch with a tattoo underneath. Closer, I leaned while imagining the black letters.

His eyes met mine with curiosity. Agent Payne shoved the sleeve of his suit over the watch as if reading my mind. He finished with my backpack and replaced the contents, including the bullets. Someone shouted his name, and he backed away, but his foot caught on Elvis's outstretched arm. Agent Payne stumbled backward, nearly falling.

Mason caught his arm. "That could have been bad."

Agent Payne smiled as he regained his balance. "Thanks for the hand."

As Agent Payne walked away with my gun in his hand, I glanced at Sylvia. "Can he see the future?"

She gave me a strange look. "Agent Payne is good with people, but he's an accident waiting to happen. He's the least likely person in this room to know what's going to happen next. Why ask?"

Maybe she was right. "What about the people who were shot? Are they okay?"

"The paramedics have signaled two are critical and the rest have non-life-threatening wounds."

"If you need to check on them…"

"I plan to shortly. We have the best medical staff in the country seeing to their needs. At the moment, I'd be in the way."

"We?"

Agent Mason gave her a look and cut his eyes to the chair next to me. Would they work together to question me like the detectives on TV? Try to learn my deepest secrets? My stomach churned as agents began to take pictures of the body of Elvis. Then they flashed a couple of me.

She sat down next to me and held out a hand. "I'm Sylvia."

"Just Sylvia? No agent name?"

"Why don't you tell me your real name?"

"It's Charlie."

"Charlie…"

"Just Charlie."

"That's the best you've got?"

I crossed my arms over my chest. "If you want to know who I am, you'll have to do your agent job and find out."

"Okay, just Charlie. Looks like I owe you my life."

"I didn't mean to cause any trouble." I took a deep breath. "He was going to kill me and I couldn't…"

"Did you hear his name?"

"Faulkner."

With a deep breath, she leaned back in the seat. "I've been tracking Faulkner for years, ever since he killed my partner. I intended to put a bullet in him myself, but you beat me to it."

"I'm sorry."

"You've saved us all a tremendous amount of trouble, along with the countless lives Faulkner would have taken. He wanted money and power and didn't care who stood in his way."

Like at the bank robbery on the news. "I heard about a man on TV robbing a bank in New York. He could move faster than the cameras."

She stared at me. "He had a power that made him special. Charlie, you seem to have an ability of your own."

I shook my head.

"Can you tell me where you learned to shoot?"

"I don't know what you're talking about."

Agent Mason sat in the chair to my other side. "You're a terrible liar."

"Seeing her take Faulkner down was spectacular," Agent Payne said, walking up. "Not a gift many people have."

I glared at him. "How could you know that?"

He hesitated. In his hand was a clear plastic bag with my gun. "No one at our agency can shoot like you. Not even our best snipers."

"Yeah, I noticed when one tried to take a shot at him." Why did I say that?

"No more games," Mason said in a voice of steel. "You took three shots. Falkner dodged the first two, but you got him with the third. How were you able to hit a person who can move faster than your eyes could follow?"

I thought about the air currents. "I aimed the gun and pulled the trigger. Guess I got lucky."

His lips twitched, and I expected a scathing rebuttal. Instead, he looked at Sylvia. "I hope this revenge scheme of yours is finally over."

Sylvia glanced at me. "Yes, but it had unintended consequences."

"You almost dying was enough."

The edge in his voice told me Agent Mason cared. It was the first hint of emotion I'd heard from him beyond cold efficiency. Despite his deep voice and harsh features, he reminded me of Dad.

No, I couldn't afford to think of this man as anything other than a cold agent. He was in a position of authority, not to mention he wasn't anyone I could imagine fighting. Without a gun, fighting any of these people was useless.

These agents could go after my family if they found out who I really was. They could capture Lorraine. The sooner I got out of the airport, the sooner I could go on with disappearing. I thought of how Agent Payne suggested I disappear when he first walked into the room.

What did he mean?

A woman approached with reddish-brown hair and sunglasses. The way her long black jacket flared around her boots made me think she wouldn't take crap from anyone, not even Agent Mason. She stood tall and walked with a confidence that told me she was taking charge of this situation.

"Looks like your babysitter is here," Agent Payne said.

I frowned. "Babysitter?"

"Yep," Agent Mason said. "Meet Agent Holmes."

Agent Holmes took off her sunglasses and surveyed me. "This is the woman who took down Faulkner?" Her green eyes met mine. "You're just a kid."

"Says she's eighteen," Sylvia said. "Her name is Charlie."

With disbelief, Agent Holmes looked over my face. "Did you make the shot that killed Faulkner?"

I nodded.

"You saved Sylvia's life. Thank you."

"You're welcome," I said.

"What did she use to kill him?"

Agent Payne held up the bag. "This was her gun."

"Still is," I mumbled.

They all looked at me.

"Emily!"

Attention shifted to another agent approaching; he'd removed his suit coat and rolled up his sleeves. His black hair was cut military-style like Mason and he wore a short, well-trimmed beard around his chin and mouth. "What did I miss?"

I studied his wrists. He wore a watch but had no tattoo. Glancing at the surrounding faces, I realized these agents were all in their mid-twenties, except for Sylvia. She was closer to my mom's age.

A pang of sorrow hit me, but I pushed the thought away.

Agent Holmes gave him a look of confusion. "Weren't you briefed?"

"I got the call thirty minutes ago. You could have given me a little heads-up."

"No one knew Faulkner would be at the airport today," Sylvia said. "When we heard, I left the base and drove straight here."

"Thank God that man is dead." He looked at me and grinned, which took the edge off my fear. "Who's the kid?"

I really wished they'd quit calling me 'kid.'

"She shot Faulkner," Agent Mason said. "Took him down with three shots."

Sylvia folded her arms over her chest. "This *kid* saved my life. Took down Faulkner better than any of our snipers could have."

"How much better?" He eyed me as the grin faded. "How old is she?"

"We don't know for sure yet, but I'd be willing to bet she's not your run-of-the-mill human."

Those words came from Agent Payne. I glared up at him. "There's nothing special about me." And why did he have to use the word 'human?' As if I'd let them call me anything else.

The new agent glanced around the room and sighed. "This is going to be a nightmare to clean up. How many people saw Faulkner?"

"Hundreds," Sylvia said. "It will take hours to figure out who saw anything useful."

"You're great with disasters, Jon," Agent Holmes said. "I told you this job would be perfect. Not boring like that Air Force garage you used to hide out in."

"I've never processed this many witnesses," Jon said.

"You'll do fine."

"What do you mean by process?" I asked.

"I'm just the resident janitor." With his arm, Jon wiped sweat from his forehead. "Come in after the action and clean up the mess. Guess we'd better get to work."

Jon turned to walk away, and Agent Payne followed. I wondered what he meant by cleaning up the mess. Would they interrogate people or maybe erase their memories like someone suggested in one of the news interviews? Maybe tell everyone a lie about how the airport had to be evacuated? I tried not to laugh at the thought of someone's memory being erased.

It wasn't possible.

Agent Payne stumbled, and Jon grabbed his arm. "Easy there," Jon said. "We've got all day."

"We've got to get this place clear in the next thirty minutes," Agent Holmes yelled. "The airport needs their building back." When they were out of range, she grinned. "The bumbling agent strikes again."

"Thirty minutes is a tall order." Mason stood. "I should help them."

"You've got surveillance duty." Agent Holmes patted Sylvia's arms as if making sure nothing was broken. "I'm glad this vendetta with Faulkner didn't end the other way."

"Thanks to this girl beside me," Sylvia said.

Smiling, Agent Holmes held out a hand. "I'm glad to meet you, Charlie."

I shook her hand. "When can I get out of here?"

Her smile died. "Were you waiting for a flight?"

"No."

"Are your parents here?"

"I'm alone and plan to stay that way."

"For now, I want you to sit here and remain calm. After we've finished the cleanup, you'll tell Sylvia everything you know, including how you ended up at this airport. Any details about how you took Faulkner down would be useful. You're better off telling her than getting locked in an interrogation room. Could make for a long night."

How long did they plan to keep me? "Can I get my gun back?"

She shot Agent Mason a humorous look.

"I let Charlie know that possessing a gun, including shooting a person of interest in an airport, was a federal offense."

"I need my gun."

Agent Holmes kneeled before me and took my hand. "I know you're scared, and I'm not sure how this happened, but we'll work together to figure out the truth."

Tears stung my eyes. "I want to go…"

"Where?" she asked.

Home, but I couldn't go back there. "I shot that man because he was about to kill me. It was self-defense."

She squeezed my hand like my mother would have. "You had the right to protect yourself. However, you being here and having the ability to take Faulkner down, a man that has killed or wounded dozens of agents… I don't believe in coincidences."

A tear slipped down my face. "I didn't come here to kill anyone."

"Hey, don't cry. We'll figure this out. Until then, know that I'm on your side."

"Agent Holmes—"

"Please, call me Emily."

"Are you going to put me in jail?"

She stood. "I'm not the person who makes that decision, but I'll do everything I can to help you."

Agent Mason gave me a look of surprise as she walked off. "Take that as a compliment. Agent Holmes usually keeps things at a business level."

Sylvia stood and followed Emily across the room to where Jon and Agent Payne had set up a table with various electronics.

Then I was alone to watch the scene play out. Injured people were wheeled away. Witnesses were interviewed. Excited voices made my headache worse, and then finally someone stopped that annoying alarm.

Dozens of people walked around me without acknowledging my existence. They cleaned every drop of blood from the floor. Agent Mason walked by with a box of VHS tapes while discussing security footage with Emily.

She gave me a wink, which didn't put me at ease.

What had I gotten myself into?

EPISODE 18

Look Inside

Exactly thirty minutes after Agent Emily Holmes arrived in the baggage claim area, the room cleared of all agents and paramedics, along with any hint of their cleanup operation. Although Jon looked overwhelmed upon arrival, his features seemed relaxed as he met Emily a few feet from where I sat.

She put a hand on his shoulder. "You did a great job. How are you feeling?"

"Like this is the worst hangover I've ever had," he said. "You continue to impress me with how you take charge of these disasters."

"Someone has to be the boss. Have you processed everyone?"

"According to Payne's list, the only remaining witness is the kid."

'Only remaining witness' sounded ominous. What did she mean by the others being processed? They both turned to me, and I wondered what would happen next. The thought of him questioning me, using tactics like in the movies to dig out all of my deepest secrets, made me squirm.

"Go back to the base and get some rest," she said to him. "I'll reach out if we need your services again."

I let out the breath I'd been holding. They wouldn't be processing me, but what about his services? What exactly did Jon do?

He nodded. "You know, when you called me about this job, I almost turned you down. Kind of glad I didn't, despite the headache."

"They need you," she said. "I like to think we're here for a calling larger than any of us."

With a last glance around the room, he headed for the exit.

She approached me. "Are you ready?"

"Can I leave now?"

"We're all leaving. The airport is opening back up for business."

"What do you mean by 'we're all leaving?'"

"You're going to lift your bag and follow me calmly to the exit. If you don't plan to go willingly, now is the best time to tell me."

For those thirty minutes, I'd sat wondering if they'd release me. A part of me wanted to teleport out of there and never look back. I'd make sure the government agents never found me.

Another small part of me felt relief she asked me to follow.

"Okay." I stood, reluctantly, and pulled the strap of my backpack over my shoulder.

Emily was taller even than I'd realized. The top of my head barely reached her chin.

"Stay close and don't talk to anyone," she said. "If you see any reporters, duck your head and don't look their way."

I followed when she headed for the main doors. Her pace was quick enough I struggled to keep up. As if her leaving signaled the end of this operation, Agent Payne and Sylvia caught up and fell in behind us. Agent Mason reached us as we walked through the doors. A crowd of anxious faces, people as far as I could see, parted as the five of us stepped outside.

Thick humidity made the air hard to breathe. I considered removing my jacket, but there was no stopping. Lifting a hand, I shielded my eyes from the bright sunlight. Nothing Emily had said prepared me for the flash of cameras or people screaming questions at us.

"How bad was the gas leak?" someone yelled.

"Is the airport safe for civilians?"

"Have the planes begun to land again?"

Pictures of me on the evening news were the last thing I needed. I lowered my face into the crook of my arm and watched the feet in front of me to keep up. Additional agents held the crowd back to either side as I peered over my elbow.

We moved toward a black car with four doors and dark tinted windows. On the other side of the loading zone were fire trucks and ambulances with flashing lights and two armored vehicles. Agent Mason opened a door to the backseat and waved me inside.

I took a deep breath. Was I really about to climb in the car and let them take me…? I wasn't sure where they would take me. Swallowing the bitter taste in my mouth, I dropped into the seat. The floor was spotless, and the air carried that coveted new car smell.

Outside, Emily turned to Sylvia. "Go with Mason and Payne so you can monitor the girl. We'll need a statement as soon as possible." She pointed at Agent Payne, who held up a set of keys. "Don't let Sylvia drive. She's been through enough today."

Emily continued to the car parked in front of us. As soon as she dropped into the passenger's seat and the car pulled away from the curb, Agent Payne tossed Sylvia the keys.

She grinned and went to the driver's side.

Agent Mason closed my door and circled our car to take the seat beside me.

"She's driving?" I asked. "I thought—"

"Sylvia doesn't ride with anyone," Mason said. "If she's in a moving vehicle, she's driving."

Agent Payne dropped into the passenger's seat as Sylvia fired the engine. "You did good back there, kid. No sudden movements, no comments for people to record."

"Why were all those people at the door?" I asked. "Why not keep them away?"

"They think we were there to clear the place after a gas leak," Agent Mason said. "There's no evidence of anyone getting shot."

"But several people were shot," I said, confused.

"Not officially," Mason said. "Our job was to convince the world nothing beyond a gas leak happened in the airport today. Now that we've deemed the area safe, people can go about their normal routines with no idea what really happened."

Sylvia pulled away from the curb and followed the signs to the highway.

"Where are you taking me?"

"To our base," Sylvia said. "There we will discuss how you took down one of the FBI's ten most wanted."

Her words made me cringe. "It wasn't that big of a deal."

Agent Payne turned around until our eyes met. "Don't underestimate your performance. The people we work for will want to know how you killed Faulkner."

"Isn't that obvious? I shot him. Why would the FBI care as long as he's dead?"

He and Sylvia exchanged a glance. "Maybe some music would be better," she said.

Mason stared out of the window. "None of that trash Payne listens to. Play my type of music."

"Johnny Cash doesn't count as a type of music," Agent Payne said.

I watched the dynamic with interest. These men were more than co-workers or even partners. They seemed like great friends. "Maybe some rock?"

The car was silent as Sylvia merged into traffic on the highway. She flipped on the radio and found a station playing Gun N' Roses. I sat back and closed my eyes, relaxing ever so slightly. For the last thirty minutes, I'd swapped between a keen interest in their efforts to clear the airport and fear at what awaited me when they finished.

"Will you tell us how you did it?" Mason asked.

"I aimed the gun," I said. "And pulled the trigger."

"Can you shoot any gun that well?" Sylvia asked. "Or is your gun special?"

When I didn't respond, Payne said, "Forensics will let us know if any modifications have been made."

Mom built the gun, but would they notice what made her design special? Despite the many guns in our cellar, that was the only one I'd shot. Would the weight and dynamics of another gun truly make a difference in my ability to hit a target when I could control air currents?

We rode for several miles in silence. Sylvia maneuvered the car through traffic, swapping lanes with gaps so small it made my stomach flip. But the ride was smooth. Unlike the way my heart hammered in my chest.

Where was she taking us?

She veered right at an exit and drove into a downtown area. While most of the buildings in Credence had only one floor, these were several stories tall and some had nothing more than a narrow street separating them. I counted more than twenty rows of windows as I stared up at a building next to a red light where we stopped. The lanes of these streets were packed with cars and buses moving in both directions. Along the sides of the streets were parked cars that made me cringe each time I thought we'd hit one. Sylvia seemed perfectly at home as she took us deeper into the city.

"That's it," Mason said, pointing at a building to our right.

My eyes widened as we slowed, and I stared up at more than a dozen floors rising against a blue sky. "Where are we?"

"Can't you read the sign?" asked Agent Payne.

Glass windows wrapped around every floor of the building. Near the top was the name of a bank in red letters. "We're at a bank?"

"Have you ever been to a big city?" Mason asked.

I shook my head. "I've seen tall buildings like this on TV and always wondered what they looked like inside. Why are we stopping at a bank?"

"Our base is above the bank," Sylvia said. "People drive past this building on a daily basis and never know what goes on inside. You'll have the chance to see what they've been missing." She drove into a parking deck next to the building and found a spot on the second level.

"Who's going to update the director?" asked Agent Payne.

"He's at a ceremony until after lunch," Sylvia said. "When he returns, he'll want to meet Charlie."

A director? Why would he want to meet me?

Agent Mason leaned forward. "First, we visit the med-level. All of us," he stressed as he glanced at Sylvia.

She gripped the steering wheel. "I'm fine."

"Then turn this car off and let's go inside," Agent Payne said with a laugh. "Problem solved." He opened his door and stepped out, then opened the door for me.

I climbed out and lifted my backpack. Mason came around the car, followed by Sylvia. They kept me between them as we walked through the parking deck, down a flight of stairs, and to the bank's front entrance. Maybe they were afraid I'd bolt, given the chance.

These agents thought they could keep me here when I had the ability to teleport anywhere. Good thing for them I wanted to see inside this building.

At the bank's front entrance, the glass doors slid open to reveal a path of shiny tile with carpet to either side. Chandeliers that hung from above gave the lobby a warm ambiance. To my right were rows of teller stations with customers waiting in line, their voices conversational and mingling with a soft musical tune. Elevator music, Dad would have called it. To my left were desks and offices surrounded by glass, most occupied by people working at a computer. The air smelled like a crisp dollar bill.

"What are we doing here?" I whispered.

No one said a word until we reached a row of elevators. Not a single person from the lobby acknowledged us as we passed through. Sylvia scanned her badge on a black pad next to the first elevator.

"Where are we going?" I asked.

"Up," Mason said.

"Only the first floor is a bank," Agent Payne said.

The doors opened and Sylvia stepped inside; Mason put a hand on my arm, guiding me in behind her. With his strength, he barely exerted any effort to keep me moving, but the message was clear. No turning back.

On the keypad, she chose a number and a letter. What an odd-looking keypad when I'd expected just numbers.

Four walls of metal surrounded us, the polished surfaces reflecting our image. We rose until the screen above the keypad said med-level. The three agents stared at the door in silence, neither of them moving from where they'd positioned me at the elevator's center. The elevator slowed so gently I jumped when the door opened.

Hesitantly, I walked out as they moved, while reminding myself I could teleport. Remembering that fact was the only way I'd get through this.

In front of me, windows stretched from floor to ceiling. At either end of the windows was a wall of brick. This room looked like the lobby of a hospital, though much larger than the one in Credence.

"I thought the glass went all the way around the building," I said.

"It does," Mason said. "But few windows are open to view. On most floors, more than two feet of concrete with re-bar sits behind that glass. If every building on this block was destroyed, this one would still be standing."

"We're in a hospital?"

Sylvia waved at the person behind a small window on the opposite wall and a set of double doors opened. A man in white scrubs approached with a clipboard in his hand.

Mason put a hand on my arm, but this time I ducked away from his grip. "I'm not going to run."

He looked at Agent Payne, and his partner shrugged. "I don't think she's going anywhere," Agent Payne said. "She hasn't tried to leave yet."

"It's important that you don't cause a scene on our med-level," Mason said. "People here are receiving medical help, some who were shot this morning."

"I won't cause any trouble."

As the man in scrubs reached us, I realized he couldn't have been over eighteen or twenty. The badge hanging from his collar showed his picture, and the name Kyle Bronson. He gave me a warm smile. "I have some papers for you to fill out."

"We'll handle the paperwork," Agent Payne said. "Get her in a room and start an evaluation."

"Got it," Kyle said.

"Order Sylvia an eval, too," Mason said. He and Sylvia exchanged a glance. "Let them do their jobs."

She nodded, and we followed Kyle down a long hall. The clean smell didn't put me at ease. This place had enough light to chase away shadows and reveal a person's darkest secrets. The gleam of the floor should have made me feel better. Instead, I tightened my grip on the straps of my bag.

Some rooms were empty; some were packed with people dressed in white while working on patients. Their voices rose above machines that beeped and gave alarms that made me wonder if people were dying. With all the tech, it was like a futuristic version of the emergency rooms I'd seen on TV.

We passed a nurses station where people in scrubs discussed patients and looked over glowing monitors. All voices stopped as we walked by and some of them whispered discreetly. One woman turned to the person beside her and said, "That's the one who killed Faulkner."

I glanced at the agents, but no one said a word. Was everyone in this building talking about me? The thought angered me; I'd arrived at the airport determined to disappear. By saving lives, now everyone here would know my name. They'd all know I was different.

How could I mess up this bad?

Kyle motioned Sylvia to a room and then put me in a room across the hall. He closed the door and his muffled voice drifted into the room, along with the voices of Mason and Agent Payne, though I couldn't make out any of their words. I sat on the examination table, which was covered with paper. On the opposite wall was a counter with a sink and a cabinet hanging from above. The counter held the same instruments I'd seen during my yearly checkups at the clinic while growing up.

For the first time since the airport, I was alone. I closed my eyes and pictured myself in my bedroom back home. Within seconds, I'd teleport out of here, leaving those agents scratching their heads.

But picturing my room wasn't enough. No matter how hard I tried to take myself home, the air still chilled my skin and the smell of alcohol swabs filled my nose.

Was I stuck here? My pulse quickened with the fear that rushed through my veins. No, this wasn't right. All I had to do was picture myself at home, and I'd open my eyes to the safety of our house. Instead, I opened my eyes, heaving and unable to catch my breath. Stumbling from the table, I dropped to my knees and put a hand on my chest.

The door opened and a man in a white coat with bifocals stepped inside. Kyle followed, and his smile swam before my eyes. Then a look of concern took over. He dropped to his knees beside me and held my arm.

"Deep breaths," he said. "Slowly."

Something about his voice felt soothing, and a part of me didn't want him to stop talking. I followed his instructions until my heart slowed enough for me to catch my breath. My chest felt as if I'd run laps on the track at school.

"You're going to be okay," he said.

The man with him reached for my other arm.

"We're going to help you to the table," Kyle said. "Do you think you can manage?"

I nodded.

"Take it easy." Kyle and the man in the coat lifted my arms until I stood and sat on the table. Paper crinkled beneath my legs.

"Good," the other man said. "I'm Dr. McIntyre. Charlie, I believe you may have been suffering from a panic attack just now. How are you feeling?"

Alone. Terrified. "I couldn't breathe."

"It can happen to the best of us in scary situations. We'll run a series of tests to be sure."

Kyle patted my arm. "This has been a rough day for many of us. We're here to help."

I didn't want their help. I wanted to go home, and now I'd become an emotional wreck. Mom said strong emotions could keep me from using this power but why now? What I needed most was a way to get out of this room.

"Do you have any medical conditions?" the doctor asked.

"No."

"Have you had any sickness in the last thirty days?"

I shook my head and felt the pulse at my neck. My heart beat at a faster pace than I could count.

"When is the last time you ate?"

"At the airport for breakfast."

"Do you have any family?"

"No," I said. "Do I have a choice in taking these tests?"

"Charlie, we're here to help you." Kyle flashed the same disarming smile from earlier. "If we don't run tests, how can we figure out how to help you?"

A voice inside told me not to trust him. "What if I decide to run?"

Dr. McIntyre gave me a stern look over his glasses. "If you make it past Agent Mason, this entire floor with go into lock-down mode and the air will fill with a neurotoxin to disrupt your brain function. You'll be out in less than a minute."

"What about everyone else?" I asked. "You wouldn't poison them to stop me."

His smile was sad. "Everyone being treated on this floor is a part of this agency. Antibody protection is a part of our day-one regimen."

"You're making this up," I said.

"When you regain consciousness, you'll have to learn to walk again. By then, you'll be locked in a room with white walls."

Tears filled my eyes. "I shot a man to save lives."

"Which is why you're here. These tests are a thousand times less painful than the alternative."

EPISODE 19

Interrogation

These tests are a thousand times less painful than the alternative. Those were the doctor's words before they put me through five blood draws, x-rays, a full body scan, and even a physical where he made me breathe into a machine and checked my reflexes. Why did doctors always insist on hitting the knee when that felt like the worst part?

While the doctor worked, Kyle asked a series of questions from a list on his clipboard and filled in my answers. They wanted to know where I was from, how old I was, medical history, etc.

Most of my answers were lies or a refusal to answer.

"Why are the two of you running all the tests?" I asked. "Some of the other rooms were filled with people."

Dr. McIntyre motioned to Kyle, who jotted a note. "The fewer people exposed to you the better, at least until we know what we're dealing with."

"Have you found anything wrong with me yet?"

He smiled. "Not yet, but we've got plenty of tests left to run."

I groaned and turned to Kyle. He gave me a smile and the dimple in his cheek did something strange to my stomach. *No*, I told myself. *Now isn't the time to fall for the cute nurse.* Maybe there was something wrong with me.

"Did everyone make it out of the airport alive?" I asked.

Both men stopped working and looked at me. "I believe so," Dr. McIntyre said. "Thanks to your ability."

They didn't know where this ability came from and probably wouldn't stop studying me until they found the truth. I sighed as the doctor shined a light in my eyes for the third time. "I place her age at sixteen."

Kyle wrote on his clipboard.

A knock sounded, and the door opened. A woman in a white coat stepped inside and approached me. "I had to see her for myself."

"Here is our latest find, Agent Lockhart," Dr. McIntyre said. "The sharpshooter who took down Faulkner."

She looked over my face. "There must be some mistake. This is a child."

"A child who shot a gun perfectly," he said. "Her bullet struck Faulkner's skull at a weak point with a miniscule window of opportunity."

"They've done an autopsy already?" When the doctor nodded, she said, "Yes, it was for the best. We had to know."

"Had to know what?" I asked.

Her eyes narrowed as she watched me. "This was more than a simple kill. You think she has a power."

"That's right," Dr. McIntyre said. "You're the one who can determine where this power comes from."

She gripped my chin. "Does anyone in your family have this power?"

"No." I pulled away. "Are you a doctor?"

"Not as you would imagine. My focus is genetics." Agent Lockhart reached for my hair. "Tell me about your power. How does it work?"

I shoved her hand away. "I never said I have a power. This man, Faulkner, was going to kill everyone in that room. I pulled out the gun and fired."

"Of course," she said. "I suppose you carry a gun wherever you go."

The way this woman stared at my face, as if taking in every minute detail, gave me the creeps. "I'm not sure how to explain."

She turned to the doctor. "Have you found anything that makes her different?"

"No," he said.

"How long will she be staying?"

"That answer is above my pay grade."

Agent Lockhart crossed her arms over her chest. "Tell me what happens when you shoot a gun."

"I aim at the target and pull the trigger. My dad taught me how to aim." Although this conversation was deadly serious, I bit my lip to keep a laugh from escaping.

"I'd like a sample of your DNA," she said.

If I gave her a sample, would she determine I was part alien? "Do I have a choice?"

She shook her head. "Since you don't seem to have any answers, perhaps I can find some for both of us."

With a groan, I offered her my arm. "They've already taken enough blood to fill a coke bottle."

Agent Lockhart held up a syringe, which I was sure she hadn't held when she walked into the room. She tied my upper arm and slid the needle beneath my skin. While the other needles had hurt, this one felt like barely a prick.

She filled the syringe with blood and removed the band around my arm. Then, with the same careful touch, she removed the needle and pressed a wad of gauze to my skin, covering it with a piece of tape.

I'd looked away during the other blood draws, but seeing the blood in her syringe made me shake. Maybe it was the thought of a syringe jammed into Mom's neck. Or maybe it was memories of dumping bodies in a lake that came rushing back. My stomach lurched, and I put a hand over my mouth. The breakfast I'd eaten hours ago came rushing back as I threw up down the front of Kyle's scrubs.

Now I felt like dying of embarrassment.

Kyle grabbed a roll of paper towels from the cabinet above the sink and tore some off for me. Then he wiped himself and laid a few on wet spots on the floor.

Agent Lockhart looked at the doctor. "You thought she was faking, but now you're not sure."

"I'm doing my job." He frowned. "Why don't you find the lab and do yours?"

Her lips twitched, as if fighting a smile. "You think I don't have feelings, but you're wrong." She turned and left the room with the syringe of my blood gripped tightly in her hand.

"I'm sorry," I muttered.

"It's not a problem." Kyle's smile shined brighter than before. "Now, if you'll excuse me, I'll get changed."

Dr. McIntyre turned to me when we were alone. "I'm glad to see you didn't run."

As I wiped my face, I thought of how he warned me not to run. "When I pulled that trigger, I never imagined any of this."

"That's a good thing."

"Why?"

"If you'd imagined any of this, you might have hesitated. A year ago, Faulkner killed the agent I planned to marry. With his speed, she didn't have a chance of stopping him." He glanced at the floor as tears threatened in his voice. "Maria didn't fear rushing headfirst into battle to save lives. It was her job." With a deep sigh, he raised his eyes to mine. "What I mean to say is thank you."

"You're welcome," I whispered.

With a nod, he lifted his glasses to wipe his eyes and left the room.

Agent Payne came in, followed by Sylvia. "Finally, the smell of something other than antiseptic."

The teasing in his voice made me feel better. "Seeing the blood got me sick."

"It's not an issue," Sylvia said. "Seeing blood makes ten percent of the population sick."

"That's a completely random fact," I said with a laugh.

"Since I have an excellent memory, random facts make good conversation starters."

"She's great at parties," Agent Payne said, which brought a grin to my face.

"Did they finish the tests?" I asked.

"For now," Sylvia said.

I glanced around the room. "What happens next?"

"We talk," she said. "And we determine your motive for being in that airport."

"I didn't have a motive."

Agent Payne reached for my arm. "Let me help you down. Then we'll go somewhere quiet and talk, maybe a place that smells better."

* * * * *

The room where Agent Payne wanted to talk smelled much better. It was a small conference room at the end of a long hall on floor 16B, whatever that meant. The long wood table had eight office chairs but reminded me of the table in my kitchen.

Glancing around, I couldn't find a clock. What time was it? Had Dad called the cops or started a search for me yet?

"What are you looking for?" Agent Payne asked.

"The time."

He checked his watch. "Three-fifteen."

"Take a seat." Sylvia waved at the chairs across from where she sat. "Need to be somewhere?"

"No." I sat directly across from her. As I sank into the chair, I slapped my forehead.

"What's wrong?" she asked.

"I forgot my backpack."

"You'll get it back," she said. "We have no reason to keep your belongings."

Agent Payne and Agent Mason leaned against the wall to either side of the door, both crossing their arms as they stared.

"Where are we?" I asked.

"Protocol states I take you to an interrogation room," Sylvia said. "I thought this would be more comfortable."

I looked at the men. "Could you sit down? It's like you're looming over me."

They exchanged a glance. Agent Payne shrugged and took a seat next to Sylvia. Mason remained standing.

Sylvia opened a manila folder and held it up. The folder contained one piece of paper with a picture of me from the airport clipped to the top corner. "This is our file on you. Pretty thin so far."

I said nothing, simply stared as she spoke.

"We know you call yourself Charlie and you shot a man at the top of the FBI's most wanted list."

While she waited, I felt their eyes on me. "I'm not sure what you're asking."

Agent Payne leaned forward. "Tell us what makes you special."

"I'm not special."

"What's your last name?" When I didn't respond, Sylvia said, "I appreciate you taking down Faulkner, more than you'll ever know. But we all have a job to do."

"You're part of the FBI, right?"

"Not exactly," she said. "Our organization handles the stranger cases. A man who could move as fast as Faulkner is a prime example. Now we have a person who took him down, which is equally amazing."

I gripped the arms of my chair. "I wasn't in the airport to hurt anyone."

"What *were* you doing in the airport?" Mason asked.

"I ran away from home."

"Care to tell us where home is?" He slid a hand through his dark hair. "Don't say Texas, kid. Treat us like we investigate some of the world's most intricate crimes for a living."

"You can't make me go back there."

"Go back where?" Sylvia asked. "Did someone hurt you?"

"No." I tried to stay strong, but dreaded tears filled my eyes.

After several moments of silence, Agent Payne said, "Tell us how your power works."

"I told you before; I aim and shoot."

Sylvia's voice was emotionless. "Why were you carrying a gun in an airport?"

"Because my mom gave me that gun to protect myself. She made me promise to keep it with me at all times."

"Where is she?" Mason asked.

"Dead," I said.

Another moment of silence passed. "Could she shoot like you?" Agent Payne asked.

I hesitated. "She taught me." With all their technology, did they already know who I was? Did they have my family under their control, waiting for the right time to threaten me? "What do you want from me?"

"The truth," Sylvia said. "Our team is resourceful. If you don't answer our questions, we'll learn what brought you here."

"Better to come clean now," Mason added.

"My mother gave me the gun and told me not to show anyone I could shoot. I had no intention of shooting the man you called Faulkner. But I didn't have a choice when he tried to kill me."

Sylvia nodded. "Your mother knew it would attract attention."

"After she died, I had nowhere to go and ended up at the airport."

"You had less than two hundred dollars in your bag," Agent Payne said. "How long did you think that would last?"

"Long enough to find another home. Then I planned to find a job so I could eat."

Agent Payne rubbed the back of his neck, and Sylvia gave me a look of sympathy.

Mason walked to the table. "If you want another home, you have one here."

Sylvia closed the folder. "Offering her a place to stay is one thing. A home is something else entirely." She looked at me. "Can you replicate what you did at the airport?"

Why would they offer me a place to stay? The voice inside my head told me they wanted my power. They wanted to control me for the same reason the government of Golvern sent soldiers after my mom.

But maybe I'd be protected in this building, which seemed more like a fortress. Maybe I could hide here until I found a better situation. "Yes."

"Then we're done." She stood, and so did Agent Payne. "The rest is up to the two of you."

"What's the rest?" I asked.

"We have one more stop," Mason said.

With a sigh of relief, I rose and slid the chair against the table. At least this interrogation was over. "Where to?"

He opened the door and led the way outside. "To see you shoot."

Sylvia took the folder and started down the hall. "I'll let you know when he's ready."

When who was ready? Did she mean the director they'd mentioned? At the elevator, she chose a series of five numbers and letters. We rose, and I wondered how many floors this building had. Smoothly, we stopped, and she stepped off.

Mason typed the number five and the letters S and R. He stepped back and watched the screen above the keypad.

"Are we going up or down?" I asked.

"Down this time." He turned to Agent Payne. "This morning you said our day would be interesting, but I never imagined seeing Faulkner wiped out. Thought you were whining about the politics again."

Agent Payne gave me a smile. "Thanks to the kid's timing, I was right."

The elevator stopped and the doors opened. Mason led us down a hall and into a room with ceilings that reminded me of the gymnasium at school. Several targets hung on the far wall, each shaped like a person. Some were full scale, and some only showed a chest-up form. Dividers split each section like lanes at a bowling alley.

Several men and women, some dressed in suits and some in black sweats, fired at the targets. Mason walked across the room to the last lane, which was open. A few people noticed me and watched with interest.

Facing the target, Mason lifted his gun and gave it to me. "Show us what you can hit."

"Where?" I asked.

Agent Payne handed me muffs to protect my ears. "I'm sure you know the best spots."

I put on the muffs and faced the outline of an upper body. Having a gun in my hand felt amazing; for the first time since arriving, I had a rush of confidence. It didn't matter this wasn't my gun. I pulled the trigger and twisted the air currents around the bullets, forcing three at the chest and three at the head.

Mason stared at the target while I shot, but Agent Payne watched me. He shifted his focus to the target as quickly as our eyes met.

With a smile, I handed Mason his gun. The exhilaration of firing his weapon had my heart pumping with adrenaline, in a good way this time. I wasn't about to lose my breakfast again.

A screen next to us came on and showed the marks I'd made. "Not bad," Mason said. "So, it wasn't the gun. It was your power all along."

"I still want my gun back."

He laughed. "Show this power to a few more people and we might can arrange that."

Agent Payne pulled a pager from his pocket, which vibrated in his hand. "Time to meet our director."

My stomach sank. What would their boss have to say about me?

I stayed quiet on the elevator ride to a floor with yet another strange combination of letters and numbers. If they feared I'd figure out how to control this elevator, they'd be mistaken.

They took me to another room with a table, this one so brightly lit I had to squint as I stumbled to the chair Mason pulled out for me. He sat to my right and Agent Payne took the chair to my left.

The man at the head of the table was older, maybe around sixty. Sylvia sat next to him with her hands on the table in front of her. With fingers laced, her posture was identical to his. Her black hair was the same color, tied in a bun at the back of her head while his was cut as if he'd spent years in the military. He didn't wear a black suit like the other agents; instead, he wore a Navy uniform with decorations on the chest.

"How was the presentation?" Agent Payne asked in an upbeat voice.

"It finished on schedule and the weather held out." The director looked at me. "I hear appreciation is in order for you, young lady."

I opened my mouth but couldn't find any words.

"How did the target practice go?" he asked.

"She hit every mark perfectly," Mason said.

"Good. Charlie, while you're here you can call me Hamilton or simply Director."

My breath caught. "How long will I stay?"

He looked at Mason. "You will train her to fight. With the ability to take down Faulkner, she'll make an excellent agent."

"You can't be serious," Sylvia said, glancing his way.

"You have much to learn about sitting in this chair," he said.

She stared him down. "I have no ambition to sit in that chair."

His voice became harsh. "Then my efforts have been for nothing. You don't want to be an agent, and you don't want to take over my job one day."

"I never said I don't want to be an agent."

"It shows in your work. This business with Faulkner showed how weak you are."

Sylvia leaned forward, never breaking eye contact. "I said I wouldn't stop hunting Faulkner until he was dead or locked away. He attacked our agents, and someone needed to take him down."

Silence filled the room as the tension hit a peak.

Agent Payne cleared his throat. "Will she be working with someone on missions or simply training at this base?"

The director leaned back in his chair. "For now, you and Mason will take her along. She'll pick up the ropes quickly at your pace."

Mason sighed. "She's a kid. How can you expect her to become an agent?"

"This *kid* has a gift our agency needs. The rest she'll learn as she goes." He glanced at me. "Has she told you her full name?"

"Her mother is dead, and she's on the run," Sylvia said. "Charlie refuses to give us anything else."

He watched me for several agonizing seconds before laughing. "Good. If she won't tell us where her family is, we have no door to knock on if she dies."

EPISODE 20

New Job

We have no door to knock on if she dies. Beneath his laughter was a harsh tone. The director meant those words.

"No," Agent Mason said.

"No?" The director leaned forward and made a bridge with his hands.

"I didn't take this job for kid duty," Mason said in a tone harsh enough to rival the director's. "Sylvia's the one with experience in that department."

The director turned his head. "I don't think Sylvia is the right person for this job."

"What if I say no?" I asked.

Any trace of humor disappeared from the director's face. "You have until six a.m. tomorrow to decide." He stood and lifted a briefcase from the floor. "I have a meeting in ten minutes. Work out the rest of the girl's details between yourselves."

He left the room, and the remaining men exchanged a glance. Sylvia leaned her head back and closed her eyes.

"What happens if I refuse?" I asked.

"You'll trade one box for another," Agent Payne said.

Sylvia opened her eyes. "The director is wrong about this."

"Agreed," Mason said. "What can we do about it?"

"Nothing at the moment," Sylvia said.

Agent Payne lifted his pager. "Trouble on the isolation floor." He looked at Mason. "You take the girl and I'll deal with the mess."

"We should flip for it," Mason said.

With a grin, Agent Payne stood. "I'll see you later." Before Mason could argue, his partner was out of the door.

"Give me a minute." Mason stood and left the room.

Sylvia sighed. "I'm sorry about you being stuck here. Maybe if you had cooperated and told us who you are—"

"I'd rather not."

"You must think all of this is strange. When you woke up this morning, you didn't know any of us existed."

"I woke up at the airport. I didn't have a plan for what to do or where to go."

"If you pick up any phone in this building and ask for Sylvia, someone will find me. Don't feel you're all alone here."

"Thanks," I said.

She stood, and I followed her into the hall. Mason stepped out from another room. "I've got this under control. Get some rest," he told Sylvia. "You should sleep better tonight than you have in years."

"I hope so," she said, but her eyes told me she wasn't sure. Sylvia headed for the elevator, and I looked up at Mason. He stood at least six feet tall, his solid frame towering over me.

"There's something you should know," Mason said as he watched her walk away. "Sylvia is the director's daughter."

"What?"

"Stay long enough and you'll learn all the relationships and history of this agency."

"I don't know how to deal with half of what I've heard, and now you're telling me more secrets. If I don't take this job, what will they do to me?"

"If we need to cross that bridge, there's an alternate plan." He looked down at me. "Anytime I run a mission, I always analyze strengths and weaknesses before taking the first shot. I'm assuming you did the same as you watched Faulkner."

"I didn't plan to shoot, but I couldn't let him kill me or anyone else. Do you consider that a strength or weakness?"

He sighed. "Having the power to save lives and using it is a strength."

"If you were me, would you take the job?"

"You can save lives. In your shoes, I'd take the job and proudly serve my country."

"Were you in the military?"

"Special Forces. Volunteered for rescue missions overseas, some with no way out. I made my own exit and fought the politics, but some things never change. When the director invited me to work at this agency, I needed a change in my life."

"Are you happy here?"

Mason started for the elevator. "The hours are long enough I don't sleep much. Can't have nightmares if you don't sleep."

I almost ran to keep up. "Can I get my gun back?"

"What's so special about that gun?"

"It was a gift from my mother."

"What would she think about you firing it in an airport?"

"Since she's dead, it doesn't matter."

"I'm sorry," he said.

Although he was an agent, and it was probably his job to lie to me, I believed Agent Mason. He hit a button at the elevator and the doors opened. "You look hungry."

As if on cue, my belly growled. "How did you know?"

"What have you eaten in the last twenty-four hours?"

"Food from the airport."

His face twisted with disgust. "You need real food. We have an entire floor dedicated to restaurants."

"Will you eat with me?"

He checked his watch. "I have a meeting to attend and a report to write afterward."

"Report?"

Agent Mason grinned slightly. "I also have to catch a flight to Toronto, but I wasn't supposed to tell you that. I'll be back by morning."

"Not like I can tell anyone. Unless you'll let me make a call?"

"If there's someone you need to call, tell me who. Otherwise, no contact with anyone on the outside."

"Am I supposed to eat alone?"

"I thought alone was your motto."

I put my hands on my hips. "You're doing a terrible job at convincing me to stay."

"Don't worry. I arranged a dinner date for you."

*****

Mason took me to a floor with fifteen restaurants. When we stepped off the elevator, the smell of food hit, and my stomach rumbled. I looked at all the lighted signs with amazement. It was like the food court at the airport, but bigger and with fancier names for the restaurants. Names I'd never heard of.

He stopped and opened one of the doors. Blue lights on the wall next to the door glowed with the name Hugo's.

"What kind of food is this?"

"A mix of American favorites, with a sample from each of the largest cities. Has a twenty-eight-page menu."

My eyes widened. "I can order what I want?"

"Here, you can have whatever you please."

"What about money?"

Mason gave me a sideways glance. "As long as you're with this agency, everything is taken care of." Across a room where nearly every table was packed, he spotted Emily and waved for me to follow.

The agent who managed the airport chaos smiled as we walked up. "I thought a quiet dinner would be nice."

"Hope you enjoy the food." As soon as his words were out, Mason hurried away.

"Is he okay?" I asked.

Emily put a hand over her mouth, covering laughter. "You'll have to excuse Mason, he's not good with kids." She motioned to the seat across from her. "Please, sit down."

I took the seat, and a server appeared with a glass of water.

"You can have something else to drink," she said. "They have coffee and tea, plus several kinds of soda."

"This is fine." I drank most of the glass as they watched. I'd never felt so thirsty.

"What would you like to eat?" asked the server.

"Mason said the menu has twenty-eight pages."

Emily smiled at the server. "How about a Memphis burger with fries? Bring two."

I nodded with relief as he moved to the next table. "I'm starving."

"When is the last time you ate?"

"This morning at the airport."

"We'll have to do a better job at looking after you," Emily said. "I heard the director made you an offer."

"He said I had a choice, but I don't think he meant it."

She took a sip of her drink, a dark amber liquor, and sloshed the ice around. "If you're going to be a part of our team, you need to know who we are."

"You're an FBI agent. We're in an FBI building."

"Guess I'll start at the beginning." She tipped up the glass and finished the drink. "First, this isn't the FBI. You're at the global headquarters for an agency called Earth Under Fire."

"Never heard of it."

"You wouldn't have. This agency began with the Department of Defense. It was originally called America Under Fire. A group of patriots started the project to protect U.S. citizens from threats such as people with powers."

"Like Faulkner."

"Yes, great example. The director you met was one of our founders. As this agency became a worldwide network of resources, they renamed it Earth Under Fire. At that point, our founders realized we need to focus, not just on human threats, but threats from space."

I took a deep breath. "Aliens?"

"Do you ever watch space shows?"

"Yes."

"Have you ever looked at the night sky and wondered about life beyond those stars?"

"Often," I said.

"Then you believe in the possibility?" She sighed. "Sometimes my hardest job is convincing new agents of the truth. Aliens exist, but some people won't believe no matter what I say."

I sipped what was left of my water. "Have you ever met an alien?"

"No, but I've read reports from agents who confronted people that weren't human."

"Should you be telling me this?"

"You're worried about hearing too much information?" Emily tapped her chin as she considered. "From your view, I can understand the danger. When I'm finished explaining about our team, you'll see why it's not an issue."

The server appeared with more water and a loaf of bread with butter.

"Go ahead," she said. "You eat while I talk."

I buttered a slice of the bread and groaned at the wonderful taste. What would Emily say if I ate the whole loaf?

"You might shoot with precision, but Sylvia has the power to move with precision. She goes into some kind of power mode, and her brain takes over; she thinks like a computer. Super speed, super-fast thinking. In this mode she won't talk to you, but she can save your life."

"What do you mean by 'thinks like a computer?'"

"She never forgets a fact or figure she's seen, which could be a blessing or curse. Depends on how you look at it."

"Why doesn't she have an agent name?"

Emily blinked. "What do you mean?"

"Why does Sylvia use her first name only?"

"Since her father is our director, Sylvia grew up with this agency. Her power is his legacy."

"Oh." Maybe Sylvia and I were more alike than I thought. "What about Agent Mason?"

"Donald Mason doesn't need a gun or a power to kill. His bare hands are enough. For years, he did special forces missions, but lost it the night his team was ambushed. Our government abandoned the team and Mason found his way back to the States on his own. Everyone thought he was dead."

"Why work for this agency if he hates the government?"

"He's still a patriot. Willing to do whatever he can to protect the American flag and the freedoms it represents. He doesn't like politics and prefers missions with no way out. Mason enjoys a challenge."

"And Agent Payne?"

"Noah is a good agent, a decent shot. He knows his way around technology, but not enough to make him an expert. More than anything, he gets these intuitions about people. It's like he can see a bigger picture than any of us."

I thought of Keva. "Do you think he can see the future?"

She hesitated. "Noah can be a bumbling agent, but people like him. He once saved Mason's life by causing them to arrive twenty minutes after an explosion."

"How did he explain that?"

"Laughed it off in true Noah Payne style. Said he read the directions wrong."

"They make a good team."

Laughing, she reached out as our server stopped with a fresh drink.

"What's so funny?" I asked.

"For a year, Mason trusted no one to be his partner. Anyone the director assigned to him would run screaming the other way."

I raised my eyebrows.

"He literally made an agent cry. It was a defining moment for all of us."

"But he likes Agent Payne."

"Mason requested him, but no one knows why. Some days it seems as if they barely tolerate each other."

I buttered my third slice of bread.

She sipped her drink, laughter still in her voice. "It's obvious Noah cares about the team, especially Sylvia. If he saw the future, he could have prevented her from being held hostage and almost dying. Noah Payne is clueless at times, but God help him he has a heart of gold."

"Then you wouldn't have found me."

Her laughter died. "What?"

"If he'd prevented Faulkner from attacking Sylvia, I never would have shot him."

She considered my words. "Now that I think about it, Noah had a run-in with one of the chefs. Saved the man's life when he cut an artery by accident. If Noah hadn't been there, the man would have bled out in minutes. Now that chef calls him Eightball."

"Like he knows what will happen."

"I'm sure he's just lucky. We all have those days every once in a while."

"So, only Sylvia and the director have a power?"

"Agent Lockhart has the power to erase memories and bring them back."

I thought of a news interview where someone's memory had been erased. Then I thought of the genetics specialist. "I met Agent Lockhart on the med-level. She took a sample of my blood."

Emily thought for a second. "That was his wife, Francine. You met Jon Lockhart at the airport. He has the power."

"I remember. How does his power work?"

"He touches a person and erases what they've seen over a specific time. Or he brings back forgotten memories. According to Jon, memories during times of stress can be altered at a conscious level. It's a coping mechanism, but the brain never truly forgets."

"Then he's a doctor."

"He's actually a damn good mechanic. If you feel you can't trust anyone here, you can trust Jon."

"You trust him?"

"With my life. I was the only one who knew about his power. After landing the job with this agency and learning others were using their gifts to help people, I convinced Jon to fly to Atlanta for an interview. He'd been working as a mechanic with the Air Force for five years, wasting that power."

"Okay, you've mentioned a power like a computer and a power to erase memories."

"You haven't met Hannah yet, but she can absorb your power and use it herself."

"That would be weird."

"It only lasts an hour or two, but she's been able to borrow some of the most dangerous powers and use them to help the team."

The server laid a plate in front of me with a burger so big I didn't know if I could eat it all and enough fries for a week. "Anything else?" he asked.

"Thanks, no." Emily lifted the burger from her plate as he walked away.

"What about you?" I asked.

"Me?"

"What's special about you?"

She chuckled. "Haven't you noticed? I'm the glue that holds this band of misfits together."

For the next few minutes, we ate in silence. Noises intruded from the other tables, but I focused on the taste of the food. Emily finished her plate completely; I ate the entire burger but could only eat half of the fries.

"So, what do you think about the job?" she asked.

"After everything you've told me, I don't see this director letting me out of here."

"Jon could erase your memory, but that's not the objective."

"Mason said there was an alternate plan. That's Jon?"

She nodded.

I thought about her words. "What's the objective?"

"Your gift can save lives." She watched my face. "You can't be older than what, fifteen? Sixteen? You belong in school, but it looks as if national security will take precedence."

"If I wanted to say no, could I?"

She shook her head. "I've found it's always better to at least give the appearance of a choice."

I thought about Mom leaving Golvern because she didn't want the government there to force her to kill. It was why she stayed on Earth and died to protect me and Lorraine. She didn't want this life for herself and she didn't want it for me. Mom had warned me what would happen if the government here learned of my power.

Now they knew, and I couldn't undo revealing my power. If I went home, they would hunt me down along with my family. "Where will I live?"

"We'll set you up with a room on this base. The agency will provide your meals and a tutor for your educational needs. You'll train as an agent while we study your ability to shoot."

I pushed my plate away. "That was the best burger I've ever eaten."

"Charlie, if you need anything, let me know. Don't let Mason scare you."

Something told me Mason wouldn't be a problem. "Where do I go now?"

She stood and lifted her jacket from the chair. "If you'll follow me, I'll show you to your room."

With everything she'd told me, I stayed silent as we took an elevator to yet another floor. The doors on this floor were closer together, and there were no windows like on the floor with the offices and meeting rooms. She scanned her card on a square pad next to my door.

The lock clicked, and she pushed open the door. Inside, Emily turned on a light above us. We stood in a living room with a couch and TV, and a small kitchen to my left. To my right were doors to a bathroom and a bedroom.

"I believe someone delivered clothes for you," she said. "Check the bed."

I spun around, taking in my new home. Already, I missed my home in Credence.

"Charlie?"

"Yes?"

"My room is directly across the hall. Wake me up if you need to." She put her hands on my shoulders. "Will you be okay?"

"I'll take a shower and get some sleep. Maybe watch TV."

"Mason will be here to collect you at eight-thirty in the morning. Make sure you're ready." Emily turned to leave. She closed the door slowly, watching me with concern as she stepped into the hall.

A stack of clothes sat on the bed, all in my size. They'd left my backpack next to the bed, but the bullets had been removed. I showered and put on a pair of black sweats, then laid on the bed while trying to digest everything Emily had told me about the agency. Government agents who tracked aliens and people with powers. Guess that made me a double whammy.

How long would it take them to figure out my alien legacy?

A phone sat on the table next to the bed. A sticker that said 'Dial 0 for Operator' sat next to the cradle. If I dialed home, would they put the call through? With a number, they'd trace my family. I inspected the ceiling and wondered if they watched me now. Were cameras hidden in every room?

I turned off all the lights and stood in the dark bathroom. With the lights off, maybe they couldn't see me. Would this work?

Closing my eyes, I pictured myself in the kitchen back home. I wasn't scared or in emotional distress; I just wanted to go home.

When I opened my eyes, a single light shined. The bulb above the stove in my kitchen.

A relieved chuckle came from the doorway.

I spun to see Dad watching with a cup of coffee in his hand.

"That didn't take nearly as long as I thought."

EPISODE 21

New Purpose

My heart leaped as I looked at Dad. Before I realized what was happening, my feet were in motion and I'd thrown my arms around his waist. He wrapped me in his arms and held me tight, careful not to spill the coffee cup still gripped in his hand while kissing the side of my head.

"I'm sorry for leaving," I said.

"I know."

Our shadows stretched across the floor of the kitchen, formed by the soft yellow light of the bulb above the stove. The window over the sink gave a dark view; I imagined the garden and Mom's bench, though I couldn't see it. The house was silent, and I wondered if Lorraine was asleep in her room. A lingering smell of bacon brought my attention to the table, where an unused plate and silverware waited at my seat.

"You had breakfast for dinner?"

His voice was a gentle sob before he released me and dropped into a seat at the table. When he spoke again, his voice was harsh. "It's what Lorraine wanted. There was no one else to argue."

"I deserved that." Better to get this conversation over with. The pain on his face didn't make me regret coming back. "I didn't know what to do, but I'm back now."

"As if those words can fix everything." Dad took a sip of the coffee as he watched me. "Will that change when I wake up tomorrow?"

"No."

"You can't find answers by running, and one day is hardly enough time for peace."

"I made a mistake by leaving."

"Where did you go?"

Red crept into my face. "It's a long story."

As if on his command, the grandfather clock in the hall chimed. Ten o'clock. "We have plenty of time," Dad said.

A strange emotion had crept into Dad's voice. Maybe anger at me for leaving or pity that I made the wrong choice. Maybe guilt. "Where should I start?"

He leaned back in his chair. "I read your note. Did you write that yourself or did someone put you up to it? I haven't heard of any new friends from school, and you never mention places you'd like to go. Went to see Carmen at her mother's shop and she didn't know why you left. Couldn't tell if she was more worried or angry you'd run away."

Carmen probably hated me for leaving. "I didn't tell her."

"Her boyfriend was there. He promised to do whatever he could to find you."

Joel was resourceful, especially with the way he got rid of Steve. Good thing he wouldn't have to follow through on his promise. "I needed to get out of this house. I can't explain. But I didn't plan to come back this soon."

"What *did* you plan?"

"To pack a bag and run as far away as possible."

"You can teleport anywhere."

"That I know. You and Mom never took me anywhere, and I've never seen a place on TV I'd like to visit."

"Why run?"

I closed my eyes. "The running part was about getting away, not where I went. I couldn't stay here a moment longer and think of her."

"What do you think I've been doing? Or Lorraine? Should we run away too?"

His words made me flinch. "I didn't think about you or Lorraine."

"Because you were only thinking about yourself. Charlie, I've never known you to be selfish. Guess I didn't know my daughter as well as I thought."

My eyes shot open. "I can't deal with her being gone."

"And you think dealing with your mother's death will be easier somewhere else? Where no one knows you?"

"I didn't think that far ahead. I only knew I had to leave."

We sat in silence with me staring at the table while he drank his coffee. Other than the empty plate at my seat, the kitchen looked the same as it had the night before, when I'd grabbed my bag and locked the front door. Had I ever planned to return? This one day felt like years had passed.

"When I found your note, I felt angry. But also sad for you. The fact you didn't trust your family, knowing you'd leave us at this time, seemed almost unforgivable. When Lorraine read the note, she cried."

Tears filled my eyes. "I'd never hurt her."

"But you did. She wouldn't go to school. We drove around most of the day looking for you; she even insisted we drive halfway to Atlanta in case you were trying to hitch a ride on the highway."

"She was right."

"What?"

I wiped the tears that slipped down my face. "Lorraine was right. When I left last night, I went to Atlanta." Turning, I met his glare under the glow from the stove. "Do you hate me for leaving?"

His voice softened. "Running is a natural reaction. Sometimes we all want to escape."

"I'm sorry." Saying the words again didn't make running out on my family seem any better.

"Tell me about your day."

He'd said those words many times over the years, but they'd never carried such weight. My gut twisted as I considered the best place to start. "I packed a bag, left a note, and started walking."

"In the middle of the night?"

"When I left, it wasn't midnight yet. I walked until I reached the pavement and turned right. Two men stopped to offer me a ride. The first gave me a bad feeling, so I aimed my gun at him and he drove off."

Dad's eyes widened. "Didn't you consider what would happen if he reported you?"

"I wasn't getting in his truck, even when the man tried to force me."

"Force you? Charlie, this world is dangerous. Haven't you figured that out?"

I nodded. "The second guy was a college student on the way to fly home for break. I accepted his ride, and we reached the airport before sunrise."

"Then what?"

"He caught a plane to Denver, and I went inside to find breakfast. At that point, I didn't know what to do or where to go. I threw my license in a trashcan, so it's not like I could catch a plane."

"Why throw away your license?"

"That way no one could find out who I was and make me go home."

His hands shook where he gripped the cup. "You didn't plan to come home." The voice was soft, yet his anger cut right through me. "There's irony in the fact someone with the power to teleport anywhere in the world chose an airport. Then what?"

With a deep breath, I looked into his eyes, which held the same anger as his voice. "I ate breakfast and fell asleep. When I awoke, the airport was empty."

Dad rubbed his chin as recognition lit his features. "The gas leak."

"Gas leak?"

"The news this evening said there was a huge gas leak at the airport. Everyone had to clear out, and all the planes stopped landing and taking off for two hours. The aerial view looked like mayhem on TV. What did you see?"

I thought of the explanation the agents gave as we were leaving the airport. "There wasn't a gas leak."

"I don't understand."

"Do you remember the news story with the man who robbed the bank in New York? He moved faster than the cameras could record."

"Yes. I wondered if it was a trick of technology or he really had a power."

"His name was Faulkner, and he had the power of speed. He showed up at the airport and tried to kill several people, including me. A government agency cleared everyone out to protect them. The gas leak story was a cover."

"And you know this because…"

"Because I shot Faulkner and made sure he won't kill again."

If I thought the silence before was thick, the air between us had become unbearable. "You showed your power?" he asked.

"I didn't have a choice."

"You killed a man? Now this agency knows you exist?"

"I saved one of their agents."

"Is this the FBI?"

"It's an agency called Earth Under Fire. They handle cases of aliens and people with powers. They keep it hidden."

Dad took fast, shallow breaths. "They convinced the world there was a gas leak. How?"

"By erasing the memories of everyone who saw Faulkner in the airport. One of the agents has that power."

He swore, something Dad rarely did.

"Faulkner was going to kill me. He pointed a gun at my face, and I froze." Fresh tears filled my eyes. "Mom made me promise to teleport away if I ever got in trouble, and I broke my promise."

"You're saying they saw you shoot, but they don't know you can teleport?"

"They took me back to their base and asked questions I refused to answer, and they never saw me teleport. No one knows my real name, and they don't know I'm your daughter. I told them to call me Charlie. They want me to work for the agency."

"They want you to…"

I stared at the table. "She made me promise and I—"

"Forget about that promise," he snapped. "You kept your cool and stayed with the agents. They didn't erase your memory. How did you get here just now?"

"They assigned me a room in their base, which is really a high-rise bank in downtown Atlanta. I went into the bathroom and turned out the lights before teleporting. That way if there were cameras, they couldn't see me."

"I'm sure there are methods they can use, like thermal imaging." His tone became thoughtful. "If you stay gone long, they'll figure out you left."

"I'm not going back there."

"You have to."

I looked up. "What?"

"This isn't as bad as it seems."

"How can you say that? It's worse."

"Hear me out."

The shock of what he was suggesting made my teeth chatter. "I can't go back."

He put a hand over mine. "Charlie, you didn't surprise me by running. You've always been independent and wise beyond your years."

"I don't feel like either of those." I squeezed his fingers. "I'm here now and things will be like they were before I left."

Dad's eyes drifted around the room as he seemed to consider. He finished his coffee and studied me until I pulled my hand away. "Now that you've left, I don't think you can come back and be satisfied."

"That makes no sense."

"Your mother gave up what made her special to stay here with me. Sometimes I could see the longing to be free of this life and be herself."

"She's part of me, but so are you."

"But the part like her you can't deny. You have a greater purpose that I can't help you find."

How could I possibly agree to this? "What about Lorraine?"

"She'll get a little more time to grow up," he said. "You'll buy her that time."

"How?"

"Since your mother died, I've struggled with the question of how to protect you."

"I don't need protection."

"If Golvern soldiers return, are you prepared to fight them? If they trap you, they could drag you across the galaxy and I'd never see you again. Neither would Lorraine."

"No one will take me, and I'd never leave here on my own."

"You already have."

I shook my head. "You know what I mean. I'll never leave the planet, I swear."

"Don't make a promise you can't keep."

"You think I'd leave the planet?"

"Last night, you walked out of our front door without a word. You could have disappeared without me knowing where you went or with who. Someone could have slit your throat—"

"No one hurt me."

"What about your alien legacy? If the government finds out, they could lock you up and start their experiments. It's better to play their game and let them think they're in control."

Hearing him say those words hurt. "I'm a person and I'm human. It's my life and I don't want to go back."

"If you don't, those agents will come knocking on our door. Then they'll *force* you to use your power."

"They plan to force me now. Their director wants me trained as an agent."

"Let them think they're forcing you. Do their training and use your powers to help the innocent." Dad put an arm around my neck and hugged me. "I can't protect you if Golvern's government sends more soldiers. Maybe this agency can."

"What if they come for Lorraine?"

"No one knows she has the power. Maybe by then you'll be in a better position to protect her. Go back and do their training."

"You're really sending me away?"

He leaned his head against mine. "You have a way back. Now you'll have to be careful and make sure they don't find out you're gone. Wait at least three days before coming back."

"Do you know how to reach Keva?"

"No. Your mother told me she'd return only when needed."

I glanced around the room as if seeing it for the last time, again. "Our talk wasn't supposed to go this way."

"Think of the lives you saved today. Of all the people you can help by using your powers. It's hard for me to send you back, but it's our best hope. Make me proud, Charlie."

Nodding, I stood and pictured myself back in Atlanta. I teleported to the dark bathroom and found my way to the bed without turning on the light.

The look of sorrow on his face had me tossing and turning for hours.

*****

The next morning, the phone by my bed rang. When I picked up the receiver, an automated voice said, "This is your wake-up call."

Groaning, I slammed down the phone and glanced at the clock radio. Seven-thirty. Mason would be here at eight-thirty to pick me up. Leaning back on the pillow, I stared at the ceiling while remembering how I teleported home. Dad insisted I return and train as an agent while trying to help people, but I'd never felt more unsure of my abilities.

I splashed water on my face and stared at the girl in the mirror. What happened to the person who walked into the airport twenty-four hours ago? Yesterday, I wanted to run from everything I knew, and now I wanted my life back.

How ironic that I could teleport anywhere but couldn't leave this base.

Near the bed lay the pile of clothes left by the agency and a pair of black dress shoes with one-inch heels. I'd never put them away before falling asleep. The thought of them lying on the dirty floor all night made me flinch. But I examined the tiled floor and realized it was probably cleaner than our kitchen floor on most days. No matter how hard I looked, there were no traces of mud.

Black suit pants and jacket. White shirt. Black sweats to sleep in and maybe train? Maybe I could find a store in this place that stocked jeans.

At promptly eight-thirty, Agent Mason knocked on my door and I opened it.

He looked over the black suit I'd chosen with the black shoes and nodded his approval. "I assume this means you've accepted the director's offer."

I smoothed my hands down the sleek black fabric of my suit jacket. "I thought I didn't have a choice."

"It's better if the choice is one you want to make."

His words were no better than Emily's nonsense about the appearance of a choice. With another groan, I pulled the door shut. "You agents keep talking about choices when it's just an illusion."

A smile crossed his face. "You had a productive talk with Emily."

Mason would never know about Dad asking me to stay. "I put on the suit. What now?"

"Seems like it fits. You and Sylvia are the same size. She loaned you a couple of her suits in the event you chose to take the job. Not that she was advocating keeping you here."

"She didn't think her father was right in forcing me."

"No one does." He cleared his throat as we walked. "Did you sleep well?"

Hearing this agent who towered over me, dressed in a black suit, ask this question in a caring voice felt strange. Was it an act? "Yes. What about you?"

"Me?"

"Did you sleep well?"

He stared ahead as we approached the elevator. "I haven't been asleep in over forty-eight hours. No reason to try now."

"Is this how you start every morning?"

"This might be the start of the morning for you, but I've already attended two meetings and filled out a report about what happened at the airport." Mason checked his watch. "I've got thirty minutes before meeting number three."

"Another meeting?"

"We have meetings to discuss threats to this agency and the public. People with powers, aliens…"

His voice drifted off as we stepped into the elevator. Mason punched the code for the floor that held the restaurants. We rode in silence as I watched him out of the corner of my eye. He stared straight ahead with shoulders squared and hands linked at his front.

Could he know I left last night? Had anyone seen me teleport?

When we reached the hall of restaurants, Mason chose one that served pancakes. He sat across the table that seated four and told the server he wanted his usual. I ordered three pancakes with two sides of sausage.

"That's quite a meal," he said as the server walked off. Mason's voice boomed over the crowded tables around us. "I should have asked for what you're having."

"Yesterday you said I could order anything."

"The kid's right. You've got to watch what you tell her." Agent Payne dropped into the seat to my right. In his hands were a plate with bacon and another holding a stack of pancakes. "Before you know it, she'll be asking to drive."

"You've got food already?" I asked.

He smiled. "Saved the life of one of the chefs, and now they all look after me. Always get my plate first."

Agent Mason rolled his eyes. "Smug about it, isn't he?"

I grinned. "If I save someone's life, does that mean I get my plate first?"

"You've already saved Sylvia," Agent Payne said. "But I wouldn't recommend eating anything she cooks. Stick with the grub-level."

"Grub-level?"

"That's what most agents call this floor," Mason said.

"Suit looks good on you, kid." Agent Payne dug into the pancakes as he glanced at Mason. "Might need to order your food to go. Director's in a bad mood, from what I hear. Not sure why."

"Attend the staff meeting and you'd know." Agent Mason seemed to relax when the server appeared with our plates.

"Meetings are boring," Payne said. "Well, most meetings. This next one…" He glanced over me. "I think the nine o'clock will put many things in perspective."

Mason hesitated, his fork and knife hovering over his eggs. "You know I don't like when you speculate. Either tell me how deep in the weeds we are or keep your mouth shut."

"Pretty deep now that we've got a tag-along."

"Tag-along?" The pancakes tasted almost as good as the ones Mom used to make. "I think I liked you calling me 'kid' better."

"A reminder," Payne said. "Not for you. Sometimes the director forgets he works for this agency. He also forgets some of us are innocent."

Mason laughed. "Maybe the kid, but not us."

Payne laughed with him. "Speak for yourself, but I plan to retire on my own private island. I'll be buying the stairway to heaven."

The tune of "Stairway to Heaven" came to mind, and I mouthed the words, instantly feeling better. If this agent liked rock music, maybe he wasn't so bad. He gave me a wink, as if reading my mind.

"Damn, you're worse than I thought. Why do I get the feeling you're not joking?" Mason's laughter faded. "I know how you like playing the battle of wits but don't challenge him today. I need you to have my back in the meeting. Jump in if I look like I'm about to say 'to hell with it all' and take off my badge."

"What's this meeting about?" I asked.

Both opened their mouths, but neither spoke as they stared at me with looks of pity.

"Is it some big secret?"

"No." Agent Payne gave a thin smile. "The meeting is about you."

EPISODE 22

The Team

The conference room for the meeting about me was full. It was larger than the one from yesterday, with an agent seated in every chair except for the three in a row waiting for us and one at the head of the long table. White walls surrounded us. The only smell I recognized was the familiar twang of coffee. People looked up as we walked in, watching me follow Agent Mason, but the noisy chatter continued.

Agent Payne trailed behind me, and I wondered what he'd do if I turned and ran. What had I gotten myself into?

I forced myself to take deep breaths as we headed for the three empty seats. Mason took the one to the right and pulled out the center chair for me. Slowly, I sat, and Payne sat on my other side.

Mason sat and rested his elbows on the arms of his chair. He glanced around the room with caution; his hands sat unmoving, and his body remained tense, ready to fight at a moment's notice.

From this close-up view of his face, he had to be older than Agent Payne. Probably late twenties or maybe even thirty. While Payne seemed charming in his demeanor toward the other agents, along with a playful smile he gave someone across the table as he laughed at a joke, Mason's face was hardened as if he'd fought in a war, and he had the build of a soldier who didn't back down from a fight.

His words came back to me. *Can't have nightmares if you don't sleep.* Perhaps he had fought in a war and that's what he meant about nightmares. From what Emily said, his own government left him abroad, and he had to fight his way home.

The people talking around us reminded me of a meeting I helped with for the teachers at school. These agents had a camaraderie in the way they interacted that made them seem almost normal. A meeting of co-workers who spent eight hours a day together, maybe more since they seemed to live in this building. Did everyone have a room here like me? Some conversations were about recent cases and at least two were about what happened at the airport.

I eyed the woman Payne was talking to and listened as her shrill voice rose above the others. She wasn't taking any of his teasing and demanded he produce proof of whatever he'd suggested. Looking closer, I realized this was the woman from the med-level who took my blood sample, only she wasn't dressed like a doctor today. Her black suit mirrored the other agents. Next to her sat Jon Lockhart, the man from the airport who Emily said could erase memories.

Leaning toward Mason, I whispered, "Wasn't she on the med-level?"

He nodded. "You met her yesterday. She's Agent Lockhart."

Yes, that's what the doctor had called her. I swallowed the bile in my throat. She had a sample of my blood, and I could think of only one reason she'd attend this meeting.

Although I stared at her while the banter between the agents continued, she never looked my way.

"Two people named Agent Lockhart in the same room?" I asked. "Doesn't that get confusing?"

"Sometimes," Mason said. "Since they're married, we have no other choice."

The woman's cold retort to one of Payne's questions had several people around us laughing. Down the table, Emily sat to one side of the director's empty seat and Sylvia sat to the other. Emily glared at Agent Payne, and he dropped his teasing of the female Agent Lockhart.

"When is this going to start?" I asked.

"When the director arrives," Mason said.

Every voice in the room quieted when the door opened, and the director walked in. He took the seat at the head of our table, dropping his briefcase to his side.

"Glad everyone could make it on time," he said in a gruff voice as he pulled out a black folder and spread the contents on the table. "We're here to discuss our newest find." The director looked down his glasses at me. "Oh, there you are. With the suit, I assume you accepted my offer."

Like I had a choice. Instead of opening my mouth, I nodded.

"Good, then we'll get this meeting underway. Have you shared any details of your identity?"

"No," I said.

He laughed and thumbed through the pages. "Charlie, with no last name. How old are you?"

When I didn't answer, he slid off his glasses and put them on the table. He linked his hands in front of him. "Agent Lockhart, have you finished the assessment of her blood sample?"

"Yes," she said.

"Well, this sample can't give us a name, but you can tell us about her."

For the first time, she looked my way. "I have a presentation ready."

Several agents around us let out a sigh, and she frowned.

"Your presentations tend to cover more than necessary," he said.

"I like to be thorough," she said.

The director leaned back in his chair. "Hold old is Charlie?"

She glared at him. "From my analysis, around sixteen."

"Is her power genetic?"

"There are markers that make her different," Agent Lockhart said impatiently. "These markers are perhaps the source of her power and could have been inherited. I can show you the comparison slide."

Emily spoke up. "Is there anything to show she's a danger to this base?"

Again, Agent Lockhart looked at me. "No."

"Is she human?" Sylvia asked.

I held my breath.

"Yes," the doctor said.

The director looked at me. "Are you sure?"

"One hundred percent, sir."

Slowly, I released the breath, though Agent Payne glanced my way. Did he see my relief? Agent Lockhart focused on genetics yet had found nothing strange. But shouldn't the sample reflect my mom was from another planet? We'd studied DNA in school. Although the test wasn't as easy as checking for my blood type, everything about this agency told me they had first in class technology. How could she have missed the truth?

Mom looked human, as much as me and Dad. Maybe our DNA wasn't as different as I'd thought.

The way Agent Lockhart stared in my direction made me squirm. Her eyes were piercing, as if she could decipher every secret from the next words I spoke. Well, she'd be disappointed since my only plans for this meeting were to keep my mouth shut and stay out of the spotlight.

The agents discussed me, including Emily's description of what happened in the airport and how I'd acted since. Hearing her declare I wasn't a threat made me relax slightly. The men to either side of me agreed with her assessment.

"Unless anyone else has something of relevance to add," the director said, "we'll continue with Agent Liu."

All eyes moved to a woman who sat halfway between us. She had black eyes and silky black hair that hung just above her shoulders. Evenly-cut bangs hung above her eyes; her face was pale and free of any blemish. Her age was more difficult to determine than with the other agents, but I guessed around Sylvia's age, maybe mid to late thirties. She wore gloves that matched her suit, and her body remained rigid as she watched the director.

"You want me to test her power," she said in an emotionless voice.

"Yes," he said. "I won't be convinced until someone determines how this power works." The director looked down the table at me. "Unless you'd be willing to enlighten us."

When I said nothing, he stood, his voice rising. "Don't dare disrespect me. If you can't follow orders, we have a less comfortable room for you to stay." He closed the folder and reached for his briefcase. "If that threat isn't enough to scare you, we'll find what you care about most and destroy it."

My family. Was he threatening to go after them now? My heart pounded as I thought of agents breaking down the door to our home.

"Agent Vickers," he said to a man on the other side of Emily. "Get our recruit a badge and make her official. She'll have access to the standard list, but nothing classified."

"I need a background," Agent Vickers said. "A history. Are you saying you want me to make her appear out of thin air?"

"If that's what it takes." The director turned to leave. "Get to work, everyone."

Several agents stood and followed him out of the room. Mason and Payne stayed behind, along with Emily, Sylvia, Agent Liu, and both Agent Lockharts. Agent Vickers closed the door and returned to his seat.

"I don't know how much longer I can stand this insanity," Agent Liu said.

Agent Vickers nodded. "For once, you and I agree. Forcing a child to play agent is no laughing matter."

"Careful, Phil," Emily said. "We have our orders and for now we will follow them." She looked to Agent Liu. "Hannah, do you think you can unlock Charlie's power?"

"I'd like to give it a try, but holding this girl here against her will is unacceptable." She slammed a fist on the table. "How long does he plan to keep her?"

"He offered her a job." Emily looked my way. "She's not being held against her will."

I swallowed. "Is he doing this to make me kill people? Or is there another reason he yelled at me?"

"In case you're ever in doubt, our director doesn't like women," Hannah said with disgust. "We're a nuisance to him."

Agent Lockhart leaned forward, her eyes fixed on Hannah's face. "He doesn't like people who challenge his authority. Gender is irrelevant."

"Enough," Emily said. "This discussion gets us nowhere." Again, she looked at me. "Will you give Hannah access to your power?"

I thought back to Emily's words about Hannah and nodded. She could absorb powers and use them herself. Would this work on my power since that part of me wasn't human? Even worse, what if she realized I could teleport?

Emily looked around the table. "Okay, everyone ready to start the day? Hopefully, we'll have a better start than yesterday." Everyone laughed as she looked at the other Agent Lockhart. "Big job today?"

He nodded. "Had another earthquake, this time in California. Few witnesses of who caused the event, but I'll find out what they saw and erase what's needed."

An earthquake caused by a person? Like when the news reported an earthquake shook Atlanta and claimed it was a cover-up? An agent who could erase memories was the perfect person to cover up an earthquake.

"Good." She looked at his wife. "Are you finished with the analysis of Charlie's DNA?"

"As far as the director is concerned, my work is done. Today, I plan to investigate more of the samples taken from Faulkner. If we could harness what made him special…"

"Agreed," Emily said. "I'll be in the office today, but please reach out if there's anything I can do to help." Everyone stood but Emily. "Donald, stay behind. There's something we need to discuss."

He sighed and dropped into his chair. "I only kill when absolutely necessary. Last night I had no other option."

The room went still.

"Hey, easy on my partner," Agent Payne said.

Emily's face showed she didn't buy Payne's charming act, but her tone was light. "We can talk about this after the room has cleared. Everyone, let's have a great day and show this agency what we can accomplish as a team."

With a glance at Mason, Payne nodded. "Guess that leaves me with kid duty."

Mason reached for my arm as I turned to leave. "Don't let what the director said bother you. He's yelled at me plenty of times. One day you'll realize it's a badge of honor."

I nodded and followed Agent Payne out of the room. Next to him walked the agent who wanted to borrow my power. As we approached the elevator, she complained about an argument she had with the director last night.

"Are you sure you should talk about that here?" Payne asked as we stepped inside.

"What could the girl possibly do about what I've said? She doesn't know anyone here, and she doesn't have access to the outside. Our director has to learn how to control his temper."

"Agreed," Payne said. "Well, let's get to the shooting range and show some teamwork. From the mouth of our cheerleader."

She shoved a finger in his face. "Don't talk that way about Emily. She's never said a word to hurt anyone here."

"Just because the two of you are friends doesn't mean she should have power over you."

"Could you name a better boss in this place?"

He hesitated. "No."

"You'd be lucky to have a woman half as smart as Emily Holmes. Too bad she'll never give you the time of day."

"You know the agency's rules about fraternization with coworkers," he said. "She's our boss."

"Since when have you been one to follow the rules?"

The door opened, and we stepped into the hall.

"Agent Liu—" I said.

"Call me Hannah."

"Okay, Hannah."

"Now that we're on a first-name basis, I want to know who you are and where you came from."

Payne laughed. "Since no one else could get it out of her, you think you can?"

She nodded. "Her past can't be as bad as mine. Tell me, Charlie, where is home for you?"

I shrugged. "Where is home for you?"

With a slight smile, she looked at him. "She's a natural at this. Now I'll tell her about fleeing China and how my family was murdered. Then I'll tell her what I did to those bastards who took them from me. Give her some ideas. Maybe even show her the life she ran from wasn't so bad."

A pang of sorrow tugged at my heart. "You lost your mother?"

Her smile faded. "Let me give you the best advice of anyone here. The only way you get hurt is if you allow it. Survival isn't about the fittest; at this agency, it's the smartest who flourish."

I followed them to the shooting range from yesterday. They found an empty stall and Hannah surveyed the target. She removed her gloves and held out a hand for me. I put my hand in hers and she gripped my fingers while closing her eyes. After a moment, she released my hand.

"That's it?" I asked.

"Do I have to touch the gun with my bare skin?" she asked.

"No."

"Good." She replaced her gloves and lifted a gun from the holster inside her jacket. "We'll see if this power is real."

Real? Didn't she mean we'd see if she could access it? I stood back and watched from Payne's side. He gave me a sideways glance before watching Hannah square her shoulders and aim the gun.

"How long will she have my power?" I asked.

"It's not permanent," Payne said.

"What Agent Payne means to say is it depends on the strength of your power. An hour, maybe two, but it drains me. All powers have their own kryptonite of sorts, including mine. Now stop talking while I concentrate."

Almost every target in the place was in use. How she could concentrate with all that noise but not ours made me laugh. I stilled my laughter and considered what would happen if she teleported.

Hannah emptied the clip as she aimed for her target. When Payne checked the hits, he laughed. "You're supposed to aim at the target, not away from it."

She frowned. "There's nothing wrong with my aim."

"Obviously," he said.

Turning, she pointed the gun at him, and he dropped to his knees fast enough I sucked in a breath. I'd wondered about his fighting skills compared to Mason, and now I considered he might not be a fighter at all. No one in the room bothered to glance our way.

She spun to dodge his kick, and he rose to grab her in a chokehold. The fight continued back and forth as they kicked, spun, and punched, neither backing down. With a grunt, she holstered the gun and twisted his arm. This woman, who was no taller than me and probably weighed less than half of what he did, dropped him to the floor in an effortless move. Hannah put a foot on his chest and drew the gun to point at his face. "Too bad you have no power for me to borrow, Agent Payne."

"Yes," he bit out. "We should get this close more often."

"Not a chance," she said in disgust. "The only thing I'd like to do this close is put a bullet in your head."

I took a step back in surprise. Still, no one bothered to interfere, though a few people were now watching and laughing.

"You hate me that much?" he asked.

"Try me."

He held up his hands in a show of surrender. "I know when I'm fighting a losing battle."

Hannah removed her foot from his chest. She offered him a hand, which he refused, and she smiled. A cheerful face didn't suit the deadly image she'd crafted so far. Did they fight like this often? Obviously, since none of the other agents seemed interested in stopping them.

"Can you teach me to do that?" I asked.

Her face turned serious. "You want to learn how to fight?"

I nodded. "You're half his size and you dropped him like he weighed nothing."

"Fighting is not about size," she said. "You teach me how to use your power and I'll teach you to drop Agent Payne to the floor."

Standing, he rubbed his chest as if her foot had left a mark. "Nice touch. Does she have a deal, kid?"

"For me, shooting is not about aim," I said.

Hannah re-loaded the gun and handed it to me. "Show me how you shoot."

I aimed for the target and fired six bullets, each in a diagonal line across the target.

They checked where my bullets landed, and she reached for the gun. "Did you mean to miss the center?"

"To make the power work, I focus on the bullet while bending the air currents around it. I make it land where I want."

She took a deep breath and focused on the target. This time, Hannah fired three shots, each of them making it close to bullseye.

"I didn't get it the first time, either," I said.

For an hour, I helped Hannah learn to shoot like me. I explained the air currents but didn't talk about the book with the kill shots or those designed to take a person down without killing them. By the time we'd finished, she seemed to believe what I said about the air currents, even said she could feel them. "I guess your power is real," she said. "Who taught you this?"

My mother, I wanted to say, but couldn't. Instead, I shrugged while wondering if she'd shove me down on the floor like she did with Payne. How long could I hold out if they tortured me?

She sighed and lowered the gun. "We all have secrets. The director may hold you here and use your power for his agenda, but never forget you're a person like the rest of us."

EPISODE 23

Threats

After loaning my power to Hannah, Agent Payne took me to a security area where Agent Vickers was waiting. Thin screens hung on the walls of a room larger than the gym at my school. Wider than any TVs I'd seen, each screen appeared to show a live video. If the time stamps were to be believed, it was almost noon.

One wall of screens showed cars moving on the streets outside the building, various angles of the parking deck, and the entrance to the bank. Another wall captured feed from the med-level and agents walking along various halls. The resolution of this video startled me. It was so clear, I swore they could see a bug crawling across the floor.

Agent Vickers had his team take my picture and fingerprints. For nearly an hour, they showered me with questions about where I came from. Finally, they seemed to give up and handed me a badge with the name Charlie Kidd. On the back were the letters F and A.

"What do these letters mean?" I asked.

"F means you're approved for field duty, and A means you're trained for ammunitions."

The picture made my face look older, like I'd survived an event that changed my life. Could it be a trick of the light? "That name isn't funny."

Agent Vickers huffed. "If you'd tell us your real name, you'd save us all a lot of trouble."

I shook my head and glared at Agent Payne. "You did this."

Payne laughed. "Thought the name suited you perfectly."

"Kidd isn't even a name, is it?"

"Yes." While Payne acted like this was a joke, Agent Vickers frowned. "We take security seriously here," the security agent said, "and this has never happened on my watch."

"We're all doing our jobs," Agent Payne said. "Don't forget who makes the rules here."

"Will you show her around the base? Point out every shadow she should stay out of?"

Payne nodded. "She's seen all she needs to so far."

We walked out of the security area and through an area with desks separated by partitions. Pictures hung on the walls of these cubicles, much like they had in the office at my school. Polaroids of kids and drawings made with crayon. Awards and certificates for years of service. These simple items made the agents seem more like people who did their jobs and cared about their families than walking, talking mysteries in black. Along the far wall was a thin slice of windows about my height. I walked to the windows and watched cars move through the streets of downtown Atlanta.

"We must be near the top of the building," I said.

Payne watched from behind me. "Next to last floor. I've got to grab a file from my desk. We'll sit in one of the conference rooms, and you can help with my report about the airport."

I followed to his desk, which was devoid of all the pictures and certificates that made the other agents seem human. It contained a computer with a wide, rectangular screen that reminded me of the ones in the house where Joel lived. Glancing behind the screen, I did a double take at the thickness.

"What's wrong?" he asked.

"I've never seen a computer screen this thin."

"We have the best technology here."

I glanced at the square computer that sat on the desk next to the screen. We had a few of these at school, but not one in each classroom. This room had a computer on every desk. "I've seen computers, but never this many."

He flashed a grin that put me at ease. "Have you used a computer?"

I shook my head. "My math teacher won't even let me use a calculator."

"Better to use some of that brainpower than get lazy and depend on a computer." He pointed to the back, where a gray cable plugged into the wall. "All of our computers are connected."

"To what?" I asked.

"The Internet," he said.

I looked at him in confusion. "What's an internet?"

"Not *an* internet, *the* Internet." Payne laughed. "You'll find out soon enough."

So far, the other agents all seemed to like Agent Payne. He carried on a conversation with everyone who passed, like Lorraine. Keva's words came back, and I shivered.

My oldest son was like her. Never met a stranger.

Why did I think of Keva just now? A phone rang across the room, the noise repeating seven times before stopping.

Looking around, I realized the room was empty except for us. For some strange reason, fear rose in my throat. "Where is everyone?"

"Working," he said. "Most of the agents here have field jobs. Sometimes I go a week or more without seeing my desk."

"The other agents have pictures and certificates. Where are yours?"

He shrugged. "I don't mix my home life and work."

"From what Mason said, he doesn't have time for a home life."

"I'm not Mason."

Next to his keyboard sat a black device. "What is that?"

"A phone." He laughed, lifting the phone. "I told you we always get the latest technology."

It didn't look like the cordless phone I'd asked for last Christmas, one that talked wireless to a base. No, this device was thin and sleek, like the communication device Keva had used. Could it be possible…

Next to me, Payne raised his hand to check his watch. The cuff of his shirt rode up above the gold metal band on his wrist. I grabbed his wrist and shoved the fabric up, but there was no tattoo.

The laughter died as he shuddered and wrenched his arm away from me. "You overstepped a line, Charlie."

It was the first time he'd used my name instead of 'kid.' "What line?"

His tone was cold, murderous. "No one touches me. If you were anyone else…"

I took a step back, shrinking from the depths of his brown eyes. Two beacons that reminded me of Keva, but with a flash of calculated fury she never showed. "Hannah touched you."

"Did she?"

I thought of the gloves she wore. Maybe she didn't touch him, but why worry about me? He didn't have the tattoo, and his anger made no sense.

A smile crossed his face as his tone changed to warm and friendly. "We value personal space here. I suggest you stick to your own secrets."

* * * * *

The meeting with Agent Payne couldn't get over fast enough. I refused to eat the lunch he ordered as we reviewed details for his report. When I returned to my room that evening, my hands still shook from the shock of how he'd turned on me.

If you were anyone else…

What did he mean by anyone else? And why had his threat affected me more than the director's?

I opened the cabinets in my small kitchen but found only a few plates and glasses. Nothing to eat, which meant I'd have to make my way to the floor with restaurants or go to bed hungry. I removed the black suit and button-down white collared shirt that felt like a noose around my neck. Why had I agreed to this job?

Other than the fact Dad insisted, I had nowhere else to go. I'd been so stupid to walk out the door that night without a thought of how I'd survive in this world alone. If Mom could see me now, she'd either laugh or remind me how many people my actions had hurt. This was my life, though on this base I had no control.

Maybe I could teleport somewhere else and disappear from everyone. Would the director hunt down me and my family? I shivered. What if they already knew who we were and didn't say? Making me work at this agency, an unknown teenager, made no sense despite my gift.

How badly did they need me to kill people?

From the scene at the airport, pretty bad. Especially if Faulkner almost killed the director's daughter. Sylvia had the same power as him, could think like a computer and move fast, but not fast enough to take him down. Was the director worried it wasn't enough?

After a long, hot shower, I slid on a pair of jeans and a t-shirt from my bag. I'd just laid across the bed when a knock came from the door.

Emily stood outside, still dressed in her agent suit. "I thought we might have dinner again." She glanced over me. "You look so young in that outfit. Where did you get the clothes?"

"They were in my bag from the airport."

"You looked good in the suit this morning, so grown up." She cleared her throat. "Sorry, I didn't mean to linger. How about we have some comfort food tonight? It's been a long day."

I stepped into the hall and closed the door. "Is there any way I can get more clothes? Maybe something other than a suit or sweats?"

Next to me, Emily stood even taller than I remembered. "That can be arranged."

"When can I get my gun back?" I asked.

"Our forensics team is examining your gun. From what I hear, your power works with any gun."

"I want *my* gun."

"What makes that gun special?"

"It was a gift. If anything happens to it—"

"Nothing will happen to your gun. I promise."

Emily stayed silent until we reached a restaurant with menus that showed familiar southern food like collards and fried chicken. Were only half of the tables in use because it was after dinner or before? Being inside the base with no windows was messing with my internal clock.

"This is what you meant by comfort food?" I asked.

"I grew up in Detroit, but my mom was from Mississippi. She cooked the dishes she grew up on."

Staring at the menu, I wondered what dishes my mom grew up on. She'd cooked the same dishes as other families in our small Alabama town. Thoughts of her smiling as she taught us to make gravy rushed back, and I fought tears.

"Are you okay?" she asked.

I wiped my eyes. "It's nothing."

Luckily, a server appeared and asked for our orders. I chose slow-cooked roast beef with mashed potatoes and gravy, a side of green beans, and a coke. She asked for the same, but with a tonic and gin.

"Do you drink every night?" I asked.

"Maybe not every night." She thought for a second and chuckled. "Well, maybe every night. It's my way of dealing with the stress."

"Your job is hard?"

"You'll find that hard and stressful aren't always the same but both wear you down."

"But you like the job."

"Oh, yes. Best decision I ever made."

We talked until the food arrived, mostly about her observations from the morning meeting. She asked basic questions, sometimes so warmly I almost forgot her job was to dig for information. I fed her useless answers and felt like I'd won a victory when the food arrived.

Except I didn't feel like eating. My stomach churned as I thought of Agent Payne's face when I checked for the tattoo. I took a small bite of the roast beef. Tasted good, but I couldn't swallow. What if he was one of Keva's sons? I'd felt so sure he'd have the tattoo like her—the same tattoo as the agent who showed up at the flower shop. Payne even fit the deputy's description with his brown hair and height about five-eleven. Now I wasn't sure of anything.

Emily put down her fork. "I need the truth. How old are you?" When I didn't respond, she sipped her drink and leaned over her plate. "I can't help you if you don't help me. If you're going to have an extended stay here, you'll have to trust someone."

"What about Mason?"

She raised an eyebrow. "Mason doesn't trust anyone."

"That doesn't mean *I* can't trust him."

"You're a strange girl, Charlie. Most people gravitate to Payne, not Mason."

"I don't trust Agent Payne. He has secrets."

"We all do." Emily took another sip and started on her food. "Eventually, you'll have to tell us who you really are. The director won't play your game for long."

"Why is he playing at all?"

She downed the rest of her drink and motioned for the server to bring another. "I asked him to play this one slow. He understands the value of your abilities."

"He listened to you?"

"In this case. He wasn't the best at raising a girl. I told him from experience we'd be better off if you worked with us rather than against us. I'd help make your life easier, and you'd do the same."

"Why help me?"

She waited for the fresh drink before answering. "You remind me of my sister."

"Does she work for this agency?"

"She's never heard of this agency. Thinks I'm a paralegal for a big-shot law firm." Emily smiled. "Fits with her idea of me. She's studying marine biology at a college on the East Coast. Can't wait to graduate and save the planet."

"Sounds as if you two are just alike."

"After our parents died, I made sure she could achieve her dreams. Whenever I work overtime or am faced with a life-or-death decision, I remind myself of why I'm here."

"Saving people means something."

She nodded. "And speaking of school, I've ordered tutors to keep your education on schedule."

"How do you—"

"Know you haven't finished high school? Just a guess. You'll take their assessments to determine your grade level and comply with their assignments without argument." She watched me. "This isn't negotiable."

I nodded. "Would the director really find what I care about most and destroy it?"

"He doesn't make empty threats."

"What did he mean about a less comfortable room for me to stay?" I asked.

"Prisoners of this base are housed in a secure location. We call it the isolation floor."

"Like the med-level?"

She shook her head. "You need to see it to understand. People with abilities that make them dangerous to the public are locked inside a cell."

"How long do they stay in this cell?"

"Indefinitely."

The roast beef was looking less appealing by the second. I put down my fork. "So that's his threat? Lock me up? Don't I have rights?"

"People without powers have more rights, I will admit."

"The director has a power."

Emily scraped mashed potatoes from her plate and lifted the fork to her mouth. "This was supposed to be a calming meal."

"Why doesn't he scare you?"

"The director rules by fear and intimidation. Backing down would only justify his actions."

"But you work for him."

"I work for this agency," she said.

"You said you don't have a power."

"That's right."

"How does a normal person get a job for this agency?"

The server stopped for her empty plate and sat another gin and tonic on the table. He turned to me. "Is something wrong with the food?"

"No." I lifted the fork as if to take another bite.

"Tell you what," she said when he was gone. "I'll give you my story as long as you eat."

Reluctantly, I took a bite of the potatoes. The taste made my insides twist, but I wanted to know about Emily.

"I went into law enforcement after a good friend disappeared. I wanted to help find him and the local police told me to leave it alone."

"Did you ever find him?"

"Years later, I found out he'd run away from home and joined the Air Force. He was a mechanic for helicopters and almost anything else that flew. Or helicraptors, as he called them. Never had a good opinion of anything made by or for the government."

"Were you a police officer?"

"I studied psychology and then criminology. After a few breaks on profiling cases, an agent approached me for a collaboration. Bodies were disappearing at a resort in Florida. I thought he was FBI and didn't realize the suspect had strange abilities until we'd nearly solved the case."

"What abilities?"

"A woman could breathe underwater and hear ultrasonic waves. They nicknamed her The Mermaid."

I finished the potatoes and moved to the green beans. "Sounds like a movie."

"Maybe a horror flick. She used her power to drown tourists and rob them blind. She'd disappear into the canals around the hotels before anyone was wise to her. After her capture, the agent's director was so impressed he asked to meet me."

"The same director?"

She nodded. "Didn't know what I was getting into, but unexplained cases were the reason I went into law enforcement. He asked me to lead a case, which I solved, and he offered me a job. The director said I had a talent for reviewing crime scene data and connecting the dots. But he also wanted me to teach his daughter about being a better agent."

"That's an amazing story."

"No more than yours. Now that you're finished, I guess so am I."

I looked down at my empty plate. "Hannah said you're the boss."

"My position wasn't written in stone when the director hired me. His style is to load employees with work until they break. I don't break."

The force of her words stunned me. "How long have you been here?"

"Long enough to take on half of his responsibilities. He enjoys reminding me he's in charge, but he also likes to hit the greens with military leaders around the world."

I gave her a confused look.

"He plays golf. Really, Charlie, where *did* you come from?"

Slowly, I finished my coke. One person in this base could know the answer to her question. "What about Agent Lockhart? The one from the med-level?"

"Francine is the best in the world when it comes to genetics. Dead last when it comes to bedside manner."

"Did she find anything in my DNA?"

"You got the same report we all did." Emily laughed. "I suppose you'd like to know more about your power, same as the rest of us."

"She's married to the man who can erase memories, right?"

"They met while he was working on a cleanup operation. His orders were to erase her memories regarding a potential viral attack."

"Guess he didn't follow orders."

Emily shook her head. "Jon brought her into the mission, and she helped identify several contagions the agency had never seen. The director offered her a job and two months later, Francine married Jon. She's brought us a great deal of understanding for how powers work."

"Then she's smart."

"The correct term is genius. Her understanding of DNA is years ahead of anyone else."

I stared at my empty plate. "Last night you mentioned aliens. Has she ever studied their DNA?"

"That's a question out of left field, but yes, I believe she has."

If she knew about alien DNA, why didn't she see the evidence in the sample I gave her? Or did she realize and not say anything at the meeting? She'd given me a strange look. But keeping the information to herself made no sense.

The server removed my plate. "Anything else?"

"No, we're done here," Emily said. When he walked away, she said, "We need to talk about tomorrow."

Dread filled me. "What's tomorrow?"

"Although I don't feel right about the timing, the director wants you in the field. Usually, agents train for six months before stepping out."

"You think I can't do it?"

"Jon needs help with his job in California. Mason and Payne will fly out at six a.m., and you'll be tagging along. Do *you* think you can handle this assignment?"

"Do I have a choice?"

She leaned back in her chair. "Pretend you have a choice."

"You want me to shoot someone."

"Possibly. They can give you the details en route."

"This is my job now, right?" I asked with more confidence than I felt.

She sighed. "Remember, this isn't a movie. You can die out there."

*****

As soon as I reached my room, every bit of the food came back up. I spent the next thirty minutes on my knees in the bathroom.

After I'd thrown up all of dinner and felt too tired to move, I laid across the bed. Dad told me not to come back home for at least three days, but there was nothing I wanted more than my bed.

Except my old life back.

Not to mention my mom.

The walls had no windows and must have been thick enough to block out all sounds. Even the air blowing down from vents in the ceiling was quiet. I pulled the blanket tight as I cried myself to sleep, unsure if this mess could ever be fixed.

I was even less sure of who to trust.

EPISODE 24

Earthquake

The next morning, I threw the pillow over my head when the phone rang. Groaning, I answered the call and immediately slammed the receiver down. 3:30 am. I'd barely slept. My eyes were crusty from my crying and my mouth felt like I hadn't brushed my teeth in days.

Stumbling into the bathroom, I found the toothbrush along with the bag of supplies someone had left on the counter. I brushed until the taste of puke faded and turned on the shower. This day was going to last forever.

After the shower, I put on another of the black suits left in my room. In the bathroom mirror, I stared at someone who looked nothing like me. I tied my wet hair at the back of my head, in a bun like Sylvia wore. Emily said I'd fly to California with Mason and Payne. It would be my first flight. Would I be good to pass through security with my new badge?

I clipped the badge on the right front of my jacket. Charlie Kidd. Maybe the old me really was gone now.

A knock came from the door, and I wondered what else I should take with me. I lifted the straps of my backpack over my shoulders. This bag was all I had, but I wasn't leaving it behind. Who knew where this first mission would lead me?

Mason waited outside the door, dressed in a black suit that looked the same as the others he'd worn. "Taking your bag?"

"It's mine," I said.

"We'll return after the mission, unless you have other plans."

Since I didn't respond, he shrugged off the conversation and led me to the elevator. He chose the buttons G and 1. When the elevator stopped, we stepped out into a brightly lit hall and walked to a set of doors where Agent Payne stood. Cameras that hung from the ceiling recorded every move we made. As we approached, Payne opened one door and steamy air spilled in.

Outside, the parking deck was only half filled, mostly with black vehicles of all shapes and sizes; everything had a similar Georgia license plate and no markings. A guard house with two men dressed in military uniforms was the only hint this wasn't a normal parking lot. They held automatic weapons across their chests.

"We didn't come in this way," I said.

"The bank doesn't open until eight." Mason hit a button on his key chain and the lights flashed on a car to our left. "We pass through those doors during working hours and these at other times."

"Fancy." I'd never seen a car flash the lights on its own, but Dad had always been a fan of older trucks.

Payne opened a door to the backseat and motioned me inside. "If you think that's fancy, you didn't notice the security system in the bank lobby. You had a full body scan by the time we reached the elevator."

Mason dropped into the driver's seat as Payne took the seat in front of me. He cranked the engine and turned around. "Have you ever flown, Charlie?"

"No."

"Well, this day should be fun." He looked over at Payne, who shook his head and stared out of his window.

The tension inside the car felt so thick, I wished I'd never climbed into this car. These men were partners and mostly seemed to get along. Had they been arguing? I put on my seatbelt. "I can't believe you used the word fun."

"Believe it," Payne said.

The streets of Atlanta were silent as Mason drove us to the airport. Even the highway seemed quiet; only a few cars were out this early. The clock on the dash showed five o'clock by the time we reached the airport. Mason parked the car, and we walked into the airport as if we belonged there, the men to either side of me staying close enough to grab my arms if necessary. Maybe they thought I might run if given the chance.

No, I'd walked into the airport for the first time, determined not to go home. I'd eaten breakfast and observed the people entering and leaving this airport as an outsider. Today, I would be on a plane myself.

I barely kept up with Mason's pace as people rushed around us in all directions. He didn't stop at the ticket line; no doubt this trip had been planned methodically. As we reached the security area, Agent Payne handed me an envelope with a plane ticket in my new name and a passport, complete with a fake birthday.

"This says I'm nineteen."

"Couldn't make you any older," Mason said. "It has to be believable, though the suit helps."

With the envelope in one hand, I gripped a strap of my backpack in the other. "At least with the suit I look like I belong here."

He reached in the duffel bag he carried and handed me a pair of sunglasses. "With these, you'll look like one of us."

One of them. I'd never had a job or finished high school, and now I was about to fly across the country on a mission for a government agency. I didn't have time to put away the sunglasses as Mason led us around a dozen lines with people who waited for metal detectors snaking around the room. Payne waved to a security agent who opened a lane for us. He chatted with the man in a black-and-white uniform while the agent reviewed his credentials.

"Go ahead, Agent Payne."

Payne put his bag on a conveyor and walked through the metal detector. On the other side, he reached for his bag while the security agent checked my credentials.

"Proceed, Agent Kidd," he said.

When I didn't move, Mason leaned in. "That's your cue."

"Does he work for the agency?"

"We have people everywhere," he said. "Now, put your bag on the conveyor and walk to Payne."

Right. Everything had been taken care of for this trip, the same way Emily had made plans for my schoolwork. They would manage every part of my life in the agency's methodical way. If I refused to play along… What if I ran for the doors instead of getting on this plane? What if I teleported in front of all these people?

That would cause a scene, and that was the last thing I needed. I tossed my bag on the conveyor and walked through the metal detector.

On the other side, Payne smiled without humor. "Glad to see you're not packing."

"Packing what?" I asked.

"Any weapons." Mason walked up from behind and grabbed his bag from the conveyor, along with mine. "They're not allowed on a plane."

"You have my gun."

"Could you please refrain from the use of that word in here?" Mason asked.

I glanced at the security agent, who stretched a rope with a 'closed' sign across the lane and disappeared through an unmarked door along the wall behind us. "How do you fight without a… weapon?"

"That will be taken care of by the time we get to California." Mason put on his sunglasses and began the walk to our terminal. "It's easier this way."

Sliding on my backpack, I followed as Payne donned his sunglasses and walked next to Mason. I tried my sunglasses but put them away because I could barely see. The two spoke about a previous case as we went down an escalator, caught a train to our terminal, and took another escalator to the walkway leading to our gate. I focused on the ceiling high above me, the planes outside the long windows, and their backs, if necessary, to avoid eye contact with anyone in the airport.

I was out of breath by the time we reached the gate. Mason motioned for me to sit in one of the empty chairs. Instead, I stood near him and Payne until the call to board our flight. As we waited, I kicked off one of my shoes and rubbed my heel. A blister burned beneath my sock.

"Okay there?" Mason asked.

"These shoes aren't comfortable. Can I go back to wearing my sneakers?"

He shook his head. "Those won't meet the agency's dress code. We'll find you some more comfortable shoes."

When our row for the plane was called, I followed the agents down a covered walkway and onto the plane.

Payne checked his watch. "This plane might actually depart on time. Flip you for the aisle seat."

Mason sighed. "You can have it. I'd rather watch what's going on outside the plane."

"What about me?" I asked.

"Stuck in the middle," Payne said.

"Are you always going to put me in the middle? It's like you think I might run."

"You could," Mason said. "Not that I would blame you, but we have orders. If you run, the agency will hunt you down and the rules will tighten."

"I won't run."

"I believe her," Payne said. "You haven't given her a reason to leave… yet."

I followed as Mason found our row and stowed his bag in the compartment above our heads. He shoved my backpack in next, along with Payne's black duffel bag. Our row on the right side of the plane had three seats. Mason took the window, I sat in the middle, and Agent Payne took the aisle seat. More people boarded the plane until every seat was full.

Looking around, I observed the exit signs and where the flight attendants stood, while trying not to look like an inexperienced girl who'd never climbed on a plane before. I had alien DNA, which made this whole situation laughable.

The voice of the pilot came over the intercom, welcoming us, and an attendant demonstrated what to do in the event our plane crashed into water. They showed an oxygen mask, and I put a hand over my mouth as my stomach turned.

"Do they say that every time?" I asked.

"Every time," Mason said. "Pay attention. You never know when you might need the knowledge to survive a plane crash."

"Survive?" I gripped my seat arms. "How often do planes crash?"

Mason laughed. "Don't worry, full planes never crash."

"A myth," Payne said. "Planes with empty seats crash as often as those at capacity."

Behind us, a woman stood and leaned forward. "Could you not talk about planes crashing?"

He gave the woman a stern look. "This plane isn't crashing today. I was merely illustrating a point."

She sighed and sat down. Within moments, the plane jerked and moved backward. Outside the window, the sun glowed on the horizon. Other planes moved to form a line as we stopped and began rolling forward. The control tower rose against the sky. After stopping and waiting for several more moments, we moved forward and picked up speed until the plane rose off the ground.

My fingers dug into the arms of my seat as the world tilted outside the window. While we rose skyward, the pressure made me feel as if my stomach dropped. The plane bounced and dipped to our side, making me cry out. The wing near us lowered and buildings became visible below.

"It's nothing to worry about," Payne said.

Nothing to worry about? I didn't like this feeling at all. Was it the movements that made me sick or how high we'd risen? Again, the plane shook, and I wondered what flying on a spaceship would feel like. Hopefully not as bumpy and my stomach wouldn't want to heave. After last night, I didn't trust myself not to throw up, even though I hadn't eaten breakfast. The decreasing air pressure made my ears pop.

Payne pointed to a paper bag tucked into the seat in front of me. "If you get sick, don't do it on me."

"This feeling doesn't bother you?"

He shook his head and closed his eyes, leaning back against the seat.

To my other side, Mason stared out of the window. "Can he really sleep during this?" I asked.

"Yes." Mason opened a menu. "Hungry?"

I put a hand over my mouth.

"Okay, take it easy. We've got four hours in the air, so get comfortable."

Four hours? I groaned. Teleporting back to Atlanta after the mission was sounding better by the minute.

*****

Those four hours were some of the longest of my life. At least landing wasn't as bad as taking off. The motion made my stomach lurch, but I was so ready to be on the ground, I held back the urge to puke. How had my mother traveled in a spaceship across the galaxy when I wasn't sure if I wanted to get on a plane again? But I'd have to fly to get back to Atlanta, unless I teleported, which wasn't an option.

Agent Payne conveniently slept until our plane came to a stop at the airport in California, where he stretched and looked at me. "What did you think about flying?"

"I hated it."

"You'll get used to it," Payne said.

"It's a requirement of this job," Mason added. "You don't have a choice."

"Thanks for reminding me. I don't have a choice about anything."

"You'll have a choice," Payne said. "At some point. Don't waste it."

After leaving the plane, we rushed through the airport and bypassed the baggage claim area where several of the passengers stopped. We headed for the main exit. Agent Payne led the way outside, where the sun sat lower along the horizon than I'd expected.

"What time is it?" I asked.

He checked his watch. "Eight fifty-seven. Don't forget you've lost three hours, kid. Different time zone."

Keeping up with all these facts would make this agent job tough work. "Where are we going now?"

"There." Payne pointed to a car waiting along the curb.

A man in a black suit stood at the rear of the car. He tossed a set of keys to Payne with a nod and walked away.

I looked around, but no one had noticed us. "What was that about?"

"That," Payne said, "was using my people skills. If you want things to happen in this business, you've got to construct and maintain relationships."

"You mean make friends?"

"That's not what he means." Mason took the keys and climbed into the driver's seat.

Payne opened the door behind Mason, and I climbed in. He took the front passenger's seat.

"Friends won't hesitate to shoot you in the back." Mason found my eyes in the rearview mirror. "Relationships require some level of give and take from both parties. An understanding that supersedes any other objective."

"What kind of objective?"

"Start with staying alive." Mason cranked the car. "I'm sure you've heard the rumors by now. Everyone wants to know why I insisted on Payne as my partner. To be honest, he's good at relationships and I'm not."

I looked at Payne. "You don't seem like a good friend."

"I'm not," he said. "Haven't you been paying attention? Mason is the muscle and I make things happen."

We pulled away from the curb. Payne lifted a folder from his bag and handed it to me. On the first page was a picture of a man with hair that shined with a mix of brown and gold, cut above his ears, and dressed in a gray suit. His smile made his face look attractive. The name under the picture was Augustus Hertz. "Who is this?"

"Our target," Mason said. "We call him Bishop."

A shiver passed over me. Target. This job was getting real, fast. "You want me to kill him?"

"Yes." Mason slowed to a stop at a red light. "That's why the director suggested you go on this mission."

"Suggested?"

"*Strongly* suggested. He wanted you to take down our target without additional casualties."

On the next page of the folder were photographs of people with open wounds and some with bones broken and protruding through the skin. My stomach lurched again, and I closed the folder.

"What did he do to deserve death?"

Mason hesitated. "According to our director, simply existing with the power to kill people is enough."

"What is his power?"

"He causes earthquakes," Payne said. "By slamming his fists together, he can make the ground shake and bring buildings down."

"The news had a story," I said. "There was an earthquake in downtown Atlanta, and they interviewed someone who mentioned a cover-up."

Payne glanced my way. "That would be Bishop. Recently, he caused a scene in Atlanta before our agents ran him out of town. The director believes that having powers means having a target on your back. Sometimes he seems to forget he has a power and could be considered deadlier than some of those on our list."

"Where am I on this list?"

"Near the top, but I don't think being born with a power should mean you're a threat. It's how you use the power."

I handed the folder back. "Why not arrest him?"

"It's not that easy," Mason said.

"Does he move fast like Faulkner did?" I asked.

"No."

"Why can't someone else from the agency shoot him?"

"Part of his anomaly." Mason took a left and went down a hill that had my stomach doing flips.

I rolled my window down just in case. "Can you stop making me sick?"

Payne handed me a bag he'd swiped from the airplane. "Bishop's able to cause vibrations in the air and the ground. He can make the bullets stop before they reach him."

Weird. "Like how I use the air currents to manipulate where the bullet goes?"

"According to Hannah's report," Payne said, "your skill in manipulating the air currents is far beyond Bishop's, but on a rudimentary level I suppose they are similar."

"So, he got away and now he's in California. Has he caused an earthquake here yet?"

"One large enough to scare people but with minor injuries," Mason said. "The next could be worse. People here are already on edge because of an earthquake last year. It's like pouring gas on a fire."

"Agent Mason?"

His voice was harsh. "I told you before. Just call me Mason."

"Did you get in trouble at the meeting yesterday?"

"It's nothing for you to worry about. My job isn't the same as yours. Neither is how I handle pressure."

"I thought the director wants you to train me."

Mason stopped at another light and turned to me. "To be an agent, yes. Not to be a killing machine like I was trained. Our government spent years trying to make the perfect soldier. Some of those experiments were performed on me and my team, though I didn't learn the truth until after I came to work for the agency."

"Does that mean you have some kind of power?"

"Not a power. What makes me different is my mind never stops going over a mission. I study every angle until I can't sleep at night and, to tell you truth, I don't need much sleep anymore."

"What did they do to you?"

He stared ahead as he hit the gas. "The mission went sideways, and locals killed my team, except for me and one other soldier. I got him out when I made my escape."

Payne pointed to a conversion van along the sidewalk to our right. Mason approached the van and slowed to a stop behind it.

From the outside, it looked like a normal van. The back doors opened, and Agent Lockhart jumped out, revealing surveillance equipment and two other agents. Payne climbed from the car and took the seat next to me, leaving the front seat for our new addition. As soon as Agent Lockhart was in, Mason put the car into drive and merged with traffic. The entire exchange took less than thirty seconds.

While Agent Lockhart gave a situation update, Payne pulled a gun from inside his jacket and handed it to me. The weapon looked the same as the other agents used, a basic black pistol with a standard clip.

"Where is my gun?" I asked.

"Be a good girl and you'll get it back," he said. "I'll make sure of it."

"Where did you get this gun? I never saw you pick it up."

He smiled. "I've had the gun since Atlanta."

"But the metal detectors, airport security—"

"We have ways around that."

"You tricked me. I think…" My words died as the car shook, vibrating with a strange humming sound until the glass shattered. Instinctively, I closed my eyes and turned my face away.

Mason slammed on the brakes and jumped out while drawing his gun. He leaned on the open door and pointed the gun at someone standing in the street ahead. Agent Lockhart opened his door and took the same stance as Mason.

Payne grabbed my arm. "Charlie?"

"I thought you said no touching."

"Use your power to take Bishop down, but don't kill him."

"But the orders were—"

"Do you really want to kill him?" Payne asked.

I stared at the man in the road, who was approaching our car. He looked different from the picture, older maybe, and his hair was now a mess of thick golden strands that almost touched his shoulders. Had he used a hairbrush lately? Bishop wore a ragged white t-shirt my mom would have thrown in the trash. His jeans also had holes in the knees and rips near the feet.

A pang of sympathy filled me as I looked at his sorrowful expression. What happened to change him from the clean-cut suit look to someone who'd given up hope?

"No, I don't want to kill him," I said. "I don't want to kill anyone."

"Then don't. You're an expert shot. I'm sure you know how to take a man down without killing him."

"What made him this way?"

"He killed people he cared for, before he knew about his power. It was an accident."

"Why do you care?" I asked.

"I don't, really. It's complicated." Payne wiped his face. "Do you think you can take Bishop down without taking his life?"

I nodded.

"Good, then get out. We'll see whose air currents win."

EPISODE 25

Following Orders

We'll see whose air currents win. Gripping the gun, I stared at Agent Payne. There was something fundamentally wrong with a grown man, not to mention a government agent, telling me to get out of the car and face a man who could cause earthquakes by slamming his fists together. Today was my first time flying, my first time on a mission.

And I might die today.

"Well?" Payne reached across me and opened the door. "This isn't the time to doubt your abilities."

I shook my head. "How did we get here? We just left the airport, and we were driving the street…"

"As we were leaving the plane, I received a nine-one-one page from Agent Lockhart. The situation with Bishop had degraded, but I didn't want you to worry then. Timing is everything."

"So, it's okay for me to worry now?" When I met his stare, it was like looking into his eyes for the first time. Agent Payne had joked with others, been the bumbling agent as Emily suggested, and he'd also threatened me. Today he was deadly serious to the point my heart pounded and sweat rolled down my face. "I'm not an agent."

"You are today." He shoved me out of the car, and I stumbled into the street.

Still gripping the gun, I found my balance and walked toward where Agents Mason and Lockhart had their guns trained on the man they called Bishop. The agents were shouting for him to stand down when Bishop slammed his fists together. The ground shook, and I stumbled again, this time landing on my knees. Pain shot up my legs and I wasn't sure if slamming against the pavement hurt worse or the burning from the blisters on my feet.

Slowly, I stood, bracing myself for another earthquake. As I moved closer, my eyes widened at the size of this man. Standing near the smaller agents made him look like a giant; he was at least a foot taller than both men, who seemed more like kids waving toy guns and issuing empty threats.

To the right side of the street, a woman lay on the sidewalk while clutching her leg. Part of the building's structure above the entrance had collapsed and a metal bar lay across her foot. To the left side of the street, a young girl with pigtails cried out and the man with her shouted for them to move faster.

"Stop this." Mason fired his gun at Bishop. The air hummed as the ground shook and the agents facing him stumbled backward. Bishop laughed as the bullet veered away from his body.

I held up my gun and fired a shot at Bishop. The ground shook, and I stumbled left and then right as the air vibrated around me. The air currents I weaved around the bullet lost their symmetry and faded as the bullet flew past his head.

Bishop seemed to notice me for the first time. "They sent a girl?" He bent over with laughter. "How old are you?"

Anger bubbled inside of me. Then fear. Emily's words repeated in my head. *Remember, this isn't a movie. You can die out there.*

I fired a second shot and Bishop caused another series of vibrations in the air and through the ground. As the pavement buckled between us, the bullet I carefully wove through the threads of air moved in slow motion, careening past his face, and every bit of my power couldn't force it to turn around and strike. Forget trying to go for a shot that would save his life. I'd be lucky to get in any shot against this man.

Could my luck with the agency have run out this quick? First, I faced a man who moved faster than cameras could follow and now I'd been ordered to take down a man three times my size who could affect the same air currents I depended on for survival.

Maybe the answer was yes.

Bishop sneered at me. "How many times before you realize your bullets can't touch me, little one?"

A woman escaped from a store to my right and screamed at the sight of Bishop. With the gun in my hand, I spun and ran back toward our car. The backseat was empty as I raced past, my lungs heaving for air. At the next corner, I took a right and ran down the sidewalk. Despite the aching and burning in my shoes, I didn't stop when someone yelled, "gun" and pointed at me. No, I kept going and took a left on the next street.

The heel of my right shoe caught on the sidewalk and I kicked off the shoes, not stopping as I continued in my socks. Down another street—how far would I go? I couldn't catch my breath and my heart felt like it would explode. All around, debris scattered from buildings and some sections of concrete had fallen on cars parked along the street.

Then I saw the bench—a metal bench along the sidewalk on the opposite side of the street, untouched by the damage from falling debris. I thought of Mom and ran across the street. When I reached the bench, I collapsed on the seat and tears streamed down my face.

The world shook, and I closed my eyes, dropping the gun to the ground. What did I do to deserve this? Everything around me shook and people screamed, but I couldn't move. Mom had helped people in a burning building despite the danger of showing her powers. She'd risked her life to save others when all I could do was run away.

I could teleport back to Alabama and make sure these agents never found me or my family and never have to face a man who could cause earthquakes again. If we had to move, I'm sure Dad would do whatever it took to protect me and Lorraine. He would agree I couldn't do this job. It wasn't safe. The idea of a teenager playing agent was ludicrous, though I'd proved myself at the airport. I'd saved lives.

"Get lost?"

My breath caught, and I opened my eyes. Next to me sat Agent Payne. The surrounding sidewalk was empty, and the only sounds were alarms in the distance.

"How did you find me?" I asked.

"Part of my job. I noticed your sense of direction may have been affected by the quakes."

"Or I ran."

His eyes focused across the street; his face showed no emotion. "I'll give you the benefit of the doubt."

"I can't take him down."

"Yes, you can."

"How would you know… Unless you can see the future?"

He hesitated. "I've seen you in action. I know what you're capable of."

"That's not an answer," I said. "How sure are you?"

"One hundred percent." He picked up the gun and handed it to me. "We can debate later. For now, I need you to act."

What would Mom have done?

Stop the man who could cause earthquakes and save lives.

I took a deep breath, grabbed the gun, and jumped to my feet. Without looking back, I ran toward the street where Bishop stood, wearing only my socks.

Payne caught up and ran beside me. "What happened to your shoes?"

"They were hurting my feet, so I ditched them."

He motioned toward the street where all of this started, and I nodded. A sharp edge cut into my heel, probably glass, though I didn't stop to look down. If I stopped, I might think about where I was going. If I thought about facing the giant man who laughed at me, I might never get close enough to fire my gun. I needed to see the spot on his head. This tiny patch on his skull near his ear would be the perfect way to take him down alive. It was close to a zone that would kill, but I'd do everything I could to make sure he lived. At least then he could pay for hurting others.

We reached the street, and Agent Payne grabbed my arm. I stopped and looked back at him. "What is it?"

"Don't kill him."

"I won't." I shrugged off his hand and approached where Bishop stood with his head lowered, as if in prayer. On the ground was Agent Mason, gripping his upper arm where he'd removed the jacket and rolled up his sleeve. Hot, sticky red pooled around his fingers. Agent Lockhart stood next to the van we'd seen earlier, with what looked like a phone. An antenna jutted out of the top, and it had no wires. The device looked like it weighed as much as one of the boat anchors Dad used at the lake.

Despite my approach, Bishop didn't move. I walked closer, holding the gun out in front of me. Closer, I needed a clear view of his head. The hair around his ears would have to be my guide to find this mark.

When I reached Mason, Bishop looked up. "Little one is back again."

"Don't call me that," I said.

He laughed. "What should I call you?"

I didn't care as long as it wasn't 'little one' or 'kid.' My hands shook with the gun aimed at him.

"Are you going to shoot me?" he asked.

"Yes."

"You will fail, just as your other agents failed. Why are you here?"

"To do a job," I said, with more confidence than I felt. "Why are you here?"

"To make your agency see there's nothing they can do to hold me. If you shoot, aim to kill because I will never stop."

His words made no sense. "Why won't you stop? Having a power doesn't mean you have to hurt people."

He sighed. "So young. Go ahead, fire your bullets. Empty your weapon and hit me if you can."

With a deep breath, I thought over Mom's lessons on concentration. Bishop had a way to control the air currents, which made us even. Except for the fact I knew which shots would take him out the easiest.

We'll see whose air currents win.

Maybe Agent Payne could see the future. If so, he was a hundred percent sure I'd beat Bishop. Only one way to find out.

As I reached for the trigger, Bishop slammed his fists together, and the ground shook. I stumbled to one side and then the other. Strong hands rested on my shoulder. One from Agent Payne and the other from Agent Lockhart. They were trying to steady me, and I knew this was my chance.

I pulled the trigger and focused all of my energy on the bullet. The world around me slowed as I followed the bullet with a feeling of pride. Pride that I could help people. Pride that my mother's power wouldn't go to waste. Confidence surged within me, and I forced the bullet on a path toward the small part of Bishop's skull that could render him immobile. Two lengths of a bullet to the right of my mark and he would die.

Vibrations went through the air, and I memorized the pattern. Bishop had blunt force, but I had precision. Skill. I rode the waves until my air currents were no longer in opposition. Crafting a straight line through the center of his waves, I found my opening and roared ahead unobstructed.

The ground continued to shake and the air currents spun around me, glowing blue and green as the red line of my bullet advanced. Closer, it was almost to his head. I felt the bullet as it cut through the thin layer of skin and burrowed deep into his skull. Bishop stumbled and collapsed into a heap onto the pavement.

All shaking stopped. For a few seconds, the men on either side of me looked on in awe and gripped my shoulders as if I was the only thing standing between them and a certain death.

Mason crawled forward and reached for Bishop's neck with his good arm. "This man still has a pulse." He looked up as I approached. "Did you mean to let him live?"

"Yes," I said. "Please don't tell the director."

He gave me a look of surprise.

Agent Lockhart exhaled. "You're playing a dangerous game, Charlie. If the director wanted you to kill Bishop—"

"Best to keep your mouth shut," Payne said. "Unless you plan to shoot him yourself."

The three men exchanged a glance, but Agent Lockhart looked away first. He ran to the van and got on the bulky phone.

Two agents came out of the van and approached. The street felt eerily empty, with no people and no sounds. Only the sun shining down on us. The quiet ended as another van turned onto our street and then several cars with flashing lights. Police? An ambulance arrived with paramedics. Within five minutes, the street had filled with vehicles and a mix of agents in black suits and emergency personnel.

The medics helped anyone on the sidewalk hurt by falling debris and fanned out to check the nearby stores for people needing medical attention. A team of agents swarmed around Bishop and captured the gigantic man. Somehow, they carried him to an armored truck and shoved him into the back. The agents also rushed to help people in the vicinity, with Agent Lockhart finding the woman I'd seen clutching her leg. She'd been buried in more debris, but thankfully was conscious as the medical team helped her onto a gurney and into an ambulance.

I shivered at the thought of how many more people Bishop could have hurt. But why was he so intent on hurting people? I could kill a person with a single shot and had no desire to do so.

A group of agents, including Agent Lockhart, formed a circle close enough for me to hear their words. They were deciding the best way for him to erase the memories of everyone who saw Bishop make the ground shake. Thankfully, they'd been able to keep the reporters away from the scene and effectively hidden the entire event from the public.

Agent Payne sat on the ground next to Mason. A medic kneeled to Mason's other side as she wrapped a bandage around his arm.

"How bad is your arm?" I asked.

"Just a scratch."

"Sir," the woman said, "you need stitches."

"Which can be handled back at the base," Mason said. "You've wrapped the bandage tight enough no one on the plane should notice."

Her eyes widened. "You can't travel with a hole in your arm."

"Is his wound life-threatening?" Payne asked.

She shook her head. "He'll survive the trip back to Atlanta. Though why he insists in this condition, I can't fathom."

When she stood and walked away, Mason leaned in and whispered, "Since I'm hurt, that should get us back to Atlanta faster. We'll avoid cleanup detail."

Which sounded good to me. These people rushing around us made me wary, and I'd never felt so tired. "When can we leave?"

Payne smiled and climbed to his feet. "For once you asked the right question, kid." He reached out a hand to me, but I refused and so did Mason.

The car ride back to the airport was silent. Payne handed me my shoes before claiming the driver's seat, leaving Mason to take the passenger seat and me in the back. At the airport, a ticket agent printed our boarding passes for a flight less than an hour away. I passed through security and carried my backpack to the gate without looking back. We reached the gate as an attendant called our row for boarding.

How the agency managed these details was nothing short of amazing.

Flying back didn't scare me as it had on the way to California. As I watched others board the plane, I felt empty. Numb. One attendant joked with Payne as he made a remark about a business meeting.

"Finished up early," he said with a grin, and she laughed. "Our company handles its business efficiently."

During the flight, Mason ordered me a box with a sandwich and chips, but I refused the food.

"Save it for later," he said. "Traveling on an empty stomach can ruin your day."

"I think my day is already ruined."

To my other side, Payne leaned back with his eyes closed.

"Aren't you hurting?" I whispered to Mason.

"Only when I think about it," he said in a low voice.

"How do you block out the pain?"

"It's more mental than anything. I don't let it bother me."

"Something from those military experiments?"

He looked out of the window. "No, I've always been like this. All I can tell you is ninety-eight percent of survival is about focus."

"What's the other two percent?"

"Luck," Payne said, without opening his eyes.

"Another reason we work well together. I bring the focus and he brings the luck." Mason gave a dry laugh. "You did good today, kid. Not exactly what you were told, but you saved lives. You should feel proud."

"I was terrified."

That drew a look from Mason. "You achieved our goal. People are safe because of you."

"Because of how I shoot. Without a gun in my hand, I'm nothing. I want to learn how to fight."

Payne opened his eyes. "Don't think hand-to-hand combat is in the cards for you."

"I want to protect myself. Right now, the only weapon I can use is a gun. Out there, I couldn't have fought without it."

"How well you used it made up for the rest," Mason said.

"Will they take Bishop back to Atlanta?"

"We've tried to keep him there, but he escaped. The plan wasn't to bring him back." Mason smiled. "Guess they'll have to make a new plan."

*****

The plane took longer to land on our return trip and circled the airport until I felt sick to my stomach. The sun sat low in the sky as we drove back to the base, weaving through thick traffic along the highway and in the downtown area. For the first time that day, I felt grateful for the dark sunglasses.

Mason and Payne stayed close as we entered the base through the rear doors; by this time, the bank had closed. They stood to either side of me on the elevator ride to the med-level. As soon as we stepped off the elevator, the smell of antiseptic turned my stomach.

Leaning down, Mason said, "You look a little green. I told you to eat something."

I put a hand over my mouth as I gagged.

Payne pulled a piece of folded paper from his jacket pocket, which I realized was the bag from the airplane. "Thought you might need this."

Instead of arguing, I dropped into a chair in the small waiting area and dry heaved into my bag. With a groan, I wiped my mouth and looked up in time to see Kyle emerge from the doors to the admission area and wave Mason inside.

Kyle's face twisted with concern as he noticed me. "Are you okay?"

I nodded as my cheeks turned red. The last time I'd seen this nurse, I'd puked down the front of his scrubs. "I didn't eat anything today."

He shook his head. "That's no good."

"I don't get sick like this all the time."

"Only when you see me."

His grin had a calming effect on my stomach. "I guess you're right."

"I heard you were successful today. Congratulations."

As I watched Kyle, I couldn't think of anything to say. Glancing around, I realized we were alone. Payne must have either left or went in with Mason.

"Sorry, I have to run. On the clock. If you're not sick with something we can fix, visit the grub-level and find something to eat."

I nodded as he reached for my arm and helped me to my feet.

"Maybe we can talk later," he said. "It's not easy to find friends to hang out with, especially since I'm not old enough to drink."

"How old are you?" I asked, happy for finding a complete, useful sentence to say.

"Eighteen. I just graduated high school and landed the job here a few weeks ago. Took CPR and some first-aid classes in school and found out I was a natural. If I do well as an aide, they'll send me to school for more training and this job could be permanent."

"I'm glad." As I turned and walked to the elevator, I smiled at how much better Kyle made me feel.

"Hey, Charlie!"

I spun back to face him.

"Maybe we can grab lunch tomorrow, if you don't leave the base."

"When?"

"Don't worry. I'll find you." Kyle gave me two thumbs up as he backed away, before rushing through the admission doors.

The smile on my face grew as I stepped into the elevator and realized I could breathe again. Kyle wasn't like any of the guys from school. The thought of having lunch with him gave me a rush of excitement.

Maybe I'd found a friend in this place.

EPISODE 26

The Isolation Floor

My thoughts were in chaos as I walked back to my room. Though I felt exhausted, the thrill of completing this mission pulsed through me.

I was unstoppable, despite my sick episode on the med-level. What did Kyle think of me? Well, it had to be good if he wanted to meet for lunch. Having a friend in this place would be nice. My smile faded as my thoughts strayed to Carmen and what a terrible friend I was by leaving without telling her. She had every right to hate me. Though I had no way to contact her, I wondered if she'd made it to Seattle to see her dad.

In my room, I changed into a t-shirt and pair of jeans. In the corner near my bed sat a pile of dirty clothes. How could I get them washed? This was the last clean clothes I'd brought from home.

In one of the restaurants, I ordered a grilled cheese sandwich and a bowl of chicken noodle soup, which made my stomach feel almost normal. At least it did until Emily found me and insisted we meet with the director.

On a higher floor, in a conference room with a table that seated only four, he sat across from a window as he sorted through a stack of files. He looked up as we entered. "Sit down and close the door."

Emily closed the door as I sat across from him, and she took the seat to my right.

"Your country thanks you for your service," he said.

I'd never been this close to the director and seeing him face-to-face made me shiver. His eyes held a darkness, a depth that reminded me I'd once feared the shadows in my room at night or the endless darkness under my bed. The words he'd used were honest and matched the inflection in his voice, but his eyes told another story.

"We are pleased to have you here, Charlie. But I gave you an order today."

I swallowed.

"An agent who doesn't follow an order isn't working as part of a team. There is no I in team, Charlie."

Was this man serious? Another look in his eyes told me that, yes, he was. His voice was sharper than a knife and carried a finality that made my teeth chatter.

Next to me, Emily watched his face, but her only movement was the rise and fall of her chest.

"Did you plan to kill Bishop?" he asked.

"I was told to kill Bishop. He could change the path of my bullets."

"You didn't answer my question."

"Yes," I lied.

The director watched me long enough sweat trickled down my face, before smiling. "Good. I believe we understand each other." He turned to Emily. "Assistant Director Holmes, why don't you show Charlie what happens to people with special skills who don't follow rules?"

"Yes, sir," she said.

"You are both dismissed."

She rose and so did I. After she closed the door and we'd started for the elevator, I turned to her. "You're an assistant director? I thought you were an agent like everyone else."

"People thinking of me in that way makes my job easier. I told you my duties here include many of the director's responsibilities."

"What does he want you to show me?"

"The isolation floor. That's where you'll spend tonight."

*****

By the time we reached the isolation floor, my whole body shook. This is where they locked up people with powers. People they couldn't control. Indefinitely, according to Emily.

Tonight was my turn.

I walked slowly by Emily's side; she didn't speak to me during the elevator ride or when we stepped into a long hall with white walls and a seamless white floor, though my sneakers made a squeaking sound like we walked on wet tile. She wouldn't even look at me.

Unlike the white lights that illuminated every crevice of the med-level, this floor had lights that glowed dimly from a source I couldn't locate. Not shining from the ceiling or the floor, and not from the walls either. Along the hall were windows, with a door next to each window, extending to the right and left at regular intervals. A woman dressed in a long white lab coat approached. She wore safety goggles and thick rubber gloves that covered her arms up to the elbows.

"The director asked that Charlie be assigned a room for tonight," Emily said.

The irony was I'd been issued this room as punishment for not killing a man. Sure, he had the ability to cause earthquakes that could kill dozens of people. But I immobilized him. Wasn't that enough?

Emily turned to me. "This is Dr. Lazenby. She will monitor your stay here."

I searched her words for any type of emotion. Was Emily okay with her director locking me in here?

Dr. Lazenby watched me with interest. "This is our recent addition? The girl who can hit any mark?"

"Yes," Emily said. "With a gun in her hand, she's an expert marksman. Keep that in mind and don't give her access to any weapons."

The doctor motioned for us to follow her down the hall. On the other side of each window was a brightly lit room that contained a bed with white sheets and the same white walls and floor as outside. People sat on some beds, normal looking people like me except for the solid white outfit. A woman Emily's age sat in the first room and then a man my dad's age in the next. Another younger man laid across the bed in the third room, appearing to sleep. The fourth held a woman with silver hair who sat with her head lowered. One room held a boy younger than Lorraine.

"Mason said Bishop won't be brought here," I said.

Emily nodded. "He's one of few people we can't place here. His power would cause vibrations that could reduce this building to rubble."

"Will they kill him?"

"No," she said. "He's already been moved to a secure location, and the bullet was removed from his head. Your actions may have angered the director, but he's decided

Bishop's ability could be useful under a set of controlled conditions."

"All of these people are in prison?" I asked.

"We like to think of this as a place of rehabilitation," the doctor said quickly.

A man in a similar white coat approached and handed a stack of white fabric to Dr. Lazenby, which she gave me. "Change into this." She stopped at an empty room and typed a code into the keypad next to the door. "This will be your room for the night. You can change inside."

I held the fabric to my chest as the door opened. "Is there a bathroom?"

She pointed to a toilet and sink in the corner of the room, and I gasped. This was worse than the jail cells I'd seen on TV. I'd never been arrested or charged with a crime, and now I was about to be locked in this room.

"Will they let me out of here?"

Emily's words were steel as she put her hands behind her back. "I'll come to get you tomorrow morning."

"Promise?"

She exchanged a glance with the doctor, and the woman in the white coat sighed. "So innocent," the doctor said with pity.

Emily nodded. "This is truly the worst part of our job, but we owe it to the people outside this base to keep them safe." She turned to me. "When I say I will do something, I do it. This is your punishment for disobeying the director's orders. Take heart that he has a good reason for every decision he makes. Learn from your mistakes."

I stepped into the bright light and shielded my eyes with my hand. "You think not killing a person is a mistake?"

"Change into the white suit," Dr. Lazenby said. "Take off everything, including your underwear, then hand me your clothes."

Turning away with a red face, I changed into the outfit. I gave her the bundle of clothes and she stepped into the hall.

The door clicked shut, but there were no handles or anything to grab onto, just a flat metal surface. I walked to the window, where my reflection stared back. On the other side, they could watch all night without me knowing. A memory came back of Dad explaining a two-way mirror. The see-through part needed bright light on the inside and lower light outside to make it work. At least with all the bright light, I could see how clean and shiny the floor was.

I sat on the bed and drew my knees against my chest. Even with my eyes closed, there was no blocking out the light. The room smelled clean, but nothing like the antiseptic from the med-level. The only sound was a gentle humming that never stopped, which I decided must be from the lights. There was no determining the exact light source, and I couldn't stand to look at the ceiling long enough.

With my power, I could teleport out of this room. I could hide where the agency wouldn't find me and never feel this fear again.

But the strongest emotion I felt was no longer fear.

Anger rose in my throat, anger at a man who could lock a teenager in a jail cell for punishment. Anger at this doctor for sealing the door.

Anger at Emily for telling me to learn from my mistakes.

If I left this place, he would win. The director would keep hurting people with powers to achieve his twisted goals. However, staying meant finding a way to make him pay for hurting me.

When I finally slept, I dreamed of putting a bullet through his head. The fear in his eyes as I pulled the trigger satisfied a deep need I never knew existed and felt both terrifying and exhilarating.

I woke before learning if I'd landed a kill shot.

*****

The next morning, Emily showed up as promised. In the white room, I sat on the bed while taking deep, calming breaths. I wouldn't let the constant humming get to me. They wouldn't see me broken by lights that glared so bright they felt warm. She stood outside the door while the doctor from last night checked my vitals and made notes on a clipboard.

I'd sworn to hate Emily after leaving me, but the dark circles under her eyes convinced me otherwise. She held a cup of coffee, which she drank on the way to my room. As she told me to get dressed for the morning meeting, Emily sounded as if she'd slept less than I had in that white cell.

Back in my room, a fresh suit lay across the bed, along with a brown box containing a new pair of shoes. I opened the box, with no brand name or markings of any kind, and felt surprise as I slipped on the most comfortable pair of shoes I'd ever worn. Black, with platform heels, the shoes had support and cushioning the heels from Sylvia didn't.

"Thanks for the shoes," I said.

"You shouldn't thank me for anything. I was hoping last night opened your eyes about this place."

"What do you mean?"

She sighed and shook her head. "I didn't get the shoes. Agent Payne found them for you, where I'm not sure."

"Can I get my clothes back?"

"All of your clothes have been cleaned and are now hanging in the closet near your bed."

To my surprise, the heap of dirty clothes no longer sat on my floor. She left the room for me to get dressed and waited outside my door. Emily led me to the morning meeting, filled with agents as before, though today everyone stopped talking as we entered.

Mason and Payne sat at the table; they'd saved me a seat between them. Across the table, Agent Lockhart—the woman with a sample of my DNA—leaned forward as I sat down. "I hear he had you locked on the isolation floor."

Next to me, Mason cringed. "It's not your place to get involved."

She folded her arms across her chest. "You plan to justify him holding her?"

To her side, the other Agent Lockhart put a hand over hers. "I agree with Mason. Stay out of this."

Turning, she glared at him. "And when he locks you away? Should I stay out of it then?"

A buzzing of emotion flowed through the room as many agents sat wide-eyed, and no one said a word.

The door opened, and the director took his seat with a glance down the table at me. "From what I hear, Charlie enjoyed our hospitality for the night. I hope she has a new appreciation for her role here."

Every part of me wanted to scream. My hands balled into fists under the table, but I wouldn't give him the satisfaction of seeing my true feelings. "I do."

The words came out with a sound of control that surprised me.

Across the table, Agent Lockhart raised her eyebrows and gave me a slight nod. She looked at the director and then back at me. Whatever she saw seemed to satisfy her, and she leaned back in her chair.

The time for this meeting went by quicker than before. Bishop was being held at a remote location where his powers would be out of range for causing harm. Someone mentioned Antarctica and several agents laughed. Where could they hold someone like him? The director talked of more agency business as I focused on the far wall. My thoughts stayed on how I could get back at him.

After the meeting, Mason and Payne left, saying I would spend the day with my tutor. Both seemed relieved. When they were gone, Agent Lockhart stopped by my side. "I like your spirit," she whispered. "The director will rue the day he brought you here."

I looked up with surprise. "What do you mean?"

She merely smiled and walked away.

Emily dropped me at another conference room on the way to her next meeting. The tutor who waited was a woman, dressed in a black skirt and blazer. She was older than Emily, maybe forties, and gave me a warm smile with crooked teeth. A computer sat on the small table, where she logged in and opened an interactive test.

"Can you type?" she asked.

I shook my head. Typing was a junior level class.

."This may take longer than I thought. Many of the questions are multiple choice, but there are a few written portions."

For the next two hours, I took the test, which told them I was at a senior level in high school. I hid my shock. Maybe Lorraine wasn't the only smart one in the family.

Around lunch, the tutor turned me loose with the promise we'd meet again next week. She left me with a binder of work to complete, which I took back to my room and tossed on the bed. I changed out of the suit and into a t-shirt and pair of jeans from the closet.

I found a restaurant that served Greek food and ordered a salad. There were no Greek restaurants in Credence, but why not try something new? As the server walked away, Kyle approached from across the room. I had to remind myself to breathe as he stopped and reached for the chair across from me.

"Mind if I join you?" he asked.

"How... did..." I stuttered.

"I saw you come in and thought, hey, Greek sounds good. Unless you're meeting someone else."

His laughter calmed the tension in my body. I motioned to the chair. "You can sit."

"Good." His smiled widened as he dropped into the chair. "Heard you had a rough night."

The server returned with my coke and took Kyle's order for a steak gyro. With a nod, the server walked away.

"You didn't need a menu?" I asked.

"Nah. After a few weeks, you'll have most of them memorized."

After a few weeks... I tried not to think that far ahead. "Does everyone know about last night?"

He shrugged. "Gossip travels like wildfire around here."

The conversation lapsed into silence until the server brought Kyle's glass of water. "You should switch to clear beverages. Better for you."

"Does being a nurse mean you get to irritate people by telling them how to live?"

"Irritate people?" Kyle laughed. "Technically, I'm not a nurse yet. I'm in training."

"Do you enjoy working here?"

"The benefits are amazing. At eighteen, I couldn't do much better than the retirement package they offer."

I wanted to laugh as I thought of my passport with an age of nineteen.

He took a sip of the water. "Speaking of ages, do you have one?"

"Like I said, you like to irritate people."

"Everyone has an age." Kyle took another sip. Was he nervous? "Just wondering if I'm wasting my time with jail bait."

"I was in a jail cell last night. Might want to think about that."

"I have." His eyes met mine as he gave me a charming grin. "I'm willing to take the risk."

This conversation had become too intense, far too fast. I took a huge drink of my coke and choked. Dark liquid drizzled down my chin. With embarrassment, I took the napkin Kyle handed me and wiped my face. "I can't seem to stop making messes around you."

"Could be a sign. I don't mind messes."

But I did. "Why be a nurse? Why not a doctor?"

His grin faded as he studied me. "Nursing is a critical job. My mother was a nurse and took pride in saving lives. She believed the work she did helping people was at times more important than what the doctors did."

Helping people as a nurse sounded like a good job, for honest reasons. "I think it's a job I would enjoy. What do you think?"

The grin returned. "I think you've got an even more important career ahead of you."

EPISODE 27

Sylvia

Kyle talked through most of lunch, about his job on the med-level and growing up on a farm in Nebraska. Every so often he'd throw out a question nudging for more information about me, usually when he stopped to take a drink of water or a bite of his gyro, but I dodged his efforts. By the time his lunch hour was up and Kyle returned to the med-level, I felt proud of myself for standing my ground with him.

And I longed for another lunch date.

Maybe I wouldn't call it a date. Just a meeting between two people who had the potential to become great friends. Meetings wouldn't catch the attention of the other agents. There were enough meetings around this place, and I needed someone closer to my age to talk with.

Who was I kidding? Kyle worked for the agency and probably wouldn't go to any effort to see me again. Why waste his time?

Back in my room, I turned on the TV and flipped between two soap operas, three news channels, and finally found MTV. Music might help me deal with all the stress from this place. When the commercials ended and a Tom Petty video started, I sank into the couch.

The video barely finished when someone knocked on my door. Groaning, I stood and found Sylvia waiting outside. She wore her normal suit with a pair of sunglasses perched on top of her head. Her short black hair was tied in a tight bun at the back of her head.

"Ready for a new assignment?" she asked.

"I thought I might get the afternoon off."

"Not around here. If you'll follow me, we're on a tight schedule."

"Do I have to change back into the agent suit?"

"I'll overlook your attire this time."

I grabbed my backpack from the floor by the couch.

"You won't need the bag. We'll be back in a few hours."

Good thing for her I was too tired to argue. If I didn't make it back, I could always teleport the bag. "When can I get my gun back?"

She gave me a strange look. "Who said you'd get the gun back?"

"Agent Payne."

Sylvia seemed to consider. "He could be right, but not today." She headed for the elevator, and I ran to catch up. "What's special about your gun?"

I didn't answer until we stepped into the elevator. "I told you before, it was a gift from my mom. Please tell me nothing has happened to the gun."

She hesitated while reaching for the buttons. "We still have it. Your mother…"

"I didn't lie when I told you people she died."

"I'm sorry."

After the elevator stopped, Sylvia took us to some sort of garage. Not the parking deck we arrived on, but a room filled with fancy, hi-tech cars made for racing. She chose a small two-door car with a symbol on the front I didn't recognize. "What kind of car is this?"

With a smile, she opened the driver's door and dropped into the bucket seat as I sat next to her. "A fast one." Carefully, she drove through a door barely large enough for the car to pass and down a ramp to the street. As soon as we hit the pavement, she made a sharp left and floored the accelerator.

I gripped the door handle as we flew so fast, a bump in the road would have sent us airborne.

"You haven't asked about our mission."

How could she sound this calm? "I'll ask when we stop," I yelled between breaths.

Sylvia swung the car to our right and squealed tires as we made the turn, all the while keeping us within the lines. "This mission will be easy. We visit a local hospital and interview a girl with a strange ability."

Maybe if I closed my eyes, my head would stop spinning. "What kind of ability?"

The light ahead turned yellow, but Sylvia didn't touch the brakes. "She can change the color of her skin." With another turn, Sylvia took a ramp and merged onto the highway, to the far-left lane. "Our job is to verify her power."

We cut between two cars, both so close I gave up and closed my eyes. Ten minutes later, she slowed the car and brought us to a smooth stop. Even though she stopped the car and killed the engine, my body felt like we were still moving.

"What do you think about Emily?" she asked.

I opened my eyes to a parking deck with cars on either side of us and arrows along the walls that pointed visitors to an E.R. "I hate her."

Sylvia gave me a look of surprise. "Out of everyone at the agency, she's the one person you want on your side."

"She locked me in a cell."

"Emily was following orders."

"She could have refused."

Laughing, Sylvia leaned back in her seat. "She picks her battles, a skill you need to learn."

"Can we get this over with?"

"Were you scared on the isolation floor?"

"No," I said.

"Why not?"

Because I could teleport out of there. "His threats don't scare me. What's the worst he could do, kill me? He won't do that if he wants my power."

"I was scared the first time."

My breath caught. "He locked *you* on the isolation floor? His own daughter?"

"Several times. The first was to show me who's boss. The second through sixth was to get me to stop chasing Faulkner. The ninth? Well, that was personal and I deserved it."

What was wrong with this man? "I think he was wrong to put me in there."

"You didn't follow his order to kill Bishop."

"Would you have?"

"I had the chance once and didn't. That was number seven."

"Do you hate Emily?"

"I consider her one of my best friends. She takes the bulk of my father's grief over me not training and maintaining the agent image at his level. The director's job is an optics campaign for him, if you haven't noticed." With a sigh, she opened her door and stepped out.

I followed as she walked to the E.R. entrance; the sound of her heels echoed as they tapped the concrete. Inside, she spoke with the admissions nurses and a hospital administrator. All verified the girl's parents had taken her from the hospital property before the staff discharged the patient. Sylvia asked questions and obtained relevant information like addresses and phone numbers, though the administrator seemed to think most, if not all of it, was fake. Emily had compared Sylvia's mind to a computer, which is probably why she never wrote a single note.

"We're in the business of saving people, not verifying their home address," the administrator said.

Sylvia thanked him for his time and ushered me back to the car.

When I sat inside, I asked, "Did you think she'd still be here?"

"It was a long shot, but I volunteered since driving always makes me feel better. It's been a tough week. Do you mind if we take our time going back?"

I couldn't argue with the long week, but I thought taking our time meant going easy on the accelerator. Instead, she took us outside of town and down streets with few cars. There, Sylvia could move at full throttle without having to worry about turns or traffic lights. After thirty minutes of this, I wondered if we'd end up in another county or state. Instead, she pulled into a gas station and insisted on buying us both an icee.

"Haven't had one of these since I was a kid," she said after a swig. Sylvia gripped the bridge of her nose. "My son would call this a brain freeze."

"You have a son?" I asked between sips of the frozen liquid.

She nodded. "My father doesn't like to talk about him. He's a huge disappointment, like me."

"Does he live at the base?"

"No." Sylvia dropped her icee into a cup holder. "This isn't a bad job, you know. Let my father think he's succeeded in intimidating you and life will be easier."

"Is that what you do?"

"It's a survival technique, though I believe on some level he knows better. He expects his daughter to play his game for all those watching. Now that Faulkner's gone, I've considered changing the rules of our game."

My icee cup was down to a few sips and my head throbbed. "Why was Faulkner trying to kill you?"

"For years I've tracked him, a few times getting close enough to kill him though I couldn't close the deal."

"What did Faulkner do to you?"

"Seventeen years ago, Faulkner killed my partner. Ever since then, I've fought to avenge his death."

Seventeen years ago was before I was born. I thought of how my mom left her home and fought those guards for eighteen years. Sylvia's face held the same dedication and resilience as Mom's when she'd talked about nearly two decades of fighting. "You cared about your partner?"

"I had his back and Anthony had mine. You'll see it's the same with Mason and Payne."

"No, this isn't the same."

Sylvia stared straight ahead. When she spoke, her voice sounded hoarse. "What do you mean?"

My mom fought for me all those years and didn't go back to protect me. She did it because she loved me. "He was more to you than a partner. Why?"

She turned to me. "After seventeen years of spending every waking moment tracking Faulkner, you're the only one who's ever asked that question."

I hesitated. "Will you tell me?"

"Be careful digging into the secrets of this agency. We all have reasons for keeping them." She cranked the car and drove us out of the parking lot. "Some secrets you don't want to know. Some you can't afford to carry."

*****

That night, I sat in my room until the clock by my bed showed ten. I turned off all the lights and tiptoed into the bathroom. From there, I teleported home.

When I appeared in the kitchen, Dad sat at the table and so did Lorraine. Both looked up. Lorraine jumped to her feet and ran to me, throwing her arms around my neck. "Dad told me everything."

I patted her back. "He told you I ran away?"

"I can't believe you left like you did." She pulled away and looked at me. "He told me you're working for a government agency."

"They didn't give me a choice. After they saw my power to shoot, they wanted me to fight their bad guys."

She smiled. "Sounds like a movie."

I left her and went to hug Dad. His embrace was warm, and he lingered as if not wanting to let me go. When he finally released me, I wiped tears from my face and dropped into my usual chair.

"I don't hate you," Lorraine said. "I wish you'd told me instead of writing a note."

"I haven't been the same since Mom died."

Dad cleared his throat. "None of us have. You don't have much time. Tell us what's happened since I saw you last."

"Do you remember the news report about a man who could cause an earthquake?"

Lorraine and Dad both nodded. "They talked about him again last night," he said. "There were unconfirmed reports of earthquakes in a California town."

"The reports are real," I said. "The agency wanted me to kill him."

With a squeal of horror, Lorraine put a hand over her mouth. "Did you?"

"I took him down, but he's not dead. His ability to cause vibrations also worked in the air. I had to fight against his vibrations, which the other agents couldn't do. In the end, I won."

Dad squeezed my shoulder. "You saved lives and didn't take his. I'm proud of you."

I looked at the table. "I missed the end of school. What did you tell everyone about me?"

"That you're heartbroken over your mother and are spending the summer with relatives in Virginia."

Hugh, Dad's friend, lived in Virginia. Not a horrible lie.

"I've considered we may need to leave Credence," he said. "If that's the case, we'll all go stay with Hugh."

"Why would you leave?" I asked.

He reached for my hand. "People are already talking about you leaving. As long as we can keep your abilities quiet, we'll stay here. If they find out about Lorraine, we'll have to leave."

"Would Hugh let you stay with him?"

Dad nodded. "Hugh and Wynn would both help us, even hide us if need be. Wynn has connections. Let's leave it at that. If we need to rush out of here, we've got a place to run to. Don't worry about us."

I spent the next few minutes telling them about the agency, about the cases and the people I'd met. Especially the evil director, though I left out the part about him locking me on the isolation floor. Dad watched the stove as we talked, the minutes on the clock creeping up faster than expected.

When he suggested my time was up, a letter appeared in Lorraine's hand, which she gave me. "This is from Carmen," she said.

"What did she say about me leaving?"

Lorraine shrugged. "She knew you were upset. Carmen said to give you this letter when you came back."

The envelope was sealed and 'Charlie' was written on the back in her perfect cursive writing. "She didn't tell you she hates me now?"

"Carmen is an extremely forgiving person, if you haven't noticed. You, however, haven't been the best friend."

I folded the envelope and tucked it into my pocket. "She has every right to hate me. I'm not sure if I want to read her letter."

Lorraine smiled. "Save it for a rainy day."

Which was a silly phrase Mom always used. The words brought a smile to my face.

"You're out of time," Dad said.

We all stood and hugged. "There's one more thing I need to do. Sixty seconds."

He glanced at the clock and nodded. "I love you, Charlie."

"And I love you both. I'll be back in three days."

"I'm holding you to that," Lorraine said with one more hug.

I turned away before the tears could start again and walked into the garden. My seconds ticked away as I sat on Mom's bench and stared up at the stars. I called out Keva's name, but she didn't appear.

At least for now, my family was safe. I'd do whatever it took to keep them that way.

EPISODE 28

Rogue Mission

The next morning, I dressed in one of the black suits that now hung in my closet. The letter from Carmen sat on the table by my bed unopened. A part of me wanted to hear her voice, but the other part didn't want to face her wrath for leaving. Instead of opening the letter, I slid it inside my backpack. As I tied up my hair, Mason arrived to escort me to the morning meeting.

"How is your arm?" I asked.

He held up the arm that was bandaged in California. "Good as new. The folks on our med-level do wonderful work."

Which must be why he flew all the way home before getting stitches. "Can we get breakfast before the meeting? I didn't eat last night."

He checked his watch. "If we make it fast."

Twenty minutes later, we sat at the long table in the conference room, awaiting the director. I'd grabbed a sausage biscuit from one of the restaurants and finished it in the elevator. As usual, Mason sat to my right and Payne to my left. Did they still think I was a flight risk? I smiled as I imagined teleporting out of there and the look of shock on all the faces.

Payne talked with an agent on his other side. When he stood and walked to the coffee maker near the entrance, I watched with humor as he tripped on the carpet and almost fell. The surprise turned to confusion as I thought of how he'd not tripped once on our walk through the airport or on the street that shook from Bishop's earthquake. At the door, Emily entered but stopped as she noticed him. She shook her head and took her seat. He grabbed a cup of coffee and went back to his chair beside me, just as the director stepped into the room.

'The bumbling agent' was what Emily called him, but how could this be true? The more I learned about Agent Noah Payne, the less I thought of him as able to bumble anything.

"We have a special case today," the director said. "Requiring urgency. Three of our agents have been captured in Russia. No one is claiming responsibility. Video has been released showing their torture, and we've made contact with a person of interest who claims she can return them."

"Who?" Sylvia asked.

"She's known as Diamond." He looked around the table. "I'm giving this mission to Mason and Payne. They will meet her in an hour, and Payne can use his negotiation skills to figure out a trade for the lives of our men."

"What about the kid?" Payne asked.

"Take her along," the director said. "If you're unsuccessful, we can use her to turn up the heat."

My stomach churned. The only place I wanted to go was back to my room.

"The three of you are dismissed. I want an update as soon as you have word."

* * * * *

Mason drove this time and Payne rode in the front seat, leaving me in the back as usual. The meeting point was about twenty minutes from the base, behind a movie theater. When we reached the parking lot, Mason stopped the car in the location he said gave us the best view of our surroundings. Did he think we'd be ambushed?

Payne handed me a gun, which I placed on the seat next to me. Maybe I'd ask for a holder like the ones that hung inside their jackets. "Only shoot if necessary," he said.

"Who is this contact?" I asked.

"Diamond is a mercenary," Payne said. "She sells her services to the highest bidder. No one knows her real name, but she's involved with a worldwide crime network. They steal money through hacking computers."

"People steal money from computers?" I asked. "Or with computers?"

"Technology is advancing fast," Payne said. "Before you know it, almost all banking will occur online and cyber currency will be more valuable than the U.S. dollar."

"Cyber currency?" I glanced at Mason.

"Don't look at me. If I had my choice, I'd handle all of my business in gold. Paper money is worthless, but at least you have something to hold. The thought of money based on ones and zeros doesn't sit well with me."

Payne laughed. "That's the future."

"You sure know a lot about the future," I said.

He cleared his throat and handed me a folder with info on their contact. Inside was a blurry picture of a woman with sunglasses. Her hair was tucked under a broad-brimmed hat that shaded her face. None of her features were distinct enough to recognize.

"Heads up," Mason said.

I closed the folder as a black car came to a stop next to us. The driver got out and opened a door to the backseat. A figure in a black coat stepped out, despite the warmth from the sun on my window. She wore huge sunglasses and a red scarf over the rest of her face.

Payne turned to me as Mason got out. "Remember why we're here. Whatever it takes to return our agents."

Sliding the gun into my pants, I opened my door and climbed out.

The contact's voice was low and sultry, but definitely female, with an accent I couldn't place. "It's been too long, Agent Mason."

"I'll leave the pleasantries to Payne," Mason answered gruffly. "I only care about our agents."

She turned to Payne, who approached as if in no hurry. "The director sent you to negotiate? Did he learn nothing from the last time?"

"He's set in his ways," Payne said.

"Which will seal his fate," she said.

Payne stepped closer to the woman. "What do you want?"

"You give me a favor and I get your men back to U.S. soil."

"What can we give you that you can't get yourself?" Mason asked. "You have money and connections."

"Sorry, gentleman, but I need to borrow your little hot-shot."

Mason's eyes widened as she grabbed my upper arm and shoved me down. The world faded, and we appeared in the backseat of a car. From the wide area around us and the opposing seats, this had to be a limo like I'd seen in movies.

Next to me, Diamond removed her scarf and sunglasses. "Sorry for pushing you, but it's always tricky teleporting from standing to a sitting position."

My mouth fell open. Diamond was Keva. I said the words in my head again.

"If my power was to read your emotions, this conversation would be easier. Tell me what you're thinking."

"Do the agents know who you are? That you're…"

"If they didn't know I could teleport, they do now."

Outside, signs passed that were in a strange language. With a start, I realized we were riding on the wrong side of the street. "Where are we?"

"No longer in the U.S."

"That doesn't tell me much. What's going on?"

"Charlie, dear, the less you know the better."

I pointed to another sign. "Can you read that?"

"I'm fluent in many languages. So was your mother. I have ties to Golvern, but my business happens here."

"What business?"

She sighed. "When you go back to that place, you won't want to divulge any secrets."

"Go back… Are you saying I'll go back to Atlanta? How did you know I was there?"

"I've seen your future. I always know where you'll be."

I closed my eyes and leaned back against the seat. "Are there really captured agents?"

"Yes."

"You need me to shoot someone, don't you?"

"Can I be honest with you, Charlie?"

Reluctantly, I nodded.

"To achieve my goals, you'll have to kill several people. All bad."

"Tonight?"

Keva chuckled. "Only one tonight."

I opened my eyes. "What if I refuse?"

"Work with me and I'll ensure no harm ever comes to your sister."

"How can you make that promise?"

"Because I have someone on the inside of the palace on Golvern."

My eyes widened as I thought of that other planet. Mom's home. "Palace? You mean—"

"Home of Golvern's king and queen. Someone inside is working with me."

"What if they find out?"

"The only way they'll ever find out is if you talk, and I don't think you will. At least, not in the future I've seen. My contact is systematically erasing your mother's trail."

"What do you mean by erase?" I asked.

"What she did on Earth and where she's been for the last eighteen years."

"How can anyone erase what she did or where she went?"

"We can't erase all of it, nor do we want to hide her reason for leaving Golvern. Years from now, people will fight in her name. But we can change where she went. No one else will come to that tiny town and knock on your door. That one truth protects you and your sister until she's old enough to fight."

"Then I can go home?"

She put a hand on top of mine, where it rested on my leg. "Unfortunately, going home would be a step back for you. Now you move forward."

"Hold on. Did you say Lorraine will fight?"

"She will."

Sirens sounded and lights flashed up ahead. The car slowed for an ambulance to pass. I rolled down the window and took a breath of stale, humid air as the siren blared past. While the sun had lit the sky in Atlanta, above us darkness floated with no visible stars. "Tell me something about my mom I don't know."

Keva hesitated. "Humans have ancient lore concerning four elements—earth, fire, air, and water. These elements are critical to sustaining life and must remain in balance."

"I've heard of elements, but what does that have to do with Mom?"

"Golvern has a similar lore in relation to our powers. Four powers are like four elements. Each one of these powers makes Golvern special. Throughout history, legendary figures have worked together to maintain balance. These figures are known for the strongest power levels of their generation. It has a long name in Golvern, but for simplicity we call it a Tryn, which means the intersection of four powers."

"This is Golvern lore or a real thing?"

She leaned her head back and closed her eyes. "Most people on Golvern believe the lore, though the members of a Tryn have pledged secrecy for life. They take no official credit for their efforts and only the stories told throughout history remind us of why they fight."

"*Why* do they fight?"

"To protect the future of Golvern and preserve the freedoms of its people, regardless of who sits on the throne." Keva leaned in and locked eyes with me. "For the last twenty years, I've been part of a Tryn. I've used my power to protect Golvern's future in any way possible."

"If you've pledged secrecy, why are you telling me?"

"Because your mother was our Protector. When she died, our Tryn was broken."

"Can't you find another Protector on Golvern? Mom said there were more."

"The power is rare, and Candorice's bloodline was the strongest ever known."

"What if I can't keep your secret?"

"You'll be better at keeping secrets than most people I've met. Don't forget I've seen your future." Keva stared out of her window. "I was hoping one day you could take her place."

"You've seen me take her place or want to change the future?"

She didn't answer.

"How can I be as powerful as her? I'm half human."

"Your mother was strong, and you inherited everything she had to give. You and Lorraine prove human blood doesn't dilute the gene pool as some believe, which is a fact Golvern's government would shed blood to conceal."

"You think I could be as powerful as her one day?"

She smiled. "With proper training. Tonight, we'll give you a test run."

* * * * *

Keva didn't speak again as we turned down a long drive, or as we passed homes large enough to be hotels. The car slowed to a stop, and she took my hand. We teleported to the top of a building that overlooked a large pool with cabanas on either side. We were several stories up, but the lights below were bright enough I made out a waterfall on one side of the pool, at a huge rock structure. This pool was bigger than any I'd seen, even on TV.

She looked through a pair of binoculars with an interactive screen. "That's not human technology," I said.

"No."

A high-powered rifle sat next to the edge of the roof. I dropped to my knees and lifted the gun over my shoulder, then leaned down to look through the scope.

What was I doing? I'd never used a gun like this before. "Why do you need me to make the shot?"

"Because of the distance. This bullet won't reach its target on hope alone, and the positioning must be exact. I need your power to reach our mark."

"Where are we?" I whispered.

"Are you sure you want to know?"

"This isn't like killing the soldiers that came for Mom. Who am I supposed to shoot?"

"His name is Theodore Rush. He'll be responsible for the annihilation of ninety percent of the human race. People from Golvern will come here and use the remaining humans as slaves."

"How will they come here and stay? Won't our sun kill people from Golvern like Mom?"

"Technology is constantly advancing. You'll see the answer to the problem with Earth's sun in your lifetime."

"How can *you* stay here?"

"I don't stay more than a few days for each visit. When I go home, I undergo a process to remove the radiation." She held up a hand and showed me the back.

"This is the treatment Mom should have had. Why didn't she go back?"

"Didn't she tell you?"

"She could have saved herself without exposing us. I want the truth."

Keva lowered the hand. "Candorice was my friend and I'll always honor the memory of who she was, but she made her choice years ago. Why she made the choice is a little more complex."

I thought of how Agent Payne asked me to spare Bishop's life, not because he cared but because it was complicated. "How old are you?"

"Why do you ask?"

"Are you older than Mom was?"

"By several years."

"You talked about two sons. Where are they?"

She sighed. "It's not time for us to have this conversation."

"Not time—"

"Everything must happen on time, Charlie. At least for me." She pointed to the gun. "The sooner you make this shot, the sooner your agency can get their men back."

Since when was it my agency? I swiveled the gun around as I viewed people on the ground through the scope.

"He's the only person dressed in a t-shirt with a spaceship."

I found the man with a spaceship across his chest. How ironic I'd have to shoot someone who wasn't human. He shook his head and stomped around the pool as if in a tantrum.

I could do this, but did I trust Keva? "Why are you trying so hard to help humans?"

"Because they're too weak to help themselves. I don't want to be involved with a Golvern takeover of Earth. Your mother and I worked too hard to avoid that kind of future."

"Are you sure about this?"

"One shot and don't aim for a mark you've used before. Make it an injury no one could survive."

I watched the rise and fall of his chest and determined the top edge of the ship sat over his heart. I'd aim for the picture and hit the most vulnerable part of his heart.

"Now."

I pulled the trigger before I could talk myself out of it. The bullet followed the line of air currents I manipulated, even giving it that extra push to maintain velocity. At his chest, it pierced his shirt and flesh in slow motion. Through the scope, I watched him fall. Next to me, Keva gave a sigh of relief as she watched through her binoculars.

Sitting back from the edge of the building, I felt pity for this man who would no longer live. Then I felt a sickness in my stomach.

She dropped to her knees beside me. “You did an outstanding job. Now back to the agency.”

“What if I don’t go back there?”

“You must. Their agents will shape who you are.”

“Will they hurt me?”

“Yes,” she said. “But they’ll also break your fear.”

“Do I have a choice?”

“I see two paths for you. Either you return and conquer your power or you go home and try to hide who you are. The problem with hiding? There’s no place in the universe where you can hide from what you’ll become.”

I shivered at her words.

EPISODE 29

Consequences

Keva took me back to the parking lot where Mason and Payne waited. Surprisingly, I was gone for less than an hour.

She'd covered her face before arriving. "Your hot-shot met the terms of our agreement, and your agents are on a flight to Atlanta as we speak. Until next time, gentlemen."

Mason and Payne stared with incredulity as Keva's driver opened a door and she climbed into the backseat of her car. He went around to the driver's seat, and they sped off.

"What happened?" Mason asked.

"She wanted me to kill someone."

His face was furious. "Who?"

"A man she said would kill millions of people." Ninety percent of humans? "Make that billions."

Payne held up his hands. "We should have this discussion at the base."

Mason nodded and fired the engine. Payne and I climbed in and no one said a word on the ride to the base. Nothing was said until we reached a conference room where

Emily and the director sat. Mason herded me to a chair and took the one next to me. Payne stood by the door.

"Our contact made Charlie kill a man," Mason said.

"Who?" the director asked. "Where did this take place?"

"I'm not sure." I took a slow breath. "She said he was a killer and your agents would be returned once I completed her mission."

"Did you believe her?" After my nod, he asked, "Did you learn anything about Diamond?"

I shook my head. "I was too scared to ask anything else."

The phone on the table rang, and Emily answered the call. Agent Vickers, the security lead, came over the line. "We have eyes on our agents. The mission was a success."

"Thanks, Phil." Emily hung up the phone.

The director turned to me. "Good job. You acted like a patriot. I couldn't ask for more from any of my agents."

Mason shook his head. "I don't like any of this. That woman had the power to take Charlie away from us and make her shoot a man, and we don't know who."

"We have our men back," the director said. "And Charlie has intel on our contact. We'll tap into her memory if need be."

Would they have Agent Lockhart mess with my head? My stomach lurched at the thought.

* * * * *

After meeting with the director, I recited my side of the morning's events to Emily, who took notes as I talked. I remembered Dad's advice. *The trick to lying is that it has to center around truth to be effective.* So, I gave her a true story while omitting some key details, like the man's name and the fact I knew Keva.

She seemed bothered by parts of my story but genuinely happy that Keva brought me back.

"Did you think she wouldn't?" I asked.

"I didn't know." She closed her folder of notes. "How do you feel about going out for lunch?"

"With you?"

"I'm meeting Hannah, but you could tag along. Might be a little more relaxed than your time with the men."

"Sure," I said.

Emily took us out of the base and through a drive-thru where we ordered burgers and fries, before driving us to a park with swings and benches around a huge grassy area. She parked along the street, and we found Hannah practicing some type of martial arts moves in an area shaded by trees. Emily sat on a metal bench nearby.

Hannah did a few kicks and turned to Emily. "How did last night go?"

"The director's meeting lasted until three a.m."

I dropped onto the bench next to Emily, while forcing back memories of sitting on the bench with Mom. "Do you ever stop working?"

Emily handed Hannah a bag with a chicken sandwich. "That's why the agency provides our living space. They want us on call twenty-four hours a day, seven days a week."

Despite being angry at Emily for locking me on the isolation floor, I felt a sudden closeness to her. She really did give her all to this job. "Can't you stop working for an hour?"

"I could try, but I'm not making any promises."

Hannah laughed. "The answer is no." She sat on the grass next to the bench and opened her bag.

Emily opened her burger and took a bite. "Some days I'm more tired than others. Today is one I'd like to call an end to right now."

"Then do it," Hannah said. "We could say I dedicated this afternoon to training our new recruit."

"Training me to do what?" I asked with a mouthful of food.

"What would you like to learn?" Emily asked.

"How Hannah dropped Agent Payne to the floor."

After we finished our meal, Hannah made me spend the next thirty minutes meditating. Emily joined in, and when the meditation session was done, Hannah began showing me how to stretch and use correct posture. If I could master those, she'd teach me to fight.

"Did you leave anything out this morning?" Emily asked.

How did I know that question was for me? "I told you what happened. The truth."

"Are you okay with what happened?" she asked. "Killing someone should never be easy."

I shrugged, and Hannah waved for me to copy her by stretching my arms overhead.

"There are consequences for every choice we make," Hannah said. "What's important is, can you live with those consequences."

"You mean penalties?" I asked. "Jail time?"

Hannah pointed to my chest. "All that matters is what's here. Do you feel you made the right decision? You won't always. When you make a mistake, you must live with that knowledge."

For two hours we stretched, and Hannah showed a few fighting stances. When she sat down on the bench, I asked, "What about the move you used on Payne?"

"Not today," she said. "That's more advanced. If you want to train to fight, I will teach you."

I glanced at Emily. "The move was amazing. She dropped Payne to the floor as if he weighed nothing."

"Wish I could have seen that."

"You will, one day," Hannah said. "Agent Payne hasn't yet learned when to shut his mouth."

Emily crossed her arms. "It's part of his image. I'm willing to bet he's messing with your head."

"Nonsense," Hannah said. "He thinks he's smarter than he is."

"Don't say I didn't warn you." Emily turned to me. "Tell me how you felt when you killed that man."

I looked away. "Isn't this the part where you tell me feelings are useless? Feelings get in the way and they'll get me killed? I'm better off not remembering where I came from, who I am, or why I care if others live or die."

"Look kid," Emily said, "all that stuff is great, but this is reality. The decision you made to save Sylvia was based on emotion."

"I wouldn't be here if I let her die."

"But you didn't," Hannah said. "Now you must follow where your heart leads."

I laughed sarcastically. "My heart didn't lead me here."

Emily stood. "Where was your heart taking you? You were at the airport but not registered for a flight. You didn't have identification, which meant you couldn't have bought a ticket even if you wanted to. My guess is you had no plans of taking a plane."

The grief of losing Mom hit me so fast, I choked. Tears streamed down my face. "I didn't know where to go and now I can't go home."

"What happened at home?" Emily asked.

"You wouldn't understand."

"Tell me." She grabbed my arm.

I spun back to her. "I killed my mom."

Emily blinked, and her look of shock turned into sympathy. "After knowing you, I'm sure that's not true."

No, I didn't deserve her sympathy. "I put a bullet in her head."

Her arms were around me before I could shove them away. "Why?"

"She was dying and asked me to end her suffering." I cried into the silky fabric of her suit jacket. "I murdered her."

"Euthanasia is practiced in many cultures," Hannah said, her voice neutral. "When the old are too feeble or in too much pain. It's known as a mercy killing, not murder."

Emily pulled me to the bench and Hannah slid over to make room for us both to sit. "I don't have a power. I'm not special like you."

I rubbed my nose. "I'm not special."

"You're special to me."

"I don't understand."

She sat back and looked into my eyes. "Sylvia is more to me than a fellow agent. I consider her one of the best friends I've ever had."

"How can agents have friends?"

Her lips formed a thin smile. "You haven't been with us long, but I think you can already see there are no hard and fast rules for how this agent gig works. And we're not all out for ourselves. When we work as a team, we have the backs of everyone on that team."

"Like Mason and Payne," I said.

"They are an exception to many rules," Emily said. "I can't explain why, but I think Mason actually trusts Payne with his life. They're more than partners, they're true friends. That doesn't happen often in this line of work."

"Friends like you and Sylvia?"

She nodded. "I thought Sylvia would die in Faulkner's grip. We were all helpless as he strangled her, watching in horror. I never imagined you'd show up and take him down."

"I didn't plan to do anything. I heard her scream, and I reacted."

"That's all any of us could hope for from a member of our team. You saved her life, and for that reason, I felt gratitude." She looked over my head and locked eyes with Hannah. "Could you give us a minute?"

Without a word, Hannah stood and walked away.

"Do you have any other family?" Emily asked.

"No one who wants to see me."

"What I'm about to say is off the record."

I held my breath as I waited.

"If you want to leave, I'll get you out."

"What would the director—"

"He'd fire me without a second thought."

"Why tell me to leave?"

Tears glimmered in her eyes. "You're not like us. I came here because I knew I could save lives. Nothing is more important. Jon has a skill the agency needs, but his life would be in hiding without this agency's protection. Mason was damaged during a mission in Iraq."

"Don't you mean hurt?"

Emily shook her head. "No one could hurt Mason; he's never been the same since that day. Payne has a history, but he won't talk about it. Still, I recognize the look in his eyes. It's the same as Sylvia's every time her father makes an edict we all must follow. We belong here; you don't."

"I'm damaged like Mason."

"You still have time to turn back the clock. Go home to your life and start living."

"I can't."

"If you stay here a year longer, maybe even a month longer, you'll turn into what we are. I don't want that life for you."

"You sound like my mom," I whispered.

She took my hand. "You need someone to look after you, but no one will ever replace your mother."

Tears spilled down my face. "She asked me to end her life so she could die with honor. My mom believed in something I didn't."

"What did she believe?"

"That I could make a difference. That giving her life to protect me was a worthy trade."

"Do you remember my sister, the one in college? I would give my life to protect her."

I swallowed as I took in Emily's features, really looked at her this time. She was a good person, with a warm heart. On the outside, she made a fearsome agent with her thick, brown hair with a shimmering hint of red. She was nothing like a model but beautiful on the inside. Her green eyes were so deep it was hard to look away. Maybe this was all an act, but I truly believed Emily wanted to help me.

If only she could.

* * * * *

We returned to the base around four. After she parked, Emily looked at me. "One more thing on the agenda today."

"What?" I asked.

"We visit the med-level for your vaccines."

I grinned. "Does that mean they can't lock the place down and kill me now?"

"The gas wouldn't kill you, though you might wish you were dead the next morning. Now that you're part of our team, you'll get the same vaccines issued to the other agents."

"Will you take me?"

Her laughter faded. "I'll hold your hand if you need me to."

"That's not necessary but not being alone is nice."

"Charlie, what are we going to do with you?"

I followed her to the med-level where Kyle showed us to a room. She sat in the seat beside me.

"Doc will be in shortly." Kyle winked in my direction.

Fighting a grin, I said, "Thanks."

Emily looked at me when Kyle was gone. "I don't like that look on your face. Has he turned your head already?"

"I don't know what you mean."

"Look, Charlie, this agent business is tough. My most sacred rule is to *never* date an agent."

"I'm not dating Kyle, and he's not an agent. We've talked a few times and had lunch. That's it."

Before she could respond, the door opened and Agent Lockhart stepped inside while pushing a cart with syringes on top. Emily's eyebrows rose. "Francine? What are you doing here?"

"I'm going to give our new agent her vaccines."

Emily looked over the cart. "Those needles are huge. I asked for the new formula, where it's all in one shot."

"I don't trust the new formula."

"She's a kid, Francine. Those needles would give me nightmares."

"But she's a kid with a powerful gift. She'll grin and bear it."

Seeing the needles made my hands shake, but I didn't want to seem like a kid in their eyes. "I've had shots before."

A beep sounded, and Emily checked her pager. "I have to make a call. I'll be right back."

After she left the room, Agent Lockhart turned to me. "We have little time."

"Why don't they call you doctor instead of agent?" I asked.

"Because this agency doesn't recognize my credentials."

"Agent Lockhart—"

"Please, call me Francine. What I'm about to say won't be repeated."

My stomach felt sick. At least this time Kyle wasn't around.

"What do you know about the woman they call Diamond? What she is?"

I swallowed. "What she is, as in…"

"From my research, I suspect she's an alien who has the power to see the future." When I didn't respond, she jammed a needle into my arm.

"Ouch," I yelled.

"You spent an hour with her. What are your thoughts?"

"If you suspect she's an alien, why haven't you told the agency?"

"My suspicions are none of their business. I have a natural intuition about people. It's how I knew your intentions here were good and I didn't need to tell them what you really are."

"What *I* am?"

"When I tested your blood sample, I used an advanced method to analyze your DNA. No one at this agency understands how my process works, and I'd like to keep it that way."

"You analyzed my DNA?" I blinked. "Wha-what did you see?"

"Be honest with me. I've protected your privacy and you owe me the truth. I don't like when people lie to me."

Should I keep lying or take a risk with the truth?

She watched me expectantly. "Your silence speaks truth."

"During the meeting you said I was—"

"That's where you must examine the specifics." She pushed another needle into my arm, gentler this time.

I sucked in a breath. "You told the director you're one hundred percent sure I'm human."

She smiled without humor. "If he'd bothered to look at my presentation slide, he might have seen the markers. Then again, he probably wouldn't have known what to look for."

"You said I was human."

"Aren't you part human?"

I nodded slowly, the pit in my stomach widening.

"Sylvia asked if you're human and the answer is yes. The director asked if I was sure, and I said one hundred percent. Not that you're one hundred percent human, only that I was sure you are human. That's what happens when you rush the process and don't ask for key details."

"Seems like a minor point."

"Technically, you are human. You're also something else."

My throat felt thick. "Why didn't you tell anyone?"

"This agency has a way of interrogating and dissecting anything it doesn't understand. I don't want to see that happen to you."

Relief washed over me. "Thanks."

She nodded. "When I joined this agency, I didn't know how deep the director's cruelty went. I'm doing a job just like you are."

"I didn't have a choice in staying here. He insisted I take the agent job."

"And a fine agent you've made, so far. It takes a certain type of person to want to do this job."

"Why do I feel you're not one of those people?"

"By marrying Jon, I became part of this place, whether they like me or not. I can't go back to what I was. Even if I chose to, I don't think Jon could go through with erasing my memory. He's happy here, and I do my job in the spirit of keeping the peace between him and our director."

"But you don't agree with the director."

She smiled and gave me the last vaccine. "One of these days, I'll see him suffer for every wrong he's done to people who trusted him."

Maybe we had something in common.

EPISODE 30

Subterfuge

For two days, I stayed in my room with a headache and chills. Although most people didn't have side effects from the vaccines, mild sickness was possible for the first few days. The only meals I ate were brought by Emily.

At 2 a.m. on the second night, a frenzy of knocks sounded from my door. When I didn't answer, the door opened and Emily's voice came from the living room. "Get up, Charlie. We've got a nine-one-one mission."

I groaned and pulled a pillow over my head.

She turned on the light and pulled back the blanket. "This isn't a drill. We need you in action now." Emily helped me to my feet and pulled a suit from my closet.

At her urging, I changed and slid on my new, comfortable shoes. "Where are we going?"

"A shooter has been holed up in a high-rise hotel since last night. He never left the building, and no one can put eyes on him. We're going in to secure the place."

I yawned. "Isn't that police work?"

"We've been called in as a special favor. The governor's sister is trapped in the building. Mason and Payne can tell you the rest on the way.

On the ground floor, they fit me with a bulletproof vest that weighed a ton. Over it, they threw a thin black vest that looked three sizes too big. The back of the vest said 'task force,' which would have made me laugh if I wasn't so tired.

"I don't need this vest."

Emily put her hands on her hips. "We don't need another casualty tonight. Wear the vest."

Which meant other people were hurt or killed. She took me outside into the night as Mason pulled up to the curb. I stumbled into the backseat and Emily closed the door as Mason sped off.

"That was quick work, kid," Payne said from the front seat. Both of them were dressed in the bulletproof vest with the thin black vest thrown over.

I laid across the backseat and closed my eyes. If only I could sleep for another hour.

"Did Agent Holmes give you a rundown of our situation?" Payne asked.

"Mmm-hmm," I said.

Mason slammed on the brakes, and I slid into the floorboard, gripping my head. "What was that for?"

"To get you up." He turned around and glared at me, his voice angrier than ever. "This is go-time."

I climbed onto the seat and slid on the belt. Mason hit the gas, and we sped down the empty street.

"Our shooter is hiding inside the building," Payne said. "The upper floors have been cleared. They believe he's confined somewhere from the seventh floor down. Do you have a gun?"

"No."

He handed me the standard agency weapon.

"Can I please have my gun?"

"Help with this mission, and I promise you'll get it back." Payne sighed. "If you can shoot to kill this time, do it."

For the first time, Agent Payne sounded worried, which got my heart pumping. If he was worried, this must be a dangerous mission. The rest of the ride passed in a blur. We pulled into the parking lot of a building as tall as the agency's base. Police and emergency vehicles filled the parking lot. Lights flashed from all directions. People crowded the street behind barriers erected to keep them away from the building.

Mason stopped at a back entrance where Emily and Sylvia stood. Sylvia must have driven for them to beat us. Other agents walked up as we climbed out.

With a wave of her hand, Emily called the agents together. "Everyone here has a partner, and every team takes a different floor. Whatever happens, don't leave that person in the building. We have no idea if the shooter has a power of some kind, and we've yet to hear of a motive. Stay off the radios unless you have eyes on the shooter. Get to work."

"We stay together," Mason said to Payne. To me he said, "We search room to room until we've cleared the floor. I want you ready to shoot if we make contact."

I nodded. All of this was happening too fast. Sounds, including sirens and people screaming, ran together. I gripped the gun as I trailed behind Mason, and Payne checked all angles with his gun ready. We ran up several flights of stairs, enough to get me out of breath, and took the door marked floor seven.

"Lucky number seven," Mason said. He and Payne took turns kicking in doors and checking each room. They moved fast; I'd look up and down the hall twice and they'd finish and move to the next room.

The floor was quiet and all the rooms they checked were empty. As we neared the opposite end of the hall, a loud buzzing sounded and a light on the wall flashed. Sprinklers that hung from the ceiling came on and doused the entire area with water.

"Fire on floor eight," came over the radio in Mason's jacket.

"That's right above us," he said, spitting out the water that sprayed from above.

Water soaked my hair and my clothes, and it pooled on the floor around us.

Mason kicked in a door and Payne ran into the room after him. Near the door to the elevator stood a man with blond hair hanging over his eyes. Opening my mouth, I couldn't find a sound. Then the man was in my face. Stumbling back, I dropped the gun, and he pointed his at me. The last fifteen years flashed before my eyes as I realized this was it. He reached for the trigger… the only thing standing between me and death was my ability to stop this bullet.

I should have screamed.

I should have teleported out of there.

Mason rushed from the room and slammed the man to the floor. They rolled on the floor and the blond man recovered his gun and jumped to his feet, pointing the barrel at Mason. I closed my eyes and pictured the bullet before the sound rang out. At this close range, Mason didn't have a chance, except for my ability to curve the bullet's path.

I used every bit of my energy to steer the bullet away from his heart. When I opened my eyes, Mason lay on the floor with blood gushing from his chest. I pictured a gun in my hand, the one my mother gave me, and I thanked fate it appeared with a bullet in the chamber. The man turned, but my bullet took flight before he pulled his trigger.

He fell back as my bullet struck his head.

Water ran down my face as I dropped to my knees next to Mason. Was he dead? I couldn't focus on anything else. Payne bent and touched his partner's neck. "He's still alive," he said with relief.

The lights went out, though the buzzing continued.

"Get out of here," Payne said.

"Mason—"

"I've got him. Go."

I ran into the stairwell with only the dim emergency lights guiding my way. As I reached floor five, I realized I'd killed a man and Mason was still alive. At floor three, I knew Mason getting shot was my fault for dropping the gun. At number two, I realized my mom's gun was still in my hand. With the exit sign in sight, I remembered the fact I had teleported the gun.

Above me, the stairwell doors hadn't opened, which meant Mason and Payne were still up there. My heart pounded in my chest. I took off my soaked jacket and wiped my face. Why didn't Payne's feet sound on the stairs? Maybe he couldn't carry Mason.

I had to go back. I had to—

Next to me, Payne appeared, holding Mason under his arms. "Get the door," he yelled.

Had he just… teleported?

"Now!"

I opened the door as he dragged Mason out of the building and onto the concrete. "You can teleport?"

Mason moaned as Payne dropped to his knees while keying the radio. "Shooter is dead. Agent down at the ground-floor stairway exit."

Payne looked my way. "I had no choice. Get him out or let him die." He gave me a charming smile, though his words were as cold as ice. "How did you know what I did was called teleporting?"

I hesitated. "You appeared out of thin air."

He leaned close. "So can you, I'd bet."

Before I could respond, medics surrounded us, and Sylvia pulled me back. The other teams exited the building, and everyone looked on anxiously as Mason was loaded onto a stretcher and taken by ambulance back to the base. During all the chaos, I teleported the gun back to the cellar. Explaining what happened to it might be tough, but the agency wouldn't have the chance to take my gun again.

*****

When we reached the base, Payne gave an update as the team stood around him. He insisted Mason was the hero after I choked up and dropped the gun. Mason jumped the shooter and took a bullet for his team. I made the last shot, and Payne carried Mason out, which I didn't argue with. How could I since shock held me rigid?

Agent Payne was like me. He had the power to teleport and maybe another power. All the instances where he made me wonder if he could see the future came rushing back. Obviously, he didn't want anyone to know.

Why?

Maybe for the same reasons I didn't want them to know about my power to teleport. He'd played them all and was still playing them as he talked in a low voice, detailing our narrow escape. Payne threw every bit of charisma into that speech, and the people around him seemed to believe every word. Except for me, and he never looked my way.

What would the other agents say? What would Emily say if she knew he'd been lying, how the bumbling agent routine was an act. For what purpose?

Mason. What would he say if he knew what his partner could do, that the man he spent most of his day with might not be human? What if he already knew…

"Okay people," Emily shouted. "Anything else you can read in the reports. For now, those who were at the scene get some rest. I'll take the on-call and hopefully this day will be quiet."

My mind was reeling as I walked away. Sylvia caught me on the way out and said several words before I realized she was there.

"Are you okay?" she asked.

No, I wanted to say. Did she know what Agent Payne could do? Did anyone at the agency know his secrets? Emily had told me he had no power, but he'd teleported, which meant he was probably an alien or part alien. And it also meant he could have the power to see the future. Maybe I was right about the tattoo. "Yes."

Sylvia's voice sounded tired. "I know you feel bad about dropping the gun, but we all make mistakes."

Yes, I dropped the gun, but that wasn't the issue.

"Can I show you something?"

I nodded, not paying her much attention on the elevator or the walk down a long hall to a conference room.

She stopped at the door. "Are you sure you're okay?"

"Can we do this later?"

"When we drove the other day, we talked about my son. He's about your age."

I tried to clear the fog from my brain. "Is he like you?"

"He has my excellent memory, but he can't move fast like me." She opened the door to the conference room and waved me inside. "I thought you might enjoy having someone your age to talk to."

Every thought halted as I entered the room, for at the table sat Joel Greene.

* * * * *

Please look for Legacy of Power: Season 2 and continue Charlie's adventure.

Acknowledgements

Thanks to:

Everyone who has read this book. Please feel free to contact me anytime with your feedback since I love to hear from readers. And please take a moment to leave an honest review on Amazon and Goodreads. I do read these and I appreciate the time and effort that goes into each one of them.

The people who have followed along with Charlie's story and offered their fabulous suggestions: Larry, Barbara, Robin, and Pete. Writing these books would be a lonely road without their interaction and feedback.

Christie for too many great ideas to mention them all. I'm always lucky to have your help with my stories.

Mrs. N. for your help with editing this story as a serial. I've enjoyed hearing your thoughts and I'm thankful for your continued encouragement.

Fiona for another cover I love!

My family for putting up with my obsession for writing. They might not understand it, but they cheer me on. Isn't that what love is all about?

About the Author

C.C. Bolick grew up in south Alabama, where she's happy to still reside. She's an engineer by day and a writer by night—too bad she could never do one without the other.

Camping, fishing… she loves the outdoors and the warm Alabama weather. For years she thought up stories to write and finally started putting them on paper back in 2006. If you hear her talking with no one to answer, don't think she's crazy. Since talking through her stories works best, a library is her worst place to write… even though it's her favorite!

C.C. loves to mix sci-fi and paranormal—throw in a little romance and adventure and you've got her kind of story. She's written twenty books including the Leftover Girl series, The Agency series, and The Fear Chronicles. Her serial, Legacy of Power, is a prequel to the other books.

Please visit her website at www.ccbolick.com for updates on future releases.

www.ingramcontent.com/pod-product-compliance
Lightning Source LLC
La Vergne TN
LVHW041107080826
845145LV00007B/1721

* 9 7 8 1 9 4 6 0 8 9 2 8 1 *